THE RAINBOW GATE

Helen recognised the onset of the uneasiness Rianna showed whenever she did not want to discuss something. Helen was very sensitive to it and hated to distress her. Usually she changed the subject, but this time she could not.

She said, 'Do you remember, we used to read the Narnia books together, about some children who went into another world?'

'Vaguely.'

'And we made up our own game and our own imaginary world, only we didn't go through the back of a wardrobe, we went into Bradgate Park. We'd go for miles and we'd never see a wall or a path or any other people because we weren't in the Park any more, we really were in another world.'

Helen had a preconceived idea of how the conversation would go on. Rianna would say, 'I remember,' and Helen would say, 'Well, it's just happened again.'

Instead, Rianna murmured, 'Did we do that? I'd forgotten.'

'*Forgotten?*' Helen was stunned beyond words. Rianna shifted slightly so that she was no longer facing her, and there was an uncomfortable pause. 'Rianna, how could you possibly have forgotten?

Also by the same author, and available from NEL:

A BLACKBIRD IN SILVER
A BLACKBIRD IN DARKNESS
A BLACKBIRD IN AMBER
A BLACKBIRD IN TWILIGHT

About the author

Freda Warrington is the author of the four-novel fantasy sequence which began with A BLACKBIRD IN SILVER. Born in Leicester, she grew up in Charnwood Forest. After leaving school she studied graphic design; as well as being a writer she is also a designer and illustrator. She now lives in Derbyshire.

Her latest novel, DARKER THAN THE STORM, will be published by New English Library in 1991.

The Rainbow Gate

Freda Warrington

NEW ENGLISH LIBRARY
Hodder and Stoughton

First published in Great Britain in 1989 by New English Library hardbacks

New English Library paperback edition 1990

British Library C.I.P.

Warrington, Freda
The rainbow gate.
I. Title
823'.914[F]

ISBN 0-450-53626-2

The characters and situations in this book are entirely imaginary and bear no relation to any real person or actual happenings.

Printed and bound in Great Britain for Hodder and Stoughton Paperbacks, a division of Hodder and Stoughton Ltd., Mill Road, Dunton Green, Sevenoaks, Kent TN13 2YA. (Editorial Office: 47 Bedford Square, London WC1B 3DP) by Clays Ltd, St Ives plc.

This book is dedicated to my late grandparents,
Eva Ada and Harry Travis,
with love, affection and happy memories always.

Prologue

Under a blue sky flecked with daystars, a man and a little girl sat on the bank of a river. All around them, bracken frothed away into a glittering mist, and their garments shone bright as flowers against it. Strange birds sang in the trees, bright blue fish flashed through the water. Animals watched the man and the girl with curious eyes then came to snuff at their hands, unafraid.

The man was pointing out their colours to the child, telling her the hidden meanings. A creature with short legs and star-webbed red fur pushed its snout against his arm. 'This is Aeni, the badger,' he said, stroking the creature's head. 'We call him the Maker, though he makes nothing.'

'Why?' asked the child.

'Because he is red, the colour of the hands, and the hands create.'

'My hands aren't red,' she said, laughing.

'No . . . but there is red in your hair. You will be a creator, my love. We can never hide what we are; the colour of the hair always gives us away.' He twined a lock of the child's coppery hair round his fingers as he spoke. 'The colours are symbols. Each part of the body has its own function, its own emotion, which is described by a colour. The blue fish, the blue bird; they are the colour of the heart, bringers of love.' Quietly, he added, 'The heart may hate, the hands may destroy, but the animals are innocent of that; they only bring blessing.'

A golden squirrel leapt on to the child's shoulder. The bushy tail tickled her face and she giggled. 'What does gold mean?'

The man smiled. 'Your thoughts, my little one. Your dreams. What do you dream about?'

'Huge animals like rainbows, galloping across the hills,' she said seriously. 'And about the sea. The waves are all warm and green, like bracken.'

'I shall take you to the sea. You will see such creatures there. Suis, the indigo fish that blesses dancers . . . '

A swan rose up from the river, shattering its own mirror-image in the water; a dazzling white swan, with beak and feet of silver. The child watched and said, 'Is she the colour of sorrow?'

The man's face changed. He looked disturbed, withdrawn. 'What made you think that? We call the swan Fi. She is the hidden hue of the soul. Surely you know nothing of sorrow, child. Here, where the sun always shines, where the rain falls softly through the trees at night, here it is impossible to feel unhappy.' But he spoke sadly, and the child became anxious.

'I should only be unhappy if you ever left me,' she said.

It seemed a long time before he replied, so long that she grew really afraid. 'It happens sometimes . . . that someone has to leave. Not because they want to, but because they must.'

'But you won't ever leave me, will you?'

The stab of fear was brief, easily healed as the man smiled again and took her on to his lap. 'How could I ever leave you, my little love, my light?' he said. 'No, I shall always be here.'

The lie was told. Unknown, but not far away, the vast invisible gate between the worlds creaked open and the ice of winter blew across the threshold.

Chapter One

When Rianna left, she took the enchantment with her. The colour went out of Helen's life, and although over the years she found other passions to replace what she had lost, she never ceased to be haunted by memories of what used to be.

Some people held a strange fascination for Helen. It was not necessarily sexual; it was a power of personality, a light inside – not even a light – that was the whole point, it was indefinable; the way they looked and moved, the way they spoke; they simply held the attention. You never tired of their company, though they might tire of yours. While they chose to be with you, you felt special, allowed into the circles of a secret and glamorous world.

Rianna had been such a person.

Helen had not seen her for fifteen years. When she left they had been eleven years old, and her departure had almost broken Helen's heart. They had known each other for six years, a whole lifetime to a child. Helen had taken for granted the strangeness that Rianna carried with her like an aura, a strangeness that made the world angle a few degrees from normal and took away the barriers between dreams and reality. Only when Rianna was gone did she realise how lucky she had been. Yes, privileged.

In time, of course, Helen got over the loss. She came to realise that events which had seemed real could only have been games, the response of her active imagination to her friend's fantasies. Rianna was never forgotten, but she dwindled in Helen's memory to a faint duality; sometimes just a child she used to know, sometimes the tantalising ghost of a dryad. Whatever, she was no longer real nor any part of Helen's life.

So it was a shock to Helen, as she straightened up from digging her front garden, to find herself looking over the wall and straight into Rianna's eyes.

Worse, for a moment she could not even put a name to her.

'Hello, Helen.'

'Er – ' Helen said stupidly, thinking: What a beautiful girl, I'm sure I should know her, is it the Avon lady?

'I bet you're surprised to see me.' It was an accentless voice, but with a lilt that hinted at an Australian inflexion. 'You don't remember me, do you?'

'Oh, God, this is ridiculous.' Helen raised a hand to push back her hair, forgetting her earth-clogged gardening gloves.

'Rianna Harper.'

As soon as it was said, the face resolved itself from the strange to the familiar. Refined by adulthood, it still had the same delicate, secretive features, the broad forehead and Pre-Raphaelite, russet hair. And those eyes; how could she have forgotten those wide eyes, so pale they put her in mind of opals?

'Rianna! You haven't changed at all – well, apart from being taller!'

'But you didn't recognise me.'

'I do now! I was just so surprised, you know, when you see someone out of context . . . ' Helen was half-embarrassed and half-thrilled.

'I recognised you. You look just the same.'

'After all these years. I can't believe it. What brings you here? Oh, come inside the house, I'll make some tea. How long can you stay?'

Helen's house was a terraced redbrick cottage, facing a similar row across a narrow lane. It was a modest place, but she was glad to have been able to keep it, after Nick had left.

'I'm sorry about the mess.' She led Rianna down the passage and in through the kitchen, pausing to discard her gloves and wellingtons before showing her into the front room. 'I wasn't expecting anyone.' She gathered up some magazines from the sofa and put them on the coffee table, then hurriedly plumped the cushions.

'It looks fine to me.' Rianna took off her shoes and sat down with her feet tucked under her, perfectly at home. Helen liked that. It seemed the sweetest kind of compliment.

'Would you like tea or coffee?'

'Tea, please.'

Helen went back into the kitchen and plugged the kettle in. 'I haven't got everything as I want it yet,' she called. The carpets were shabby, the furniture sparse and mis-matched, but she had done her best with fresh paint and Japanese prints on the walls. 'Nick took a lot of the furniture; we only had hand-me-downs anyway, and I can't afford to replace it yet.'

As she spoke, she grew annoyed with herself. Why was she apologising for the state of her house? She wanted Rianna to like it, she supposed, and it was an automatic reaction, explaining herself . . .

'Who's Nick?'

Helen started, and almost scalded her hand. Of course, how could Rianna know about Nick, when they had never even written to each other? Perhaps Rianna was married, a mother; anything could have happened. They were strangers.

The tea made, she carried in the tray and seated herself at the opposite end of the sofa.

'Do you take sugar? I don't, so I always forget to put it out.' She sat forward, then relaxed as Rianna shook her head. 'Have a biscuit. My mum made them.'

'I remember your mother's baking. We'd come in from playing in the Park and there were always biscuits and cakes waiting. It's a wonder we didn't get fat. We must have run it all off, I suppose.' Rianna smiled, and her lids swept down over her eyes as she sipped her tea. That was something else Helen remembered about her; she rarely looked directly at anyone. It was not shiftiness or shyness; it was part of the self-containment that formed her aura.

That had not changed, Helen noticed; nor had her childhood recollection of it been exaggerated.

She had had dreams about Rianna, all through her adolescence. Even after she had dismissed her memory of their friendship as an idealised one, from time to time Rianna would still appear at her side to run with her through night landscapes and the convolutions of unlikely dreams. There was always a feeling of intense excitement and happiness at being with her again, and with it a sense of anxiety – fulfilled when she woke and realised Rianna was not really there. But the dream-feeling would linger on for the rest of the day, giving everything a glimmer of promise and mystery.

And now Rianna was here, flesh and denim and mohair, curled up on the end of her sofa. Helen watched her as if she were watching a butterfly on a flower, trying to fix every detail in her mind before she disappeared again.

That was part of Rianna's fascination. She was elusive, capricious. She never gave anything away.

Helen had had a fantasy of her own. She and Rianna would go through life together, partners in whatever career they chose. If they acquired boyfriends and husbands along the way, that would not sunder them; they would be a team for life, Fafhrd and the Gray Mouser in female form. But real life had intruded. Rianna's parents, for their own reasons, had decided to emigrate.

'Have you been back in England long?' Helen asked, thinking that she had probably spent months visiting other friends before getting round to her.

'A couple of days.'

'Are you with your parents?'

'No. On my own.' She leaned forward slightly, her eyes fixed on the low table. Helen wished she would volunteer some information without being asked.

'On holiday?'

'I'm not sure. Perhaps for good. Can I have another biscuit? What are they, oatmeal?'

'Yes, and nuts and things . . . Come on, tell me something about Australia. You have been living in Australia for the past fifteen years, haven't you?'

'New Zealand, actually. There's a subtle difference. No snakes, more rain; pretty much like England really.' She dipped the biscuit in her tea and ate it in two bites. Helen wondered if she was too polite to admit that she was starving.

'Were you happy there? I often thought about you.'

'It was all right. I should have written to you, but children don't think, do they?'

'No, it didn't occur to me to find out your address, either. I just thought you were gone for ever, and that was it. How are your parents?'

'Fine.' Rianna was staring down at her mug now, both hands cradling it. 'They're staying over there.'

'But you're thinking of coming back here to live. Why?'

'Things change. I don't know. Helen, it really is nice to see you.' She glanced up with a smile that contained a touch of anxiety, and Helen began to sense something wrong. Unless she had misread Rianna from the beginning, her serenity was transmuting into distinct tension.

'It's marvellous to see you. I'm so glad you're here,' Helen said warmly. 'However did you find out my address, by the way?'

'I tried the phone book first. I wasn't sure you were still in Leicestershire, of course. I couldn't find you or your parents listed under Locke. So then I went back to school and found that sweet old lady who runs the Old Girls' Association, and she told me you lived in Rothley.'

'What a piece of detective work! My mum and dad have moved to the other side of Stamford and, er – well, my name isn't in the book.' Now Helen was being as cagey as Rianna, but she wasn't as good at carrying it off. 'They must have been surprised to see you at school! Did they ask all about New Zealand?'

'Yes, but . . . well, if it's in the past there doesn't seem to be any point in talking about it. I'd rather talk about you, Helen. You didn't answer my question. Is Nick your husband?'

'He was.' Helen sighed, and reached out to put her mug on the pile of magazines. Once she would almost have died of shame at having to answer such a question; for a long time, she had been unable to admit that anything was wrong with their marriage. But when the pain had built up to a certain pitch she had been forced to talk about it – to friends, to her parents – and eventually, through talking, the shame went away. She was just one of thousands. 'We're divorced.'

'That's awful. I'm sorry.'

'It's all right. I've got over it now, just about.'

'That's why I couldn't find you in the phone book. What name are you under?'

'Durham, but I'm changing back to Locke.'

'How long ago did it happen?'

'The marriage, or the divorce?' said Helen drily. 'I was twenty-one when we got married. We broke up over a year ago. But it's not a story to depress a friend with at four in the afternoon. Over a bottle of wine, maybe . . . Look, Rianna, I know you probably have to leave soon, but it would be lovely if you could stay for a meal. You'd be welcome.' Helen thought she sounded off-hand, as if she was hoping for a refusal, but Rianna answered:

'Oh, I'd love to! If it's no trouble.'

'None. This is marvellous,' Helen exclaimed. When did a butterfly promise to remain on the flower for the whole evening? 'Have you got a car? I don't want you to drink and drive, so you're welcome to stay the night.'

'No car.'

'Where are you staying, though? With friends?'

'No.' A slight smile indented her cheeks, but she seemed reluctant to admit the truth. 'I'm in a hotel near Leicester station. I came out here on the bus. I haven't any friends in England, Helen; I lost touch with everyone.' Her hands were shaking. There *was* something wrong. The enigmatic mask was slipping and beneath it, Helen began to see vulnerability. 'I came to you because you were the only person I really felt close to. I kept my fingers crossed that you'd remember me. I need a friend, Helen; you don't mind, do you?'

'Mind?' she exclaimed, stunned. 'Of course not. Quite the opposite.'

Rianna leaned her head back against the sofa cushions and said quietly, 'Thanks. It means a lot to me. It feels so strange to be here now. Everything's so different, and yet it all seems so familiar . . . Like coming home. Almost.'

There was so much Helen had forgotten, but that one word brought it back into crystal focus. *Almost* home . . . The secret of Rianna's real home had been part of their games, something easily dismissed as childish fancy. Harder to account for how real it had seemed. Suddenly Helen did not want to remember, but she could not help it.

A summer's day in the Park. Helen and Rianna were nine years old and the bracken was up to their ears, releasing the green aromatic smell that sent Helen's heart leaping. As always they had left the main path to the day trippers from Leicester, and were following the narrowest of deer tracks. Sometimes they left the path altogether and waded through the bracken as if through a sea. They liked it most when it came above their heads and they could lose themselves in a forest of secretive, glowing greens, not minding when the tough stems caught at their ankles. If they fell, the bracken bore their weight like a sprung mattress.

It was their own world, a secret kingdom.

'We are Chalcenians, very special people,' Rianna was saying. She always wove the fantasies, and Helen always went along with them. 'We are dressed like kings and queens, and we ride on special creatures. Not horses.'

'Unicorns?' Helen suggested hopefully.

'No, not unicorns! I can't remember what they're called.'

'We ought to give them a name.'

'They have a name. I just can't remember it. But they're tall and slender and they run like the wind. No one can catch us!'

They laughed, and pushed through the bracken in a kind of skipping gallop. The air was an elixir of hot sunlit dust, summer distilled, clouded with flies and gnats.

There was nothing to fear. These were still days when children could play alone in safety. There was no future, only the present. Helen's only worry – when she thought about it – was the possibility of being bitten by an adder. Now and then she would look anxiously amid the tangled stems and grass, but she had never yet seen one.

'Helen, stop!' Rianna called softly, ahead of her. 'Look at this!'

The bracken thinned out and formed a fringe round a pond, one of those wonderful secret ponds that they would stumble on once, and never find again. It reflected the perfect blue of the sky and the sharp-edged silver clouds drifting above. On its edge, framed against the water, was a snake.

Helen almost choked on a scream, but Rianna shook her arm. 'Shh! Don't move!'

'Is it an adder?' she whispered anxiously.

'No, of course not! They don't have adders here! It's Talui, the giver of grace. Look at the colour of its eye – that's the colour of the arms.'

Helen had no idea what Rianna was talking about, but she was transfixed and could not speak. As she stared at it she saw that it was not a snake but a lizard a foot long with limbs as delicate as a bird's. It was bronze in colour, with each tiny scale edged in gold. It was bizarre and beautiful, and it had – Helen blinked until her eyes hurt – it had only one eye. A central eye an inch in diameter, which glowed like a cabochon emerald.

They watched it until it lost interest in them, and slunk away into the grass.

'Wasn't it beautiful? Let's climb that hill!'

'But Rianna – '

'Come on!'

Helen was trembling, transported, aware that although they were playing a game, Rianna had somehow made it real. It had happened before. Rianna always made it happen.

Rianna made the paths and the people vanish. She dissolved walls, she spirited away the signs that said 'Feeding the deer is dangerous and contrary to the by-laws', or 'Visitors are not allowed beyond this point'. She made the Park spread out to cover the world.

From the top of the hill, no sign of civilisation could be seen; there were only bracken-covered slopes tilting down into oak forests, ancient rocks jutting against the sky. No farmland, no cars flashing along distant roads. Even the insects no longer plagued them. Only one drifted by, and that was a bee the size of an oak apple, striped in scarlet and black. Its wings were like veined glass.

'We only have to cross the forest and I'd be home,' said Rianna. She sounded solemn, not childlike at all.

'Don't be silly, Loughborough is miles away!'

'No, I mean my real home. I've forgotten the name of it, but I'll remember.'

'Is it my home too?'

'You ask such silly questions, Helen! I'd like to take you there but I can't – not yet.'

'Why not?'

Rianna frowned. Helen wished she would make her feel more part of the game; it was too much Rianna's fantasy, and she felt excluded. If she tried to take a more active part, she was kindly but firmly put down. A more wilful child might have got angry, but Helen was so much under her spell that she had to humour her.

'I don't know. I can't get back there, I can't remember how.'

'Well, make up a way.' She was worried that Rianna was about to cry, but her face cleared and she said quite kindly:

'You don't understand, Helen. I can't make it up. I have to remember.'

Helen tried to make suggestions that might jog her memory, as they wandered down the hill. Rianna shook her head at each one, sometimes smiling, but she showed no impatience with Helen and let her talk on. Helen simply wished the afternoon would last for ever.

It did not end until Rianna wanted it to. Helen was sure she could never have found her way out alone; her friend made the boundaries vanish, and only she could bring them back. That was the only thing that distressed Helen; the fact that she needed Rianna, but Rianna did not need her. That she minded, very much.

But it did not matter. They were together, and there was nowhere she would rather be than Rianna's world.

'We ought to go back,' Rianna said eventually, slipping her arm through Helen's. 'I'm hungry, and I want to go to the loo.'

'So do I, but it's miles to the gate.'

'No it isn't. It's there.' As she spoke Helen saw the wall in front of them, and beyond it the sunlight burning on car roofs, people queueing for ice cream.

Afterwards, Helen and her father spent hours trying to find the lizard in his encyclopedias. He was so sweet about it, and that stuck in her mind; he did not dismiss her description as childish nonsense, and when he had exhausted British reptiles he looked up those of every country in the world.

'Are you sure it only had one eye in the middle, Helen? It must have been some kind of marking. Tell you what, we'll look in the library tomorrow, shall we?'

They never identified the lizard, of course. It belonged in Rianna's world. Its name was Talui, the giver of grace.

Did I believe it? Helen asked herself. *We were just lost. It's not hard for children to lose themselves in the Park. I saw an ordinary creature, but my mind's distorted it into something weird and wonderful. And Rianna; did she think it was all real? Does she believe it now?*

'This is very kind of you, Helen,' said Rianna, settling herself into the front seat of the small blue Renault. 'It will only be for a day or two, I promise; I have some money but it won't last long, and I really need to find a job.'

'I keep telling you, you can stay as long as you like. I don't mind living on my own but I get a bit bored sometimes. It will be lovely to have someone else about the house.' Helen pulled out into the traffic, nosing into the lane that would take her on to the A6 and back to Rothley. 'You don't have much luggage; are you sure you've got everything?'

'Yes. There didn't seem any point in bringing much; too difficult to carry, so why not make a new start?'

Helen had persuaded her to check out of the hotel and bring all her belongings to her house. Inside, she could hardly suppress her joy at the prospect of Rianna staying with her; outwardly, she maintained a front of practicality. How did one strike a balance between being over-friendly and too off-hand? There was nothing more soul-destroying than showing affection when it was not reciprocated.

As a child, Helen had never been that confident of Rianna's friendship. Sometimes everything had been perfect between them, but at others Rianna – acting on her own whims – would be elusive and distant. Those episodes had caused Helen real agony, and left a thread of insecurity that stayed inside her into adulthood. Now, foolishly, she felt as if those fifteen years had been obliterated. She was reacting to Rianna as she had when they were five or six, with a sort of awed hero-worship. A 'crush', they had called it at school. But they were not children any more. Both had changed . . . and yet some things never changed. Her marriage had taught Helen a number of harsh lessons, but confidence in her value to others was not one of them.

Rianna was quiet in the car. It had been overcast when they had left Leicester, but now the cloud was giving way to a purple and gold dusk that lent glamour even to the dreary main road. Sandwiched in the rush-hour traffic they drifted with it, stopping and starting.

'Are you married, by the way?' Helen asked, to make conversation.

'No.'

'That answers my next question; I assume you haven't any children!' Rianna did not reply. 'Nick and I never got round to it, and it's just as well, as things turned out.'

She still said nothing. 'Are you OK? You're very quiet.'

'Oh yes, I'm fine – I was just remembering all these places and landmarks I used to know. Such a long time ago. It's strange to come back and find it's all still here!'

'Nearly there now,' said Helen, as the traffic lights changed and she turned left into the village. 'The A6 part of Rothley is awful – all that traffic – but the village proper is lovely. Not as pretty as Woodhouse or Swithland, but it has such a nice atmosphere. True Charnwood.' Helen made a detour that took her along the main street, with its Victorian cottages and tiny shops. 'I don't need to come this way, but I just want to show you – '

Rianna grasped her arm. 'Helen, stop the car.'

Helen was startled, but remembered to check there was no one behind before pulling into the kerb. Rianna jumped out as she was braking and ran across the road behind the car. Helen kept sight of her for a moment in the mirror, but in the time it took her to turn round, she had vanished.

The alarm Helen felt was irrational but horribly real, as if she were a child suddenly deserted by a parent – or an adult losing someone else's child. Was Rianna ill? A pain shot through her head, and darkness zig-zagged around the edges of her eyes.

'Damn,' she muttered, rubbing at her neck as she tried to twist into a more comfortable position. Her heart was beating fast and she had gone cold. Her anxiety was so strong that it seemed to have come from outside her; it was an emotion straight out of childhood, one which should have been left there.

A day not long before Rianna had gone to New Zealand: the two of them running through the bracken, Rianna beside her – and suddenly gone. Helen had searched for half an hour, unable to find an adult or any living soul. She had been almost frantic before she had found Rianna beneath a tree, dazed, apparently having fainted or fallen and knocked herself out. Helen had never forgotten the awful glassy vagueness of her eyes, and could not bear to think about what would have happened had she not found her. It was the last time they had played together, her last memory of being in the park with Rianna.

The village had taken on a ghost-town feel. It was a nightmare come to life, Rianna there and then gone, as if she had never existed.

'I'm being an idiot,' she told herself.

She waited. Five minutes passed, and it seemed longer. She could not stop her mind from racing ahead to visions of searching for her, calling the police and not being believed . . .

She was about to get out of the car when the sound of the passenger door opening almost made her leap out of her skin. She turned to see Rianna easing herself into the seat, clutching a bottle of wine and a frozen cheesecake.

'For tonight,' she said, grinning. 'Why are you staring at me like that?'

'The way you dashed off – I thought you were ill.'

'Oh, I'm sorry – I saw the grocer's open and I thought if I told you where I was going, you'd try to stop me.'

'No – I mean yes,' Helen said, recovering herself. 'It's good of you – I was just a bit startled, and you were gone such a long time.'

'Was I? There was a queue, and I would have been quicker but when I came out, that shop caught my eye.' She pointed ahead and to the left. 'Didn't you see me looking in the window? You must have been looking the other way.'

'Yes I was. I don't know how I missed you walking past the car. Do you mean that craft shop?'

'Yes. Honeybee Crafts. They've got some beautiful things in the window. It's a shame they're closed.'

Helen relaxed, and started to laugh. 'Well, Wednesday is my half-day off.'

Rianna looked at her quizzically. 'Why? Is that where you work?'

'Better than that. It's my shop.' The pain in her skull vanished and the world took on warmth and colour again. She could have hugged Rianna for the thoughtful gesture of buying the wine. 'I drove this way so I could show you. I must say I'm flattered that you found it for yourself!'

'So, how long have you owned the shop?'

The wine glittered in Rianna's glass as she turned it between her fingers, catching the reflection of the candleflame. Her fingernails were perfect ovals. Helen, who was long-limbed and mousy-haired and inclined to be broad in the hips, envied her petiteness. In jeans and a mohair jumper the exact autumn-leaf brown of her hair, she looked exquisite.

'It's rented, actually, but I've had it two years.' Helen involuntarily pulled a face.

'Isn't it going too well?'

'Oh, business-wise it's quite good now; I'm breaking even at last. But I've worked bloody hard for it, and the memory of that's still a slightly sore point . . . '

'Oh, why?' Rianna had been asking questions all evening, thus avoiding having to say anything about herself. Helen did not mind; it was enough to have her here, to be talking to each other as they had never talked as children. She was prepared to be patient and win Rianna's trust.

'Well, it was what broke up my marriage. Sort of. Only it wasn't.'

Rianna raised her eyebrows. 'You mean you were spending all your time at the shop and Nick didn't like that?'

'Yes. At least, that's what I thought the rows were about.' Helen swallowed some wine and refilled their glasses. 'I want to tell you about it, but it still upsets me a bit.'

'It's bound to.' Rianna looked straight at her, and Helen found her eyes disconcerting. 'But why didn't he help you with it?'

'He wasn't interested. He had his own career, he's an architect. It wasn't that he wanted me to be a housewife or anything . . . more that he didn't want me at all. We spent so much time at cross-purposes. I loved him, I thought we were happy. Meanwhile he'd decided he'd made a mistake, but he didn't seem to know any way of ending the relationship except by making my life a misery. So he started complaining that he never saw me, I was always at that effing shop, we might as well be divorced because I was more interested in the shop than in him . . . '

'From that it sounds as though he did want you.'

'No. A lot of it was nonsense. I really made an effort to organise myself so we could spend more time together. God! When I think of all the energy I wasted on trying to sweeten him up and prove I still loved him! But nothing helped. The rows just got worse. Eventually he admitted that he'd been seeing someone else all along – since a few months before I took the shop on.'

'Oh, Helen. So he was using the shop as an excuse to split up with you?'

'That's right. Dear, brave Nick. Anyway, he had his way; we were divorced about a year ago. I got to keep this place while he found a flat in Loughborough with his new girlfriend, Gina.'

'That's terrible.'

Helen sighed. Rianna's presence and the wine cocooned her against the rawness of it; it did not seem to matter so much now. 'I don't know. We've both got what we want.'

'Don't you want him back, then?'

'No. Never. I'm doing fine on my own.'

Rianna insisted on washing up, so Helen went upstairs to make the spare bed. The small back bedroom felt cold, and Helen checked the radiator to make sure it was on. Rianna had already put her bags on the bed, and as Helen moved them she saw, through a half-open zip, a small white face looking at her.

The shock made her catch her breath. She could not resist opening the bag, moving it under the light to find that her eyes had not deceived her; it was a doll about eighteen inches high, but it was no child's toy. The face was like delicate white china, moulded into a strangely blank, hermaphroditic beauty – only it was not china but silk, padded and embroidered into shape. The hair was golden, elaborately dressed, with gold beads and tiny fans glinting among the ringlets.

Helen put the bag down and lifted the doll out. She had never seen anything like it. Its costume was worked from layer on layer of coloured satins, and over that a rainbow of embroidery and glass beads. She could not place it as a reproduction of any historical costume; it must be a fantasy from the mind of the doll's creator. The workmanship was so beautiful that it left her breathless.

'Oh my God,' she said out loud. She turned the doll round and round in her hands, staring at the way the crystal beads caught the light. 'God, I wish I had a couple of these to sell in the shop!'

'Do you like it?' said a voice behind her.

Helen started and saw Rianna in the doorway. Embarrassed, she gasped, 'It's fantastic. I'm sorry, I wasn't going through your luggage or anything – it just caught my eye.'

'It's OK, I was going to show it to you anyway.' She sounded strange; not annoyed, Helen thought, but distracted.

'Wherever did you get it from? Let me guess; you must have got it on the way from New Zealand, in Singapore or somewhere.'

'No. I made it myself. I make them.'

Helen shook her head in bewilderment. 'It's just – I've never seen anything so beautiful. You know, I sometimes dream that I'm at a craft fair and I find an object so exquisite that I can't believe my eyes. Now it's suddenly happened in real life and I – oh, I don't know what to say. I had no idea you were so clever.'

Rianna came forward and took the doll from her. But she did not look at it; she held it loosely against her chest and gazed over the top of its head, pensively. 'It wasn't meant to be particularly beautiful. This is just the way they have to be.'

'Well, it is,' Helen said uncertainly. 'Why don't you bring her downstairs, and we'll give her pride of place on the mantelpiece? She's another welcome guest!'

'All right,' Rianna said, but she did not move. 'Helen . . . there's something I ought to tell you.'

At last, Helen thought. 'What is it?'

'It's about why I left New Zealand.' Her voice was quiet, her eyes downcast. 'I sort of ran away. There was a man bothering me.'

'What do you mean?'

'Watching me, asking questions about me where I worked.'

'How horrible,' Helen said, shuddering. 'Was it someone you knew?'

Rianna hesitated. 'No,' she said, with a convulsive shake of her head.

'Well, what did he want?'

'I don't know. I didn't wait to find out.' Her voice was even softer now, as if she was ashamed of what she was saying. 'It sounds silly now, but at the time I was really scared.'

'But I don't understand; why didn't you tell your parents, or the police?'

'I – I couldn't tell anyone. It was – I just couldn't.'

'You really should have done, you know,' said Helen. She was shocked and had no reason to disbelieve the story, yet something in Rianna's attitude made her doubtful. Strange how memory tended to retain only the good and filter out the bad, and that something she had forgotten for years could suddenly return with such force.

Rianna, eight years old, standing in that exact same pose, looking at the ground, her voice husky as she said, 'You must promise not to tell anyone, Helen. My parents adopted me. I was found when I was five, and I can't remember anything before that. It's because I came from another place, another world, and I can't go back.'

Helen would forgive Rianna almost anything, but she was not an idiot. She could tell the difference between truth and fantasy; there was no other world, there had only been a park and their imaginations. She had never been sure whether Rianna herself believed the things she said, or whether it was just her colourful imagination. In a child, it hardly seemed to matter. But in a grown woman – to think that she might still be inventing wild stories to dramatise her life – there was something grotesque in that. Compulsive lying, was that putting it too strongly?

'You did tell your family where you were going, didn't you?'

'Yes, of course,' said Rianna. 'Well, they think I've got a holiday job in Europe. I left in rather a hurry. I'm sorry, Helen. I didn't plan to descend on you with my problems but I just don't know what to do.'

Helen hated to distrust Rianna, but to believe her was almost worse. She drew a breath to quell her uneasiness. Whatever the truth, Rianna was upset and genuinely needed her help.

'Listen, I've said you can stay with me and I meant it. I'd

like you to think of this as your home.'

At that, Rianna visibly relaxed. 'I'd be so grateful. It won't be for long. Anything I can do in return – I'll pay you rent, of course – '

'Oh, let's worry about that another time. There is something you could do, though. I realise these dolls must be hard to make, but how would you feel about making some more, and I'll try to sell them in the shop?'

Rianna looked up, and a smile lit her eyes like white sunshine through a cloud. Helen suddenly had a feeling, not déjà vu but one uncannily similar, that the whole day had been arrowing towards this conclusion. She wished she could read the thoughts behind those veiled eyes.

'They're not as difficult as they look. I'd love to, Helen. It's the only thing I'm good at.'

They finished the evening with coffee, which kept Helen awake for hours. She fell asleep eventually; at least, she hoped she had. It could only have been a dream that she lay paralysed, staring at the door; that it stood a fraction open and that in the blackness beyond, a small white face was watching her.

Chapter Two

Within six weeks, Rianna had made ten dolls and Helen had sold them all except one.

Helen had priced them as high as she dared and wondered if it was too much, though the figure hardly seemed sufficient for all the skill that had gone into them. She need not have worried. From the day she put the first three on the shelf, they entranced everyone who came in.

For the next batch, she bought a small display case and they became the focal point of the shop, almost without her intending it. They shimmered under the lights, and she loved to see customers go straight to them, spellbound by the coloured satins sewn intricately with blue, red and green crystal beads, and by their pale, serene faces.

She had taken Rianna to every haberdasher's in Leicester and Nottingham in search of the exact materials she needed. Rianna was hard to please, but found what she wanted eventually; and Helen felt mildly surprised that the fabrics to make the dolls could actually be bought in the shops. In Rianna's hands they were transformed into something quite out of the ordinary.

When she was not busy, Helen never grew tired of looking at them. Each time she sold one, her pleasure was mixed with a distinct sadness that she would not see it again. Word of the dolls was spreading, and to her astonishment several people came in to ask about them.

'I don't know whether to take both,' said one woman, looking at the last two left in the case. 'My daughter collects costume dolls, you see, but they are so lovely I wouldn't mind one for myself . . . No, I had better only take one for now. Are they made locally?'

'Yes, a friend of mine makes them,' said Helen, wrapping it carefully in tissue paper. 'We'll be having some more.'

'She ought to be selling them in Harrods, not a little place like this with hardly any customers.'

Helen was still reeling at this backhanded compliment as she closed the till and bent down to unpack a carton of carved wooden ducks. She only heard the sharp *ting* of the bell sound once as the woman left, and she did not realise that someone else had come in until she straightened up and saw a man in a tailored raincoat looking into the glass case.

It was Nick.

'Hi,' he said in a friendly tone. 'I thought there was no one around. I didn't see you, hiding behind the counter.'

'Hello. What brings you here?' Helen asked, guarded.

'Well, that sounded better than "What do you want?" I was just passing. I had to go into Leicester to fetch some plans.' He stood with his hands in his pockets, looking round at the polished pine floor, the paintings and prints on the walls, the ferns in hanging baskets. It was a small shop, but Helen had made the best of the space. There were shelves on two sides, and in the centre was an antique table on which the display case stood with patchwork cushions and lace heaped around it. 'You've got this place looking very nice. Good God, that much for a doll!'

'I don't sell any old rubbish, you know. Don't you like it?'

'Yes, it's very nice, but who's going to pay that?'

'I'll have you know I've sold lots of them already.'

Nick looked suitably impressed. He studied the doll with growing interest, the light from the case turning his face almost as pale as the doll's. She had not forgotten why she had first been attracted to him; he could have been taken for a male model, with green eyes and abundant blond hair that any woman might have envied.

'Tell you what,' he said, 'give me a discount and I'll buy this one!'

Helen was taken aback. 'Are you sure?'

'Yes!' He was grinning as if the whole thing was a great joke. 'Knock ten pounds off.'

'Five.'

'Come on, I'm doing you a favour.'

'No you're not; people come in here asking for them.'

'Where do you get them from?'

Helen explained briefly about Rianna. Nick gave a mock sneer. 'Sounds cosy. Must be like a Korean sweat-shop in your house. Go on, then, wrap it up.'

'You really want it?'

'Yes, why not? The more I look at it, the more I like it. Is it male or female?'

'Female,' said Helen, surprised. 'That's what I've always assumed, anyway. It's wearing a dress, although that doesn't necessarily mean anything.'

'No, it's more of a robe,' he said as she lifted it from the case. It was the first time he had shown any interest in the things she sold. 'It's got a sort of oriental look to it, like a stylised Eastern print. No, I can see it as a male.'

'Well, I'm sure Gina will like it.' She had perfected the art of mentioning the pretty, dark-haired girl for whom he had left her without sounding bitter. She went to the counter and began to wrap the doll. 'I don't suppose you've got the cash on you? I don't take credit cards.'

Nick pulled a grudging face. 'I'll write you a cheque.' As he tore it out and handed it to her, he said, 'Helen, are you doing anything Sunday lunchtime?'

She paused. The doll's face peered at her from the tissue paper. 'Why?'

'I thought you might like to go out for a drink, that's all.'

'Whatever for?'

He shrugged. 'Well, we're still friends, aren't we? Friends go out for drinks together.'

Nick had a way of sounding very genuine, which made her feel a complete rat for turning him down. 'I'm sorry. I can't. I'm seeing Martin Ashley.'

'Oh, him. I thought he was working away.'

'Only temporarily. He's back this weekend.'

'Oh.' Nick sounded unimpressed. 'What about one evening next week, then?'

'No,' she said quickly. 'I'm too busy, I have to go out and buy stock in my spare time and – '

'You don't have to make excuses.' His voice had an edge to it, as if he were annoyed but still trying to be nice. 'Just a friendly drink, for Christ's sake! What's the matter with you?'

Helen felt her face turning hot. 'Well, honestly, why ask me out when we've been divorced for a year?'

'It doesn't matter. Forget it.'

'What would Gina say?'

'I said, forget it.'

Helen made a determined effort to stay calm. She hated Nick for still having any hold over her at all, but it was a conditioned reflex; he only had to say a few words for her temper to ignite in self-defence.

'There you are,' she said, handing him the parcel.

He was silent for a second. Then he said, 'If you ask me, Rianna is a bad influence on you.'

'What the hell do you mean?'

'Well, you've always lived in a bloody fantasy world. She turned your head as a kid and you've never grown out of it.'

He sounded as if he was joking, but Helen no longer found his idea of a joke funny. She felt her temper rising, blind and helpless because she knew nothing she said would change the way he thought. 'That's a ridiculous thing to say, and you know it.'

'Is it? Look at this shop. Surrounding yourself with all this stuff, pretty pictures and corn dollies and things. It's your way of hiding from life. You should try living in the real world, Helen!'

'Do you think running a business is easy? Of course, you wouldn't know, never having bothered to help me. I really don't know why you've come in here, Nick, unless it's your idea of a good time to insult me.'

'I like winding you up,' he said mildly.

'Well, good for you!' she shouted. 'Hadn't you better be going back to work?'

'Yeah.' He picked up his receipt and turned his back on her. 'I come in for a friendly chat and get yelled at. Great. Have fun with Martin.'

He walked out, slamming the door behind him. He was the wounded one, but he was taking it like a man; at least, that was the impression he contrived to give. Helen was left furious and shaking with frustration, because although it was only a pale replay of far worse scenes in the past, it brought them all back to her with a vengeance.

She should be free of it by now. She should be free.

*

The scene was still preying on her mind when she went home that evening. She found Rianna working on the dining-room table, leaning over the sewing machine with scraps of brilliant satin scattered around her. She was not a tidy worker. A splash of beads glittered on the carpet, and Helen knelt down to pick them up.

'I sold the tenth doll today. To Nick, of all people.'

'That's marvellous!' Rianna looked up with a smile. 'But I thought you and he weren't on speaking terms.'

'Only when it suits him,' Helen said gloomily. 'You must have an even more special talent than I'd thought. He's the last person I'd have expected to want one.' She pulled out a chair and sat down at the table, resting her chin on her hands.

'He's upset you, hasn't he?' said Rianna. 'Stay there, I'll make some tea and you can tell me about it.'

It was good to come home to a friend, instead of a husband who behaved like an enemy. Helen told Rianna everything.

'Why ask me out after all this time? I know what it is; I bet Gina's away for a few days and he's at a loose end. He's after me because he's got nothing better to do.'

'You're very hard on him,' Rianna said quietly. 'Some people don't know what they've lost until it's too late. Maybe he wants to make peace.'

'You don't know him, Rianna. And I hope you never do. Don't say I didn't warn you; he looks like an angel and behaves like a pig.'

Rianna curled her hands around her tea mug. 'I didn't know you had a boyfriend, Helen.'

'I haven't.'

'Who's Martin Ashley, then?'

Helen sighed. 'Just a friend. I really am seeing him on Sunday, though.'

'Come on then, tell me about Martin.'

'Not much to tell, really. He came into the shop just before Christmas. You know that lovely print of horses I've got hanging behind the counter? It caught his eye and he said, did I know that those horses were Arabs? I said yes, that's why I chose it, because they were my favourite breed. He wanted to buy it. I told him it wasn't for sale and he said that was a shame because his girlfriend would have loved it. She has an Arab mare and gelding of her own. Anyway, we got talking and it ended up with him asking me if I'd like to go over and see them. I've been over a few times and helped Martin exercise them; his girlfriend, Jo, is a farmer and she doesn't have much time to ride, so it helps her out too. To be honest, I get the impression Martin thinks more of the horses than she does.'

'So that's where you're going on Sunday?'

'Yes. I haven't seen Martin or the horses for ages. His company sent him to work in Scotland for eight weeks. He's a chemical engineer. I don't like going to the farm when he's not there.'

'Why not?'

'Oh, Jo's a bit peculiar. I don't think she likes me. She certainly doesn't trust me to take one of the horses out on my own, and I suppose she's got a point. If anything did happen, I'd feel terribly responsible. Martin's great, though.' Helen's bad mood began to lift as she thought of being on horseback, escaping work and Nick and relaxing for a few hours. 'Hey, why don't you come with me?'

'No – thanks for asking, but I don't think I will,' said Rianna, draining her mug and moving back to the sewing machine.

'Look, I told you we're just friends. You wouldn't be in the way. The farm's not far, just on the edge of Swithland. We go riding all round Charnwood and it's absolutely beautiful. You'd love it.'

'The truth is, I'm not that keen on horses.'

'Oh. Well, I won't force you, but you know you'd be welcome. God, I'm really looking forward to it!'

'It's nice to see you looking a bit happier than when you came in,' Rianna said wryly.

Helen smiled. Rianna seemed happy too; the tension Helen had noticed when she first arrived had vanished, and only reappeared if Helen tried to ask her questions that she did not want to answer. 'It's nice having you here – '

As she spoke the telephone shrilled out, making her jump.

'Hello, Helen?' said a faint voice on a crackling line. 'It's Martin.'

'Hello! Are you home? You sound as if you're at the North Pole.'

'No, I'm not back till Saturday,' he shouted. 'Look, about our ride on Sunday – I'm sorry, but I can't make it. I haven't seen Jo for two months and she insists on me spending the day with her. I'm taking her out for lunch so I thought it was best if – oh hang on, my money's running out already.' There was a pause and some indistinct swearing. 'Helen, it won't take my money. Sorry. I'll see you some time next week.'

'It's all right, give me a ring when you – ' The line went dead. She put the phone down slowly and stood over it for a moment, her mouth compressed into a grim line.

'That was Martin,' she said. 'Cancelling Sunday. Jo wants him to herself all day.'

'That's a shame. But you can go another day, can't you?'

'Oh, I suppose so. I was looking forward to it, that's all. Oh, sod it!'

Helen went into the kitchen and began to make a salad for their tea, trying to forget her disappointment in activity. When she came out again to see if Rianna had cleared the table, her coppery head was still bent over her sewing.

'Haven't you had enough for today?' Helen asked. 'You were working even before I left this morning.'

'It just struck me, if you sold the last doll you won't have any on display. I think I can finish this one by the morning.'

Helen looked to see how far she had got. 'I don't think so. Not unless you sit up all night.'

'I wouldn't mind, really. It wouldn't be the first time.'

'I know,' Helen said gravely. 'I've seen a light under your door at four in the morning sometimes. Rianna, there's really no need for you to work so hard. The dolls are doing superbly well, but the last thing I want is for you to make yourself ill over them.'

'I won't. I enjoy making them.' She picked up the doll's naked torso and it hung jointless and pallid in her hand. 'I'm happy, Helen. When I'm making the dolls . . . it's the only time I really feel at peace.'

'Oh?' said Helen, puzzled.

'I don't know why. I wish I did. Sometimes I feel as if there's a really important reason, and I just can't quite remember it.' She frowned and rubbed her forehead. Helen suddenly felt concerned. 'I wish I could work faster.'

'You're not doing badly. I thought each one would take weeks, all the embroidery . . . '

Rianna shrugged. 'The first one did take weeks. It's practice. I wish I could make thousands, and give them away.'

Helen did not know what to say. She felt vaguely out of her depth. Rianna had told her that she had made and sold the dolls in New Zealand for a number of years; that knowledge, coupled with her own observation of how hard Rianna worked, had begun to worry Helen. It seemed that Rianna's desire to make the dolls was not just enthusiasm, or even the need to make a living, but a compulsion.

'Why on earth would you want to give them away?'

'I'd like everyone to have one,' Rianna replied, simply and without conceit.

Helen could not bring herself to ask why. Perhaps it was tiredness, but the evening seemed to be taking on a strange and depressing air of unreality, and she felt that one more inexplicable answer would finish her.

'So would I,' she said lightly, 'but I'd rather they paid for the privilege. We have to eat. Look, at the risk of sounding like your mother, will you please put everything away and have a rest?'

'All right. I can carry on after tea, anyway.'

The original doll, the one she had brought from New Zealand, still sat on the mantelpiece watching over their activities like a slender-faced Buddha.

Once Helen had asked her what she called the doll. Rianna had reacted strangely; she had become uncomfortable, like a claustrophobic who was desperate to escape a room.

'She has no name,' she had replied.

'I suppose it is a bit childish to name inanimate things, but I can't help it. It doesn't seem right not to.'

'She seems to insist on being called – Ann – Annie,' Rianna muttered.

'Why not call her that, then?'

Rianna shrugged. 'I don't like it.'

Helen had not pursued the matter. Getting sense out of Rianna on certain matters was almost impossible. She had denied Nick's oblique suggestion that there was something wrong with her friend, and normally she was good-natured and refreshingly sane. But sometimes . . .

Helen looked at her, saw the way her eyes gleamed in the small bright light of the sewing machine, and suddenly had an awful suspicion that she could not stop making the dolls if she wanted to.

On Sunday mornings, Helen usually liked to lie in, but on this day she was half awake before six and lay drowsily thinking that there was some reason why she should get up early. Of course, she was going riding . . . She lifted her head off the pillow, then slumped back as she remembered that Martin had put off their arrangements.

The harder she tried to go back to sleep, the more wide awake she felt. Eventually she gave up. She got up quietly, showered and put on jeans, a thick jumper and walking shoes. As she drank a cup of tea she wrote a note to Rianna: 'Can't sleep, have gone out for a walk. Back in a couple of hours. Love, Helen.'

Her decision to drive to Bradgate Park had nothing to do with Rianna; not consciously, at least. It had become part of her routine to go there at least once a month, and when she was worried about anything she found it helpful just to walk and think. Nick had dismissed it as escapism, as he would, but the fact was that in her worst times with him the Park had given her infinite consolation.

Bradgate was a wild deer park, about eight hundred and fifty acres in area, just north of the village, Newtown Linford, where Helen had lived as a child. It was flanked by farmland, with Cropston reservoir to the east and Swithland Woods along its topmost edge.

There were car parks on three of its corners, but Helen went to the nearest, which lay by the reservoir. Loose stones crunched under the Renault's tyres as she pulled up. Although it was early there were quite a few people about already, mostly dog walkers. The car park was edged by a high stone wall, and beyond she could see the sweep of a hill crowned with ancient rocks and a dark clump of trees. Helen left the car and headed for the gate, pulling up her collar and thrusting her hands deep in her pockets.

It always seemed a couple of degrees colder here; a sharp wind cut between the hills, and she was walking straight into it. She left the main path that led through to the Newtown Linford side, and began to walk briskly up the slope to her right until she was warm. Then she paused to catch her breath and look around her.

Spring had not come to the Park yet; the trees were still naked, and it would be several weeks before the first fronds of bracken began to push up through the earth. Between two walled-off copses, she could see a wider vista of hills where last year's dead bracken had been burned off. It had left the slopes carbon-black, criss-crossed by narrow paths. With the sky a milky grey and mist softening the horizon all around her, she could see no colours except grey, black and the muted green of the grass.

Yet even in this bleakness Bradgate was beautiful. In all weathers it had a special atmosphere; something a casual visitor might not notice, that only seemed to seep into the conscious mind with long familiarity. Mist lying in the branches of ancient oaks; the scent of earth and bracken, deer wandering through the rough grass, and the dark masses of rock standing against the sky . . . all were part of it, but there was a mystery within it that defied analysis.

The Park as she remembered it from her childhood with Rianna, and the Park now, were like two different worlds. One had become a dream in which it was always summer. But through her adolescent and adult years, memory had been supplanted by reality; a cold and wild place which nevertheless bore the marks of human tending all over it. To get lost was impossible; whichever way you walked, you were certain to reach the boundary wall eventually.

Helen went deeper into the Park. The ground squelched underfoot. This winter marshiness made most people stick to the asphalt path, and she was glad of that; it meant she could walk for hours and hardly see another soul. Her thoughts turned inwards and she took less and less notice of her surroundings.

Why couldn't Nick leave her alone? Of course, that was him all over; he didn't want her, but he couldn't bear to lose control of her, either. It was a pointless exercise, yet she could not stop herself brooding about it, nor comparing him to Martin, who was the complete opposite. He was nothing to look at, it was true, but he was kind and easygoing. One thing Helen had learned was to value personality above looks. Martin liked Helen as she was. He accepted her; on the other hand, why shouldn't he? He was only a friend . . .

'What on Earth am I thinking about?' she asked herself sharply. She had no wish for another disastrous relationship, and there was no question of it anyway. Martin was devoted to Jo, although what he saw in her . . .

Helen stopped and looked around her, noticing a change in the light. It seemed darker. Iron-grey clouds were massing overhead and she cursed herself for forgetting to bring a waterproof. She was almost at the eccentric stone tower, Old John, which meant it would take her at least twenty minutes to reach the car. She resigned herself to getting wet and began to stroll back towards the Cropston reservoir entrance.

The rain did not come. Instead, the wind seemed to be detaching wisps of cloud from the sky and blowing them in swirling rags across the hillsides. Helen suddenly felt very cold and isolated. She decided to go down to the main path; it would be quicker that way, and there would be more people about.

She walked, and she walked. Old John vanished in the greyness. She knew that by now she should be in sight of the ruined house that had once been the home of Lady Jane Grey, but where it should have been she saw only a rugged slope.

'This is ridiculous,' she said to herself. She knew the Park like the back of her hand. All you had to do was head downhill and you came to the main path; you couldn't avoid it. She paused to orientate herself, and then she noticed that there was something subtly different about the colour of the landscape. The bracken here had not been burned off; it lay as it had died, in fog-sodden russet drifts.

She turned downhill, and she tried again. Still no ruins, no people, no path. She was sweating in her thick jumper and jacket, but the wind seemed to be blowing right through them, making her shiver.

Flanking the path there was a wide, flat stretch of grass

where children played cricket in the summer. Helen was crossing it before she recognised it. With relief she turned to look for the ruined house on her left, but still it was not there.

'There must be an explanation for this.' She tried to convince herself that she was in another part of the park, but there was no mistaking the familiar landscape around her. Only certain landmarks had vanished. A wall that had snaked through the park was gone; an enclosed copse now spilled raggedly across the hillside. Walking on she came to a stream, and that, too, she recognised as the Lin; but she should have crossed the main path to reach it, and the path was not there.

With Rianna, she had never been frightened. But Rianna was not here.

No point in panicking, she thought, taking a deep breath. It's only ten minutes' walk to Newtown Linford. All I have to do is follow the stream.

She fixed her eyes on the small river Lin, hoping that when she looked up again the world might have returned to normal. But the first thing she noticed was that the man-made waterfalls were no longer there; the water foamed over stones in a miniature rapid.

Helen began to run.

She ran for at least ten minutes, but when she had to slow down for breath, there was no gate to greet her, no joggers or middle-aged couples passing her. There was only the curve of a lush, tree-covered hill.

At the hill's base, on the far bank of the stream, a herd of deer stood looking at her. They looked so ordinary that she felt a pang of relief; she had seen such deer in Bradgate every time she had been there. Any moment now she would orientate herself and realise what an obvious mistake she had made.

Her breath steamed on the air as she stood watching them. They were beautiful, but she was quite glad that they were on the opposite bank. As a child she had once been chased by a bull, and had never forgotten the excruciating panic as she scrambled through a hedge to safety, tearing clothes and skin on brambles. She was not actually afraid of cattle or deer, but rutting stags had been known to go for visitors, so there was sense in being wary.

Normally, though, they were shy. Her presence was making

them uneasy and after watching her for a moment they began to move away, all except for one in the centre, one so dark that it was almost black.

It was grazing as the others scattered around it, but when they had gone it raised its head and stared at Helen.

She stared back, her breath suspended. Was this what a hallucination was like, something so vivid that the sufferer had not the slightest doubt that it was real? She knew she was awake, not dreaming, she *knew*, but she did not want to believe what she was seeing.

The creature was not a deer. For a moment she saw it as an extreme caricature of an Arab stallion, with a head so exaggeratedly refined that it resembled that of a sea-horse. The neck was too long, too curved. Its body also was horse-like, but when it moved the resemblance ceased. There was something wrong with its legs. All the joints seemed out of place, and they ended – as far as she could see – in paws.

It was coming towards the water's edge, moving low to the ground like a cheetah. The legs were long and powerful, full of the potential for speed.

Helen did not know what to do. Perhaps it would stay on its own side of the stream, and she could slip away . . . But she watched in alarm as it sprang into the dark water and waded towards her.

She backed away, certain that if she tried to escape she would only provoke it into chasing her. It climbed on to the bank and came on, shaking its head at her, while she held out a nervous hand as she would to befriend a horse. It seemed a foolish gesture. It matched her step for step, contorting its neck to study her from all angles. Its eyes were huge, black as ink bubbles.

'Steady, steady,' she said, her voice trembling. 'Stay there. Just stay there, now.'

The creature thrust its muzzle towards her and she saw a row of small square teeth as it opened its mouth and gave a sort of hoarse, barking whinny. It was the most unpleasant noise she had ever heard.

With that her nerve broke, and she turned and fled.

Chapter Three

The creature drove Helen uphill.

It was a child's nightmare distilled, running with legs as heavy as lead, her throat thick and sore. She skidded on loose stones and slimy drifts of leaves. Her pursuer could have overtaken her whenever it chose, but instead it wove back and forth behind her like a sheepdog driving a ewe.

Helen prided herself on being fit, but she was no athlete, and fear seemed to have drained the strength out of her. The hill was so steep now that although she still tried to run she was moving no faster than a walk, and every time she slipped she gasped with the effort of regaining her balance.

Now the slope began to flatten out, but she could not increase her pace. Looking up, she recognised the next hill, with its crown of dark trees, from endless leisurely walks in the past. It was still the Park she knew but it had become alien, threatening.

She was walking now, as fast as she could, breaking into a stumbling run from time to time. The ground was uneven, bracken stems and grass tussocks threatened to trip her. Every now and then the creature would lunge at her and she would dodge away with a choked yelp of fear. The teeth were bared in the razor-skulled head, and there was a terrible expression in its eyes.

Helen could not see clearly. The appearance of mist blowing across the hillside now seemed to be created by areas of the landscape shimmering, fading in and out. Nothing seemed stable. The animal drove her round a rock and on the far side there was a saucer-shaped hollow gouged out of the ground, filled with loose boulders. She knew that if she let herself be forced into it, she would not be able to climb out.

She twisted away to the left, then the right, but the creature anticipated her and it was always there, leaping from side to side to block her escape.

Helen stumbled over the lip of the hollow. Facing her, where it curved up into a near-vertical wall, she saw the black mouth of a cave. There were no caves in Bradgate, but she wasn't in Bradgate, she was . . . where was she?

The animal was trying to drive her into the cave. The fear she already felt was as nothing to the terror that welled up in her at the sight of it, and it seemed that nothing the creature did to her could be worse than being driven into that darkness.

She flung herself to the ground and lay curled up on the cold grass, gasping painfully for breath, her muscles trembling with exertion. The beast circled her. With a wrenching effort she pulled herself up, seized the first rock she could lay hands on and flung it, catching the creature full on the chest.

It shied back. The long neck undulated, then the head came thrusting towards her. A striking snake could not have inspired her with more alarm and she rolled away, wrapping her arms round her head. Yet it did not bite her. Petrified, she sensed its muzzle inches away from her ear, and she caught the strange scent of it, which was like the smell of snow. Coldness enveloped her head. There was an icy gale blowing on her and it emitted from the animal's nostrils.

'Oh God, no, don't,' she sobbed, half sitting up and trying to edge away.

The creature dipped its head lower and said gutturally, 'You. You.'

Reality was bad enough, without her imagination compounding the horror. It could not really have spoken, it was too horrible to be true.

For a moment Helen looked into its bulging eyes, and she saw a demanding hunger there which froze her. The wind it exhaled was ferocious now, and she cried out, 'What do you want of me?'

It sank down like a crouching cat. She braced herself for the leap, but to her amazement it sprang clean over her, and she had a brief glimpse of a leathery udder between its forelegs before it vanished into the cave.

Helen was not about to wait and see if it emerged again. She struggled up out of the hollow and began to run downhill. Her legs were so tired that she could not control them, and she ran wildly and in danger of falling for several minutes before she was able to slow down.

Nothing followed her.

She was shivering. Her fingers were numb. The black creature had breathed the cold right inside her and she knew that if she could not find a way to get warm soon she might succumb to exposure. She was desperate to go home. But what if she could never find her way out? Rianna was not here to guide her . . .

She looked about anxiously, but there was still nothing to give her hope. It was growing darker and more wintry by the minute. She hid in the hollow of a tree to relieve herself – as if there was anyone to see her – then decided to find the stream again. At least she could survive on water for a time. What were you supposed to do in a situation like this? Find shelter, build a fire? Helen did not smoke and had no matches, but even if she had it would be impossible to make anything burn in this dampness.

And where would she be safe? The creature might come after her again, or there might be others.

She swallowed and rubbed tears out of her eyes. 'Don't behave like a child,' she said severely. But a child was what she felt like, cold and alone and very, very scared.

On the stream's bank she knelt down and saw her reflection on the slow-moving surface. Her face was squarish, with a neat nose and deep-set brown eyes. Usually, she thought, it had a rather businesslike look, but now her cheeks were wind-reddened and her expression so wild with fear that she was shocked. She dipped a hand in to break up the reflection.

The water tasted earthy, but there was no foulness in it. She would not normally have dreamed of drinking anything that did not come from a tap or a bottle, but after the first tentative sip she swallowed it in handfuls until her thirst was quenched.

A noise so faint that it was hardly more than a movement of the air made her turn round, then throw herself flat on her stomach. Something was moving. On her side of the stream, on top of the hill, she saw the head and neck of the beast appearing.

She almost flung herself into the stream in panic, but

mastered the impulse. Then she saw that it was not the same creature. This one was a vivid apricot dappled with black, and it bore a rider.

Helen hung like a fly in a web, not knowing whether to run towards them or away. As she remained there, dithering, she saw more of the animals following the first, walking with long, easy strides. They carried their long necks high in the air, with their sea-horse heads tucked in. Their basic shape was the same as her dark pursuer's, but their colours were so bright that they shone against the dull surroundings like tropical birds. She saw brilliant reds, peacock shades, dark blue dappling into yellow. One was violet, with a mane and tail like a fall of white water. Their tails were held in exaggerated arches, horse-like except that the dock was far longer. Each animal had a rider on its back.

'What the hell are they?' she whispered. 'Oh God, are they human, or what?' She might be seeing things. She might be back in the Park, making a nightmarish vision out of ordinary riders. That would be bad enough, but if they were as real as they looked it meant that she was truly in another world, absolutely alone . . .

If there was any hope left that she was home, the next second dashed it. Behind them, cresting the skyline like a moon, came a creamy-fawn sphere the size of a house. She stared at it in blank confusion. It appeared to be lashed to the saddles of the rearmost four riders, and it came bouncing along the ground behind them as if it was of no great weight, but not buoyant enough to float. A balloon, she thought, but it was too misshapen, its surface too rough and solid-looking.

It was only then that the enormity of the situation really began to dawn on her. She could not cope. She stayed there with the terror building inside her, counting them over and over again until she established there were ten.

They were angling down the hill towards her, all she had to do was to run out in front of them . . . if she dared. The thought horrified her, but if she did not they would ride on and her only chance of help would be gone.

'This is pathetic,' she told herself angrily. 'Without civilisation around me, I can't survive one bloody day!'

Her mixed rage and fear at this knowledge broke her.

Trembling, almost out of her mind, she leapt up and ran towards them, shouting:

'Hey! Please stop!'

At once she wished she had not. The animals were bearing down on her in a whirlwind of unearthly colours, far larger than they had seemed from a distance. And the riders; surely, surely they were not human. The only things she had seen even remotely like them were Rianna's dolls. Their hair stood out from their heads and cascaded down their backs, as bright-hued as their mounts. Their clothes were bright and wild, their faces sharp and strong and as beautiful as carved angels. She felt intimidated, not by their beauty but by their exuberance. As they swept towards her, all arrogance and savage laughter, she realised that they had not seen her.

She could not believe it. She tried to leap out of their way, but too late. She saw a flash of black and apricot hair as the leading creature brushed into her, almost knocking her over, and then she was caught up with them. Their voices rang in her head, colours sang in her eyes. A scent rose up around her, spicy and raw like new-cut wood. To avoid being trampled she tried to run with them, calling out, but they did not hear her. She was overwhelmed. They were loping along at a jog trot now, overtaking her, and however hard she tried she could not keep up. She had no breath left. As her lungs forced her to a standstill and the last four riders passed her, she glanced over her shoulder. What she saw made her gasp in protest and dismay.

The great sphere came drifting along behind them, and she was in its path. All she could do was drop flat to the ground, but it was almost too late for that and the sphere knocked the wind out of her as she fell. It passed over her, bouncing on her back as harmlessly as sponge.

She found her feet, and watched it dwindling like a giant seed pod blown away through the mist. The riders had terrified her, but to be left behind was worse. Dragging energy from desperation she tried to follow, but even running her fastest she stood no chance of catching up with them.

'No! Help me, please,' she yelled, frantic. *'No! Wait!'*

Her voice cracked, her larynx felt raw. The riders were almost out of sight in a wall of mist, but just before they vanished altogether she was sure she saw one of them turn in the saddle, a pale face staring at her over the creature's plumed tail.

She waved her arms and put on a burst of speed. The fog was coming to meet her, so dense that she could not see at all. Her hands and knees took the impact as she slammed into a solid wall.

The shock winded her so badly that she slid to the ground, half stunned. When she recovered enough to stand up, her whole body was shaking with an uncontrollable tremor and her legs felt like cooked spaghetti. She could only stay on her feet by feeling her way along the cold rough surface of the wall.

Suddenly there was metal under her hands. She was looking through a wrought iron gate into a car park edged with trees. Beneath her feet, the pale asphalt of the path looked as if it had been there all the time.

It was the Newtown Linford car park. Her car was at the other end, and she could not face crossing the Park again. She slumped against the gate, hanging on to its struts like a prisoner on the bars of a cell.

'Are you all right, me duck?' said a kindly voice. She looked round and saw one of the park wardens, a tall man in a green waxed jacket, standing by a Range Rover parked just inside the gates.

'I – I don't know,' Helen gasped. Although she was dazed, she realised at once that it would be pointless to describe what had just happened to her. 'I don't feel well. I came over faint.'

'Take it easy,' he said, supporting her by the elbow. 'You look as if you need a doctor.'

'No, no,' she said quickly. 'I know what it is. It's nothing.'

'Are you sure?'

'Yes. It's – it's migraine. I'll be fine when I get home.' He seemed convinced by this. 'Oh, but my car – it's on the Cropston side.'

'Don't worry, duck. I'll drive you back through the Park,' he said, pointing along the main path. It's no trouble.' He helped her into the passenger seat of the Range Rover, then went round to the driver's side. Helen could not bring herself to ask him to leave the Park and drive round by the road; it seemed too ridiculous a request. But the moment he put the vehicle in gear and moved off, she wished she had. Venturing into Bradgate again after she had just escaped seemed insane, and awoke a terror in her that verged on phobia. She sat rigid in her seat, her palms sweating. The stream and the gnarled oaks drifted by the windows and she thought: Surely, surely it can't happen again while I'm with the warden? I'm safe now . . .

She said, 'Were there some people riding in the Park a few minutes ago? Part of a pageant, or something?'

'There shouldn't have been. Horse riders aren't allowed in at the weekend. Did you see someone riding?' he asked, a touch severely.

'No,' Helen said, improvising. 'It's just . . . I heard there might be a pageant, or a charity ride, or something.'

'Not to my knowledge, duck.'

'I must've been mistaken.'

'We had a pageant a few years ago, to commemorate Lady Jane Grey. Do you live locally? Maybe you saw it. That's her family home over there.'

The ruins were back in position again. Helen stared at the elegant, crumbling red towers and let the warden go on talking. On the path ahead of them, adults, children and dogs stepped out of the Range Rover's way with ill grace as it trundled along at a steady five miles an hour.

At the entrance, he stopped the vehicle and helped her out as if she were an old lady. She was grateful; she dared not lose contact with him until she was safely through the wooden side gate.

'Now, are you sure you're all right?'

'Yes, I'm fine now.' She forced a smile to prove it. 'My car's just over there. Thank you so much.'

'That's all right. You take care now.'

Helen half ran to her car, fumbling for the keys. It took a while for her shaking hands to do their work, but the moment she had the door open she leapt in and slammed it behind her. She sat for a long time with her head bowed on the steering wheel.

Whom could she tell?

She could imagine Nick's reaction, and the thought of his

mockery on top of the experience itself made her shudder. Martin would listen with sympathy, then suggest – very sensibly – that she ought to see a doctor. Her parents would be alarmed . . . but none of them would believe her.

There was only Rianna.

Rianna was sitting with her feet tucked under her on the end of the sofa, and there was some classical music playing softly on the stereo. For a moment Helen thought she was relaxing, then saw that she was embroidering a doll's costume. Her fingers moved with astonishing speed, creating the design as she went along.

Helen sat down in the chair opposite. She could not speak. She could feel her teeth chattering and she could not even move to take off her jacket.

Presently Rianna said, 'Did you have a nice walk?'

Helen looked at her watch. She had gone out before seven, and now it was nearly eleven. 'Didn't you wonder why I was such a long time?'

'Were you? I don't notice the time when I'm working.' She looked up, and her expression changed. 'You look as if you're frozen. Has the car broken down or something?'

Helen shook her head. Putting her work aside, Rianna jumped up to turn on the gas fire, then went into the kitchen. Helen heard her boiling the kettle, and a few minutes later she came back and placed a mug of coffee in Helen's numb hands.

'You'd better take your jacket off. The heat won't get through unless you do.' She helped her off with it, while Helen passed the mug from one hand to the other as she disentangled herself from the sleeves.

'Thanks.' She sipped at her coffee, and she had never tasted anything quite so wonderful in her life.

'Helen, you look terrible.' Rianna sat on the floor at her feet, the doll forgotten. 'What's wrong? You seem really shaken up.'

If Rianna had sometimes been off-hand with Helen as a child, she never was now. It was as if their roles had changed, and now it was she who needed Helen. They looked after each other. Helen was usually warmed by Rianna's considerateness, but for the first time she could not even respond with a smile. She felt cold, set apart.

'I think perhaps you know what's wrong.'

Rianna frowned slightly. 'How do you mean?'

'When we were at school – ' Helen paused and drank her coffee. It was so hard to begin, but she forced herself. 'We've never really talked about the past,' she said. 'I think we ought to.'

'If you like, but I don't see what it's got to do with what's upset you,' said Rianna, wrapping her arms around her knees. Helen recognised the onset of the uneasiness Rianna showed whenever she did not want to discuss something. Helen was very sensitive to it and hated to distress her. Usually she changed the subject, but this time she could not.

She said, 'Do you remember, we used to read the Narnia books together, about some children who went into another world?'

'Vaguely.'

'And we made up our own game and our own imaginary world, only we didn't go through the back of a wardrobe, we went into Bradgate Park. We'd go for miles and we'd never see a wall or a path or any other people because we weren't in the Park any more, we really were in another world.'

Helen had a preconceived idea of how the conversation would go on. Rianna would say, 'I remember,' and Helen would say, 'Well, it's just happened again.'

Instead, Rianna murmured, 'Did we do that? I'd forgotten.'

'*Forgotten?*' Helen was stunned beyond words. Rianna shifted slightly so that she was no longer facing her, and there was an uncomfortable pause. 'Rianna, how could you possibly have forgotten?'

'It was a long time ago. We played all sorts of games. I just don't remember that one specifically.'

Rianna had never made Helen angry before, but she was coming close to it.

'I don't think I ever knew you to play a game, not like most kids do. You were always deadly serious.'

'Was I?'

'You made me believe that things which couldn't possibly happen were real. You made me believe the Park could be another world.' Rianna said nothing. Helen found it harder and harder to get the words out, and the memory of the dark creature made her feel dizzy. 'When I – when I grew older, I realised . . . or rather I convinced myself that what I thought had happened couldn't have done. It must have been a game, mustn't it, but today – '

'Helen, please,' Rianna said sharply. 'I've no idea what you're talking about.'

'You must have!' Helen raised her voice, and regretted it immediately. 'I'm sorry. I'm sorry. But why won't you listen to what I'm trying to tell you?'

'I am listening. I want to hear about what's just happened to you, not what we did twenty years ago.'

Helen slumped back in her chair. It was only too obvious that Rianna did not really want to know what had happened, and suddenly there seemed no point in telling her. *Why?* she thought. How could Rianna have forgotten something that had meant so much to Helen and stayed so vividly in her mind?

Unless she was afraid to remember. She had closed in on herself and Helen could not reach her, even though she needed her help so desperately. Just as Rianna's beauty coloured everything around her, so her darker mood seeped out into the room and made Helen feel that her own house was turning grey and alien.

She thought, *Tell me I didn't imagine it. Tell me I'm not going mad* . . . but if it had not been a hallucination, if it had really happened, how much more terrifying that seemed. Suddenly she wanted to end the conversation as much as Rianna obviously did.

'It was nothing,' Helen said tonelessly. 'I didn't feel well and I got a bit lost. Now I'm going to have a hot bath.'

'That's a good idea. I'll fetch a newspaper, and make us an early lunch.'

Rather than snap at her, Helen said nothing at all.

She ran the bath as hot as she could stand it and lay in it for half an hour, letting the heat soak the chill out of her bones. Had it really happened? It couldn't have done, and yet – she squeezed her eyes shut in denial – it had, she knew it had . . .

As she climbed out and towelled herself dry, she heard Rianna's voice downstairs.

'Hello, Mrs Locke. Helen's in the bath, come in and I'll tell her you're here.'

Helen was bewildered. She hadn't expected her parents. Pulling on a dressing gown, she rushed downstairs to find her mother taking off her coat and her father methodically wiping his feet on the mat just inside the kitchen door.

'Hello, love,' he said, hugging her and placing a carrier bag in her hands.

'What's this, Dad?' It was almost impossible to switch into normal behaviour, but she made a brave effort, not wanting them to know there was anything wrong.

'An apple pie, some scones and a cake, home-made of course,' he said.

'Oh, Mum, I wish you wouldn't. I've only got to look at these to put on weight.'

'Nonsense,' said Beth Locke. 'Anyway, your father will eat at least half of it before we go home.'

Her father, tall and naturally lean, smiled ruefully. He was a college lecturer in his mid-fifties, with greying dark hair, and glasses perched on a long nose. Quiet and even-tempered, he could not have been more different to her mother, who was small and bright and outspoken.

Helen kissed her and said, 'Did you tell me you were coming? If you did, I'd completely forgotten.'

'No, darling, we thought we'd surprise you,' said her mother.

'Oh good, I'm not going mad then. It's lovely to see you, but it's a long way to come if we'd been out.'

'We're going to see an old friend of mine later, so it wouldn't have been a wasted day. You know Jill Chapman. She says she sees quite a bit of you.'

'Yes, she often comes in the shop,' said Helen. 'She even bought one of Rianna's dolls. You remember Rianna Harper, don't you?'

'Oh yes, I remember you,' said Mrs Locke, smiling at Rianna without warmth. 'Helen told us you were staying. How long are you here for?'

'I'm not sure. Helen's really made me feel at home, and we've sort of gone into business together.'

'So she said.'

There seemed to be a touch of disapproval in her mother's tone. 'I'll put the kettle on,' Helen said brightly.

'Your hair's dripping. Why don't you go and get dressed first? We're not in a hurry, are we, John?'

'No. Have you only just got up?' His tone was mildly teasing.

'I've been up since half past six,' Helen retorted. Her parents seemed to take great pleasure in implying that she was bone idle, and the next minute telling her she worked too hard. They meant no harm by it, but on this particular morning she could not help reacting touchily.

'It's all right, Helen, I'll make some coffee and look after them,' said Rianna. Helen tried to relax and smile.

'Thanks. I won't be long.'

When Helen came down again, her mother was on her own at the dining table. Although she was the same age as her husband she looked younger, with sleek black hair and a lively face. She was a ballet teacher, and as a child Helen had caused her despair with her total lack of aptitude for dancing. There had been years of conflict over it before Mrs Locke had finally accepted that her daughter was a hopeless case, and called a truce.

'Where are Dad and Rianna?'

'Making a grand tour of the garden.'

'Making sure I haven't let it run wild?'

Her mother smiled. 'How are you, dear? You don't look very well. Are you worried about something?'

'No, I'm fine, Mum, perfectly fine.'

'Well, it must be a strain on you having a guest here as well as running the shop.'

'Rianna's not a guest, really. She's working with me and it's a tremendous help having her here.'

'Oh yes, the famous dolls.' Helen had mentioned them on the phone. She looked across to see if Annie was in her usual place on the mantelpiece, then remembered that Rianna had left her in the front room.

'They're selling incredibly well, Mum. Rianna's so clever. But it's not just that; she helps in the shop and around the house as well. I like having her here.'

'Well, be careful. Once someone like that digs herself in,

you could have terrible problems getting rid of her.'

Helen could hardly believe she had heard this. 'Mum, what are you saying? She's my friend!'

'But you hardly know her. You haven't seen her since you were, what, ten? It's like inviting a stranger into your home.'

'No it isn't!' Helen was indignant. 'What have you got against her?'

'Nothing, dear. I'm just thinking of you. But I must admit I never liked her, even as a child.'

'I don't see why. She was always perfectly well behaved.'

'She was too polite. There's something odd about her. Such strange eyes. I thought she might have changed, but she obviously hasn't.'

'Why should she? I don't know what you're getting at.'

'Well, I don't know. It's just a feeling I get about her, something not right.'

Helen sat back in her chair, pressing her lips together. As she had expected, her mother could not explain what she found unsettling about Rianna. Beth Locke could be relied on to be contrary, and much as Helen loved her, she had never been able to come to terms with it. 'You seem to dislike my friends on principle. You were the same about Nick.'

'Well, I was right about him, wasn't I?'

'I suppose so, but that's not the point.'

'What is, then? I'm thinking of you, dear. You let people take advantage of you.'

'I thought you'd be pleased I've got someone staying with me.'

Her mother's expression softened. 'As long as you're happy. But you said you weren't lonely without Nick.'

'I'm not.'

'It does seem a shame that you can't find a nice young man. You haven't met anyone yet, have you?'

'No, Mother.'

'What about the one with the horses?'

'I told you, we're just friends.'

'It's his loss, then.' She placed her hand over Helen's and gave a mischievous smile. Helen could not stay angry with her.

'There's more to life than men. I'm quite happy.'

Mrs Locke sighed. 'You're like your father. You bottle things up. At least I say what I think, even if people don't like it.'

Through the window, Helen saw Rianna and her father coming to the kitchen door.

'I know, Mum, but please be nice to Rianna for my sake.'

'Of course I will, dear. Lecture over,' she said as the door opened.

'I'll fetch one to show you,' Rianna was saying. She ran up the stairs which led from the dining room, while Mr Locke came in and, despite wiping his feet again, deposited a blob of mud on the carpet.

Helen pretended not to notice. 'The garden's a bit of a mess,' she said apologetically.

'It's fine. I know you can't do much in winter, but don't let those weeds get out of hand when the weather gets warmer.'

It was her father's way of looking after her. He was not a great talker; he would never say the things her mother said. But by the simplest of comments about the most everyday matters, he showed he cared. Suddenly she was immensely grateful that her parents were there. They had changed the mood of the day completely, shifted it back to comforting reality.

'Now,' he said, 'we didn't think it was fair to expect you to feed us without notice, so how would you like to come to the pub and I'll treat everyone to lunch?'

'That would be nice.'

Rianna came downstairs with a doll she had just finished. She handed it to Mrs Locke, who was obviously impressed.

'Goodness, I didn't expect anything like this. It doesn't do it justice to call it a doll. What would you call it, John? It's more a figurine, a collector's item.'

'I don't know, but it's very well made, Rianna.'

'Good heavens, all this work. Did you really make it yourself?'

'Of course she did,' said Helen. 'There's another one in the front room, and some half-finished ones. They're all slightly different, she never makes two alike.'

'I'd like you to have this one,' said Rianna.

Helen's parents were taken aback. They looked at each

other. 'We couldn't possibly.'

'We'd pay you for it, of course,' said Mr Locke.

'No, no, I want to give it to you as a gift, if you like it.'

Helen wondered if her mother had revised her opinion of Rianna. She was obviously entranced by the doll. The beads of its costume clicked softly together, spilling over her hands as she turned it to catch the light. Rainbow dots swooped across the ceiling.

'Like it? It's absolutely beautiful. But surely you need to sell it . . . '

'They're easier to make than they look. I'd be so happy if you'd accept it.'

'Well, if you're sure . . . ' said Mrs Locke, with a pleased smile at her husband.

Helen wondered if anyone ever refused Rianna anything.

Helen went to bed early that night, and lay reading a light novel in the hope that it would prevent her from having bad dreams. But after a few minutes, Rianna came in and sat on the edge of the bed without speaking.

Helen said, 'It was nice of you to give my parents that doll.'

Rianna did not reply. She seemed very tense, downcast, almost ashamed about something. 'Helen, I wasn't very honest with you this morning. I could see you were distressed, but I just didn't know how to explain.'

Helen felt her shoulders tightening with apprehension. She had spent all day trying not to think about the morning, and she dreaded what her friend was going to say. 'Go on, then.'

'When I said I couldn't remember things . . . I was trying to be off-hand about it because it's much worse than I made out. That was cruel and I'm sorry. I've got to tell you the truth, Helen, because you're my friend and it's unfair of me not to.' Her voice, already quiet, grew fainter as she went on. 'I sort of remember, but it seems like a dream. None of it makes any sense. I can hardly remember what New Zealand was like. I know I was there but it seems so unreal, as if it had nothing to do with me. It's the same with our childhood. I can't recall a thing before I was five, not a thing, and all I can remember after that is fragments. I know we were together a lot. I recognised your mum and dad, I remember being at school, but the games we played and what happened to us when we went in the Park . . . ' Her head was bowed, but through the veil of chestnut hair Helen saw that there were tears running down her cheeks.

Her throat knotted with overwhelming pity. She had sometimes suspected Rianna of embellishing events with white lies to make them seem more glamorous, but no one could have faked the quiet misery that now poured out of her. That was what had made her moody, and she had been keeping it to herself all this time.

'It's the same with the dolls,' she went on. 'I don't know why I started making them. I just have this feeling niggling at me all the time that there's a reason. I'd do anything to know it, to know that there *is* a reason and it's not just some kind of delusion I'm suffering.'

'Oh, Rianna.' Helen sat up, put her arms round her. 'I wish you'd told me before. I'm glad you've told me.'

'I'm so scared, Helen, that there's something really terribly wrong with me. With my mind.'

That makes two of us, Helen thought bleakly. 'Oh, God,' she said. 'Listen, I'm sure there's nothing wrong with you. I forget things all the time. Oh, don't cry; it will be all right, I'm sure it will.'

Chapter Four

Helen floated in blackness, a smooth backdrop against which jewels were spinning and falling like firework sparks. But they were not soft and fiery; they were as cold and hard as diamond. They shone gold and green, electric blue, purple deepening to an indigo that was almost lost against the black, and red . . . tiny red hands carved from crystal, falling like blossoms and beckoning to her as they fell.

She woke slowly. Even when she thought herself fully awake she could still see the blurred gleam of jewels and feel the exquisite terror they roused in her. Something was lying across her chest, moving with the rise and fall of her breathing. A serene white face was pressed close to hers.

In the moments it took her to realise what it was, her breath was suspended. Then the tension was released. She started violently and knocked the doll away as she would a repulsive insect.

'Rianna!' she cried, leaping out of bed. Rianna was not in her room. Helen ran downstairs and found her in the kitchen, barefoot, an elfin figure in pyjamas that were too big for her.

'Rianna, why do you keep putting Annie in my room?' she cried.

'It's just a doll. It doesn't have a name and I didn't . . . '

'You're not going to deny putting her there? She was right on top of me!'

Rianna looked concerned and bewildered. She parted and closed her lips several times before she said, 'I'm sorry, Helen. I thought you liked her.' She turned away, and now Helen could hardly see her through the cold blue light that filled the kitchen. She knew – she *knew* that Rianna had not touched the doll, that she was pretending she had so as not to frighten Helen. But the white lie only terrified her more, and the chill of the floor seemed to be creeping right through her, freezing her where she stood . . .

Helen woke properly then, tangled up in the sheets and sweating. She got out of bed and put on her dressing gown, moving slowly to convince herself that she really was awake. Rianna's door was still closed; downstairs, Annie had not moved from the mantelpiece. Helen sighed and collapsed into a chair.

It was the first time she had the dream. In the following weeks it began to recur over and over again.

She did not mention it to Rianna. She did not want to distress her, especially as Rianna seemed so much happier since she had confided her troubles. If you could call it confiding, Helen thought; in telling her everything, Rianna had told her nothing.

Helen thought of the day when, just before her friend had gone to New Zealand, Helen had found her unconscious in the Park. Rianna apparently did not remember the occasion. Had the fall caused some damage to her brain or was the problem psychological? After some persuasion, Rianna saw the doctor, but came out saying he could find nothing wrong. It was just 'one of those things' and she would have to live with it.

Helen did her best to accept it.

Spring came, and everything went well for them. The dolls brought so many customers to the shop that Helen increased the price, and Rianna still had a permanent backlog of orders to fill. On the days Helen needed her to help in the shop she would take her work with her and sit sewing behind the counter. She made friends easily. She had a way of charming people, of making them feel better about life with just a few words and a smile. It was a gift Helen envied. Yet, she noticed, Rianna gave nothing of her self. That remained as elusive as ever, and perhaps it was why people were fascinated by her. She could not trust her memory, so she dared not show her true self; was that all there was to it?

It did no good to analyse. Rianna was Rianna, and while like the sun she drew others into her orbit, they would never be able to touch her.

Helen always had to bully Rianna into taking time off, but she usually succeeded, even if she had to physically part her from her work and say, 'That's enough. We're going to the pub.' Or it might be a picnic with their small circle of friends, or a shopping trip; but not once did either of them propose going into Bradgate Park. As long as certain subjects were not broached, Rianna was happy, and they only quarrelled once that spring.

One morning Rianna came into the shop and put a copy of the *Leicester Mercury* on the counter. Her face was solemn. 'You promised me you wouldn't do this,' she said.

The paper was open at the trade section, and framed by advertisements there was a feature about the shop and a photograph of Helen with two of the dolls sitting on the counter in front of her.

'BUSY AS A BEE', said the headline. 'Twenty-six-year-old Helen Locke has built up Honeybee Crafts into one of the most successful gift shops in Leicestershire.

'"I trained as a secretary because it seemed a sensible career," says Helen. "But I've been fascinated by crafts since I was a little girl. It was my dream to have my own shop."

'The dream came true two years ago when she gave up her job and with the help of a loan from her parents, took the plunge into business.

'"It was difficult at first, especially as I went through a divorce right in the middle of it. Now business is booming, and we have more orders for these lovely dolls than we can cope with."

'Customers come from all over the county to buy the dolls, which have to be seen to be believed. They are made by Helen's best friend, Joanna. "Almost everything we sell is hand-made. I've tried to make it an outlet for local artists and craftsmen, rather than selling stuff you can buy anywhere."'

Helen put it down and said, 'It's quite a good write-up, I suppose. Why do journalists have to put daft words in your mouth, though? "Business is booming"? I never said that!'

Rianna said quietly, 'I asked you not to mention me, Helen.'

'Yes, I know. I told the reporter, but – well, you know what they're like. He got your name wrong, anyway.'

'Yes, but – '

'I don't understand you. It's marvellous publicity, I

thought we agreed on that. You said you wanted to sell even more dolls.'

'It would've been better if you hadn't mentioned the dolls at all.'

'Why? Rianna, surely you're not thinking about the man you told me about, the one who bothered you in New Zealand?'

It was as if a shutter came down across Rianna's face. 'You think I'm being neurotic about it. You don't believe me.'

'You said yourself how bad your memory is!' Helen said, then mentally kicked herself. 'I'm sorry, I didn't mean that to sound like it did. But how likely is someone in New Zealand to see one particular copy of an English local paper and think someone called Joanna is you?'

'He'd recognise the dolls. He might be in England.'

'Have you some reason to think he is?'

She shook her head. 'You don't understand.'

'I might, if you'd explain yourself a bit more clearly! Look, don't you think you're overreacting?'

Rianna's face was set, as if she were on the point of crying. Her eyes glittered. 'Do you think I don't want to? If only I could make you understand what it's like, being in here – ' She tapped her head. 'Trapped.' With that she spun round and half ran out of the shop.

'Rianna!' Helen cried, distressed. She followed, but by the time she reached the door there was no sign of Rianna in the street.

Later, however, Rianna came back and apologised. 'You're right, Helen, I did overreact. I'm so mean to you, and I always have been. I don't know how you put up with me.'

'Don't say that. Nick used to say that.'

Rianna put her hand up to her throat. 'I don't behave like him, do I?'

'Good grief, no, never!' Helen came out from behind the counter and put an arm round her. 'You've got a long way to go to compete with him. You don't take any "putting up with" whatsoever.' They hugged, and everything was all right again. 'Help me do some dusting and rearranging, will you?'

Rianna drifted around the shelves like a spirit, someone from a Victorian photograph brought to life. It was the way she moved that gave Helen that impression; the way she caressed every object she touched, almost unconsciously, like a ghost reliving its memories. Presently she said, 'I'm pleased about the *Mercury*, really. If it brings us some more orders, that will be a good thing.'

'Yes, if you have time to fill them. What if we get a shipping order? It could happen, you know. Hey, we could always take on someone to help you.'

Rianna paused in her dusting and looked at Helen. Her eyes were startlingly pale, the irises ringed with silver and flecked with opal colours. 'Only I can make the dolls. I know how they're meant to be.'

'But you could train someone else, couldn't you, someone with some talent?'

Rianna's lids swept down, veiling her eyes. 'I don't think so,' she said thoughtfully, 'but I could try. All right, Helen, but only if we get a really large order.'

Helen was surprised. She had been sure Rianna would condemn the idea out of hand. 'That's fair enough. Anyway, when people really want something, it's surprising how long they're prepared to wait for it.' She moved round the table to rearrange some lace cushions, and saw a familiar face looking at her through the window. 'Oh, sod it!' she said, as Nick pushed open the door and sauntered in, smiling.

Seeing Rianna, he made straight for her. 'Hello, you must be Helen's friend, Rianna,' he said. 'I'm Nick Durham, I expect Helen's mentioned me.'

'Yes,' said Rianna.

'Oh dear, I'm off to a bad start then.' He pulled a face. 'Hi, Helen. I was going through my record collection and half of what I've got seems to be yours.'

She took the records from him, smiling thinly. She said nothing, but she thought: *What a feeble excuse.* He had been trying for weeks to find a chance to meet Rianna. Helen had succeeded in keeping them apart, until now.

'Anyway, it's great to meet you,' he said, draping himself against the counter. In jeans and a designer shirt he looked as if he had stepped out of a Sunday supplement. 'You haven't long been back in England, have you?'

'Not long, no.' Rianna went on polishing.

'How's it feel being back?'

'Just like coming home.'

'I should think you miss your family, don't you?'

She shrugged. 'Oh, you know. I write to them.'

As Helen listened to them, she began to smile to herself. Nick never gave the impression of being conceited, only of being very nice and genuinely interested in the person he was talking to. With his looks it made an irresistible combination. He had only wanted to meet Rianna out of curiosity, and had not expected her to be anything special, but the longer he looked at her, the more Helen marvelled that his eyes did not actually fall out. Yet Rianna seemed unimpressed. She continued to give off-hand, monosyllabic answers and remained unresponsive to his best efforts to draw her out.

He persisted valiantly for about fifteen minutes, then his charm switched off like an actor coming off-stage. 'Anyway, I've got to go,' he mumbled, looking at his watch. 'Thanks for brightening up my lunch-break.'

'I'll walk down the road with you, I've got to go to the grocer's,' Helen said sweetly. She did not want to gloat, but she couldn't resist it.

Outside, he thrust his hands in his pockets and gave Helen one of his most resentful looks.

'She must be gay,' he said sourly.

'Oh well, anyone who doesn't fancy you must be.'

'Your secret's out now, Helen. All girls together, eh? I might have known.'

'I only wish it were true,' she said wearily. 'That would solve all our problems. Anyway, what's wrong with you? First you keep asking me out, and now you're after Rianna. Isn't Gina enough for you?'

Nick looked sulky, then his expression softened to sadness. He said quietly, 'Gina's left me.'

'Oh! When?'

'Just before that time I came in the shop and bought the doll.'

'Why didn't you tell me?'

'Pride, I suppose.'

If Helen had been mean-spirited, she might have been tempted to say something sarcastic. But she was not. 'I'm sorry, Nick. Really I am. Why did she leave?'

He shrugged. 'Once we moved in together we seemed to argue even more than I did with you. She said the same things you did, that I was a moody, selfish, pig-headed workaholic who took her for granted. So maybe it's true after all.'

Helen was not sure whether he was genuinely contrite or just feeling sorry for himself, but she had never seen him quite so subdued. She almost sympathised.

'Anyway, I've got to go,' he said, kissing her on the cheek. 'See you around, kid.'

Helen wanted to be happy, and everything was in her favour: the business was going well, she had Rianna's friendship and the beauty of Charnwood in summer to enjoy. She saw Martin and the horses at least once a week. But she felt unsettled. Rianna and Nick were adults, their happiness was not her responsibility, yet she could not stop herself worrying about them.

She slept badly, sometimes afraid to go to sleep because she was so fed up with having the same dream. Recurring dreams could be caused by anxiety, she supposed; but it was not anxiety that made them begin to come true.

Three times she found Annie in her room, lying loose-limbed on the bed with the same smug expression that haunted her sleep. After the third occasion she took the doll to the shop and locked her in the glass case with a 'not for sale' sign. Rianna accepted her explanation that they needed a doll permanently on display.

The dreams ceased. Something worse began.

The first death was only a mild shock, a photograph in the paper of someone Helen knew vaguely. 'Mrs Margaret Blackley, a parish councillor for more than twelve years, has died aged 56 after a short illness. She leaves a husband and two sons.'

'My God, that's the woman who bought the first doll,' said Helen.

'Are you sure?' Rianna got up to look over her shoulder.

'Yes, I recognise her. She's been in the shop several times, and she paid by cheque. It's definitely her. Poor woman.'

Rianna sat down again and bent over her sewing. It might have been the way the light fell, but Helen was sure there was a slight smile on her lips.

In time, Helen would have thought no more of it, had it not been for a phone call the same evening.

'Hello, darling, it's me,' said her mother. 'Isn't it terrible about my poor friend?'

Helen's mind was still on Mrs Blackley. 'Yes, I saw it in the paper.'

'Jill was younger than me. She was in perfect health and they've no idea why she died.'

'What?' said Helen. 'Did you say Jill?'

'Yes, Jill Chapman. I thought you said you'd seen the announcement in the paper.'

'No, that was someone else, a parish councillor.'

'I don't know any parish councillors. Don't confuse me, dear. I thought you would've known about Jill, living so close to her.'

'Well, I didn't.' Helen was too shocked to think. 'It's awful. How did you hear?'

'Her husband phoned me. He came home from work and found her, poor man. At first he thought there'd been a break-in because there was something missing, a doll I think he said, but nothing else was touched and there were no signs of a burglary. She had just collapsed. I don't know how he's going to cope. It's just as well they had no children.'

When they finished speaking, Helen put down the receiver and turned to Rianna, stunned.

'That's terrible. I can't believe it. I only saw Mrs Chapman last week and she was perfectly well.'

'She had one of the dolls as well, didn't she?'

'Yes.'

'That's all right, then.' There was no mistaking it now; Rianna's mouth was curved in an incongruous expression of joy. 'Don't be sad, Helen. It's all right.'

'What's all right about it?' Helen gasped.

Rianna tended to close up when challenged, but this time she simply said, 'It's sooner or later for everyone, isn't it? And there might be something better.'

'You're talking to a rampant atheist. We get one chance,

and that's it.'

Rianna's mouth turned down, and she breathed out softly. 'You're lucky to have something you can believe in that strongly,' she said, and Helen did not think she was trying to be funny.

The next day was Wednesday, and Martin Ashley came into the shop just as she was about to close for the afternoon.

'I've got the day off and the weather's fantastic,' he said. 'Would you like to come and exercise Bert and Flossie?'

Helen smiled at his inappropriate nicknames for the two highly bred animals. 'I'd love to. It's just what I need at the moment.' She was delighted to see him. 'Isn't Jo riding, then?'

'No, she's busy, shearing the pigs or something.'

'Urgh, imagine trying to spin pig bristles!' Helen said, and they laughed. Martin always cheered her up. He was of medium height and slim, with curly brown hair, a beard and glasses; not her type, she would once have said, but now she was not sure. He had a quick way of moving, as if he were full of nervous energy, and he was seldom without a smile. The humour and kindness in his brown eyes had never been in Nick's cool green ones.

'Hold on while I lock up,' she said.

'I think you've got a last minute customer,' said Martin, nodding at the door.

'Oh, blast. I hope he's not going to browse for half an hour.'

'It's OK, there's no hurry.'

The door opened and a man dressed in a dark jacket and flannel trousers came in and began to look round the shop in a studiedly casual way that immediately made her think: *Police*. She exchanged glances with Martin and waited for the man to approach the counter.

When he did, his face startled her. It was strong and bony, with wiry ginger hair brushed back from a broad forehead, pale blue eyes and extraordinarily bushy eyebrows. They gave him a fierce look that made her nervous.

'Can I help you, sir?' she said.

'I'm interested in the doll in the case.' His voice was deep, very sombre.

'I'm afraid it's not for sale. We can make you one to order, though.' Helen felt her hands turning sweaty. There was no reason for it, but she felt as if she were on trial and that it was essential to give nothing away.

'Where do the dolls come from?' he asked.

'They're hand-made locally, sir.'

'I see. I would like to take a closer look at the one on display, please.'

'I'm sorry. The case is locked and I've left the key at home.'

The man looked at her as if to say: *I know you're lying, but let it pass.* 'Who makes the dolls?'

'A local person.'

'Are they made on the premises?'

'No.'

'I would be interested to meet the person who makes them.'

'Might I ask why?' Her arms were folded, her tone coldly polite.

It was the right thing to say. He could not or would not answer, which left him no option but to leave.

'It doesn't matter. I was curious about . . . such a talented person.'

'If you would like to order a doll, you can leave your name and address and I'll let you know when it will be ready.'

The man shook his head, holding her gaze. There was something about his pale eyes and colourless lashes that made her shudder. 'I'll call again in a few days.'

The bell tinged loudly and the glass rattled in the door as he shut it behind him. Helen turned to Martin.

'What a horrible, creepy bloke! What on earth was he after?'

'Search me.'

'Do you think he was a policeman?'

'Nah. They wouldn't send out a plain clothes officer with eyebrows like that. A policeman wouldn't say things like, "I was curious about such a talented person," it would be more sort of,' – he deepened his voice – '"Miss Helen Locke? I wonder if you would mind helpin' us with our enquiries. We have reason to believe that your dolls are being used as a cover for a drug smuggling operation – "'

'Don't! Oh Martin, it's not funny, it really isn't.'

'Hey.' He put his arm round her shoulders. 'What's the

matter? You seem really worked up about something.'

'Let's get out of here. I'll tell you in the car.'

They walked to the small car park by the green, where Martin had left his red MG.

'I wasn't imagining it, was I?' she said. 'He wasn't an ordinary customer.'

'No, I think you're right, but I'm sure it's nothing to worry about. You did a great job of seeing him off.'

'Did I?'

'You were brilliant.' The car pulled out on to the road that would take them towards Swithland Woods.

'As far as I can see, there are two possibilities. He might have been a trade inspector. If he was, he must have wondered why I was being so cagey.'

'Why would a trade inspector be interested in your dolls? I know they have regulations about toys, but yours aren't toys and you make that obvious.'

'Something awful happened last night. I found out that two people who bought Rianna's dolls have died.' Martin said nothing, and she added, 'Now I've said it, it sounds ridiculous. But I just have this awful feeling . . . '

'Hold on, Helen . . . are you suggesting that Rianna's dolls somehow caused their deaths?'

'I don't know. No, of course not. But what if the police made that connection . . . no, it's stupid.'

'It's not stupid, it's just a rather startling leap of logic. Think about it. They probably both bought baked beans or disinfectant or a new car, but you wouldn't immediately think there was a sinister connection, and neither will anyone else.'

'No, but – '

'So it's a coincidence.'

'Yes. Now you put it like that, it must be.'

'So what's been going on to make you think of something like that? Has Rianna been spiking the dolls with cyanide?' The way he said it made her laugh, but inside she felt it was no joke.

'It's hard to explain. When I told her about the women who'd died, she reacted really strangely. She seemed pleased.'

'Pleased?'

'She was smiling. She said, "It's all right, don't be sad," or something.'

'She was trying to cheer you up. Were you depressed about it?'

'Yes, of course, but no more than anyone else would have been. You think I'm imagining things because I'm depressed?'

'No, I'm just trying to work out what's going on,' he said calmly.

Helen subsided in her seat, aware that she was rigid with tension. She was grateful for Martin's unemotive sense. She could talk to him, because he took her seriously without indulging her. She was tempted to tell him everything, even about the Park and Annie.

Martin pulled into the farmyard and switched off the ignition. Jo's cottage – an ancient thatched building in need of renovation – fronted the road, and behind it were barns and a pigsty. A concrete path led between them to another small yard with four loose boxes and a gate to the horses' field.

They were grazing on the far side, but when Martin called them they came trotting across the field with their heads up and their tails arched over their backs. As well as the dapple grey mare and the bay gelding, there was a chestnut yearling filly, the mare's daughter. Martin opened the gate and the two older horses trotted through and went obediently into their separate boxes. The filly tried to follow, but he shooed her away and she cantered in circles, snorting.

'What a show-off,' he said affectionately. 'What was the other possibility?'

'Eh?'

'You said there were two possibilities about who that man might be.'

'Oh yes.' The mare, Destiny, put her head over the half-door of her box and Helen raised a hand to stroke the small, velvety muzzle. 'Rianna said a man in New Zealand kept pestering her, and it worried her so much that she came to England to get away.'

'Sounds a bit extreme. Why not just go to the police?'

'That's what I said. Anyway, when we had that feature in the *Mercury*, she carried on about it as if he was going to see it in New Zealand and trace her to Rothley! I know what you're thinking. That's as far-fetched as my first theory. But what if she was right?'

'He didn't have a New Zealand accent.' Martin went into the tack room and came out with a grooming kit. 'It's Rianna, isn't it?'

'How do you mean?'

'Something about her is – I don't know, worrying you, making you nervous.'

'No. Well yes, sort of. But there's no harm in her at all, and I'm so fond of her, so it doesn't make sense.'

'Maybe you liking her so much is the problem. You can't see her faults,' said Martin.

'What sort of faults?'

'I hardly know her, so I can't say. But she's . . . not ordinary. And neither was that man who came in asking about her.'

It was a relief to Helen to hear him say that. She was aware of Rianna's faults – her evasiveness, for one – but it seemed both disloyal and too complicated to explain. She went into the tack room to change into the jodhpurs she kept there, then busied herself brushing the dust out of Destiny's coat. The horsey scent, a mixture of hoof-oil and sweat and grassy breath, always soothed her.

When they had tacked up, Martin led the gelding out and paused to adjust the chinstrap of his riding hat. He said, 'I think we can ride in the Park today, if you fancy a change.'

Helen froze in the act of tightening Destiny's girth, then carried on. Martin held the mare's bridle as she mounted.

'I've told you two crazy things today, so one more should really finish you off. I'd rather not go in the Park. Something weird happened to me in there a couple of months ago and I haven't dared go in there since.'

'How weird? Stand still, you sod!' The gelding, Fikri, was dancing about as he tried to mount.

'Uhm . . . something chased me.'

'A stag? A dog?'

'Something like that. I haven't been in since.'

'Then we'll definitely go in today. You sound as if you're getting a phobia about it, and the best way to deal with that is to face it before it gets really bad.'

'No, I can't. Martin, please.'

He looked at her, concerned. He must have seen something in her eyes, heard the terror in her voice, because he did not argue. 'All right,' he said gently. 'We'll go in Swithland Woods instead.'

The Woods in sunlight were glorious, endless canopies of brilliant green and gold. They were silent yet full of sound, cavernous yet soft and enveloping. Everywhere they looked there were different colours, different falls of light through the leaves. Earth tracks wound through the trees, and on either side there were knolls thick with grass and twisted roots.

Once, thought Helen, all of Charnwood Forest must have looked like this. Now there were only pockets of woodland left between the farms and the villages, but the special aura still lived on in the sweep of fields, the trees in the hedgerows, the granite cottages. There were other places in Britain that were comparable in beauty – certainly far more spectacular – but she would not have swapped Charnwood for any of them.

To be riding through the Woods on such a day would have been heaven on earth, had she been able to stop thinking about the two women who had died. Now Martin must think she was crazy, and perhaps she was, but at least he treated her as if she were quite rational. They talked about the horses as they rode, laughed about inconsequential things. Helen felt better, until Martin said:

'I think we're lost.'

They had been riding for about half an hour. Helen always lost her sense of direction in Swithland Woods, but Martin knew them as well as she knew the Park.

'How do you make that out, then?'

'Well, we're not where I thought we were. I thought we'd go out by the car park and do some road work. So where's the car park?'

Because she was with Martin, Helen felt no particular anxiety at first. 'All we have to do is ride in a straight line until we come to the wall, then follow it round,' she said.

'Oh, I'll soon work out where I've gone wrong.'

A wind sprang up. Helen had been warm, but now she felt her ears beginning to ache with cold. The horses arched their necks and began to jib and pull at their bits.

'We could let them canter, while we're on a decent straight bit of track,' said Martin. 'Is it me, or has it gone cold?'

'Martin, I – '

'What is it?'

'Nothing.'

'Come on, then. I think the wind's spooking them.'

The horses plunged forward into a jerky canter, fighting to gallop. It was all they could do to hold them back. There was sky through the trees ahead of them and Martin said, 'Slow down, Helen. The road's ahead.'

But Destiny and Fikri set their mouths against the bit, pulling harder and harder. Helen had never known Martin to be unable to control the gelding before. She ducked a low branch, gasping as it struck her spine, then sat down hard in the saddle and struggled to slow down. But the normally gentle mare seemed oblivious to her; the muscles around her ears and eyes were bunched up in fear and she pounded on as if possessed. It was all Helen could do to hang on and dodge the trees. No horse had bolted with her since she was a child, and now she rediscovered how frightening it could be. Destiny's behaviour was so abnormal that she seemed mindless, and Helen had the dreadful impression that she was not on a horse at all, but being carried away by the dark, alien beast that had pursued her.

Side by side, Destiny and Fikri burst from the edge of the trees. There were no cars parked; the low wall bounding the Woods, and even the road itself, were not there. There was only a slope of rough grass sweeping up to an undulating skyline. The horses ran on, carrying them up the slope and deeper into a landscape that was familiar yet wholly strange.

'Let them have their heads,' Martin called. 'Just don't fall off. They'll have to slow down eventually.' He sounded breathless, shaken. Helen could not find the breath to reply. The landscape was swooping past her, the chill wind bearing her to somewhere that she did not want to be.

It was ten minutes before the possession loosed its hold on the horses, and they slowed down of their own accord. All around them were gentle hills, mottled with bracken and outcrops of rock. Destiny and Fikri stood with their heads down, trembling and sweating.

'I've never known either of them bolt like that, even when they were youngsters,' Martin said. 'Are you all right, Helen?'

'Yes. Just a bit shaken up.'

'This is really strange. We're in the Park, aren't we? This looks like Old John but without the tower and the monument.'

The double-peaked hill was unmistakable, but the copse between the two peaks was no longer contained by a wall.

'Yes. That's how it looks to me, as well.'

'But that's impossible. Swithland Woods are separated from Bradgate by a road and some fields, agreed? And we didn't cross a road, we didn't go through the gate and up the bridle path, so how can we possibly be in the Park?'

Helen was so frightened that she felt numb, but at the same time she was glad he was with her. If it could happen to someone else it meant – she was not sure what it meant, but she was glad.

'Martin,' she said hoarsely, 'this is what happened to me in the Park. I couldn't tell you because you would have thought I was making it up. But I wasn't. All the roads and walls vanished, just like now.'

He looked confused. 'No. It's impossible. There's a perfectly sensible explanation.'

'That's what I thought, but there wasn't.'

'I don't get this. Look, let's dismount and cool the horses off. It's not far to the top and I'll be able to work out where we are from there.'

They led the horses slowly up the hill that had once been Old John, and as they walked they became aware of a faint rushing noise. It sounded familiar but totally out of place.

'Is that the wind? It feels like we've walked into winter. God, this is weird, Helen. Look, if we're in the Park, we'll be able to see the top car park from the hill and then we can have an ice cream to warm us up . . . '

But when they reached the top there was no mark of civilisation to be seen. They were not even sure that they recognised the landscape at all. With all signs of cultivation gone and woods spilling wildly over the slopes, it looked different.

'Perhaps we're not where I thought,' said Martin.

'But if we'd left the Woods any other way, we'd have come

out into fields.'

'I know. No, this is the Park, Helen – or was. I can see Beacon Hill over there. How did you . . . er . . . get out of this before?'

'I don't know,' she said, shivering. She told him about the strange folk she had encountered, without embarrassment, because she was beyond caring whether he believed her or not. 'Then I was suddenly back in the normal world again. I almost knocked myself out, running into a wall.'

'Were you scared?'

'Absolutely bloody terrified.'

'OK,' he said thoughtfully. 'OK, we'll walk slowly towards Beacon Hill. Don't worry, Helen, at least we'll be able to panic in stereo.'

The horses were quiet now, and went with them obediently. It was a walk of about three miles, and all the time they kept looking about them for signs that the world had returned to normal. There were none. Instead the rushing noise grew louder, rising and falling rhythmically. The wind carried a scent that they recognised, and the further they went the milder it blew, until they began to feel the warmth of the sun again.

They were walking up a long ridge, unable to see anything beyond it. Martin broke into a run and Helen followed, trying to keep up, but he reached the top first and she heard him say, 'Jesus.'

'What is it?' she called. Destiny was tired now and did not want to trot.

'How far is Leicestershire from the coast?'

'About a hundred miles.'

'That's what I thought.'

She caught him up, and her ears were filled with the crashing of waves, her nostrils with the smell of salt and seaweed.

'Oh my God,' she gasped, hanging on to the mare's neck.

The ridge ended in a cliff, and below them stretched a green, glittering, impossible sea.

Chapter Five

It looked like the world they knew, but at the same time it did not. The landscape was sharper, more vibrant. The sky sparkled with daystars, amethyst-blue sweeping down into the turquoise of the sea. There were birds wheeling above the waves, but their cries were not like any seagull that Helen had ever heard.

They stood on the edge of the cliff, speechless. Eventually she reached out towards Martin and he found her hand and clasped it so tight that she almost gasped with pain.

'Well, this is it, then,' he said.

'What?'

'I've run out of possible explanations for this. There's no way. Unless half of England has just collapsed into the ocean without making a sound, we have to be . . . somewhere else.'

'Yes. I know. I don't think there's much hope in trying to be rational about it,' said Helen quietly. 'God, I'm so thirsty.'

'When you got out the last time, are you sure you don't know how it happened?'

'I told you, one minute I was running after those riders, the next everything was back to normal. The appearance of the Park didn't change, but the fog grew thicker and suddenly there was the path and gate. It was nothing I did.'

'So it could happen any time. Or not at all.'

'I suppose so. Martin, you sound very calm. You're not suddenly going to panic, are you?'

'I won't if you won't,' he said, grimacing. 'First one to go mad has to buy the other one a drink when we get home.'

'Yes. Oh, hell.' She pulled off her riding hat and rubbed her face. 'What are we going to do?'

He did not answer. He touched her arm and pointed to their right, to a place where sea and beach met the horizon, and there she saw shapes moving on the waves.

'Boats?' she said.

He shrugged. 'We can't stay here for ever. I think we ought to go down to the beach and see if we can find help.'

What sort of 'help' they might find, Helen did not like to speculate. They walked along the cliff edge until they found a place where it sloped gently enough for the horses to negotiate, and they picked their way down to the sand. It reminded her of the Norfolk beaches she had played on as a child, wide and smooth and tawny-gold. The sand sank beneath their feet as they walked.

'I'm worried about the horses,' said Martin. 'At least there's plenty of grass up there, if it's normal grass. But I'd be happier if they hadn't been dragged into this.'

'I thought it was them who dragged us,' Helen said morosely. 'Why does this keep happening to me? I'm sure it's Rianna's fault.'

'Oh?' Martin sounded astonished. 'Why blame her?'

'There's a lot you don't know. Nobody knows, because it's not the sort of thing you tell anyone, unless you want to be carted off to a mental ward.'

'This might be a good time to tell me.'

Helen hesitated and began quietly. 'Rianna and I used to play in Bradgate Park. At the time it seemed real, then for years after I wasn't sure whether it had just been my imagination. It was as if we had walked into another world. Oh, we never saw the sea, it still looked like the Park – that's why I wasn't sure, but . . . after this, how can it not have been real?'

'I believe you, Helen. Did it only happen when you were with Rianna?'

'Yes, in those days. After she went abroad it never happened again – not until she came back. Don't ask me why it should've happened to me just because she's back in the country again, I haven't a clue.'

'She wasn't with you, the most recent time?'

'No. Without her it was different. Horrible.'

'Have you spoken to her about it?'

'Oh, I've tried!' Helen groaned. 'She denies all knowledge. Says she remembers hardly anything. I think she's telling the truth. I wish I could have got her to come to Bradgate Park with me to see if it happened again, maybe jog her memory and find out what was going on, but I daren't suggest it – for her sake and mine.'

'You poor kid. I didn't know all this was going on. Rianna always looks so cheerful, but I don't know what to make of her now.'

Helen sighed. 'If only I could get through to her. It just tears me apart, wondering what's going on inside her. She sometimes makes me so angry.'

'She means a lot to you, doesn't she?'

'I love her, I can't help it. She has that effect on people.'

'Mm,' said Martin.

They could see the boats clearly now. They were primitive in design, like coracles with double sails, yet they might have sailed out of a fantastical painting into life. Their hulls were glittering blue, the sails green as snakeskin and held in elegant shapes by delicate, curved masts. The rigging shone like spider silk.

The horses pricked their ears at the sight of them and began walking sideways, sweating. Helen and Martin paused to calm them down. The four vessels appeared to be riding at anchor, and there was no one in sight.

'When you were . . . wherever you were with Rianna, did you ever see any human beings?'

'No, not one. There were sometimes weird animals, never people.'

'So when you saw that lot in the Park, it was the first time?'

'Yes. I don't particularly want to see them again, either.'

'Why not? Did they look dangerous? Were they carrying weapons?'

'They didn't look like something nasty from *The Lord of the Rings*, if that's what you mean. I don't know how to describe them. They were – a bit like Rianna's dolls.'

'Floppy?' Martin said, and Helen began to laugh. There was a touch of hysteria in it, a massive release of tension. She could not stop, even when Martin held her arms, smiling but concerned, and said, 'Come on, it wasn't that funny.'

When she stopped it was very sudden, as if she had been punched in the diaphragm. Shock sobered her; the shock of seeing a group of people walking along the beach towards them.

'No,' she said faintly. 'They were more like that.'

The four figures approaching them moved like dancers, all energy and exuberance. Their clothes were as bright as butterfly wings, their hair long and thick and bright, flowing out on the air in halos of extraordinary colours. Helen and Martin moved close to each other, holding tight to the horses' reins. It was too late to hide now so they stood their ground bravely, feeling as uncomfortable as if they were faced with a crowd of drunken hooligans at the end of a dark alley.

'Do you think they've seen us?' said Helen.

'I don't see how they can miss us.'

'The last time, the riders just looked straight through me, they almost mowed me down, like I was invisible.'

'Not this time. Unless they're staring at an extremely interesting piece of sand that happens to be right where we're standing . . . '

'What do we say?' she exclaimed. 'Do we try to explain where we really come from?'

'Helen . . . '

'We'll have to, I mean how can you tell lies in a world you know nothing about?'

'Helen, I hardly think they're going to understand us,' Martin said nervously. 'Are you any good at drawing pictures in the sand?'

There were two men and two women, although they were hard to tell apart; they were all as tall as each other, and dressed in equally flamboyant colours. Again their faces took Helen's breath away, with their pale carved features like Rianna's dolls brought to life. Like Rianna herself. But their eyes and lips were painted in a way that made their angelic beauty seem predatory.

They came right up to Helen and Martin then spread out and began to circle slowly round them, staring at them, cautiously trailing their fingers along the horses' sides. Their clothes rustled, sand hissing on silk. Helen's eyes were filled with green and violet, ruby and blue and gold. They carried a strange scent with them, not unpleasant, like sandalwood and fresh sawdust.

When they began to speak at last, it was in a language Helen knew. It was not English, she had never heard it before, yet she understood it as if she had known it all her life.

'They are Gallahs,' said one of the women.

'No they're not, Sheyde,' replied a man with a cascade of platinum-white hair. He was leaning casually, almost arrogantly on Destiny's saddle. That annoyed Helen, but she felt too intimidated by them to speak.

'They must be. They look like Gallahs. Colourless, like things out of the earth.'

'Ugh, don't!' said a scarlet-haired woman, shivering.

'But it's true,' the woman called Sheyde said mockingly. 'That's what death is, didn't you know, Corolea? You lie suffocating in the cold earth until all your beauty's drained away, then you're ready to crawl out again.'

'Stop it!'

'Leave her alone,' said a quiet voice. Helen looked round and saw a slender man whose hair was a wild, glossy mixture of blues. His eyes had a sleepy look, his mouth a permanent slight smile that made his face seem all upturned crescents.

'Well, she asks for it,' said Sheyde. 'They must be Gallahs. Who agrees with me? Ananthis?'

'They cannot be,' said the blond man. 'When did you ever see any Gallah wearing such strange clothes – or any at all, for that matter? And these animals. I have never heard that they bring animals with them.'

'Shall we ask them?' Sheyde came so close to Helen that she drew back, overwhelmed. The spicy wood-scent was all around her, and within it the perfume of hyacinths. The woman's indigo hair, heavy dark brows and red lips were startling against her white skin. She was smiling, but Helen did not know what to read into the smile.

'You could try, Sheyde,' Ananthis said languidly. 'Sometimes they can speak.'

They exchanged what seemed a significant look, a private joke. 'Some of them are just like us,' said Sheyde. She moved to look at Martin. 'This one isn't, though. He has circles of glass over his eyes.'

'Don't touch those, I can't see a damn thing without them!' he exclaimed, stepping back. Fikri shied, and the blue-haired man hurriedly moved to avoid being trodden on.

Sheyde gave Ananthis an amused look. 'See, they can

speak.' The other two lost interest in the horses and came to stand with Sheyde, but Ananthis remained leaning on Destiny's back, affecting boredom. Helen wished Destiny would bite him, but the mare was too well mannered. 'Can you understand me? Are you Gallahs?'

'I – I don't really know, it depends what Gallah means,' Helen stammered.

'Extraordinary. The savages are philosophers,' said Ananthis.

'If you were not so busy making clever remarks, we might find something out,' Sheyde said mildly. 'Look, they're trembling. Poor things. We should be kinder to them. What are you?'

'Bloody fed up of being patronised,' Martin said under his breath, but Helen squeezed his elbow.

'We – er – we're lost,' she began. 'I don't know how to make you understand this but we're from another world and we don't know where we are.'

'This is Tevera, of course. The sea is Halaranthe. We are from the Heart of Life. Don't you know these places?'

'No. We came here – sort of by accident, from our own world. We're from – where are we from?'

'England,' said Martin. 'Earth. The world.'

'Another world!' exclaimed the man with blue hair. Their gasps were half-mocking, half-curious.

Ananthis walked round to Sheyde's side and looked down at Helen. His clothes, of complex design, were predominantly gold, accentuating the whiteness of his skin. Beautiful as he was, there was a certain affectedness in the way he moved, which Helen found irritating at first, then increasingly fascinating. She could not take her eyes off the long, ivory curve of his throat.

'How can we not believe them?' he said. 'Look at them. Their clothes are alien, and what are these beasts?'

'Horses.' 'Arabs,' Helen and Martin said simultaneously.

'They are lovely creatures,' said Ananthis thoughtfully, running his hand down Fikri's neck. 'Small, though.'

Martin pulled the bay's head towards him possessively. 'Look, we need your help. I can't explain how we came to be here but all we want to do is go home. Is there anything you can do?'

'You want to go back into death?' said the red-haired woman, Corolea, frowning.

'What? What are you talking about?' Helen exclaimed.

'Ignore Corolea,' Sheyde said soothingly. 'She is one step behind the rest of us. We have established that you are not Gallahs, so it must be true that you are from this other world. But we know nothing of it. So how can we possibly help you to return there?'

'We would help you if we could,' added the blue-haired man. 'Ananthis, they are very frightened. Wouldn't you be, washed up on the shore of an alien world? Let's show them some friendship. I am Tasnian.'

He reached out and took Helen's hand, which he raised to his forehead. She was so surprised by the gesture that she could think of nothing, except that they were perhaps not as bad as she had first thought.

Beside her, Martin said, 'Oh – er – my name's Martin, and this is Helen.'

'Surely these are not your full names?' said Sheyde. She raised an eyebrow, then laughed. 'We also do not speak all our names to strangers. So, it is enough. I am Sheyde, and this is Corolea, and our disdainful friend is Ananthis.'

They nodded, the blond man with a cold smile and Corolea with a touch of wariness, but neither repeated Tasnian's greeting.

There was a silence, wide and bright-edged as the sea, in which all Helen's fear, all her awareness of their inconceivable situation, seemed to be swirling towards her out of the sky. There was nothing there yet she could feel it, something loud and cold and physical. She caught her breath to cry out and run.

'Now what do we do?' asked Corolea.

At the sound of her voice, the scream subsided and Helen breathed again. The panic had passed, she had not broken. Yet.

'We don't want these strangers with us,' Corolea went on, 'but what can we do with them?' She was a tiny bit like Rianna, Helen thought, though taller and more colourful. Her brilliant red hair was swept back from her face and there was a nervous edge to everything she said and did. 'We can't just leave them here.'

'Can't we?' said Ananthis off-handedly.

'Of course not.' Sheyde put her hand on Martin's shoulder, making him jump. 'I find them fascinating, and so do you, if you'd admit it. We can't send them home, so it's our responsibility to look after them. They need food and drink and shelter, just as we do.'

'I am not sacrificing this afternoon for their sake.'

'No one requires you to. We'll take them with us.'

Ananthis gave Sheyde a long look, then smiled broadly. It did nothing to make him appear more human. His face was angelic, shimmering, but there was demonic mischief in his eyes. 'Why not?' he said. 'It would be amusing.'

'Where are you going?' Helen said, alarmed.

'Where do you think?' Ananthis pointed at the boats swaying against a brilliant sky. 'To sea, of course.'

Helen and Martin looked at each other. 'No – no, I don't think so,' she said.

'Are you afraid, intrepid travellers from another world?' He put his hands on his hips, still grinning. 'Afraid of a few hours on the open sea? I don't know what you might imagine could happen.'

'Couldn't we wait on the beach?' Martin sounded calm and reasonable, but his hand was tight on Helen's. 'Or couldn't you tell us where there's someone else who could help us?'

Sheyde stepped between them, putting her arms round them both and excluding the others. She spoke softly and her expression seemed kinder now. 'Ananthis thinks it is fun to frighten people. There is nothing to be afraid of, I promise.'

'All the same – ' Helen began.

'It is something we do often, for pleasure . . . and for something more than pleasure.' Sheyde's voice was warm, persuasive; the promise of unimaginable experiences rose in it like bubbles through honey, and she was not to be denied. Helen felt herself growing less averse to the idea. 'It is a very special thing, to sail upon the waves of Halaranthe and to see the Oa. I want you to share it with us. It's only for a few hours, and there is no danger. See how calm the sea is.'

'Yes, well,' said Martin, 'I can't leave the horses.'

Helen felt an unexpected pang of disappointment. He was right, of course.

But Sheyde said, 'Can you not tie them up? They'll be quite safe.'

'No, I can't. I haven't any rope and I'm not risking them breaking their reins.'

Sheyde laughed. 'Ah, but we have rope.' She turned and called, 'Tasnian, bring us some rope!'

They watched in amazement as Tasnian ran towards the sea, skidding in the wet sand as he went, and plunged fully clothed through the tide to the nearest boat. It danced and canted as he hauled himself up on the side. He retrieved the rope and let himself back into the water, vanishing completely below the surface for a few seconds. Then he reappeared and ran towards them, laughing, his clothes and hair plastered to him, scattering water in droplets of pure sunlight.

Helen stared at him. With his hair flat to his head, he looked more than ever like a sculpted being.

He handed the soft, sea-bleached rope to Martin, who turned the coil round in his hands and said stubbornly, 'I can't leave them on the beach. There's nothing to tie them to and they need to be fed.'

'Then take them to the top of the cliff,' Sheyde said patiently. 'Surely you can tie them to a tree, and they can eat the grass. They eat grass, don't they?'

'Yes, but – '

'They will be safe,' she repeated firmly. Martin was losing the argument. 'If you come with us you will understand why you would have regretted missing it for the rest of your lives. And we take food and drink with us; aren't you hungry or thirsty? Helen?'

'Yes, I am, actually – '

'Whose side are you on?' Martin exclaimed.

With difficulty, she pulled away from Sheyde and took him to one side. 'Look, I don't know what we should do,' she said. 'But I don't really feel they mean us any harm, do you?'

'No. I suppose not.'

'Well, what shall we do then? Wait on the cliff until they come back?'

'You want to go with them, don't you?' From Nick it would

have been an accusation of nameless crimes, but from Martin it was just a question, a need to get things clear.

'Yes. I think so.' Helen shivered as she said it. 'Don't you?'

He took off his glasses and polished them on a tissue, holding Fikri's reins under his arm. 'It wouldn't be a good idea to separate. And I would like to know what's so wonderful that we mustn't miss it.' He turned to the others and said, 'All right, we'll come with you, if it's not for too long.'

'We'll return before sunset,' said Tasnian. 'I'll help you take the horse-arabs up the cliff. We shouldn't lose any more time.'

'I'll drink an ocean of wine to that,' Ananthis said, and yawned.

Helen watched uneasily as Martin and Tasnian led the mare and gelding up a steep cliff path. They were out of sight for an age; she tried to go through all the actions in her head, imagining Martin running up the stirrups, removing the saddles and finding somewhere safe to put them, fashioning makeshift headcollars and tethering the horses so that they could graze . . . surely it could not take this long . . . Sheyde was speaking to her but she did not take in a word of it, keeping her gaze fixed on the green rim of the cliff. Ananthis and Corolea moved away towards the sea's edge. There was no visible danger yet it sang inside her, clear and sharp as the air.

'Here they are,' said Sheyde. The two men appeared on the cliff path and Helen breathed again.

'Everything all right?' she said as Martin approached her.

'Fine,' he said, patting her on the shoulder. 'I think Tasnian's OK – for someone with hair that colour.'

Ananthis and Corolea had pulled one of the boats up through the tide, oblivious to how wet they had become in the process. They had taken off their outer garments and left them on the sand, and now Sheyde and Tasnian did the same, walking to the boat dressed only in thin, silky tunics. Helen and Martin, with several nervous glances at each other, removed their boots and waded out to the vessel. The water was transparent and diamond-cool. Tasnian vaulted into the boat, then he and Sheyde helped them in while the other two held it steady on the water.

Within, the vessel was shaped like a large coracle, with room for eight people to have stretched out comfortably. There were no seats, only a false bottom that appeared to be made of closely-woven wicker work, stained a smoky deep blue. Helen and Martin sat with their legs stretched out, their backs braced against the side.

'It's hardly more than a canoe with a sail,' Martin said uneasily.

'But with the wind in her sail, she flies,' said Sheyde. The boat dipped violently as the others climbed aboard. Ananthis and Corolea took an oar each, and the vessel began to glide through the transparent waves.

As soon as they began to move, Helen felt her tension lessening. Boats had always had this soothing effect on her, and this journey was pure enchantment. She leaned her head back, taken out of herself by the vastness and brightness of the sky, the crystal lapping of waves. The breeze and a gentle current took them, and the rowers laid down their oars and relaxed. No one was steering, and no one seemed to care.

There was a gentle swell, enough to make the boat rise and fall soporifically. Helen lost track of time, until she was roused by Sheyde saying, 'Time to eat, I think. Helen, are you thirsty?'

'Yes, very,' she said, lifting her head. She had almost been in a trance. Sheyde and Corolea were taking things from a bag that was made of a soft material like chamois leather, and she could not help smiling. It put her in mind of a boating party, with only the parasols and the chilled champagne missing.

Sheyde took out an odd container, shaped like a giant poppy head, and poured liquid into a leathery cup. She handed it to Helen, who looked at it dubiously.

'It's all right, Helen, it's water!' Sheyde said, laughing. 'Quench your thirst with that, then I'll give you some wine.'

'They tell you never to drink the water,' Helen said to herself, but she drank it anyway, relishing it in long, cold mouthfuls.

'Martin?' said Sheyde.

'Nothing for me, thanks,' he said in an odd voice. Helen looked at him for the first time since they had set out, and was alarmed to see that his face had turned greenish-white.

'What's wrong?' she said.

'I get seasick in the bath,' he said faintly. 'I always tell myself that it won't happen this time, but it usually does.'

'Oh Lord,' said Helen, helplessly distressed for him.

'Is he unwell?' asked Ananthis. 'You should have said something before. Here, take a sip of this.' He picked up a smaller container, poured out a little fluid, and held it out to Martin.

'I don't think I could swallow anything,' he said, regarding it suspiciously.

'Please try,' added Tasnian. 'It will make you feel better.'

Martin obviously did not trust Ananthis, but he was prepared to take Tasnian's word for it. He took the cup and drained the contents with one gulp. The effect was startling. His eyes bulged, his lips disappeared and he went completely white. Then the blood rushed back to his face and he let out a gasp that was halfway between a choke and a cry of pain.

'Feel better now?' Ananthis enquired. Martin nodded mutely.

'What was it?' said Helen.

'About two hundred per cent proof,' Martin managed to say.

'Too good to waste on those who don't appreciate it.' Ananthis poured a drop of liquor for each of the others, but added a generous amount of water. 'Wine from the Heart of Life,' he said, raising his own cup.

Even watered, the drink was still fiery. It had an almost instant effect on Helen, relaxing her more than ever.

She had been apprehensive about what sort of food they would be given, but while it was strange it was not too alien to be edible. There was a sort of white curd with seeds stirred into it, a salty cheese like feta, and large spongy fruits that tasted of honey. After a few minutes Martin managed to eat something, and there was a healthy colour back in his cheeks.

When the picnic was over, Helen felt so euphoric that she wondered if the drink was not alcohol but a drug. It was like being in paradise, in the company of angels.

'Are you glad we brought you now?' Sheyde asked. Above her, the sail stretched itself on the wind like a dancer, vivid as a leaf against the sky.

'Yes, oh yes.'

'So am I, believe it or not,' Martin said with a smile.

'It is not over yet.' Sheyde leaned languorously back over the side and trailed her hand in the water. 'This boat is called *The Wings of Chalceny* and she is well named.'

Before she could think twice about it, Helen said, 'I've heard that word before. Chalceny, or Chalcenian . . . '

'How?' said Martin, but she felt she should not have said anything.

'From Rianna, of course,' she said under her breath. 'Sheyde, what does Chalcenian mean?'

The woman opened her arms wide. 'We are Chalcenians, Helen. Can't you tell?'

'Well . . . yes.'

'But Helen and Martin are not Chalcenic, are they?' said Corolea, her voice edged with acid.

'But they might become so. I think they are on the edge . . . on the edge, like you.'

The sudden rage in Corolea's face was frightening. 'I am not! Look at this!' She pulled at her hair, which ran like red flames through her fingers. 'This is what matters – to create, not just to be always smiling and laughing. Any fool can do that.'

'Well said, my dear.' Ananthis had been lying full length on the deck, but the argument seemed to capture his interest and he stirred himself to lean on one elbow.

'That was the gravest insult you could give me, Sheyde,' Corolea said. 'To bring these colourless folk with us and then accuse *me* – '

'I don't have the slightest idea what you're talking about,' Sheyde retorted coldly. Corolea glared at her, apparently lost for words.

'If you can't manage a more interesting argument than this, be quiet. You'll bore us to death.' Ananthis lay back again, giving Sheyde an unpleasant look that Helen was glad he had not turned on her. The air almost shone with the tension between them, making her only too aware that she was intruding on the lives of people of whom she knew nothing.

'It's Sheyde, not me.'

'I know, Coro dear, it's you I'm defending,' Ananthis

replied. 'Her brains are in her feet.'

'Stop it, all of you,' Tasnian said gently, and after a second the tension vanished as if it had been discharged. Helen realised where she had seen his face before; it was that of a da Vinci saint, with whom she had fallen in love when she had seen the painting reproduced in a school book. Tasnian moved to sit next to her. His hair was dry now and she marvelled at the colour of it, sky blue and royal blue. He said, 'What is your world like?'

'Not so different to this,' said Martin. 'We name our boats, too.'

'I'd rather you told us something about this world,' Helen added.

'What can I tell you of Tevera to make it seem less strange?'

'I don't know. I don't know where to start.' She glanced at Martin but he had his head back and his eyes closed, a smile just visible through his beard. 'Why do you dye your hair such strange colours?'

'Dye?' Tasnian sounded amused. 'My hair is its true colour – true to my nature.'

'I'm sorry, I don't see what you mean.' She felt warm, weightless as a seabird diving through a watery golden mist.

'Indigo is the colour of the feet, the colour of swiftness and dancing. Sheyde is a dancer, but there is purple in her hair as well, if you look.'

'What's purple?' Helen asked sleepily.

'That is the colour of the legs and loins, and it means life and passion.' His voice was like a spoken lullaby. 'My hair is blue, and that is the colour of the heart.'

'Love,' said Helen.

'Yes, but all other emotions as well, which may be bad as well as good. And green – '

The colour of the arms. The Giver of Grace, she heard Rianna say in her head, and she opened her eyes wide, just in time to see Ananthis and Sheyde in the middle of pulling each other's tunics off and flinging them into the sea. The boat began to rock.

Martin sat up, gripping the side, and said, 'What's going on?'

Naked now, Ananthis and Sheyde grappled each other on

to the bottom of the boat and began to make love with unashamed enthusiasm. The two other Chalcenians did not turn a hair; Corolea went on sipping her drink as if nothing was happening, and Tasnian continued in the same gentle tone, 'Green is for grace, forgiveness, the greatest benediction of all. The embrace of the arms.'

Helen had broken out in a sweat of embarrassment and could not look at anyone, least of all Martin. She closed her eyes and felt sweat in the creases of her eyelids.

'Corolea's hair is red and that is for hands and creativity. And the head is gold, the colour of thought. Ananthis fancies himself an intellectual.'

'I *am* an intellectual!' Ananthis retorted gruffly, without pausing in what he was doing. Tasnian went on talking and Helen kept her eyes tight shut, trying to concentrate on what he was saying and block out the lovers' gasps. She failed.

Perhaps two or three minutes went by, then Tasnian's voice ceased abruptly. She felt a movement beside her, a tipping of the boat, then heard a splash. She and Martin both looked round, startled, but Tasnian was no longer in the boat.

The others took no notice. Ananthis and Sheyde were now lying loosely tangled together, looking very pleased with themselves.

'Where's Tasnian?' Helen cried.

'He dived in,' said Corolea.

'I don't believe this is happening,' said Martin. 'Where is he? He might be drowning!'

'No, not him,' said Sheyde, sitting up and pushing her hair off her damp shoulders. Martin was trying to look and trying not to look at her at the same time, and Helen felt a touch of what she hoped was not jealousy, but which probably was. 'They're here. Look.'

Sheyde was pointing at the sea. They turned, and saw that there were creatures swimming all around the boat, glistening animals the size of dolphins but slender and covered in shining jade-green scales. They poured through the water like silver. Helen had never seen anything like them before. Their beauty stole her breath, but it was their joy that made them beautiful, their unbounded delight in life as they cavorted and dived. Watching them, she forgot everything else.

'They are the Oa,' said Sheyde. One rose right out of the water and for a split-second Helen was nose to nose with it, marvelling at its delicate face and its eyes, which were soft and golden as a frog's. 'They are what we came to find. Ananthis and I called them.'

Tasnian was swimming with them. His hair trailed in the water and his arms flashed white through the waves. Helen watched him, then glanced round a moment later to see the other three lowering themselves into the water, Corolea still wearing her tunic.

'They're mad, they're all bloody mad,' said Martin, but he and Helen were clinging together as if to stop each other diving after them. Helen felt an incredible joy pushing up under her heart, and with it a longing to fall into the sea and join the rippling dance. The Oa swam round them and past them, breaking the waves into cascades of light.

One minute they were everywhere, the next they were gone. The Chalcenians could not keep up with them. They swam back to the boat, laughing like children, and almost capsizing it as they climbed back in. Corolea retied the sail and, without a word, she and Tasnian began to row back towards the beach.

They were quiet now, but their eyes were glazed with a joy that was almost mindless. Helen half shared it but she still felt excluded and she longed with all her soul to be part of it completely, to understand, to become *Chalcenic*.

There was conversation on the way back, but she could not follow much of it and did not take it in. She and Martin kept looking at each other, laughing silently in delight and disbelief, but neither could have put a name to what they felt. What had happened? They had seen the Oa, and everything had changed.

The vessel drifted safely back to the shore. Tasnian and Sheyde anchored it, then they went up on to the sand to retrieve their clothes which they put on regardless of wet hair and the sand clinging to their legs. Ananthis and Corolea began to walk towards the cliff with their arms around each other, to Helen's confusion, but Sheyde took no notice.

'Now, will you come with us?' she said to Helen and Martin. 'We are going back to the Heart of Life, and we would be pleased to have you as our guests.'

'Yes, we'd love to, thank you,' said Helen.

'If we have to stay here, I think I can bear it,' Martin said into her ear, and took her hand in a firm, sandy grasp. At that moment, Helen did not care if she never went back to Earth again.

They walked along the beach for several hundred yards, then made their way up an uneven path to the cliff top. The light was fading, the sky turning a clear mauve against which the daystars shone as bright as planets. Beyond, fields of paler stars were appearing, forming spider-web constellations against drifts of white and coloured seeds. Sheyde and Tasnian were otherworldly yet comforting presences at their side, shedding joy and silent laughter with every step.

A cool wind blew from inland, carrying the scent of bracken. Martin stopped suddenly and said, 'Oh my God, the horses!'

Helen gave a small cry of dismay. 'Oh no, Martin, how could we have forgotten?'

'I was walking along in a bloody dream, that's how. It's no good, I'll have to go back and fetch them.'

'Can you remember where they were?'

'I think so . . . '

'They should not be hard to find,' said Tasnian. 'Just walk straight back along the cliff edge, and you'll see the trees where we tied them. Shall I come with you?'

'No, there's no need for that, but don't go too far, will you?'

'We shall wait here,' said Sheyde, unperturbed.

'I'll come with you,' said Helen. 'It'll be quicker with two of us.'

They ran back along the cliff, shaken out of their complacent mood. It was further than Martin had anticipated, and it was a good five minutes before they reached the clump of trees and saw the mare and gelding grazing contentedly.

'Thank God for that,' Martin sighed, getting his breath back. Destiny and Fikri raised their heads and whickered a greeting. Helen was relieved, but at the same time she felt an increasing sense of panic. It had become like one of those dreams in which she was in a mad hurry, desperately trying to achieve something before she woke up and never quite managing it. If they took too long, would Sheyde and Tasnian grow bored with waiting and go on their way? They might never find them, and they would be stranded.

Martin put Fikri's saddle on, while Helen saw to Destiny. Every buckle, every flap conspired against her. Her hands were shaking, but Martin took even longer, and then he could not untie Fikri's rope.

'Hurry up!' she said.

'Don't worry. They said they'd wait.'

'I know, but . . . '

Finally they were both in the saddle. It was still light enough for them to see where they were going and they set off at a brisk canter. Three minutes . . .

'We should have reached them again by now,' Martin said, slowing to a trot. 'Perhaps a bit further.' But the sky was darkening, the air thickening around them. The loss of clarity was not mist but a sort of granulation, a breaking up of the landscape.

'Oh God, Martin, no,' Helen gasped.

They knew what was happening but they could do nothing to stop it. The granulation was moving now, quivering like a mass of atoms and then beginning to slant downwards across their eyes. Moisture condensed out of nowhere to wrap itself round them, and through it they saw the outlines of farm buildings, a gate and a wire fence, all dripping with rain in the half light.

'It's no good, Helen, it's over,' Martin said gravely. 'I think we're home.'

Chapter Six

'Where are we?' said Helen. 'I don't recognise this at all.'

'We're at the back of the farm.'

'Jo's farm?' she said incredulously.

'Yes. I think so. Come on, we'd better get Bert and Floss back to the stables.'

She followed Martin towards the dark farm buildings in a daze. Nothing was distinct in the blue-grey gloom, and her eyes hurt with trying to see through it. She felt shaken, as if grief or anger had poured through her and left her drained white inside.

Martin was right. They were in the paddock behind the loose boxes. As he opened the gate, the yearling put her head over the half-door of her box and nickered a welcome. Jo had stabled and fed her . . . Helen and Martin looked at each other apprehensively, but neither voiced their thoughts. They went automatically through the process of stabling the horses, untacking them and rubbing them down without speaking.

Martin filled buckets of water, Helen put the tack away and measured out feeds. Eventually Martin came out of Fikri's box and said, 'What time is it? It's nearly dark.'

'My watch has stopped. It wasn't waterproof.'

'We must have been away for hours. If it's still the same day. I suppose we've been lucky.'

'Lucky? How d'you mean?'

'Well, how have we come back here?' he said. 'Imagine, we could have found ourselves in the middle of Katmandu, stranded with two horses and no money and no way of getting home. Or bobbing about in the Atlantic Ocean. We might have ended up anywhere. I call this luck, or something.'

Helen paused in scratching Destiny's neck. Martin was looking at her over the door. 'It really happened, didn't it?' she said. Suddenly all the words, all the questions came flooding up inside her. She saw it reflected in his eyes, the need to talk and talk until they could make sense of what had happened. 'I didn't want to come home.'

'Neither did I,' he said softly.

Behind him, a very cold and very angry voice retorted, 'I'm sure you didn't.'

Drizzle glinted in a thin yellow torch-beam. Jo came into view, her short blond hair so tousled that it stuck straight up from her head, giving her a punk-like, aggressive look. Helen had never seen her so angry. Her face, never gentle, was all hard planes and she seemed luminous with rage, burning yet terrifyingly self-controlled. Helen almost fell apart just at the sight of her.

'*Where the hell have you been?*' Jo began. 'What the bloody hell do you think you've been doing? Do you know what time it is? It's half past nine, and you've been out since well before two.'

Helen tried to vanish in the shadows behind Destiny. Martin seemed at a loss for words. 'I know, but – '

Jo yanked open the stable door and Helen jumped back, but she only had eyes for Destiny. 'I've been driving round looking for you all evening,' she said, running her hands down the mare's legs. 'I called the police. I mean, what were you thinking of? I thought you'd had an accident. Is that what happened, and if so, why the hell didn't you find a phone and ring me?'

'There wasn't an accident,' said Martin. 'We're not hurt.'

'I'm not concerned about you, I'm thinking about the horses!'

'I was including the horses.'

'But if there was no accident, what have you been doing? Martin, how could you just take my horses out for nearly eight hours; are you trying to kill them or what?'

She stormed out and into Fikri's box without even acknowledging Helen's presence. There was an excruciating silence as she checked him over.

'They seem OK,' Jo said shortly. 'No thanks to you two.'

'Jo, I can explain – ' Martin began.

'Too damn right you will.' She turned and began to walk briskly away.

'Where are you going?'

'To ring the police. To tell them you're back. I suppose it didn't occur to you that you were wasting their time as well as mine?'

'Will you wait a minute?' he said, hurrying after her. 'Look, I know you must have been worried sick and I'm sorry, but . . . '

Their voices dwindled to nothing. Helen was left on her own. What on earth could they possibly tell Jo?

Helen hated scenes. That was part of the reason she had broken up with Nick, because he thrived on arguments and she loathed them. Faced with Jo she felt like a child hauled before a monstrous headmistress, and the reason was simply that Jo's anger was fully justified. There was nothing they could say in their own defence – nothing that was credible, at least – and if Helen had been in Jo's position she would have reacted in the same way.

She finished settling the horses, made sure the tack room was tidy, and locked it. Then, gritting her teeth, she made her way towards the cottage. If only she had brought her own car; she could have slipped away unnoticed, but that was the cowardly way out and she could not leave Martin to face Jo alone. She felt like two different people badly merged together, one still floating in another land, one shamefacedly trying to readjust to reality.

'I've ordered you a taxi,' Jo said abruptly as she entered the kitchen. There was a red tiled floor, a square sink and an old pine table across which she and Martin were facing each other.

Helen blinked in the raw light. She knew Martin would gladly have given her a lift back, and she had been relying on that as a chance to speak to him alone. But obviously Jo did not want Martin out of her sight for the time being. God, Helen thought, does she think that Martin and I have spent all this time rolling around in a hayfield, or that we tethered the horses outside a hotel? How could she think we'd conduct an affair so ineptly? On the other hand, in the absence of any explanation, it was all she could think.

'Thank you,' Helen said quietly. 'When will it be here?'

'Very soon, I hope.' Jo had made Martin a cup of tea, but she did not offer Helen any. She gave the impression of being furious only about the horses, but she would not be human if there was not some jealousy in there as well. Helen did not feel like reassuring her. It would sound patronising, and totally out of place in the icy atmosphere.

Helen had been basking in the illusion that there was only her and Martin, no one to intrude. She resented Jo, with her spiky hair and her hard eyes, resented being reminded that Martin's loyalty was to her.

'I've locked up,' she said, putting the key on the table. Jo snatched it, meeting her eyes for the first time.

'You don't – you just don't go out with someone else's animals and not bring them back for eight hours. I expect people I trust with my horses to behave like responsible adults! You town people – you think a farm is a bloody playground, that you can just hop on the horse and off again and leave some other bugger to do all the hard work. When did you last have to get up at five in the middle of winter or stay up all night with a sick animal?'

'Don't go on at her,' Martin said soothingly. 'It wasn't her fault.'

'I don't care whose fault it was. I thought I could trust her, and that was my mistake.'

Helen could not bring herself to apologise. It would have meant nothing and changed nothing; to do so would only draw further scorn from Jo. Neither did she have the energy to make an argument of it, because Jo was in the right and she could shout louder. She left Helen feeling exactly one inch high.

'Martin, I think I'd better leave,' she said quietly.

'I'm still waiting for an explanation,' said Jo, 'but it can wait until she's gone. Where's that damn taxi?'

There was a long silence that almost ate Helen alive. Then they heard the muffled swish of car tyres, and Martin said, 'Here it is. I'll see you to the front door.'

Jo did not follow them. They had a few seconds to themselves, but things had changed.

'I'm sorry about her throwing you out like this, but it's probably best you go home,' Martin said in a low voice.

'It's OK, I understand. I just don't know what to say to her.'

'Neither do I. There's not a lot you can say, when she's like this.'

'But you'll tell her that we – I mean, she knows there's nothing between us, doesn't she, it's so ridiculous – '

Martin scratched his head. He was distracted, impatient for her to leave. It was not the right time to talk. 'I don't know what she thinks, Helen, but mainly she's annoyed about the horses. I can't really blame her, can you?'

'No, but what's going to happen now?'

'I don't know. You'd better go.'

'Yes, right,' Helen snapped. It was important to her to retain her dignity, but inside she felt rejected, cold.

'Here's a couple of quid for the taxi.' She was about to refuse it, but he added, 'Please take it, I feel bad enough already.'

'Oh. OK, thanks.'

Martin opened the door and Helen stepped out into the darkness. As she made to climb into the taxi something caught her eye and she glanced back at the cottage. The headlights shone on the leaded window, and through the reflection she saw the softer gleam of red, blue and green jewels. One of Rianna's dolls was on the window sill, its white face pressed up against the glass and a tiny smile on its lips.

When Helen arrived home Rianna was standing in the front doorway with light streaming out around her, shining through her loose white shirt and through her hair. She was a silhouette figure from a painting or a dream.

'Helen? I've been really worried about you,' she said as Helen paid the driver and crossed the small front garden. 'I couldn't remember if you'd told me you were going out or not, and I couldn't understand why you hadn't taken the car. A policewoman came round a couple of hours ago and said – '

'It's all right, Rianna, I'm fine and so are Martin and the horses.' Helen walked into the front room and collapsed on the sofa. It was only then that she realised how tired she was.

Rianna carried on into the kitchen. 'Do you want some hot chocolate?' she called.

Helen sensed it at once. Rianna had been worried, she wanted to ask Helen what on earth she had been doing, but she did not want to hear the answer. Helen sighed, and said grimly, 'In a minute. Rianna, will you come in here, please? We've got to talk. We have *got* to talk.'

Rianna obeyed, and sat down on the sofa with her feet tucked under her, uneasy. 'What is it?'

'Do you remember ever saying the word Chalcenian to me? When we were children, it was part of our game. I remember it distinctly. You said, "We are Chalcenians, very special people," or something like that.' Rianna shifted uncomfortably. Helen suspected she was about to make a run for it, and she grabbed her arm. 'I am going to tell you what happened and you're going to listen!'

She hardly raised her voice, but the sharpness in it seemed to pin Rianna to her seat.

'Yes, I'm listening. But I don't know what you want of me, Helen. I don't remember the name and I don't know what it means.'

Helen, ashamed of bullying her, spoke more gently. 'But you have a feeling that it means something, don't you? Otherwise you wouldn't have said that.'

Rianna was silent. Her lips parted, closed again. Her gaze flickered round the room.

'Rianna, give me some help, please. There are strange things happening to me and I'm sure they're connected with you.' This time it was not the experience itself that had upset Helen, but coming back to Jo – that and the dark possibilities that she could not yet bear to consider. She went on, 'This afternoon I met the Chalcenians. They looked like your dolls and they looked like you, all at the same time. Doesn't that mean anything to you?'

'I'm not sure.'

'Please tell me the truth. I'm not making this up, Martin was with me.'

'I am telling you the truth! I'd do anything to remember, Helen. Just trying to think about it is like a black weight pressing on my eyeballs. It hurts, I can't see anything.' There was panic in her face, but Helen was determined not to relent.

She spared Rianna nothing. Rianna sat very still, with flight in every curve of her body, like someone trying to relax in the dentist's chair. Only when Helen reached the scene with Jo did her tension begin to fade, as if they were back on safer ground. What had happened at the farm really had no connection to what had gone before, but Helen related it anyway, if only to release her frustration.

'I can imagine how worried she must have been about the horses, and how angry she must have felt, but, God, the way she looked at me. I don't know why she hates me so much. Perhaps it's because she's a tough farmer and I'm not, I don't know, but I swear she's got no cause to be jealous of me. Martin's so loyal to her, and she treats him like – ' Helen shook her head, ran a hand through her hair. It felt greasy. 'She doesn't deserve him. I've got no right to say that, and if you ask me if I'm jealous I'll deny it until I'm purple in the face, but . . . I just don't like her, I suppose. I doubt that she'll ever let me near the horses again. It's all so crazy.'

'You can't like everyone,' said Rianna. 'Can I go now?'

'Where?' Helen asked sharply.

'To make a hot drink. I need it, if you don't.'

Rianna returned after a few minutes with mugs of hot chocolate and a plate of sandwiches. Comfort food, Helen thought wryly, but there was no doubt that she felt more human after she had eaten. After a while she said, 'Rianna, you're not saying much. Did any of it sound familiar to you? The Chalcenians, Tevera, the colours?'

Rianna sipped at her drink, then settled back on the sofa, leaning against Helen. 'The colours, a bit. When I'm making the dolls, the colours seem so important . . . Helen, the time you came back from the Park, shaken up, had it happened then too?'

'Yes. I saw the Chalcenians that time as well.' Helen did not mention the creature that had chased her. Rianna seemed quite tranquil now, and she did not want to cause her any more alarm.

That thought, however, brought back a sudden and jarring memory. She had completely forgotten about the strange man who had come in asking about 'the person who makes the dolls'. Had it really been less than twelve hours ago? It seemed to have happened in another lifetime.

Helen decided not to tell Rianna, at least not for the time being. There was no point in frightening her for what was probably no reason. But the image of the man was like a weight, pulling her tired mind down into the darkness of other anxieties.

'You were saying about the colours,' she said, trying to shake herself out of it.

'Do you mind if we don't talk about it any more? I need time to think.'

'Oh, Rianna. What am I going to do with you? You've got to face it, sooner or later. You can't keep trying to pretend nothing is happening.'

'Face what? What *is* happening?' said Rianna, and neither she nor Helen could answer that.

Helen was in the shop the next day, trying to deal with an unusual number of customers, when Martin rang from work.

'I'm sorry about last night,' he said. 'Are you OK?'

'Yes, I'm just so tired I can hardly stay awake. Whatever did you tell Jo?'

'What could I say? I told her we rode further than we meant to – '

'You can say that again!'

He laughed. ' – and we met some friends of yours and had a picnic. We forgot the time and couldn't hurry back because the horses were tired. It was sort of true.'

'Did she believe it?'

'I don't know. I think she had to. I'm really sorry about the way she was with you. She's not actually as tough as she seems.'

'I don't suppose Attila the Hun was either.'

It was not the right thing to say. 'Look, Helen, I know she's not an instantly likeable person, but that's because she's had to struggle for everything she's got. She lost her mother when she was four and spent all her time when she wasn't at school helping her father run the farm. Then he died when she was sixteen and she had to fight her own relatives to keep the farm. She's done it all on her own.'

The more Martin extolled Jo's virtues, the more Helen felt like saying something unpleasant. *Bravo, give her a medal!* It still did not explain how Martin could love somebody who had absolutely no sense of humour. 'It's all right, you don't have to defend her. I think she was quite right to be angry. It's also not her fault that she can't stand the sight of me. The feeling's mutual.'

It was not Martin's style to lose his temper. He became regretful and rather formal instead. 'Look, I understand the way you feel. I really think it would be best if we didn't go riding for a while.'

'Don't beat about the bush. Jo doesn't want me anywhere near her horses ever again, does she?'

'Well, she didn't say that exactly, but . . . '

'It's OK, I said I understand. But Martin, we really must talk, and we can't over the phone.'

There was a pause. 'I'm sorry, Helen, I gave Jo my word I wouldn't see you. Not for a few weeks, anyway. Give her a chance to cool down.'

Suddenly Helen could hardly speak. She knew so little about Jo and Martin, really. She did not even know how long they had known each other. They did not live together; Martin shared a house in Loughborough with some colleagues from work, so it was hard to tell how serious he and Jo were about each other. Did they plan to marry, was Martin going to give up his job and move to the farm? It was none of her business. Someone else's life.

'Great,' she said. 'Who can I talk to? Rianna can't help me, she just doesn't know anything about it, and now you're deserting me. I'll be crying on Nick's shoulder at this rate.'

'Oh, look, Helen, I'll come round and see you. Jo won't find out.'

'No,' she replied, trying to sound cheerful and unconcerned and succeeding too well. 'No, you mustn't break your word. I'll be fine, really. It's probably best if we just forget it ever happened.'

She put the phone down. If she had not been in the shop, she would have burst into tears. It hit her now that she might not see Destiny and Fikri again, and they had been such an important part of her life for the last few months. And she might not see Martin, but that was her fault for deciding to be a martyr.

Sometimes, Helen thought, I am my own worst enemy.

*

After the article in the paper the shop became busier than ever, and there were more and more orders for the dolls. Helen was grateful to the extra customers for keeping her too busy to do much thinking, but as the days went by, everything seemed to set her more and more on edge. As soon as she shut the shop each evening her mind began to whirl with grim thoughts.

She had thought she could only be drawn into Tevera from Bradgate Park. But it had happened in Swithland Woods too, and they had returned to the farm. What if she could cross the barrier from anywhere in Charnwood? She might be walking along the street in Rothley one moment, stepping over a cliff in Tevera the next. It might even happen in her own house. It gave her an almost permanent feeling of vertigo which she could not reason away.

The black animal haunted her dreams. Rianna's dolls danced on a beach, laughing at her, filling her with terror. When she woke up, there would be other anxieties to fill her mind: the connection between the dolls and the two deaths, Martin, the prospect of the ginger-haired man finding Rianna . . .

The man had said he would return in a few days. So far there was no sign of him, but she felt she could not relax for a second in case he reappeared. She wanted to protect Rianna from him, but how was she to do that? Insist she never came in the shop, make her lock herself in the house? There was nothing she could do without alarming Rianna, so Helen worried for both of them.

She knew she was depressed. She had felt this way with Nick sometimes, but then there had been straightforward reasons. Now her head felt like a crackling radio, switching dizzily between stations, none of which made any sense. If she had a breakdown she would be of no use to anyone, but nothing any doctor or psychiatrist could do would even touch the real root of the problem.

The more depressed Helen became, the more brightly Rianna seemed to shine, like a comforting angel.

Imagined fears were bad enough, but the realisation of them was often more oblique and more shocking. On a dark, thundery afternoon, about three weeks after she had last seen Martin, a London store rang up and put in an order for ten dolls.

Rianna was thrilled, and dashed home to make an immediate start on them, but Helen could not share her enthusiasm. For some reason, the idea of the dolls being more widely available made her nervous. There was no reason, of course; only the coincidental deaths of two women who had bought them, a vague resemblance to a wild and strange people in another world . . . No reason at all.

Just before Helen was about to close the shop and go home, she saw a face watching her through the door. Dismay trickled coldly through her as she recognised the broad forehead, the fierce eyes under tangled eyebrows. She wished fervently that she was not alone in the shop.

Go away, she thought, but the man was already opening the door. As he walked in, the darkness seemed to come in with him, fogging the lights and trailing a humid chill through the air. Helen's hand drifted along the counter towards the phone, but she did not actually touch it; she was only too aware that she was probably panicking over nothing.

'Good afternoon,' she said as he approached the counter. He was wasting no time pretending to look round.

'The lady who makes the dolls . . . Is she here?' he said.

'No, she isn't, I'm afraid.'

'Could you tell me where I can find her?'

Helen swallowed. She was not sure whether it was the man himself who was so menacing, or the idea of him hunting Rianna that made him seem so. She said politely, 'No, but if you tell me what it's about I could give her a message.'

'No. I must speak to her in person.'

'Well, if it's about the dolls, all business is done through the shop anyway, so there wouldn't be much point.'

The way he stared at her made her glance around for something she could use as a blunt instrument. 'It isn't business. It's personal.'

'Oh. Well, again, if you'd give me some idea of why you want to see her, I could perhaps get her to ring you, but – '

'I see. You're protecting her. Of course. Perhaps I should explain that I know her. Her name is Rianna Harper, isn't it?'

'Who told you that?' The situation seemed to be slipping out of her control.

'I did not need to be told. I would recognise her dolls anywhere and it is very important that I speak to her about them.'

'Look, would you mind telling me who you are? It really would make things easier all round if you'd explain what you want.'

He shook his head. His eyes blazed through her as if she was nothing, a presumptuous upstart between himself and Rianna whom he could blow away like a piece of straw. 'Mrs Durham, I did not expect you to be so obstructive. Forgive me for wasting your time; I'll find her another way.'

He left, but the darkness remained, lying like drifts of dust in the corners. He knew Helen's married name. Any of the other shopkeepers could have told him, of course. He could easily find her home address from the phone book, and if he did not already know that Rianna lived with her, he only had to go round there to find out . . .

Helen locked up and began to walk briskly through the unnatural gloom. The air seemed to cling round her like a plastic skin and her head ached with the electricity. Summer storms always oppressed her. It seemed this one would never break.

She passed a couple of neighbours, mumbled 'Hello', but saw no sign of the ginger-haired man. As she came in sight of the house she almost broke into a run, her heart looping up into her throat.

The back door was locked. She banged on it with one hand, fumbling for her key with the other. 'Rianna! Are you all right? Let me in!'

She pushed the door open, almost fell through and ran from room to room, crying breathlessly, 'Rianna! Rianna, are you here?'

The house was dark and quiet. There was no sign of her in either of the bedrooms. The man had found her while she was here alone and . . .

A sound made her freeze. There was someone moving about downstairs, a bag rustling, the fridge door creaking open. Then a voice called out, 'Helen, are you home?'

She went shakily to the top of the stairs and stared down, not believing her eyes.

'Hello,' Rianna said cheerfully. 'Have you just come in? We must have missed each other by seconds.'

'Where have you been?'

'To the shop, to fetch some cotton and something for tea. We ought to celebrate. The dolls are going to London!'

'Yes. Yes. Oh, God,' said Helen, sitting down on the top stair.

'What's wrong?'

'Nothing.' Helen waited for her heart to slow down. He had not been here. Not yet. If she told Rianna, what good would it do? It would only frighten her, and she might run away again. I'm being selfish, Helen thought; I don't want her to leave. On the other hand, it would be better to face the man and find out what he was after – with the help of the police if necessary.

'Are you sure you're OK?'

'Yes, I – er – hurried home because I thought it was going to rain and I'm a bit out of breath, that's all. Rianna . . . '

'Yes?'

'There have been a few break-ins round here lately. We ought to be very careful about locking up, especially if either of us is here on our own.'

'I don't know what we've got that's worth stealing! But I always lock myself in, anyway.'

'Good. Just to be on the safe side, you know . . . '

Helen was on edge all evening, oversensitive to the slightest noise outside. After they had eaten, Rianna sat down with her sewing, apparently quite happy, but Helen could not relax. To her, the atmosphere crackled with greyness like an untuned television and there was nothing she could do to dispel it.

'It's not like you to sit about doing nothing,' Rianna commented.

'I know, I'm just tense.'

Rianna put her sewing aside. 'So am I. I can't concentrate, I keep sticking the needle in my finger. What's wrong with us? It's like . . . waiting for something to happen.'

'Must be the weather,' Helen said, twisting her fingers together. 'If only that wretched storm would break – '

She almost sprang off the sofa as the telephone rang. Her heart raced. She went to answer it with undignified haste, praying that it was her mother or someone else she knew.

Lifting the receiver, she heard a voice mumbling, 'Helen – Helen, it's in the bedroom now, it knows my name, how does it know my name?'

Something in the voice made a lump of fear congeal under her breastbone, and she held the receiver away from her ear.

Rianna said, 'Who is it?'

'It's Nick. I think he's drunk. Listen.'

Rianna came and put her ear to the other side of the receiver.

'Nick?' said Helen. 'Hello, it's me, are you all right?'

'It's dark. Bloody dark. Helen, help me . . . ' There was a muffled sound like something falling, then a groan.

'Nick? Nick, can you hear me?'

'Stop it! Don't keep saying my name, it keeps saying my name.'

'Have you been drinking?'

He said something she couldn't make out, then broke into sobs so desolate that they sent electric chills shivering across her skin. She had never heard him cry before.

Rianna said, 'I don't think he's drunk. I think he's ill.'

'Nick, will you please tell me what's wrong?'

'No good. Can't see.'

'Is Gina with you? Nick, is Gina there?'

There was a pause, then he slurred, 'No, only the doll. Rianna's doll.'

After that, he was silent. There was no dialling tone; he had not put the phone down. She heard a faint clicking sound, something that might have been breathing or just crackles on the line.

'Nick! Nick! Are you there? Say something, please!'

Eventually Helen put the phone down. She was shaking, but she felt oddly calm as she sometimes did when she had stopped trying to fight a crisis and had decided exactly what she must do.

'Rianna, I'm going over to Nick's flat,' she said. 'And I'd very much prefer it if you came with me.'

Chapter Seven

Nick's flat was in a converted Victorian house, just outside the centre of Loughborough. Helen parked raggedly on the forecourt, ran to the door and pressed the bell.

As she had feared, there was no answer.

'Maybe he wasn't ringing from home,' Rianna said as she joined her. Everything looked grey in the cold orange street lights, and lightning flickered drily in the distance.

'I'll try a neighbour,' said Helen, looking down the list of names. 'Mr and Mrs Harley. I'm sure Nick said Mrs Harley was the landlady or caretaker or something.' She pressed the bell, and after a few seconds, a female voice responded through the intercom.

'Hello?'

'Hello, I'm Nick Durham's wife, I need to see him but he's not answering.'

'His wife?' The woman sounded half asleep.

'Ex-wife.'

'Oh, I see. I expect he's out, then.'

'No, I don't think so. He rang me and I think he might be ill. I'm rather worried.'

'Oh. Oh dear,' said Mrs Harley. 'You'd better come in then. Hang on – ' The door buzzed and clicked. Helen thrust it open and ran up the stairs two at a time, with Rianna close behind her. On the first landing, a thin, round-shouldered woman of about forty came out and looked at Helen as if puzzled. 'Oh, I thought you were the other girl.'

'No, I'm not Gina. She wasn't his wife,' Helen said shortly.

Mrs Harley shrugged and pushed back her limp brown hair. 'I get confused, all these different women. Wish I got a look-in, I'd swap my husband for him any day.'

She led them up to the second landing, trailing a scent of talcum powder and cigarette smoke. Helen was too worked up to take any notice of her remarks, and shifted impatiently as the woman knocked on the door of Nick's flat.

'Mr Durham!' she called, knocking again. There was no answer. Mrs Harley tried the door, then drew a bunch of keys from her pocket. 'I have spare keys to the flats, you see, although – ' she began, but as soon as the door was open Helen rushed past her, not listening.

All the lights in the flat were on, making everywhere seem glaringly shadowless.

'Nick?' Helen called, running through the hall and the sitting room, reminded horribly of the way she had searched for Rianna earlier. This time there was no cause for a sudden rush of relief, only the thread of fear tightening and tightening.

'His car's there,' said Mrs Harley, looking out of the window. 'He doesn't usually go anywhere without it, unless he's just gone for some milk.' She was hugging a flowery cotton dressing gown around herself, absently dipping into the pocket as if searching for a non-existent packet of cigarettes.

'Nick, are you here?'

They found him in the bedroom. He was lying backwards across the bed, dressed in jeans and a white shirt, with one leg stretched out and the other dangling on to the floor. His eyes were closed, his blond hair spread out on the pillow. He might have been asleep, except that there was no movement about him at all, not even the slightest rise and fall of breathing.

Rianna moved to the foot of the bed as Helen went to him, but Mrs Harley stayed in the doorway.

'Nick, wake up,' said Helen. There was no response. 'Come on, wake up.' She shook him, gently at first, then harder. His body rocked limply in her hands. 'Nick, please!'

She straightened up abruptly, her hands clawing at her hair.

'What's wrong with him?' said Mrs Harley.

'I don't know. He's unconscious,' Helen said in a faint voice, while inside her a voice screamed: *No no no no no . . .*

'Ooh no, I can't look at this,' said the woman, retreating to the sitting room. 'Call an ambulance, dear, I should.'

Helen looked at Rianna, whose face was unreadable. She might have been in shock, or totally unmoved; it was impossible to tell. 'Yes, I'll do that, I'll get an ambulance,' said

Helen.

She had to take the receiver from Nick's hand to make the call. Her voice was brisk and urgent as she gave the address, but hysteria bubbled underneath. What had he been going through when he rang her, what had he seen? The memory of him crying was terrible. He had spoken of Rianna's doll, but looking around she could not see any sign of it.

'What did they say?' Rianna asked.

'They'll be here in a few minutes.'

'I'll go downstairs and watch for them,' said Mrs Harley from the other room. 'I'm sorry, dear, I can't stand anything medical. If my kids are ill, my husband has to look after them. Oh Lord, I hope it's not serious.'

'Rianna, please stay with me,' Helen said.

She replied softly, 'Of course. Don't worry, they'll soon be here.'

While they waited, Helen sat on the bed and held Nick's hand. It felt warm. She thought she could feel a pulse, but it might have been her own, fluttering against his skin. Everything seemed pallid white and yellow; his face was as white as the pillow, his hair bleached straw-gold in the cold electric light. Every unkind word he had ever said to her, every betrayal, it was all forgotten, all forgiven. *Please don't die*, she begged him. *You can't . . .*

Afterwards, she remembered the night only in fragments, painfully vivid pools of light surfacing from a mesh of darkness. There were ambulancemen in the room, dark uniforms bustling round her and a faint but invasive medical smell.

Someone was lifting her away from him, saying, 'Have you any idea what he might have taken, love?'

'What?'

'Tablets, you know, sleeping pills or anti-depressants or something? It really would help if we can find out.'

'I don't think he's taken anything,' she said, stunned. 'I never knew him take drugs of any sort, prescribed or otherwise.'

'We thought it was an overdose.'

'I never said that,' she gasped, watching them lift him on to the stretcher. 'He phoned me – he sounded ill so I came over and found him. I don't know what's wrong. He'll be all right, won't he?'

'Well, love, it doesn't look good.'

Rianna's hand was warm on her arm, supporting her. Helen had always driven them everywhere; she did not even know if Rianna had a driving licence, but she did not argue at being guided to the passenger seat. Rianna took the wheel and, driving quite competently, followed the ambulance.

The journey was one of the lost times, all darkness and dazzling headlights. But Helen remembered the endless wait in the hospital corridors, drinking bitter coffee and wandering up and down looking at strange paintings of rainbows leaning against walls. After a time the pattern on the carpet began to make her feel physically sick.

She was glad Rianna was with her, saying little but always at her side. It did not strike Helen as odd that she seemed so calm; it was enough not to be there alone.

Eventually a doctor came and led Helen to a side room. 'Sit down, Mrs Durham,' he said. 'You are Nicholas Durham's wife, aren't you?'

'We're divorced.'

'Oh, I see. Well, I have some very bad news, I'm afraid. We did everything we could to revive him but he did not respond.'

'You mean he's in a coma or something?' she said blankly. 'You don't mean – you can't mean he's dead?'

'I'm sorry, Mrs Durham, but I'm afraid he is dead,' he said gently. 'You did the right thing, calling the ambulance so promptly, but he was already deeply unconscious and we could not save him.'

'But I – but if I'd called the ambulance sooner, before I left home – '

'Even if they'd arrived any earlier, I doubt that it would have made any difference. You acted rightly,' he said, but Helen hardly heard him. It was as if the whole evening had been spiralling towards this bleak conclusion, and suddenly her impending dread and grief burst up through her chest.

'Oh no,' she wailed, like a child. '*No!*'

'It's all right, Mrs Durham, take your time,' said the doctor. She shook with tears, an awful convulsion beyond her control. His kindness made her worse.

'He can't be dead, he was only twenty-seven.'

'I know, but it happens sometimes. The cause of death isn't clear, but it may have been a cerebral haemorrhage. We'll have to find out.'

He meant there would be a post mortem. The images flashed into her mind and stayed there. She saw Nick leaning gracefully on the counter in her shop, trying to chat up Rianna, and she saw him lying on a cold metal trolley with knives cutting his flesh as if it were candlewax. Her head buzzed and the room swam into grainy whiteness. Yet as close as she came to falling apart, somehow she did not; the feeling passed and she felt herself shuddering down into a state of wretched calm.

In a gentle voice, the doctor said, 'Now, we need to know who else to inform. Does he have any family?'

She blotted her eyes on a tissue and twisted it between her fingers. 'Yes – yes, parents and a brother and sister. I'll give you the address.'

'Would you prefer to tell them yourself?'

'No. I couldn't, I'm sorry.'

'It's all right, we'll let them know. You can stay here for a while, and a nurse will bring you a cup of tea.'

But Helen only wanted to escape, to take Rianna and go home. All she could think of now were Nick's family, what they would suffer. She couldn't grasp what had happened.

As Rianna started the car, Helen said, 'God, what about Gina? I know she'd left him, but she's still got a right to know.'

'I know, but don't worry about it now,' Rianna said sensibly. 'You're tired. Tomorrow will be soon enough.'

'No. I've got to tell her as soon as we get home.'

'It's the middle of the night. Anyway, you don't know where she is, do you?'

'I know her surname. I can get her parents' telephone number from directory enquiries,' Helen said stubbornly.

It was another of the dark, confusing parts of the night. The storm broke as they drove back to Rothley, and by the time they arrived the rain was coming down like a monsoon. Helen went to the phone without even bothering to take off her coat.

It was a mistake; she should have waited until morning, or at least until she was calmer. Yet nothing could have made the call easier, nor softened the rawness of what she had to say.

Afterwards, she could hardly remember a thing she and Gina said to each other. It was like talking to herself at a distance. Disbelief, followed by shock and grief. Gina wept, distant and tinny on the other end of the phone, and Helen wept with her, although they hardly knew each other and might never speak again.

Only one thing Gina said remained clearly in her mind.

'He told you I'd left him? We'd had a few arguments, but I hadn't left him. My mum broke her leg and I had to help look after her for a few weeks. I was coming back in a couple of days!'

So, Nick had left Helen with a lie.

Helen looked blankly around the room. *He lived in this house,* she thought. *He lived here and now he's gone and he'll never come back* . . . and she leapt up and ran out into the back garden, turning her face up to the clouds.

She was so angry she could not speak. She hated Nick for lying; hated him for making her love him, for leaving her, for dying. The rain was torrential, misery pouring from the sky, and she stood sobbing in it, feeling that if it fell for ever it would never wash out her grief. She would have stayed there until dawn, if Rianna had not come out and gently led her inside.

Helen slept until the following afternoon, and woke feeling exhausted. She made an attempt to open the shop, but when she arrived her mind was in a whirl and she could only bring herself to put an apology under the 'Closed' sign, and lock up again.

'I've got to go back to Nick's flat,' she said. 'I expect his family will come to take his things away' – she struggled against tears for a moment – 'and I'd rather get there before they do.'

'Why?' asked Rianna.

'I must find that doll.' Rianna said nothing, but Helen sensed a closing of shutters. 'He was on about the doll, you heard him! I've got to know why!'

'All right. I'll come with you.'

Helen had been too wrapped up in her thoughts to notice

how Rianna was reacting, but now she began to realise how little she had said, how little emotion she had shown. In a way Helen was relieved. If Rianna went on behaving normally – perhaps abnormally, in the circumstances – it made it easier for Helen to cope. But she could not help wondering how Rianna could appear so untroubled.

'I'll have to ring my parents and tell them,' said Helen as she pulled up in front of the flats. The thought was unbearably oppressive. 'I should have done it already, but I keep putting it off. They'll make such a fuss. Oh God, I don't think I can face it.'

Mrs Harley let them into the flat and left them to it without question, apparently too shocked by Helen's news to say much. Helen began in the bedroom and searched the whole flat from top to bottom, but she could not find the doll anywhere. Rianna made a show of helping her, but Helen had an odd impression that when she was not actually watching her, Rianna was standing still and looking into space. The situation had a shivering air of unreality. She did not believe Nick had killed himself, not for a moment.

Eventually she sat down on the edge of the bed, where she had sat and held Nick's hand only a few hours earlier. Had he known she was with him? Would it have meant anything to him if he had?

'I can't understand it,' she said. 'He said the doll was with him in the bedroom. He collapsed while I was speaking to him, so he can hardly have moved to hide it. It should still be here. Rianna, are you listening to me?'

Rianna was gazing out of the bedroom window. She turned round. 'Yes, I'm listening.'

'Well, where's the sodding doll?'

'I don't know, Helen. I don't know why you're so concerned about it.' Her face was serene, her head tilted slightly to one side and the daylight glowing red through her hair. Helen, already on edge, began to feel angry with her.

'Don't you, don't you really? I'll try to explain, shall I? Two people bought your dolls and then they dropped dead. Nick is the third. He was always in perfect health! OK, if he'd died in a road accident I could accept it, but just to collapse like that – I know the doctor said "It happens", I don't need him to tell me that, I know it happens, but not to Nick – I just don't believe it, it just feels so wrong!'

Rianna's eyes widened slightly. Without inflexion, she said, 'Do you think the doll I made killed him?'

'I don't know, Rianna! I know it sounds totally ridiculous, but what am I supposed to think? Three times can't be a coincidence. My mother' – she took a breath to steady herself – 'my mother said that when Jill's husband found her, he thought there'd been a break-in because the doll was missing! I might have thought you'd hidden Nick's doll yourself, if it hadn't been for that.'

'Well, I didn't, Helen. I didn't even see it.'

'I believe you, but it doesn't explain how the doll could just vanish. For God's sake, even if you can't find some sort of explanation or excuse, at least tell me that you understand what I'm upset about!'

'I understand, but there's no need for you to be upset about it,' Rianna said. Her voice was tranquil, but she was looking everywhere except straight at Helen.

'Why not? Why shouldn't I be upset? Is everybody who bought one of your dolls going to die, do you poison them or what?'

Rianna looked startled. Guilty? Helen wondered. 'I don't know how you can say that to me, Helen.' She turned away, lowering her eyes. 'That was a terrible thing to say.'

'It's a terrible bloody thing to happen, as well!'

'No, don't say that.' Rianna suddenly knelt down on the floor, leaning on Helen's knees and looking up at her. 'If I could remember anything, if I knew the reasons, I'd tell you. All I have is a feeling, but it's such a strong feeling, Helen.'

Helen sighed, rubbing at her face. 'Rianna, what are you talking about?'

There was a strange confusion of messages coming from Rianna. She was smiling – elated and trying to hide it – but underneath her radiance there was anxiety. It was as if she was desperate to believe that she had done nothing wrong, but feared otherwise. 'I know I'm making the dolls for a reason.'

'What reason?'

'I don't know, I'd tell you if I did, but – ' Rianna shook her head. 'Whatever it is, it's working, it's all beginning here.'

'You're mad, you're completely out of your mind!' Helen cried, struggling to believe what she was hearing. 'You mean that the dolls really do kill people, and you think that's *right?* You knew – you knew Nick would die, and you don't even care, you don't care!'

The happiness and the anxiety suddenly seemed to fuse in Rianna, making her seem slightly deranged. 'I do care,' she said in a low voice. 'But what happened to Nick – it – it doesn't matter.'

'Doesn't matter? You as good as killed him, and that's OK, is it?'

'No, Helen, it's not like that, I wish I could explain – '

Helen pushed her away roughly. 'Shut up! If I hear another word out of you, I'll strangle you!' With tears streaming down her face, she leapt up and ran blindly through the flat, down the stairs and out to the forecourt.

But when she reached the car, she waited for Rianna. She felt helpless. Why is it, she thought, that everyone I love turns out to be half crazy? Why do they use my love like a shiny little knife to cut me to pieces?

They did not say a word to each other in the car. The sky was luminous steel-grey, with wisps of cloud standing out very white against it, the air so clammy that Helen was sweating. What was she to do about Rianna? It was like trying to communicate with someone who spoke a different language . . . but then, Rianna was an alien. If Tevera existed, Helen could believe that she came from there. But what was she trying to do, what did she want?

Helen had to park a few yards away from her house. As they walked towards it, she said, 'Don't go crazy on me, Rianna. This is how it used to be with Nick, trying to reason with someone who was totally deaf to what I was saying. I never thought it would be like this with you. I really can't stand any more of it, not now.'

'I'm not crazy, Helen,' Rianna said tightly. She was hurt. 'You're the one who won't listen. I thought if I tried to explain my feelings to you it might make you less unhappy. Instead I get called a murderer.'

'Look, if you do come from that other place, from Tevera, and you can't remember anything about it or why you're here, how do you know you're not doing something incredibly evil?'

Helen had hit on the exact cause of Rianna's unease. 'No!' she cried, her face pale with distress. 'No, it's impossible. Helen, how can you say that to me, how?'

'Easily! People buy your dolls and they die! What else can I say, what can I think?' She found it unbearable to shout at Rianna. The need to do so was tearing her apart, but she could not stop herself. 'I needed your friendship so badly, then I find out that if it wasn't for you, these awful things wouldn't have happened in the first place!'

Rianna broke away from her, on the verge of tears, and vanished into the passage alongside the house. Helen caught her up and brushed past her to unlock the kitchen door. She marched into the dining room and threw her bag on to the table, but Rianna stayed on the threshold, her arms wrapped round herself. Her whole attitude had changed. She was standing very still, shaking slightly, as though she had just been drenched in ice water, and her face was sallow with fear.

'What the hell's the matter?' Helen snapped.

In a voice hardly above a whisper, Rianna said, 'He's been here.'

'Who has?'

'The – the man I told you about.'

'What man, for heaven's sake?'

'I told you about him, Helen, he was following me about in New Zealand! He's been in this house.'

Helen felt her skin turn into a sheet of gooseflesh. The scornful words that sprang so easily into her mouth died there. She knew only too well that a man *had* been looking for Rianna, but Helen had never mentioned it to her . . . 'How do you know?'

'I can tell,' Rianna said. 'I can feel him, a sort of cold, dark feeling . . . I just *know*. I suppose you'll tell me I'm mad again.'

'Rianna, this man,' Helen began, her voice unsteady. 'What does he look like?'

She looked startled. 'He has reddish hair, light eyes, a fierce face . . . very bushy eyebrows.'

'But he doesn't speak with a New Zealand accent?'

'No. How did you know that?'

'Because he's been in the shop twice, asking to see you.'

Rianna closed her eyes, shuddered visibly. 'Helen, why didn't you tell me?'

'I didn't want to worry you.'

'You should have told me!' It was the first time Helen had ever heard her raise her voice. 'If only you'd told me the first time, I could have escaped, and he wouldn't have found me! Now he knows where I am! Oh God, why didn't you say something?'

'What are you so scared of? Who is he?' Helen said.

'I don't know. I don't know. He just terrifies me, I think I'll die if he comes near me.'

Helen, having met him, could understand her fear, but she was in no mood to sympathise with it. 'You should stay and face him,' she said harshly. 'We'll call the police, if you like. Unless he *is* a policeman. If you were on the run I shouldn't be the slightest bit surprised.'

Rianna glanced up at her, a look that reflected Helen's own feelings of terror and betrayal. 'I'm going, Helen. I can't come inside the house, not after he's been in here.'

'Don't be so stupid.'

'I can't. There's no point in me staying anyway, after what's happened. I'm going.'

'Good!' Helen yelled. 'Why don't you just sod off! Don't bother coming back!'

Without a word, Rianna turned and walked away. Helen heard her footsteps retreating along the passage. After a few seconds, she ran out after her, shouting, 'Rianna! You can't just wander off. Take the car.' She threw the keys at her. Rianna picked them up, looked at her for a second, then went on her way.

'And for God's sake, phone me.'

Alone in the house, Helen felt more wretched than she had thought possible. She would have done anything to have Rianna back again. How could she have accused her of such dreadful things? The doll could not have caused Nick's death, it was unbelievable. She had been half out of her mind, irrational, and poor Rianna had become the victim of her misery. She wept, hating herself, feeling that everything that had gone wrong was her own fault. That, too, was a familiar feeling that she thought she had left behind.

She stood in the dining room, wiping her eyes and trying to get a grip on herself. Then the dreadful implication of Rianna's words hit her. *He's been in here . . .* Rianna thought the man had actually been in the house, but that could not be, the door had been locked and no one had broken in . . . had they?

The house seemed cold, full of shadows. What if he had found a way in and was still here, hiding upstairs or in the front room? Helen looked at the telephone. It hardly seemed possible that she could fear making a fool of herself more than she feared an intruder, but it seemed so stupid to call the police without definite cause.

Feeling terrified and foolish at the same time, Helen picked up a bread knife from the kitchen and crept from room to room, flinging back doors and flicking light switches before venturing in. No one was there. She slid into Rianna's room last, so much on edge that her legs were trembling. A few half-finished dolls lay heaped on the chest of drawers, watching her, their eyes glittering.

Helen closed the door on them, shivering. Rianna must have been mistaken. No one had broken in. Perhaps the man had knocked at the door and gone away; he certainly had not been in the house.

Helen went downstairs, put the knife away, and began to make herself a cup of tea. Her tongue felt as dry as a rug. She had not eaten all day and still had no appetite, but at least a drink might help her to calm down. Last night's rain had cleared the air, but the clouds were making darkness draw in early.

With the mug in her hand she went to the phone, intending to ring her mother. She lifted the receiver several times, only to put it down again. Tomorrow. Tomorrow she would tell them about Nick.

She knew she was alone in the house, that the doors were locked, yet she could not relax. The slightest sound made her almost jump out of her skin. She could not bear to do nothing, but she could not concentrate even to read a magazine, and however many lights she left on she felt as if she could not see properly. The house looked wrong, felt wrong. Something had been inside and pulled the walls out of shape . . .

'Oh, Rianna, please come back,' she said aloud. 'This is dreadful, I've got to shake myself out of this mood.'

She made more tea, then found she could not drink it. Instead she collapsed on the sofa and switched on the television, hoping that the cheerful babble would clear the darkness from her mind. It did not. None of it seemed to have anything to do with her; there was no human contact, only moving colours and shapes that mimicked reality. There was something sinister in the mindlessness of it.

Helen told herself she was being a fool, and tried to concentrate on a detective film. A well-dressed couple were having an interminable conversation on the drive of a stately home. She attempted to make sense of it, but her attention kept wandering to the sweep of green fields in the background where a black horse was cavorting.

Something about the horse looked wrong. Helen leaned forward, frowning, then recoiled. It was so tiny on the screen, yet she could see quite clearly that it had a razor-thin head, a sinuous neck and the muscular limbs of a cheetah. The couple went on talking, and behind them the dark animal danced and postured and mocked Helen.

'No!' she cried, lurching forward to change channels. The reception had suddenly deteriorated and the picture was fluctuating and ghosting on all of them.

'Must be the weather,' Helen tried to reassure herself. She fiddled with the tuning, but her efforts only resulted in static crackles that set her nerves screaming. The picture was breaking up into swirling dots, and across the screen – fuzzy as a foreign channel picked up by freak reception – she saw the creature galloping in slow motion. Then it stopped, faced Helen, and she heard a faint voice say: '*You.*'

She almost knocked the set over in her hurry to turn it off. The screen went blank and she sat back, breathing shallowly, so shaken that she could not think. The television was dead but the static hissing was all around her now, while the room seemed at once too big and too small. The ceiling looked cavernous. Everything had turned the non-colour of cobwebs.

It could not be grief that was doing this to her. Helen was so scared that she could not even think about Nick, nor about Rianna. *I'm having a nervous breakdown*, she thought. *Is this what it feels like? There's nothing wrong, it's just me, just a fit of depression.* But the fear seemed to be flowing in from outside her, too real and physical to be imagined.

'I'll go to bed,' she told herself. 'I'm overtired. However bad things are, they always seem better in the morning.'

She checked all the doors and windows again before she went upstairs, and left the landing light on, like a child afraid of the dark. She lay fully clothed on top of the covers, sensing that she would not be able to sleep and would probably feel compelled to get up again in a few minutes. Instead, she dozed off.

She did not know how long she slept for. It might only have been a few minutes, but she was suddenly awake again, her pulse going wild, the weight of the doll lying on her chest suffocating her. Its face was close to hers –

She leapt up with a shout. There was nothing there, no doll, but she flew downstairs so fast that she stumbled to her knees at the bottom and stayed there, shuddering with pain and shock. When she moved, the greyish darkness seemed to hold her like glue. It took her for ever to find the light switch and the phone.

'Please be there,' she said, dialling the number with a shaking hand. 'Martin, please don't be at Jo's.'

More often than not he was at his house in Loughborough, but she knew he sometimes stayed at the farm. He had probably been there most of the time since the argument. She had to speak to him, but she hated the idea of having to ring him at Jo's.

The phone rang and rang. Eventually a sleepy voice answered.

'Martin? No, he's not here. At his girlfriend's, I expect. G'night.'

Helen put the receiver down, dismayed. What time was it? Her watch said one o'clock. She hesitated, not wanting to face Jo's fury at being dragged out of bed by Helen, of all people. But fear got the better of her. She had to speak to Martin or go mad, and she no longer cared what Jo thought.

She looked up the number, dialled, waited. After a few

rings, a wide awake male voice answered and she almost wept with relief.

'Martin, it's Helen, thank God you're there. I didn't get you out of bed, did I?'

'No, Jo's asleep but I was watching a late film. What's wrong? You sound awful.'

At the sound of his voice, the house seemed to shake itself back into its normal shape. The colours came back, she could see and hear clearly again. 'I don't know, Martin, everything's gone wrong, Nick's dead and Rianna's left me and I feel terrible, I'm so scared – '

'Helen – Helen, calm down. Tell me one thing at a time. What was that about Nick?'

She told him everything. As she spoke she felt her tension draining away, the pressure lifting. She could breathe again. She even felt a tiny thread of hope that she might recover and the world return to normal.

'You sound as if you need some company,' said Martin. 'I'll come over.'

The mere sound of his voice had made her feel stronger. She was even beginning to wonder why she had been in such a state.

'No – no, don't worry, it's very late,' she said.

'Do you want to come here, then?'

Helen was startled. 'What about Jo?'

'She won't mind, not if it's an emergency.'

'It's not, honestly,' Helen said, embarrassed. 'I wouldn't dream of it. Anyway, I can't, I let Rianna take my car.'

'Sort of like trapping her braces in the door so she gets so far then pings back?' said Martin. She couldn't help laughing.

'Yes. Something like that. It was really because I didn't want her wandering around on foot, with that man around.'

'I'm worried about you. I think I should come over.'

'No, Martin, please don't. I'm perfectly all right now. I feel a bit silly. I panicked. I just needed to hear a friendly voice.'

'Are you sure?'

'Yes, really. I'm so tired. A hot drink and a good night's sleep are all I need.'

'Well, OK, if you're sure,' he said. 'Take care, Helen. I'll ring you tomorrow to make sure you're all right.'

'I will be. Thanks so much. 'Bye.'

Helen felt fine while she was talking to him. As soon as she put the phone down the fear returned. It leapt out at her like jeering ghosts from the walls and ceiling; it scratched at the windows, clawed at her skin. Her hand was still on the receiver, but how could she ring him again after she had told him so firmly that she felt better?

'Please come over, please, I'm so scared.'

She couldn't do it.

'This isn't happening,' she said out loud. 'I'm all right. Everything's fine.' She forced herself to go and sit on the sofa, but her terror was fast going beyond the reach of reason. Trying to take deep breaths only made her feel dizzy, suffocated.

The borders of another world were bulging into her house, melting the plaster, pushing up under the carpet.

From the side of the sofa, where it almost touched the wall, there came a noise like the scrabbling of a rat on newspaper. Helen did not want to look. Something was squeezing her lungs tight as she moved slowly towards the side of the sofa and peered down.

The breath burst from her in a short, hoarse yell. One of Rianna's dolls was lying there on top of a magazine, smiling up at her.

It was Annie. There was no mistaking it for one of the newer ones; it even had the 'Not for sale' notice still pinned to its robe. Helen had left it locked up at the shop, she had seen it in the display case that very afternoon, so how could it be here?

She did not know, she could not think. It was enough to drive her over the edge into uncontrolled terror, and she no longer cared what Martin or anyone thought if she rang again. She leapt up but she was too late; the scuffling sound began again and the doll appeared round the end of the sofa, walking upright like a tiny ballerina. The beads on its costume clicked softly as it came towards her.

Helen stared at it. She was suddenly reminded of a puppet drama that she had seen on the television when she was very small, which for no particular reason had given her nightmares. Now she had that feeling again. The thing approaching her was like a graceful and perfect mannequin, operated so skilfully that it seemed truly, humanly alive. But there was no puppeteer. It *was* alive.

'You,' it said. Its voice was a whisper that filled the room. 'You are the one.'

'No!' Helen scrambled back on the sofa. 'Get away from me! What are you?'

'Forgotten me. They all forget. I am – ' Helen thought it was going to say *Annie*, but the name ended in a hiss. 'Annis.'

Perhaps Rianna had called her that, and Helen had misheard. If it mattered, it was too late to worry about it now. The doll's appearance was changing as it advanced on her, its rainbow-coloured beads darkening until they were the near-black of clotted blood. The serene face had taken on an ugly expression.

Helen flung herself away, through the door and towards the phone, but she did not reach it. The floor was dissolving around her, the room folding in on itself. She was swimming through quicksand, then sinking, then drowning.

'Help me,' she whispered, gagging. 'Help me.'

Black suns swirled painfully across her eyes. Everything was spinning into darkness, but with what little sight she had left she saw the doll's serene white face close to hers, and she felt its tiny hands on her flesh.

'It's time now,' said Annis. 'Time to come back.'

Chapter Eight

Slowly, as if she were coming round from an anaesthetic, Helen became aware that her surroundings had changed. She did not feel that she had been unconscious so much as half-dreaming for years, and all the time rising gradually through an inky liquid.

Shadows fluttered across her mind. In a strange dream that flickered like a film, she saw the doll lying jointless on the carpet, staring upwards. The beads were regaining their sparkle, while the clotted-blood colour drained from them and curled upwards in a wisp of darkness. The doll's fresh hues burst across her mind in a pool of rainbow silk, and were gone; the carpet lurched and fell away into space, but the dark wisp remained, swelling and thickening. Helen witnessed the metamorphosis with a ghastly sense of the inevitable.

The darkness put out limbs and began to prance. It shook its sea-horse head at her in mockery, and she thought, *It came and found me in my own house. It's brought me into its cave, that awful cold cave . . .*

The feeling of rising became one of dizziness. Her eyelids were too heavy to be opened. She was disoriented, but after a time she realised that she was lying on a hard flat surface which seemed to be tipping beneath her as the bed sometimes did just as she was falling asleep. The creature was standing over her; she could feel its breath icing her cheeks, and she whimpered and tried to pull away. But it was treading on her wrists, she couldn't move –

Helen drew a sharp breath, which was stopped short by a stabbing pain through her ribs and back. The shock made her open her eyes. It was dark, but there was just enough dim illumination for her to see that there was no strange beast leaning over her. There was a draught blowing on her, and her wrists and ankles were bound to the surface on which she lay.

Terrified, she coughed and gasped until the pain subsided. It did not feel like an injury, only a muscle spasm from lying in one position for too long; so how long had she been here? She could not even begin to guess. She felt like a small child waking scared in the night without knowing why, and at the same time as if she had been squeezed through a sieve.

'She wakes,' said someone, making her heart race. It was the language of the Chalcenians, strange yet as natural to her as English. But the face which drifted into her field of vision, reflecting a dim glow against the blackness, was not a Chalcenian face. It was a sombre, male face with a long nose and heavy eyebrows, and deep lines scored around a grim mouth. The dark hair hanging to his shoulders made him look like a medieval engraving brought to life.

Behind him, Helen could make out very little of her prison. There were dark archways between pillars that had a faint sheen, like ebony. She was lying on a floor of polished black wood.

'There is too much light in here,' said a deep, female voice. Helen exclaimed in protest as what little light there was dimmed further. Turning her head to one side, she saw the woman as a tall black triangle, with a cloak flaring out from narrow shoulders. Helen could not make out her face, but she was holding a glowing white sphere. Her hand half covered it, and the light shone red through her fingers.

'Do you hear me?' said the man. There was a rustle of cloth as he and the woman both sat on the floor beside her.

'Yes,' said Helen. 'Please help me, I don't know where I am.'

'You have been brought back,' he said.

She blinked, her eyes stinging and watering. She remembered being alone in the house, the doll coming to life, the terror she had felt. 'Back where?'

'Think carefully. You know where you are.'

'Am I in Tevera?'

'Yes.'

'Are you Chalcenians?'

The man and woman looked at each other. There was a long pause. 'You are well aware that we are not. You cause us grave offence by saying so.'

'I didn't mean to,' Helen said, bewildered. 'Look, please could you untie my hands, I can't move.'

'We do not want you to move,' said the woman. Suddenly she thrust her head at Helen, like a cobra striking. Her face was pointed and hard, the brows indented over fierce, cold eyes.

Helen recoiled. The bonds cut into her wrists.

'You will not be released until you talk to us!'

Helen's own tongue felt like a snake, going all the way down into her stomach, sour and thick. 'I don't know what you want. I don't know where I am, or who you are, or anything.'

'My name is Artienter,' said the man.

'And I am Sydra.' The woman drew back a little as she spoke. 'We are Aulanti, the deepest level of Domendri. You are in the Vale of Peace, also called the Vale of Death in Life, the city of the Domendrans. Now do you understand?'

Helen felt her mouth filling with water. She swallowed. 'No, I've never heard of the Vale of whatever it was! I'm from Earth, I don't belong here. Why am I here?'

'It will not help, pretending that you don't know,' said the woman, Sydra.

'I'm not pretending, honestly.'

Artienter and Sydra looked down on her, cold and alien, until her skin crawled. 'You claim to have forgotten? But there were the Pelu. You cannot have forgotten all you knew, when there were the Pelu. What you have done is both wicked and wildly foolish. How can you not remember?' Artienter's tone was quiet but full of menace.

Sydra added, 'Surely you remember how you were brought back here?'

'I don't know,' said Helen. 'I'm totally confused. I was in my house. A doll, a doll made of cloth stood up on its feet and said its name was Annis, and I – I felt that it pulled me through into Tevera. You should be telling me how and why!'

The two looked at each other again. 'Artienter, perhaps she speaks the truth,' said Sydra. 'Her memory may have been taken. Black Annis is capricious, never to be trusted.'

'I agree, but not in this case. I do not believe she has forgotten. I believe she is lying, hoping that will save her. It will not, of course.'

'Save me from what?' Helen said, alarmed.

'That remains to be decided,' Artienter said heavily. 'What punishment can atone for your wickedness? To take a life is a small thing. To rob souls of peace is a crime beyond punishment.' He looked so mournful that she thought he might start weeping.

'Please, I really don't understand what this is about,' she said, struggling against her bonds. 'I haven't done anything. Please let me sit up.'

Sydra leaned towards her, her face as pale as a mushroom grown in the dark. 'We seek a confession from you, child. We cannot decide what to do with you until you admit to your actions and explain them.'

I've died and been sent to hell, she thought. *Oh, why didn't I go to church, why didn't I believe in God?*

Artienter said, 'I don't know what you hope to gain by holding out against us. What little spirit you have left can be taken from you very easily, in a few short hours, and presently you will be enough like us to understand. Then you will repent and talk to us.'

Folds of cloth slid over each other as he and Sydra stood up.

Helen cried, 'Where are you going? You can't just leave me here!'

Sydra leaned over her, her mouth turned down at the corners. 'It is to help you as well as us. You think you are so far above us, still? No food, no water, no light. Taste the darkness, Rianna. Become one of us, and you will understand.'

Shock made Helen gasp for breath. *Oh God, they think –*

'No, wait! I'm not Rianna! You've made a mistake!' But they only looked down at her with a terrible, cold pity before gliding away between the lightless arches. 'I'm not Rianna! Please come back, please help me . . . '

She was shouting at silence.

After the two Domendrans had gone, Helen learned how slowly time could pass. Waves of panic ebbed and flowed like the livid colours across her eyes. The floor fell and spun beneath her. She went through periods of half sleep which gave her no relief from the awareness of how hard the floor was, how much her back hurt, the overwhelming need to relieve her bladder.

The discomfort became indistinguishable from the fragments of black thought that tormented her. Nick's death, the terrible grimness of the last few days. Her life had been normal, then Rianna stepped back into it and distorted normality into something weird and dreadful. *Did Rianna know this might happen to her?* Helen wondered. If so, it explained why she had been so frightened. Perhaps she had only pretended to forget, or blocked it out. Helen prayed hopelessly, trying not to wish that they had found Rianna instead of her.

She had no idea how long she was left alone. When the Domendrans came back again, she lay in a pool of her own urine, and was so famished that she had gone beyond hunger and felt sick.

The two faces loomed over her, like vampires with bruised eyes. Suddenly she saw their characters with hallucinatory clarity. Artienter was sombre, self-righteous, pitying Helen in the worst, most contemptuous way. Sydra's cobra-sharp face betrayed a tension verging on madness, as if she had been in pain for so long that her bitterness at it had turned into masochistic glee.

'Have you had time to think, Rianna?' said Artienter.

Her lips cracked as she tried to speak. There was a foul taste in her mouth. 'I hope you're pleased with yourselves, doing this to me,' she said hoarsely. 'I told you, I'm not Rianna. You don't know what she looks like, do you?'

'No,' Artienter said grudgingly.

'If you did, you'd know that I'm not her. I'm Helen Locke. All I can think is that I've been mistaken for her . . . '

'Helenlocke?' said Sydra, as if it were all one word. 'If you are not Rianna, where is she?'

'I've no idea.'

'So, Annis made a mistake?' said Sydra.

'Perhaps not,' Artienter said slowly. 'Rianna was not there, so Annis brought one who is close to her instead. To help us.'

God, they'll use me to find Rianna! Helen closed her eyes, wishing with all her heart that she had said nothing, or even pretended to be Rianna. 'Please let me get up. I don't feel well.'

Artienter's hand stilled her feebly struggling wrist. 'Where is Rianna?'

'I don't know! She ran away, and I don't know where she is now. Why do you want her anyway?'

'If you were her, you would know,' replied Artienter. 'If you are not, it's no concern of yours. You must tell us where she is.'

'I can't, truly I can't. I just don't know.'

Artienter put his face close to hers, like a sinister judge speaking more in sorrow than in anger. 'Listen to me. Rianna is doing something terrible beyond words, committing a blasphemy against life itself that is too appalling for your small mind to comprehend. It is for your benefit that we leave you here. The closer we bring you to despair, the more you will see the wisdom of helping us.'

'No, you can't,' Helen exclaimed, but the way they looked at her told her that her pleas would not be heard. She raised her voice. 'Don't leave me like this, please. This is torture! There are laws against this where I come from!'

'But you are here now,' Sydra responded softly. 'We have our own laws. You have a long way to go into our darkness before you understand.'

With that they glided away from her, black sails outlined against a glow that vanished with them.

Helen hung on the edge of hallucination, not sure whether she was still sane or only imagining that she was. She remembered books she had read about people who had endured similar or far worse experiences with incredible bravery, but her own soul seemed empty of such strength. She felt terrified and wretched. Even shame at her own cowardice, she thought, would not stop her from pleading with her captors and telling them anything they wanted to know.

She thought of her parents, and wondered what they would think had happened to her. They might think she was dead. If she had simply vanished, they would have no way of finding out what had become of her. *They'll never know, they'll never know* . . . and she thought of their unhappiness, and wept for them.

She tried to still her panic by going through songs in her head, trying to remember every item in the shop . . . *Oh no, I should have gone to buy some stock today, and there's no one to open up for me! They can't keep me here, I've got to open the shop . . .* She struggled, suddenly angry, but her rage achieved nothing; except, perhaps, to help her survive a little longer. She could not let herself believe that she would never go home.

Her senses became distorted. For a long time she was convinced that she was a piece of paper being pegged on to a washing line, and then it came to her that there was a moon shining near her feet, and someone was cutting her bonds.

A gentle voice said, 'It is cruel, I know, but there is no place here for those who are not Domendric.'

Someone pulled her into a sitting position. Pain shot through her shoulders. Her limbs were painfully numb, and her jeans hung clammily on her. Suddenly aware of the state she was in, she felt humiliated. She stank. There was such a thin line between dignity and degradation; a few hours without food or sanitation were all it took to reduce a human to this pathetic state.

A cup was held to her lips. Helen swallowed the water with desperate thirst. Her stomach rebelled, and she took deep breaths until it settled and began to make loud protests of hunger.

'I am Cadreis,' said the Domendran at her side. Still supporting her with an arm round her shoulders, he leaned over to pick up the spherical lamp and move it in front of them. In the steady white glow, she saw a young man with dark colouring and a sad expression. He had shaggy black hair falling to the shoulders of a shirt that was hardly more than rags tied together.

'Who?' she said.

'Cadreis,' he repeated, watching her with large, dark eyes. 'They have appointed me to guard you.'

'Guard?' said Helen suspiciously.

'Yes. I will stay with you while Artienter and Sydra are not here.'

'My own personal prison warder,' she said, half to herself.

'You are not imprisoned any longer. It's my task to feed you, to see that you are comfortable. Don't be afraid of me.'

Helen stared at him. She had almost gone beyond being afraid. His manner was gentle, he did not look like a brute, but what would he do if she tried to escape? The idea was laughable. She did not even have the strength to sit up unaided.

'Oh my God,' she said with quiet despair. 'You're the nice one.'

'I am what?'

'I've heard about this trick. When they've finished torturing you, they send in someone nice and kind who pretends to befriend you, and they swap between torture and kindness until you break.'

He frowned slightly. 'I don't know what you mean. Is this what they do where you – where you dwell? It must be a very terrible place.'

'You don't call this terrible?'

'It was only to bring you into the darkness. To make you understand. I think you still don't understand, but you won't be bound again. We don't want you to die; not until you wish it.'

Helen shivered, not knowing how to interpret the last remark. If he meant they would bring her to a state in which her only desire was to die, she dared not think about it. She said shakily, 'I don't understand, because no one will explain anything to me. I want to go home, you've got no right to keep me here.'

She put her head in her hands. His arm around her did not feel at all comforting.

'I'm sorry. But it is Artienter's decision. I must guard you.' Helen did not speak. She hurt all over.

After a few moments he said, 'I am to take you to bathe and eat. Are you strong enough to walk?'

She sighed, shuddering. 'I'll try. It would be good to wash. Are there any clean clothes I can have?'

'Yes. Come with me. I'll help you.' He lifted her to her feet, and as she leaned on him she noticed his warm, clean smell. It made her horribly aware of how filthy she was, and she could have wept with humiliation. Cadreis, however, did not seem to notice the state she was in. 'They said your name is Helenlocke.'

'Just Helen,' she murmured.

The place where she had been shackled was not a cell. She

could not define it as any kind of room she knew, nor was it a cave. As far as she could see it was roughly dome-shaped, with strange twisted pillars forming archways around the edge. Even with the light from Cadreis's lamp, it was too dark to make out anything clearly. She had thought the arches must enclose solid walls, but as he led her between them she realised that some of them gave on to passageways. A cool draught smelling of earth blew into her face.

'Where are we going?' she asked.

'To the river,' said Cadreis.

'Oh, good, I can't wait to see daylight,' she said. But the black twisting tunnels through which they walked seemed to go on for ever. Her head began to throb with the effort of trying to see. Colours zig-zagged round her eyes, and she recognised the onset of migraine with dismay.

Cadreis said, 'We have to climb downwards here.'

'I don't think I can climb anything; my legs feel like pieces of string.'

'Lean on me. I won't let you fall.'

There were steps spilling down into a lightless hole, carved out of earth. Helen found herself hanging on to the walls as she went, but the surface was irregular and treacherous. Sometimes there was soil under her hands, sometimes rough wood.

From below, she heard a hollow rushing of water and saw a faint light. The stairway widened, then opened out and she found herself staring dizzily into a vast river-cave.

The truth hit Helen then. She might have realised sooner, had she not been so dazed.

'We're underground,' she said breathlessly. She had been hanging on to tree roots on her way down. 'Is it far to the surface? I want to go outside, I don't like this.'

'We don't go outside.'

'Why not?'

'We have no need to. Everything we want is here. This is the city of Domendrans; didn't Artienter tell you?'

'No, he said we were in the – the Vale of something . . . '

'The Vale of Peace, the Vale of Death in Life. That is the name of our city.' He held her arm, guiding her down towards the floor of the cavern. 'There's nothing to fear, Helen. Come down to the river bank.'

The river, some thirty feet wide, flowed out of the darkness to their right and vanished where the cave curved away in the distance. The water gleamed like pewter. Giant shadows moved across the rock of the walls and roof, spangled with flecks of light. Helen saw that the light came from fires burning here and there along the bank, and from white lamps clustered like mushrooms on the walls. There were figures on the river's edge, almost all solitary, moving in a kind of listless slow motion.

'You have to wash in the river?' she said uneasily. The prospect made her shiver.

'There is nowhere else.'

He took her towards one of the fires, which was tended by an old woman sitting hunched up under a voluminous cloak. A large container was suspended over the flames. As Cadreis spoke to the woman, Helen saw that there was a deep, water-filled hollow in the bank, a few yards away from the edge, and she realised with relief that she would not have to bathe in the river itself. But if it was a bathing place, it was a very public one.

The old woman rose as if it was a great effort and began to ladle water from the container into the pool. When she had finished, she looked at Helen as if to say: *What are you waiting for?*

Then Helen realised, with shock, that she was not old. She was young and sweet-faced, but her eyes were dead, and apathy seeped from her like a miasma. Chilled, Helen turned away and looked at Cadreis.

'She has warmed the water for you,' he said. 'Afterwards, she will dry you and bring you a cloak.'

'I see,' said Helen, still looking at him. He was showing no inclination to allow her any privacy. There was only one thing for it. She sat on the edge of the pool and sprang in fully clothed.

The cold knocked the breath out of her, sent pains shooting through her neck to lodge in her left eye. The hot water had barely taken the chill off. Submerged in the water, she began to strip her clothes off as fast as she could, rinsing them and throwing them on to the bank. Her head hurt so much now that she could hardly see, and modesty seemed pointless.

The woman gave her a piece of rough sponge, which was apparently designed to take the top layer of her skin off. She washed swiftly, and when she began to climb out, the woman – girl, almost – was ready to wrap her in a large dark cloth. When Helen was barely dry, a robe was pulled over her head and a cloak wrapped round her. At least they were warm, but the pain through her left eye was making her shiver. She knew from experience that if she did not lie down, she would pass out.

She bent to pick up her wet clothes, but the girl said, 'Leave them. I'll dry them.'

Helen was surprised to hear her speak. 'Thank you,' she said. 'Is this your job?'

The girl looked at her as if absolutely stunned to be asked a question. 'Yes. I attend the bathers.'

'How long have you worked here?'

'A long time,' the girl said. Helen sensed a withdrawal, as if she did not know how to cope with someone showing any interest in her.

'So you live in the city?' Helen persisted, but the girl turned away.

'I must go on with my work,' she said, and proceeded to sit by the fire and do nothing except stare into the flames.

Cadreis came to Helen's side and took her arm. 'You must be very hungry,' he said.

'I – I'm not, actually,' Helen said weakly. 'I'm going to have to lie down somewhere. I get these terrible headaches sometimes, I feel sick and I can't do anything at all until it's gone off.'

'You can lie down and sleep if you wish. It will be warmer above.'

'I'd rather stay here. I couldn't climb those steps again.'

He looked at her grimly. Despite his gentleness there was no real warmth about him, and he seemed incapable of smiling. Perhaps he might turn nasty and start bullying her, but at the moment she did not care; if he tried to make her do anything she knew she would faint, so he would be wasting his time.

But he said, 'As you wish. You had better lie by the fire.' He found a smooth stretch of rock and borrowed some of the girl's rough towels for a makeshift mattress and pillow, and fussed over her until he was sure she was comfortable.

Helen was infinitely, almost pathetically, grateful. She probably would have managed the stairs if it had been essential, but the truth was that she did not want to return to the claustrophobic darkness. At least the river held some promise of escape to the outside. The noise soothed her. At first she wished Cadreis would leave her alone; it embarrassed her, having him watching over her while she was feeling ill. Later, though, she was glad. When the pain was at its worst he held her hand and stroked her forehead as her father might have done.

As the migraine eased, some hours later, she slid into the tranquillity of convalescence, watching the figures moving along the river bank, dimly aware of people bathing in the hollow, the girl coming and going from the fire as she helped them. All the Domendrans moved like mourners at a funeral; some gave the impression that they had simply lost interest in life, others that they were burdened with inexpressible grief. They were so different to the Chalcenians, whose joy Helen remembered like a bright sharp light; they emanated misery, sucked life from everything around them.

'Is this a prison?' Helen asked.

She felt Cadreis's hand twitch in hers. 'Did you say something, Helen? I think I was asleep.'

She almost managed to smile. 'So, you are human. You should be more vigilant. I might run away.'

'No, you are too weak,' he said quickly.

'I was joking. It wasn't very funny, I know. Doesn't anyone have a sense of humour? Why is everyone so miserable?' Cadreis did not answer, and she sensed that she had offended him. 'I mean, if this is all part of the prison, it would explain it.'

'There is no prison, Helen. This is part of the city, as I told you.' He moved away to the fire, and she heard him exchanging a few words with the girl there. When he came back, he helped her to sit up and put a wooden cup in her hands.

The drink within it was warm, milky and slightly sour, but it seemed the most delicious thing she had ever tasted. When she had finished it, she managed to eat a square of a dark, sticky bread. Its flavour was slightly earthy, thought not unpleasant.

'Do you feel better now?' he asked.

'Yes, a lot better. Still a bit shaky, though. Cadreis, how long have I got to stay here?'

'You don't have to stay here. You may go about the city, as long as I am with you.'

'No, I meant how long are Sydra and Artienter going to keep me in Tevera? I mean, I shouldn't be here, I've got things to do, a shop to open, my parents must be worried sick. I can't exactly send them a postcard, can I?'

She was not sure he understood her. She was mixing in English, where she could not find the right word.

'I don't know,' he said. He was sitting next to her now, his head bowed and his dark hair hiding his face. 'I'm sorry, Helen. I think it is a terrible thing that you have been brought here, but there is nothing I can do. You haven't eaten enough.'

She accepted another piece of the bread from him. 'This is so weird. One day everything is normal, the next I'm sitting in a cave talking to someone from another world.'

He raised his head and looked sideways at her. It was then that she noticed how startlingly beautiful he was, despite the sad expression. 'It is strange for me, too. Knowing where you come from, but seeing that you are the same as us, yet not the same.'

'You know I'm not Rianna, don't you?'

'Yes.'

'Do you know why Artienter and Sydra want her? What has she done?'

He turned away again. 'You should not be asking me these things, Helen. I can't answer them.'

'Why not? Have they told you not to? Or is it because you don't know?' She felt stronger now, strong enough to argue with him. Whatever the Domendrans had intended, they had not yet broken her spirit.

'Both,' he said quietly. 'There are levels of wisdom. You surely do not think I am on Artienter's and Sydra's? I am only Sfaia, not Aulanti.'

'I don't know what to think.' She sighed. 'Look, Cadreis, if you really have to watch over me all the time, the least you could do is talk to me. I need to understand why this is happening.'

'We're not allowed to speak of such things, not even to each other.'

'Well, what are you allowed to talk about?' she said, exasperated. He looked unhappy at being questioned, but as long as he did not silence her by physical violence she was determined to persist.

'You are . . . you are different to us. We talk very little here.'

Helen drew her knees up and rested her chin on them, watching the river. 'Well, tell me about the city, then.'

'It would be better if I showed you. When you feel well enough to walk.'

She did not relish the idea of returning to the dark tunnels, but they could not stay in the cavern for ever. In an odd way she was glad that Cadreis was not allowed to leave her, because she hated the idea of being alone. The people on the river bank, with their lifeless eyes, would offer her no friendship.

'Not yet. I think I need a good long sleep,' she said. 'How long have you lived here?'

He shrugged. 'A very long time, I think.'

'All your life?'

'No, not all of it.'

'Where were you before?'

Cadreis pressed his fingers to his forehead briefly. She sensed that she was distressing him. 'Nowhere.'

'Something else you're not allowed to talk about?' He said nothing. 'I've been in Tevera before, Cadreis. I don't know how it happened, but I came through and I met the Chalcenians. Do you know them?'

'You came through before?' Surprise briefly animated his face. 'How could that be?'

'I haven't the faintest idea. But it happened. I met these tall, beautiful people with brightly coloured hair, and – '

He cut across her sharply. 'They – the others – they are not to be spoken of. They are opposed to us. Surely you understand that.'

'You mean you are enemies?'

'Enemies,' Cadreis echoed, as if to himself. She was not sure if he had answered the question.

'Is that it? Rianna is a Chalcenian, and Artienter thinks she has done something against the Domendrans?' He made to stand up, but she caught his arm. 'Cadreis, please! She was my friend, and whatever she's done I don't want her to get hurt. I should have let them think I was her. Then they might have punished me and left her alone.'

'You don't know what you are saying.'

'No, I don't! Some dreadful things have happened to me and I'm going mad trying to make sense of it. Why won't you help me?'

There was pain in his eyes, which was better than seeing nothing there at all. 'You are right to be angry. They are being unfair to you. If you knew Rianna, you should be told what she has done.'

Her heart turned over like a lump of dough. 'Will you tell me?' she said softly.

'I can't. I don't know, and that is the truth. But I know that it was something very terrible.'

She could only just hear his voice above the sound of the river. 'How terrible? As bad as – as killing people?'

'There are worse things than that,' he said.

'Worse? How? Like what?'

He shook his head. 'It is only my guess, why Artienter and Sydra want her. I've no right to speak of it. I cannot.'

'Please,' she said, but he fell silent and would not answer anything she asked him. Helen gave up, helpless. She suddenly felt overwhelmed by tiredness and lay down again. Her body craved normal sleep. She did not even know she had fallen asleep until she woke suddenly, confused and feeling that everything had changed.

All the fires were out and there was only the dim fungal glow of the lamp-clusters. The river bank was deserted. A sense of desolation, of many hours having passed, made her sit up violently.

'Wake up, Helen Locke,' said a deep, female voice. 'We are with you.'

Artienter and Sydra were sitting on either side of her. There was no sign of Cadreis; she was alone with them. All the apprehension that sleep had soothed away returned, and she felt suffocated by the velvet darkness of their cloaks.

'Where's Cadreis?' she said, breathless, trying to shrink back so that she was not touching them.

'He is permitted to rest while we are here.'

Helen was frightened, but she was also angry. 'So you've come to tie me up and interrogate me. You won't degrade me like that again.'

Sydra looked at her companion and said, 'There is still spirit in her.'

'Let it be,' said Artienter. 'Let her find her own way into quietness. She is unhappy enough.'

'Indeed,' Sydra said acidly. 'As you would expect of one from Anatevera.'

'Where's Anatevera?' said Helen, but they ignored her question. Their attitude to her seemed graver and not quite so unsympathetic, but if anything Helen found it more sinister.

'We can see now that you are not Rianna, that you could never have been Rianna,' Sydra went on. 'You are not a creature of Tevera. In that we pity you.'

'I don't want your pity, I just want to go home.'

'You cannot go home,' said Sydra.

'Why not?' Helen cried. 'You've no right – '

'Because Black Annis brought you through. We cannot command her to take you back. She is not ours to command.'

Helen floundered. She could not find the right questions. But her deepest fears thrust up inside her and like a patient asking a doctor for news he dreads to hear, she said, 'Am I dead? In my world, I mean? Is that why I can't go back?'

'Why do you think that?' said Artienter.

'The doll I told you about – other people had those dolls, and they died.' It was only the seed of a hope, that Nick might also be here and not truly dead after all, and it had no chance to germinate.

Sydra was silent a moment. 'No, you are not dead. Annis brought you through bodily. The doll, the Pelu – she only borrowed its form. She likes to play such games.'

'So what happened to me did not happen to the others?' Sydra gave a single shake of her head. 'Was it different?'

'Yes.'

'So I'm not dead . . . but what about those others who *did* die?'

'They are dead,' said Sydra, turning her face away. Her profile was flat, almost oriental. 'Black Annis keeps the boundaries between our domain and yours. We had an agreement with her that when Menenthonis found Rianna, Annis would open the boundary and bring her through. She brought you instead.'

'It's not the same, then. Nick really is dead.' Shaken by sobs, Helen put her hands to her face. Then came the most terrible thought of all.

She had been blind in not seeing it before. Suspicion of the dolls had been an abstract idea; the obvious, most personal connection had been lost in her preoccupation with other problems. Now it might be too late.

'My parents,' she said. 'Oh, Rianna gave my parents a doll. Sydra, you have to let me go back. I've got to warn them, I must get the doll from them before anything happens!'

'We told you,' said Artienter. 'We cannot send you back.'

'You've got to!'

Helen had angered him. 'Do not raise your voice to me! Respect our ways. This is the Vale of Peace; we are not Chalcenians, to shout like children.'

'How can I make you listen? My parents are in danger . . . '

She felt as if she were swaying on a ledge. She was not getting through to them. They looked at her as if she was talking gibberish, as if they did not even know what 'parents' were.

'For God's sake . . . ' she said weakly.

They were quiet for a moment, and the rushing of the river seemed deafening. Then Artienter said, 'With your questions, Helen, you have told us more about Rianna than ever we could have learned by questioning you. She claims to have forgotten Tevera, yet she remembers enough to make the Pelu. Why do you defend her, yet weep for those the Pelu have destroyed?'

The thought that she had betrayed Rianna horrified her; but if Helen protected her friend, what was she protecting? Threads of panic stabbed through her. At every turn she seemed to do or say the wrong thing, and she hated herself for it. 'I don't know! How am I supposed to know, when no one will explain anything to me?'

'You are not Domendric. It would be a mockery to explain our beliefs to you,' Artienter replied scornfully. 'It grows from within; it is not a given knowledge, and if you are devoid of understanding that is your own loss.'

'But what has Rianna done? And why?'

Artienter and Sydra looked at each other, and there was an unspoken communication between them that made Helen feel she had ceased to exist. They were not going to tell her. She was not on their 'level'. She felt intimidated, as if she was a child who had had the nerve to ask a serious theological question of a priest.

She thought: *You bastards. This is ridiculous, I didn't ask to come here.* But it seemed nothing she said had the power to make any difference.

'I hope you will come to understand, for your own sake,' said Sydra. 'It would impress upon you how important it is that we find Rianna. But you are not Domendric. Not yet. Do you think you are missed in your own world?'

'I should think so. I don't know how long I've been here.'

'If Rianna missed you, would she seek you?'

Helen met Sydra's eyes, her own suddenly wide with suspicion. 'No. No, I'm sure she wouldn't.'

'But your face tells me otherwise,' said Sydra. 'It's reason enough for us to keep you here. To draw her to us.'

Suddenly Helen was no longer sitting between them. She was on her feet and running. The darkness rushed to meet her, flowed all around her; she could not see where she was going, could hear nothing but the voice of the river. All she knew was that she must escape, and that the river cave must lead to the outside.

The cold rock hurt her feet and jarred her ankles. Her chest was aching with fear. She ran perhaps twenty yards before someone stepped out and caught her.

Her heart almost stopped with the shock. She struggled, but the grip on her arms was unbreakable.

'It's no good, Helen. You must not try to escape,' said Cadreis. His voice was flat, sad, distant. 'It's a very long way to the outside.'

Chapter Nine

Helen could not endure her captivity, but she had to.

Cadreis took her away from Artienter and Sydra, up the earth staircase to the higher levels of the city. He led her through long earth tunnels that wound between tree roots, and up further steps edged with flint. All the time she feared that he was going to bind her again. If he was not, another attempt to escape might change his mind.

In the upper levels, roots as thick as pillars arched up into darkness, forming rooms and halls which were linked together without any true walls. Black wood lined the floors. There was still very little light, only a few round lamps to guide the way. Cadreis had called this a city, yet Helen could see no divisions between public areas and living quarters. There was only the cavernous warren of roots. Here and there she saw the dark figures, some asleep, others sitting apparently in meditation.

'They can't keep me here,' she murmured. Cadreis said nothing. 'They wouldn't tell me anything. It's ridiculous, how could Rianna possibly think I was here? How could she come here if she did? It doesn't make sense. Cadreis, can't you talk to them, persuade them to let me go?'

'You torment yourself by asking these things,' he said. 'You know I can't.'

'Where are you taking me?'

'To Bayn. It is a place where we find peace. I hope you might also, Helen.'

Other Domendrans were moving around them like wraiths, wrapped in dull cloaks. When they had first come from the river, the tunnels had been deserted. Now figures were appearing from the darkness in ones and twos until Cadreis and Helen were walking with a stream of people into a low, wide passage. They went in utter silence.

The passage led downwards, then opened suddenly into a

chamber like a crypt. It was too dark to perceive its exact boundaries, but dull illumination picked out carving on ebony pillars. The mustiness of rock and earth was so strong that it made Helen's throat sore, brought tears to her eyes.

'Sit down,' said Cadreis.

'Where?'

'It doesn't matter,' he replied. He led her to the centre of the chamber and sat by a pillar, so that she could lean back against it. Pews would not have looked out of place, but there were no seats as such. All around them the Domendrans positioned themselves on tree roots, rocks or the floor itself.

'Is this Bayn?' she whispered.

'Yes. Hush.' His hand was on her arm, and she could not envisage shaking him off and bolting out of the place. There were too many people there, and the air was heavy with a grave, expectant silence. Helen looked around, deeply uneasy. No one acknowledged anyone else; all their faces had the same hopeless look, and there was no life in their eyes. Some were expressionless, others seemed on the verge of weeping.

She wanted to ask Cadreis why they were so wretched, but she had already tried once. He could not answer, because he was one of them.

They might all be prisoners, she thought. *Perhaps that's what they are . . . prisoners of the Chalcenians?*

A woman entered and stood before them under a carved arch at one end of the chamber. For a moment Helen thought it was Sydra, and she quickly pulled up the hood of her cloak, hoping she would not be noticed. But this woman was smaller, with a strong, bony face and a mass of crinkly black hair.

The woman raised her arms and began to chant.

The sound was sinister, paralysing. Helen looked at Cadreis, but his eyes were closed and his lips were moving in time with the chant. It grew in volume as other voices joined in, all in the same monotone.

At first, she could not make out the words. Then it began to sound like, *Anatever Anatever Anatever Anatever . . .*

She did not want to listen, she needed to escape . . . She tensed as if to leap to her feet, then heard Cadreis whisper, 'Don't fight it, Helen. Close your eyes and listen.'

She did as he said. After a few moments she became used to

the drone, let herself relax into its rhythm. It was more a mantra than a prayer, and it drew her down into a state of torpor where she no longer wanted to strive for anything. She felt nothing. She slid to rest in a grey harbour where there was no pain and no joy, and she could look at her own predicament with the mild interest of an observer.

I am in another world. I am under a different sky, with stars and planets that no one from Earth has ever seen. The people around me are more alien than the remotest tribe of South America, and this city . . . The Vale of Death in Life . . . I am so privileged to be in a place that no one else knows exists. I feel like an explorer. How old is the city, how big, why is it here, what is outside? Am I the first human to have been brought here? There is so much to find out, yet all I can do is think about myself . . .

No, not just myself. My parents . . .

She opened her eyes. The chanting had faded – though she had the strange dislocating sense that it had gone on for years – and the woman-minister was speaking. Her voice had no rise and fall, no expression, yet there was a weird and soothing beauty to it.

'To peace we bring our spirits. In peace we empty our souls. Let our souls be emptied into the void, no more to struggle on earth or below it, no more to walk in Tevera nor in Anatevera. Our pain shall be eased. Our striving shall cease. All things shall be one. Seal the mouth of Anatevera against us, and let us pass through the veil into the soft darkness of sleep, into oblivion, into eternal peace. To this we bring our spirits . . . '

The words went on and on. The atmosphere was different now, as if they had all accepted what sorrows they had and let them go. She closed her eyes again and let herself sink down with them, her mind empty of everything except the grey tranquillity.

Then the peace was shattered by a shout.

'No! *No!*'

Helen jumped violently. Some were too deep in the trance to react, but she was not the only one to look round. Cadreis was alert at once, his hand tightening on her arm.

To their right, a girl was on her feet and stumbling between the seated Domendrans, sobbing as she went. Her arms were stretched out in front of her as if she were blind. Several times she fell over people, but none of them made to help her, or even cursed her as she passed. They only watched blankly.

'No, I can't, it's too dark,' she was gasping. 'Help me, let me out!'

In panic she scrambled through the last of the seated Domendrans and fled into the tunnel. Her hair and cloak flew out on a draught as she went. No one tried to stop her.

The minister waited until she had gone, then turned to the assembly and said, 'Did anyone here bring that girl into Bayn?'

There was silence for a moment. Then a thin, hollow-faced man stood up and said quietly, 'I take responsibility for her.'

'Did you not know she was a transient?' The woman's voice was mild, but it echoed from the cold walls.

'I did not. I would not have brought her, had I suspected it.'

'Had she been long in the Vale of Peace?'

'No,' the man replied uncomfortably, 'but she was almost Nohmic; I thought she was ready.'

'It was too soon. You should not have brought her. Now follow her, see that she goes to the proper place.'

The thin man obeyed. Now there were sighs as he pushed his way to the tunnel; the atmosphere had been lost, and the minister looked gravely at the seated Domendrans.

'I am sorry,' she said. 'Responsibility for the peace of our gatherings must rest with me. I think it is too late to begin again. We will end with the Chant of Tranquillity, but any others who are not truly Domendric may leave now.'

Cadreis drew Helen to her feet and led her out of the chamber. She felt many pairs of disapproving eyes on her, but she was not sorry to leave. In retrospect the trance she had slid into seemed unhealthy, and the girl's panic had shocked her back into her anxiety.

'You should not be here either,' he said quietly as they walked up through the tunnel. 'You are not a Domendran.'

'No. I suppose you're right,' she said. 'What was wrong with that girl?'

He looked at her. His eyes were so beautiful, so haunted. 'Whatever made you want to leave Bayn when we first sat down, it was the same for her.'

Helen was slightly stunned. It seemed too simple a reason. She tended to assume that the Domendrans' emotions must be alien and far removed from her own, and it was hard to believe that they were not. 'What did they mean by calling her a "transient"?'

There was a breath-long pause before he replied, 'A traveller, in a way. Someone who tries to stay here when they do not really belong.'

'You mean people *want* to live here? They must be out of their minds. Do they have a special name for people who are desperate to leave?'

'Don't mock us, Helen. You are different.'

She nodded. 'Sorry. What will happen to her?'

'She will be taken to the outer levels of the city. She may be sent outside.'

'Is that a punishment?'

'Helen. Oh, Helen,' Cadreis said sadly. 'Is that what you think of us, that we are ruled by fear and punishment? I wish you could understand. We are not cruel. It is life that's cruel, nature that punishes us.'

There was no night and no day in the Vale of Peace. The Domendrans seemed to have no way of measuring time, and Cadreis was vague to the point of being evasive if Helen tried to establish how long she had been there. They had no rhythm of working and resting. They apparently slept whan they felt like it, which meant that nothing ever really changed. There were always sleeping bodies curled around the roots of trees, others wandering about or engaging listlessly in essential tasks.

In her everyday life, Helen had always complained at how fast time went, that there were never enough hours to get everything done. Now she discovered just how painfully slowly time could pass. Nothing was required of her. She could only be grateful that she could pass the hours in relative freedom, not locked in a cell.

Cadreis was her gaoler, yet if it had not been for him she would have gone mad. He showed her the city. He talked to her. As the days (hours? months?) went by, he talked to her more and more.

He also needed to rest, of course. Sometimes Artienter or Sydra would watch over her in his absence. They said very little, but they always had a brooding, expectant air, as if they were waiting for her to produce Rianna from nowhere at any given moment. She hated their presence. There was another guard, too, who seemed harmless and did not speak to her at all. Cadreis was with her the most, so when he was not she tried to spend as much time as she could asleep.

Her dreams were haunted by Rianna.

She grew used to sleeping on hard surfaces, making the best of earth hollows and tree roots. There were no beds, let alone private rooms in the city. Sheer mental exhaustion enabled her to find oblivion almost as often as she wished . . .

And Rianna waited there, in a green and gold world where it was always mid-summer. She and Helen sat together in a glowing cave of bracken, their knees tucked up to their chins, hidden in their secret land. They were children again.

The scent of grass and bracken mingled was unspeakably poignant, holding for Helen the promise of everything that was good in life. The air was speckled silver with tiny insects. Crickets chirruped around them, never seen. They might be in Bradgate Park or they might be in Tevera, or both at once; it didn't matter. She and Rianna were together, and everything was as it should be.

Rianna was telling her something very important, something she must not forget, but the words were going away from Helen as fast as she said them. She was not listening. She was watching a creature that had wandered among the bracken stems, as long and graceful as a polecat, as blue as a kingfisher. *Blue, the colour of the heart . . .*

It scampered around Helen's feet, then reared up to rest one forepaw on her foot, the other dangling as it snuffed at the air.

'Look, Rianna!' she whispered.

'That creature's called Halat, Bestower of Love.'

'He's tame!'

'Don't touch him, Helen. They sometimes bite.' Rianna was smiling, but Helen suddenly began to feel nervous.

'We are in Tevera now, aren't we?' she said.

'I was trying to tell you, Helen, weren't you listening?'

Rianna's smile vanished. Her forehead creased, tears shimmered in her eyes. 'We're on the boundary of your world and mine, but I can't go back, I can't remember how. I can't remember. I mustn't cry!' she said, scrubbing at her eyes. 'I mustn't be unhappy, or they'll send me away.'

Distressed, Helen put her arms round her, but Rianna squirmed and beat her off.

'No! I've got to go back!' Rianna cried, leaping to her feet.

Helen's heart ached with love and the bitter pain of rejection. Rianna plunged out of the green cave and vanished from sight. Helen followed, only a second behind her, but as she surfaced from the sea of bracken, Rianna was nowhere to be seen in any direction.

Helen walked and walked. Summer lay thick and heavy on her, almost suffocating. The dream was more vivid than memory, as vivid as reality. She had always been here, walking, searching for Rianna and never finding her . . .

The dream pulled itself out of phase. Time leapt ahead, and she suddenly found Rianna lying unconscious on the grass, her autumn-red hair tangled, her eyes closed.

'Rianna?' she said fearfully.

Her friend did not stir. Helen knew she was dead, and began to sob; but the dream made another leap, and suddenly they were talking again as if nothing had happened. Rianna was saying, 'Black Annis tried to take me, but she couldn't. I don't want to go back, Helen. I'm scared.'

'I thought you came from Tevera, and you wanted to go home,' said Helen.

'I did, but now I don't,' Rianna exclaimed bitterly. 'I don't ever want to come in the Park again!'

Helen was on her own, and she was crying. It was over. They would never play in Bradgate Park again. There would be no more endless summers. Rianna's parents would take her to New Zealand, and Helen would never see her again . . .

She went home, and now she was no longer a child, and Nick was waiting for her.

'Where the hell have you been?' he said. He was looking at her in that not-quite-sane way that presaged a flash-fire of temper.

'With Rianna, in the Park.'

'Oh, Rianna,' he sneered. 'You think more of that stupid cow than you do of me. She's a bad influence on you, it's her fault you live in a bloody fantasy world!'

'But we were only children, I haven't seen her for years – '

'You knew we needed some food! I had to go to the sodding supermarket myself, which means I'll have to go back to work until midnight to catch up! Can't you ever think of anyone except yourself?'

Helen could not make herself heard. Nick went on and on, and all the time his eyes glittered, utterly uncompromising, striking an unbearable pain into her heart. It was a bad dream, but it had been real . . . and suddenly she woke up, shaking and panting for breath.

Cadreis was with her. Dark roots twisted around her and above her. The lamp-glow barely touched the shadows.

'Oh God, this is a bloody nightmare,' she gasped.

'Is it?' he said quietly. He sounded despondent. 'Sometimes I dream it's over.'

'What?' she said, coming fully awake. 'You dream what's over?'

'Nothing. This is just the way we live. There's nothing else.' He put his arm round her, warm and strong, and she leaned into him, closing her eyes. He was the only comfort she had. He asked, 'What were you dreaming about?'

'Oh – about my – ' She could not find the word for "husband". 'A man I knew, who died.'

'He has gone to Anatevera, then,' Cadreis said thoughtfully. 'Sometimes I think that however bad things may be in Anatevera, they can be no worse than here.'

'Cadreis, what is Anatevera?'

'You must know,' he said, surprised.

'But I don't. I thought it might be the name you give to my world, but I'm probably wrong.'

'Anatevera is the place to which our souls go when we die,' he said.

'You mean an afterlife, like hell, or limbo?'

'Yes, limbo. We call it that sometimes. A terrible place where people live on in torment. You told me this yourself.'

'I did what?' Helen said, confused. 'Wait, surely you don't think Artienter and Sydra conjured me up from limbo? I come from Earth. I'm as alive as you.' She held up her arm and pinched the skin. 'Look, solid flesh and blood.'

Now Cadreis looked uncertain. 'Earth?'

'Yes, another world, like this only different.'

'Well, I only know of Anatevera.'

'And you believe it exists?' she asked.

'Of course. I don't know whether I should speak to you of these things.'

'Oh, please go on. It's hard enough being here, without knowing absolutely nothing about you.' By degrees, Cadreis was becoming friendlier towards her. She was learning how far she could push him for information, and the boundary seemed a little further each time.

'It's so difficult to explain in words. If you told me about your world, I probably would not be able to comprehend it. In dwelling here, you will come to know us.'

She shivered. 'I don't want to dwell here.'

'Come down to the river, Helen. You can tell me more about yourself, as well.'

Although she still could not have found her way about on her own, she was growing used to the great networks of halls and the tunnels that connected one system with the next. Much everyday life was conducted along the underground river, Shabdaranth. From upstream they took their drinking water. Midstream was the bathing area, and far downstream the river acted as a self-cleansing latrine. There were no other sanitary arrangements. It made for an existence more austere, inconvenient and uncomfortable than a monastery. The Domendrans seemed to care nothing for privacy, and Helen had had no choice but to get over her embarrassment. She wondered why they forced such hard conditions on themselves unless they were, as she had speculated, captives of the Chalcenians.

When Helen had bathed, Cadreis took her upstream and they sat on the bank, eating pieces of dark, earthy bread and drinking what tasted like warm yogurt. Helen thought with longing of tea and her mother's home-made scones. Distribution of food seemed random. Cadreis would not tell her where it came from, except to hint vaguely that it was from the taboo place, 'outside'. Some of the Domendrans were so thin she was sure they hardly ate at all.

After a time she asked softly, 'Cadreis, why do you go to Bayn?'

'Don't you know?'

'When I jump to conclusions, I'm usually wrong, but it seemed as though it was to find spiritual peace.'

'Yes. You are right.'

'How often do you go there?' She was half hoping for a tangible answer like 'Once a week'.

'Whenever we wish it. There is no set time.'

'You don't seem to have any way of measuring time here at all.'

'What is the point?' said Cadreis. 'Time is only a reminder of the length of our lives. It's better to suspend it than count our hours of misery.'

'What I truly don't understand is why the Domendrans are all so unhappy. Perhaps it's being in the Vale itself that causes it . . . ' Almost imperceptibly, he drew away from her. She had touched on a sensitive subject and had a powerful feeling that she must not pursue it. 'Cadreis, am I stopping you from going to Bayn? I don't mind going with you if you want. I won't leap up and run out like that poor girl.'

'I know, but I should not have taken you, all the same. It's all right, Helen. I can find peace in other places.'

'Well, if you're sure.' She rested her chin on her knees, watching the half light ripple dully on the water. 'If there's no set time, how do they know when to hold the meeting?'

'It is an unspoken thing. When enough people gather, one of the Aulanti will come and begin it.'

'Who are the Aulanti?'

'Domendrans of the deepest level. Artienter and Sydra are Aulanti. They are changeless. They are the only ones who possess true wisdom.'

'And you're not Aulanti.'

'No.' For some reason, Cadreis was no longer quite so reluctant to talk. 'My level is Sfaia. Most of us are Sfaian; we are the ones who serve the Aulanti and do all the necessary work. Then there are the Luthnei, whom we call transients. They are not allowed into the city proper.'

'Why not?'

'Because they are only superficially Domendric. They are wanderers, feckless. They don't know where they belong or what they want. They are permitted only in the outer levels of the Vale. We turn no one away, but if they become . . . troublesome, they are exiled.'

Helen wrapped her hands round her knees. Softly, she said, 'If they can go outside, can't we?'

'It's impossible,' he said sharply. 'And it wouldn't help you, Helen; we explained that you cannot be sent back to your own . . . Earth.'

'But I might find my own way back.'

He shook his head, then looked at her questioningly. 'Why do you say that? Is there some reason you think you could?'

'Didn't I tell you? I've been in Tevera before, and met the – '

'Yes, yes you did,' he said quickly.

'I was only here a few hours. After that time I sort of faded back into my own world. I feel that if only I could go outside and walk, eventually I'd be drawn back.' He said nothing, but his expression was grim. 'Cadreis, it's worth a try. Help me, please. We – we've become friends, haven't we? It's not for me, it's for my mum and dad, I think they're in danger and I'm worried sick for them. Please. Do you really wish it on me to stay here?'

'There are many here who have even less choice than you. I'm doing Artienter's will. I can't help you.'

Helen had felt quite calm for a time, but now all her distress at her impossible situation swept over her. She tried to fight it down. 'Don't you have parents, Cadreis?'

'Parents?' He was frowning. 'No. I never knew them.'

That shook her slightly, but she went on, 'What about brothers and sisters?'

'If I had, I do not know them.'

'Don't you have any family at all?

'None of us have families.'

'But you must have someone,' she exclaimed. 'How can none of you have any relations?'

'We are Domendrans. We are all one people.'

'Oh no you're not. You're all alone. You don't even speak to each other unless you have to. I don't see any love between you, nor even hatred. There's just nothing. Apathy. There's something wrong.'

'Don't, Helen. You don't understand us,' he whispered.

'I'm not pretending to, but how can I make you hear what I'm saying? There must be someone you love. If there is, wouldn't you go mad to save them if they were in danger? That's what I'm doing, Cadreis. I'm going mad. Please help me.'

'No!' The anguish in his voice shocked her. 'Don't ask me again.'

'What else can I do? I'm sorry if I'm distressing you. I'm none too happy about being here myself.'

He bowed his head. His fingers gripped the edges of his cloak, white as the fungal lamps. 'If you think we don't care, you're wrong. I'd help you if I could. I can't.'

Helen sighed and pushed her hair back. 'Oh, God. This is worse than talking to Rianna. I wish you'd tell me the truth about this place. Are the Chalcenians forcing you to live here, because you surely can't be doing this to yourselves?'

'Helen, you must not keep speaking of the – the others. Only the Aulanti are allowed to speak of them.'

'Oh, are they? You still haven't answered my question.'

'The Vale of Peace is not a prison,' he said in a low voice. 'The Chalcenians do not share our beliefs, that's all. As far as we're concerned, they do not exist.'

'But they do. And they're alive. They laugh and talk to each other and argue. They hug each other. They make love. They're not scared to go out in the sunshine.'

'You know nothing about them!'

'How much do I need to know?' Helen exclaimed. 'I've got eyes. They took us out on the ocean . . . ' The memory calmed her, very suddenly, as if a wave of blue sunlight had washed over her. She began to describe the voyage and the beauty of the Oa. She closed her eyes and her memories were projected on the darkness; the sequin green of the sea, the glassy flash of the Oa slipping through the foam, their golden eyes. She was aware that Cadreis was desperate for her to stop, almost on the verge of putting his hands over his ears, but she felt detached from him. The less he wanted to hear, the more vividly she conveyed the beauty and awe of the experience . . .

Until Cadreis leapt up, dragged her to her feet and shook her. 'Stop! I wish Artienter damned to Anatevera, for bringing you here!'

She was more angry than frightened. 'What are you so scared of?' she shouted back. Her voice rang along the river cave. In the distance, she saw one or two heads raised to stare at her.

'Helen, it's not a question of fear.' He released her. The pain in his eyes was so far beyond her that she felt ashamed of having provoked it. She wished she could soothe it; but how could she, when she did not even comprehend what she had done?

He said, 'Forgive me, Helen. How can you respect our ways, when you don't know them?'

'And why should I, when I don't even want to be here?' She hugged herself, rubbing at her arms. 'I don't mean to upset you. I only want to go home.'

They stood looking at each other. There seemed to be a chasm of misunderstanding between them, an odd feeling that they were trying to throw ropes to each other and missing every time.

'I haven't shown you the deepest places of the city,' said Cadreis. 'We'll go there now. Since you came, Helen, quietness has been slipping away from me. I need to find it again, and I seek it for you as much as for myself.'

The hall seemed as boundless as a forest at night, but the twisted trees were roots as thick as trunks, and they vanished not into the sky but into a roof of earth. Figures blended with the shadows but here and there a head, an arm or a shoulder was outlined by a light fainter than candleflame.

Helen hesitated, but Cadreis drew her deeper into the hall to walk among the figures.

Some were seated, others lying down or standing. All were motionless. Except for the rise and fall of their breathing, Helen would have thought they were waxworks. Many had their eyes open and were blinking, but they all had the same glassy look of being in a trance or coma.

A few Sfaians moved silently among them, tending to their needs like nurses. The frozen Domendrans showed no reaction, although Helen saw one accepting food without ever ceasing to stare straight ahead of himself. They seemed utterly unaware of their surroundings or of anyone around them.

'What's wrong with them?' Helen whispered.

'Nothing is wrong. They are Domendrans of the fifth level, Nohm,' Cadreis replied.

'But they look as if they're – we'd call them catatonic, I think. Can't they do anything for themselves?'

'No. That is why the Sfaians tend to them.'

Helen felt as disturbed and out of place as she might on walking into a mental ward. There was some profound truth here, but she could not grasp it; she saw with her eyes, but inside she was blind except for one sliver of understanding. However deep they buried it, the Domendrans cared for each other. Her heart ached.

She said, 'What has happened to them, to make them like this?'

'Nothing has happened. Any Domendran may become Nohmic; it is a mystic state. We revere those who achieve it.'

'You mean it is something you strive for? Is it deeper than Aulanti?'

'Perhaps.' Cadreis was taking her to the far side of the hall, and she saw a narrow tunnel leading into darkness. The Nohmics had taken no notice of them at all, locked inside their private visions. 'It is a separate state. No one strives for it, but when it occurs, it is venerated.'

Helen felt cold. 'Because you fear it?'

He did not answer for a while. His eyes were too bright. In that dead place they brimmed with life, flickering from side to side as if he felt as trapped as she did. He pulled a round lamp from the wall and placed it in her hands.

'Yes,' he whispered. 'Because we fear it.'

The tunnel beyond the hall went down into rock, and she noticed the faint cold smell of the river. The lamp felt light and papery, like a puffball.

As they walked, she said, 'There are no children in the Vale of Peace, are there? I haven't seen a single one. Although that girl by the bathing place isn't much more than a child.'

Cadreis said nothing. She fell silent, almost beyond asking any more questions. The tunnel was long, and she hung nervously on to his arm, suddenly dreading what lay at the end.

The stench that swept up to meet them was so horrendous that she would have stopped in her tracks, had Cadreis not pulled her on. They came out into a grey, echoing cave. They were on a rim of rock that formed a natural balcony. Below them stretched an uneven floor, dotted with rocks. Helen's eyes had become used to the dim light provided by the luminous fungi, but it was several seconds before she realised what she was seeing.

The cave was full of corpses. Some were skeletons, dislocated and begrimed with sandy soil. Others were in varying states of decay, but each one had a rock on its chest, and in many the ribcage had collapsed under its weight.

'This is the Centre of the Vale of Peace,' Cadreis said in a remote voice. 'Quietness is here.'

'Oh, God,' Helen exclaimed. She drew backwards, swallowing her words. If this was the way the Domendrans buried their dead, she must at least show respect.

'I find peace here,' he said, 'and so do others.' She looked around the rim of rock and saw several people, each on his or her own, looking down at the bodies. He went on, 'It's enough to live once. Must we die, only to go through another life, and another, with no hope of it ending?'

The desolation in his voice sent dread shivering through her. She tugged at his arm and he faced her, seeming to understand the questions in her eyes.

'Life is unhappiness,' he said. 'Sometimes it is so black that there is nothing to comfort us except thoughts of death. Bayn teaches us and reminds us that death will come, and that if we can still our spirits we will eventually find peace there. But . . . there is still Anatevera. If – if the soul lives again in Anatevera, how shall we ever find rest?'

I'm not hearing this, Helen thought, hugging herself. *I can't stand it, I've got to go home*. 'That's awful. That's all you want, to die? I always thought people were lucky to believe in an afterlife. They believed they'd get a second chance.'

Cadreis was not really hearing what she said. 'Death is all that can relieve our pain. We put rocks on the dead to keep the soul from going down into Anatevera. So that they can rest for ever.' His voice was so quiet now that she could barely hear him. 'But we all know it is a false hope. A rock cannot prevent the soul from flying out and continuing in its misery.'

Almost unconsciously, Helen had begun to shake and sob. She looked at the bodies and she saw Nick down there. She saw her parents. She saw herself.

'Cadreis,' she gasped. He turned and looked at her as if he was suddenly seeing her properly for the first time, understanding what she felt. 'Is that going to happen to me? Please help me, I know you told me not to ask again but I can't help it. I have got to go home.'

Some hours later, when Helen surfaced from sleep in one of the upper halls, she found Cadreis kneeling by her. Her old jeans and shirt were bundled up in his arms.

'Helen, wake up,' he whispered. 'Are you well?'

She tried to moisten her lips, but her mouth was bone dry. 'I'm still alive.'

'Put these clothes on quickly, and come with me.'

She sat up, yawning, thinking of the long walk down to the river before she could relieve herself. 'What's the hurry? Where are we going?'

'You'll see. Put the cloak over them, to hide them.'

She turned away from him to change. He did not seem to understand her need for modesty, but at least he respected it by averting his eyes.

'Cadreis, I really must go down to the river.'

'There isn't time.'

She was puzzled by his manner. He seemed on edge and very serious at the same time, as if he was about to do something he should not. She protested feebly, but his hand on her shoulder was compelling.

From the ebony halls he took her into a tunnel that wound upwards, and branched into a warren-like confusion. At the threshold of one, a grave-faced Domendran man stepped out and confronted them.

'What is your business here?' he asked mildly.

'I'm taking this transient Luthnei to the upper levels,' Cadreis replied.

'Very well. You may pass.'

Helen had thought the upper city might be like the lower, only less dark. If anything the darkness was worse; there were none of the glowing fungi to light the way. The tunnels were low roofed and smelled rank as compost. Massive tree roots blocked the way rather than forming part of the structure, and as they squeezed past, Helen noticed Domendrans sitting in the shadows, some as motionless as Nohmics, some weeping.

'Where are you taking me?' she whispered anxiously.

'Hush.' He paused at a junction of tunnels. 'This way, I think. It's hard to remember the way.'

The passage became smaller. They had to bend almost double as they went, and earth sifted on to them from above. Helen was about to suggest nervously that they turned back, when she suddenly found she could see.

A few more steps and the light blinded her, like the molten flash of sunlight on water. She was not prepared for the brilliance of daylight, nor the intensity of colour.

She closed her eyes against the light, basking in the warm redness on her eyelids. She breathed sweet, fresh air. She knew how a prisoner felt in his first moment of freedom: ecstatic.

Cadreis helped her from the end of the tunnel, though he too could barely open his eyes. The entrance was half overgrown with grass, hardly visible.

'Go, then,' he said softly.

Helen was not sure she believed what was happening. 'Are you – are you letting me go?'

'You wanted to leave,' he said shortly.

'Yes, I do, but – '

'So, I am setting you free.'

Helen knew the sensible thing to do would be to run, not to stand asking questions. But she was bewildered, and she still could not see properly.

'Cadreis, why?'

'You don't belong here.' He spoke abruptly, as if he could not bear to be asked the question. Perhaps he had taken pity on her, perhaps he had changed; she was not sure, and nor did she know what he might be risking by disobeying Artienter and Sydra. It seemed ironic to thank her gaoler for keeping her sane, but she did not want to part from him without expressing her feelings. She was desperate to say something to him, but he was turning away, hostile. He did not want to hear.

'Thank you,' she said, her heart turning over. 'I don't know what else to say – '

'Say nothing!' he cried roughly, giving her a push. 'Go!'

And Helen plunged half blind into the sea of dazzling green light, while all around her the trees sighed endlessly in the wind.

Chapter Ten

Even when Helen had grown used to the light, it still hurt her eyes. The pain felt wonderful.

Above ground there was no sign that the city of the Domendrans lay below. There was a forest of huge, wide-spaced trees, though they were not as massive as their root system had led her to imagine. The existence of the city, however, was not a secret. She passed several Domendrans – transients, she assumed – trudging through the forest like pilgrims. They watched her with glazed eyes as she ran by.

It was a warm summer evening. At the edge of the forest she sloughed off her cloak and wiped her forehead. Then, shielding her eyes, she paused to study what lay beyond.

The landscape of Tevera. A cloak of bracken lying in folds, soft as velvet. In the distance, hills shimmering into a clear sky.

'What if I can't find my way back to Earth?' she said to herself. 'What if there isn't a way any more?'

She ran into the bracken, heading downhill, her eyes half closed and her mouth open as if she were drinking light.

'I'm going home,' she said out loud. She began to repeat it between breaths, like a mantra. 'I'm going home. This isn't Tevera. Sod you, Annis. Sod you!'

She broke from the edge of bracken on to a grass path, almost collided with an oak tree, and stumbled down a sudden drop. She came to a halt, swaying, not comprehending why there was a red and white cloth at her feet, covered in bowls and plates and cups.

A few feet away, she heard a child giggle.

Sitting on the grass round the cloth were a large woman in dungarees, a thin man with a moustache, and two boys aged about nine or ten. They were all staring at her, open-mouthed. In the silence, a toddler came running up and launched a large, brightly striped ball at Helen.

She caught it by reflex and threw it back, but her hands were shaking and the ball bounced on the edge of the cloth, upsetting a bowl of salad. From their faces, they must have heard her talking to herself and swearing. She dreaded to think what was going through their minds, but suddenly it no longer seemed to matter.

'I'm terribly sorry,' she said, backing away. 'Sorry.'

Then she was away from them and running down the path. Behind her she could hear the woman's voice: 'You could've said something, Gary, but no, you just sit there – ' Then it faded and she saw the drystone wall ahead of her, and beyond it the crowds of children playing cricket, and the main path that would take her back to civilisation.

With the asphalt under her feet she halted, as if it could hold her in place on Earth. Bradgate Park. People and dogs strolled by her on all sides, the stream ran softly over the rocks, deer grazed among the bracken on the far side. Everything was as it should be, as if Tevera had never existed.

'So I'm back. Now what do I do?'

The most urgent task was to contact her parents and tell them to dispose of the doll – if there was any way of disposing of it. But she had no money, no means of transport other than her feet. It would take an hour or more to walk back to Rothley. There must be someone she knew closer at hand who would help her . . .

Jo's farm was only a few yards from the Park gates at the Swithland Woods side. Whatever she thought of Helen, surely she could not refuse to help her in such a desperate state. And Martin might be there.

Half walking, half jogging, Helen headed for the car park, keeping to the exact centre of the path.

Fifteen minutes later, exhausted, she crossed the road and entered the farmyard, looking round to see if Jo was outside.

The first thing she saw was a blue Renault, parked next to Jo's Land Rover. It was Helen's own car. She had lent it to Rianna, the evening they had quarrelled.

'Rianna!' Helen said under her breath. 'What's she doing here?'

She ran to the house and hammered on the kitchen door. A

moment later it opened and Jo stood in the doorway, wiping her hands on a grimy teatowel.

'Bloody hellfire, it's you,' said Jo.

'Is Rianna here?' Helen did not even think to bother with civilities, but if anything Jo seemed to prefer a direct approach.

'No,' she said with a sarcastic lift of her mouth that could not be called a smile. 'Rianna is not here. Neither is Martin.'

'Well, what the hell's my car doing outside? What's going on?'

'That's a good question. I wish I knew. I wish someone would think to tell me!' Jo said bitterly. She seemed in only a slightly better mood than when they had had the row about the horses, but Helen was past being frightened of her.

'Look, Jo, can I use your phone? It really is desperately important. Say what you like to me after, but I've got to ring my parents.'

'Yeah, all right. You'd better come in. Phone's on the dresser.'

'Thanks,' said Helen.

Entering the cottage was like entering another time; everything was still as Jo's parents, even her grandparents, must have left it. It smelled of saddle soap, dogs and boiled cabbage. An elderly terrier sniffed at Helen's heels as she went to the phone.

'You look as if you're in a right state,' Jo commented as Helen dialled. 'Didn't Martin find you?'

'No, I haven't seen him.' Helen crossed her fingers as she heard the ringing tone. *Come on, Mum, answer it, answer it.*

'Martin reckoned he'd gone to look for you,' said Jo. 'He said you'd vanished. I suppose it must've been true because there was a bit in the paper about it.'

'About me?'

'Yes.' Jo sat down at the kitchen table and pulled her wellingtons off. '"Mystery Disappearance of Local Shop Owner", or something. Usual sort of thing.'

'Oh God. How dreadful,' said Helen, mortified at the thought. The ringing tone went on. 'How long ago was I supposed to have – er – disappeared?'

'About a week. Six days.'

'Jesus,' said Helen under her breath.

'So what the hell happened to you?'

Helen did not know what to say. Had Martin told Jo the truth, or anything approaching it? She did not want to sound like a lunatic, babbling about other worlds, but she did not feel up to inventing a convincing story. Meanwhile her parents' phone rang and rang, and she felt panic building up inside her. She put the phone down, dialled 100, and asked the operator to try.

'There is no fault on the line,' said the distant, rather condescending voice. 'Perhaps they're out.'

Helen dialled again for herself. She let it ring for another minute, before Jo said, 'There's no point in hanging on like that. They're obviously not there. Come and sit down. I'll make some tea.'

Helen dropped the receiver back on its cradle. Should she ring the police? The thought of having to answer their questions was too daunting. She needed to collect her thoughts.

'Thanks,' she said. 'Do you mind if I use your loo? I'm absolutely desperate.'

'Do you know where it is?'

'Yes,' Helen said, moving towards the back door.

'Oh, don't use the outside one. Bathroom's off the passage to the sitting room.'

As she washed her hands, Helen looked at her face in the mirror. It was a shock. She looked thin and pale, like a drug addict, and her hair was lank and full of knots. No wonder those picnickers in the Park had stared at her. She looked as if she had been sleeping rough for a week.

Which, in a way, she had.

As she went back into the passage, she glanced into the sitting room and saw Rianna's doll in its place on the windowsill. What had Artienter called the dolls? *Pelu.*

She returned to the kitchen and sat down opposite Jo, who was now pouring mugs of tea from a huge brown pot. 'Jo, that doll in the other room. Get rid of it.'

'You what? You mean the one Martin gave me, that your friend made?'

'Yes. I know it sounds stupid, but I'm not joking.'

'Get rid of it how?' Jo asked, spooning sugar into Helen's

tea without asking if she took it.

'I don't know. Burning it might be the safest.'

Jo's face was set, like a schoolteacher who had been pushed too far. 'You know, the way I feel at the minute, I really would like to tear that doll limb from limb, jump up and down on it and leave it to fester in the muck heap, but that wouldn't get me very far, would it? For God's sake, Helen, what are you on about?'

'The dolls can sort of . . . hurt people. Oh, why am I being coy about it? They kill people. I don't know why or how, but I'd rather you just got rid of it before it's too late.'

'Well, now I've heard just about everything,' Jo said flatly.

'What do you mean?' Helen asked, between sips of tea. Despite the sugar, it tasted like nectar.

'Well, I've had every cock-and-bull story under the sun from Martin. Someone's trying to pull the wool over my eyes, and I'm not having it.'

'What has he told you?'

'A load of rubbish about another world; what really happened when you two went off with Destiny and Fikri, he called it. And to round that off, an even bigger load of shit about your friend Rianna.'

'What did he say about her?'

Jo shrugged irritably. 'I can't remember the half of it. Something about her being followed by a man. He made it sound like a John Le Carré novel. Now you come here, trying it on as well. What is the idea? I'm warning you, I won't take this crap, Helen, not from you or anyone.'

It was the first time Helen had seen any sign of vulnerability in Jo. How could things look to an outsider, except crazy or made up? She had a feeling that the more she tried to explain, the worse Jo would feel.

'I don't know how to ask you to believe it, but it's true,' Helen said. 'Some very strange things have been happening. Look, would you please tell me why my car's outside? I quarrelled with Rianna and she stormed off. I made her take the car because . . . well, there really was someone following her. I didn't want her wandering about on foot.'

'OK.' Jo sighed and sat back in the chair. 'The whole story. Last week – must've been the day after you "vanished" –

Martin was supposed to come over. Instead I get a phone call. Helen's friend Rianna has left home because some weird man has tracked her down and she's scared. She's been driving around all night, wondering where to go, when she suddenly gets the bright idea of going to Martin's house. The man won't know she's there, will he? So then, says Martin, they try to ring you, but there's no reply. He goes to your house and shop; nobody's seen you. So, he says to me, he can't come over because he's got to race around trying to find you.

'Fair enough, I thought. It'll be sorted out in a few hours. But that was all I heard for two days. That was when I saw the bit in the newspaper. The next thing I know, Martin and Rianna turn up here, her in your car and him a few minutes later in his MG.' Jo paused, drumming her fingers lightly on the table. 'Helen, I know I'm difficult to get on with and I was bloody angry about the horses that time. But I never wished you any harm. I was quite worried when I realised they'd got the police looking for you, and I wanted Martin to find you.'

Helen nodded.

'Anyway,' Jo went on, 'here are Martin and Rianna in my kitchen, and she's got her hand through his arm, and they say they've got something to tell me. Then I get all the spiel, Martin has always believed in being totally honest with me, he never thought this would happen, it was so sudden, he doesn't want to hurt me but . . . and so on, you know the sort of thing.'

Helen was staring at Jo, but Jo did not meet her eyes. Instead she bent down to hoist the terrier on to her lap and let it lick the tea dregs out of her mug. Helen glanced at her own mug and grimaced. 'You mean Rianna and Martin . . . '

'Yes, marvellous, isn't it?' Jo said savagely. 'They hardly know each other. In the space of two days they decide they've fallen in love and want to do the decent thing, that is come and announce it to my face. I mean, what do they want, a bloody medal?'

Helen was almost too stunned to speak. So much for Martin's loyalty to Jo. She suddenly felt ashamed of herself for the times she had wished Jo out of the way.

'What happened next?' she said. Then, 'Oh Lord, Jo, I'm really sorry.'

'Yeah. So was I. Anyway, then they come out with all this stuff about this other world, and they said they were really worried about you and had to go off looking for you. So it was goodbye Jo; they didn't know when they'd be back, but it had been great knowing me and all that. They went off in Martin's car, just in case "The Man" spotted yours and recognised it. So that's why your car's there. I hope that's answered your question. More tea?'

'Oh, yes please, why not,' said Helen, beyond being fastidious about sharing crockery with dogs. As Jo reboiled the kettle, Helen said, 'I – I don't know what you thought about Martin and me, but there really was nothing between us. I never thought he'd leave you.'

'You just lived in hope, eh? Oh come on, Helen. I'm sure it's not for my benefit, you looking as if you've just had a death in the family – ' Jo audibly choked on the last word. 'Oh shit, Helen, I'm sorry. I'm completely tactless – I didn't mean anything.'

'It's OK. We seem to be doing a lot of apologising.'

'Yes, well. Maybe we've both had our little dreams dashed. I'll get on fine without him. I'll just have to find someone else to help with the horses.' Jo spent an unnecessarily long time with her back to Helen, stirring the tea, but when she turned round her face was dry. Helen could not imagine her crying in private, let alone in company.

'Jo, about the things they told you. I don't want to push it because I know how hard it is to believe, but they weren't trying to play some awful joke on you, I swear.'

'I don't know. Martin thinks all sorts of stupid things are funny.'

'But not this,' said Helen. 'I was taken to another . . . well, call it a strange place, and I've been held prisoner there for what I now know was six days. They took me in mistake for Rianna. She really was in danger, and still is.'

Jo said slowly, 'But she's been making dolls that kill people?'

'I don't understand it, either. But I'm damn well going to. Do you mind if I try and ring my folks again?'

'Help yourself.'

There was still no reply. Helen glanced out of the window.

The sun was setting.

'Did they leave my car keys here?'

'Yes,' said Jo, reaching behind her into a drawer. 'They're in here somewhere. Here you are.'

'I'm really worried about my parents. They've got one of the dolls in the house.'

At that, Jo suddenly seemed to realise that Helen was deadly serious. She went white. 'Maybe I will throw mine out, to be on the safe side. This is weird. I'll stick to my animals, people are nothing but trouble.'

Helen nodded, trying to smile. 'Anyway, I'm going to drive over to their house. Maybe they're just out for the evening . . . I've got to find out, I don't know what I'd do if anything's happened to them.'

'I'd come with you, but I can't leave the farm . . . '

'I know. It's all right, Jo. Thanks for your help.'

Jo opened the back door for her. As she did so, the terrier waddled out into the yard and began barking, apparently at nothing.

'Smarty, *get* back in here!' Jo shouted. The dog looked at her hesitantly, then went on yapping into the dusk. 'What is it, is someone out there?'

On the far side of the yard, near the gate, Helen saw a familiar figure. It was a slender young man dressed in dark trousers and ragged shirt. His face was half hidden by his shaggy black hair.

'Who's that character?' said Jo. 'If he looks like causing trouble, I'll fetch the shotgun.'

'No, don't,' Helen said quickly. 'It's someone I know.'

'Are you sure?'

'Yes.' Helen walked towards him, aware of Jo hovering suspiciously behind her. 'Cadreis, what on earth are you doing here?'

He looked at her from under his fringe, his eyes very large and very dark. Outside his own city, he seemed a raw creature from another land or time.

'I followed you, Helen.'

'Why?' She was angry and afraid and inexplicably pleased to see him, all at the same time.

'I was worried about you. And I was curious to see whether

you really could just walk back to your own world, as you said. I kept you in sight. You stayed the same, but everything around me was different . . . ' He looked around nervously, as she had done when she had been drawn into Tevera.

'You're not planning to try to take me back, are you?' she said.

'I could not if I wanted to. I don't know the way back.'

'What are you going to do, then?'

He shrugged and gave a slight shake of his head. 'I would like to help you, Helen.'

'Good grief,' she said, agitated. 'Look, I'm in a hurry, I'm on my way to my Mum and Dad's. I can't leave you here. You'd better come with me.'

She turned and went towards the car, but neither Cadreis nor Jo moved.

'Cadreis, what are you waiting for?' said Helen. She unlocked the doors and climbed into the driver's seat. He approached the Renault warily and stood looking in at her, running his fingers along the metal edges of the window.

'I thought you were seeking your parents. Why are you sitting in this box?' he said.

Helen jabbed a finger at the seat beside her. 'Sit there and you'll understand in a minute.'

He obeyed, but as Helen shut the door, Jo strode up to the car. 'Surely you're not going to drive off with this weirdo?'

'It's OK, Jo.'

'But he doesn't even speak English. What on earth was that language you were talking to him? It sounded like Icelandic or something. I didn't know you were bi-lingual.'

'Neither did I,' said Helen, starting the engine. The fuel needle rose to half; at least Rianna had left her some petrol. She had no money to buy any more. 'He's sort of a stranger here, like I was in the other place . . . '

Jo's expression changed, as if she had guessed where Cadreis came from, but still could not bring herself to believe it.

'If Martin comes back, I'll tell him I've seen you,' she said.

'Yes, OK,' said Helen. 'Thanks, Jo.' Hesitantly, with a touch of awkwardness, they shook hands through the window. Then Helen reversed the car and drove out of the farmyard into a twilight streaked with grey and gold.

Darkness came slowly as they sped along the main road towards Stamford, but the oncoming headlights were blinding. Her eyes were still sensitive from the enforced darkness of her imprisonment. It was over an hour's drive to her parents' house in daylight, and without a map she was not sure of the way. She had only made the journey a couple of times. Her mother and father had not long moved to a small village near Stamford, and they usually came over to see her.

Beside her, Cadreis was pressing himself back in his seat, his hands gripping the edge. He said nothing, but Helen could imagine what was going through his mind: incomprehension and alarm. She had suffered too much of it herself of late to feel much sympathy. Her only concern was her mother and father.

Surely Rianna would not have given the doll to her mother, knowing it might kill them . . . but she had done exactly that to others. Helen tried to banish the visions of Nick, but they came back relentlessly. The road stretched out, grey and endless, and the oncoming headlights splashed painfully on to her retinas. The Renault's small engine was whining at sixty.

'Cadreis, why did you follow me?' she asked.

'I told you.' His voice was hardly more than a gasp. 'I – I could not believe that you could simply walk through the boundary . . . '

'OK. Now tell me the real reason.' He did not reply. 'Tell me Artienter didn't send you, hoping I'd lead you to Rianna.'

His silence was enough. Angry, she put her foot down, and the car accelerated sluggishly to sixty-five. 'Cadreis, tell me the bloody truth!'

'Helen, it was the only way I could make them let you go,' he said. The car's speed seemed to extract the admission as effectively as a knife at his throat. 'They knew it was unlikely Rianna would come to find you. But if you came back to Earth . . . '

'Yes, right,' Helen snapped. 'You were nearly in luck. For a few minutes, I thought she was at the farm. I hate to disappoint you, but I haven't the faintest idea where she is now. I couldn't lead you to her if I wanted to.'

'I am glad. It will give me time to think,' Cadreis said.

Helen slowed down slightly, trying to read a signboard. 'Think about what?' When he did not reply, she said, 'I wish I knew whose side you're on. I don't know why I'm defending Rianna. I don't even know whether she's my friend any more. But I still love her. You can't work for Artienter and Sydra, and pretend to be helping me.'

'You speak of them as if you hate them. But they are doing what they believe is best for all people, not only the Domendrans.'

'You mean they told you that, and you trust them?'

'In everything I say, there is truth,' he said. 'I have never told you a lie. There may be several different reasons for any action.'

'So it's true they sent you, but it's also true you want to help me?'

'Yes.'

Helen took a deep breath and released it slowly. 'I give up. I can't make you out at all.'

They were driving through Stamford now. Cadreis stared out at the buildings and glaring street lights as if hypnotised. Each time another car approached them, he seemed to rear back in his seat. 'This world is not as I had imagined. It is far more terrible.'

'Now you know how I felt in the Vale of Peace,' she said.

'When I followed you from the Vale, I saw no change in the landscape. Suddenly there were people and children everywhere, dressed in strange clothes. I had never seen anything like them. Where was the boundary, Helen?'

'The what?' She was desperately trying to remember which road she should be taking.

'The boundary between your world and mine. Black Annis is its guardian, but I did not see her. How is it that we could just walk through, and not attract her notice?'

'Don't ask me. Rianna and I used to go in and out quite often when we were children, only I didn't realise what was happening. I think she said we were on the boundary . . . Or was that something I dreamed? I don't know. It only used to happen from Bradgate Park, that's the place where we came through just now, but lately it's happened from other places.

It's scaring me to death.'

She pushed her hair back. She was sweating. She turned on to a country road, fairly certain that she was going the right way. But there was a web of narrow lanes to negotiate before she reached her parents' village. Half of them were not sign-posted, and in the darkness every junction looked the same.

'We should not be able just to walk through,' Cadreis said quietly. 'I think it means the boundary is collapsing. I was afraid when I followed you. I thought I was coming through into Anatevera. But surely Anatevera itself couldn't be worse than this.'

They drove on in silence. Helen found the turning she had been looking for, a lane only wide enough for one car. She remembered it, she thought . . . But as she drove on she did not recall it being so long, with so many blind bends. She slowed down to thirty-five, and still the hedges flew past with dizzying speed, pale as stooping owls in the headlights.

The lane went on and on. Helen tried not to contemplate the possibility of running out of petrol. They should have been there by now. Wasn't there a left turn somewhere? Much as she dreaded what she would find when she reached the house, the anticipation seemed worse.

'God, I think I'm lost,' she said shakily. 'I'll have to carry on, there's no room to turn round.'

Cadreis did not reply. She had the impression that he was no longer there, that he had dissolved like a reflection into the night. She looked round quickly, and took a shuddering breath. Her mind was playing tricks. She put a hand on his knee to reassure herself that he was solid, and he closed his fingers over hers.

'It's all right, Helen,' he said, as if he knew what she had been thinking. 'I'm here.'

As he spoke, the lane vanished. There was mud under the car wheels. Shocked, Helen braked and brought the car roughly to a standstill. She could see nothing in the range of the headlights but a flat expanse of grass.

'We're back in Tevera,' she said. A scream of frustration and terror rose up inside, fell away without being voiced. She gripped the steering wheel. 'It can't be. All I want to do is reach my Mum and Dad, why can't Tevera leave me alone?'

'Helen.' Cadreis sounded concerned. 'The path turns to the right. You went straight on. Did you not know?'

'I did what?' She turned round to look out of the back window. In the faint glow of the rear lights, she could see what Cadreis meant. There was a sharp bend. Helen had driven on to a farm track. Putting the gear in reverse, she pulled on to the lane and drove on the way she had been going.

'It's because I'm tired,' she said, trying to lighten the mood and failing miserably. 'This lane has to lead somewhere.'

Ten minutes later, she saw street lights twinkling ahead. She accelerated towards the village, craning her neck to read the name on the sign.

It was her parents' village. It looked unfamiliar, but after a few moments she realised that she had entered it on a different road.

'I must have gone wrong somewhere, and found another way round,' she said. 'I'm not sure where I am. I'll know which way to go, once we reach the middle . . . '

Once she spotted the village shop, she was able to orientate herself. A right turn, a quarter of a mile along a tree-lined lane, and she came in sight of the bungalow, which was set back from the road in a large garden.

There were no lights on.

'They might have come home and gone to bed,' Helen said, pulling up and leaping out of the car. She did not wait for Cadreis to work out how to open the door. She was on the front doorstep, ringing the bell with one hand while she sorted out her keys with the other.

Cadreis came to her side rather diffidently, looking around him.

'I've got a key,' she said. She was so choked up with anxiety that she could hardly speak. 'I'd better let myself in, if they're in bed it'll take Dad ages to wake up and get to the door . . . '

In the hall, she flicked on the light and blinked against the white glare. A pleasant smell of wood and polish greeted her. The walls were painted cream, the furnishings were a homely mix of old and new. There was no sign that anything was amiss.

Helen glanced round the door into the sitting room. The room was dark, but in the corner she saw the glitter of violet jewels. The doll sat in a glass-fronted cabinet, lifeless and benign. She switched the light on as if making the sign of the cross at it.

Then she went down the corridor that led to the bedrooms, calling, 'Hello, it's me. Is anyone there? Mum, it's only me!'

Her heart was hurling itself repeatedly into her throat, but she did not pause at her parents' bedroom door. She knocked, pushing it open at the same time. In the glow of street lamps through the curtains, she could see that the bed was smooth and flat, and had not been slept in.

Mechanically she checked each room in turn, but she already knew that her parents were not there. She went through the kitchen door into the garage, and looked at the patch of oil where their car had stood, and breathed the cold concrete smell.

She came back into the kitchen and leaned against a wall, dizzy.

'Helen?' said Cadreis. He stood in the doorway, touching the frame on either side of him and looking up at the ceiling. 'Your own parents live in this – this structure, alone?'

'Yes.' She was so exhausted now that she could hardly think.

'Where are they?'

'I don't know. They've gone, the doll's still here, so they must be all right.' She moved towards the telephone on the hall table and lifted the receiver. She paused for a moment, then began to dial her own telephone number.

'What are you doing?' Cadreis asked.

She could not be bothered to explain. There was just a faint chance that Rianna might have gone back to Helen's house, if only briefly. She did not expect a reply. It made her jump when after two rings it was snatched up and a male voice said, 'Hello?'

'Hello, who am I speaking to?' she said, thinking that she must have dialled the wrong number.

'This is John Locke speaking.'

Helen almost dropped the phone in astonishment. 'Dad,' she said breathlessly, 'Dad, it's me, Helen.'

'Helen! Where are you, love, are you all right?'

'I'm fine.'

She heard him calling urgently, 'It's Helen, she's on the phone, she's all right!' and her mother replying indistinctly in the background.

'Where are you?' he asked again, but before she could answer, her mum had taken over the telephone.

'Darling, is it really you?'

'Yes, Mum. Are you and Dad all right?'

'Of course we are, darling, but we've been desperately worried, what's happened to you, where are you?'

Thank God, oh dear God, thank you so much, Helen thought. Tears began to roll down her cheeks. 'I'm at your house.'

'*Our* house? Whatever are you doing there?'

'I thought you'd be here. What are you doing at mine?'

'Darling, we came to Rothley as soon as the police told us you were missing. We've been so worried.' Mrs Locke was sniffing as she spoke. Helen had not known her to cry for years. 'It was as though you'd vanished off the face of the Earth. The police tried to make out you might have just gone off somewhere without telling anyone, but we told them, you would never, ever do that, whatever the reason. We've hardly slept, we've just been waiting by the phone all the time in case there was any news. Oh John, can you – ' Her voice broke, and her father came back on the line.

'Helen, love, you're not in any danger, are you?'

'No, Dad. I'm OK, I promise. I'm perfectly safe.'

'But, love, why didn't you contact us before? What's been going on?'

Helen had no idea what to say. She could tell Jo about Tevera, perhaps because she felt Jo could cope with it, but there was no way she could ever explain it to her parents. Whatever she said would make it sound as if she were losing her mind, but she could only think of one convincing alternative, and that would seem almost as bad. 'I . . . it was Nick, Dad. I was so depressed about it, I couldn't face anyone. I just wanted to be on my own. I didn't realise how much time had gone by. I'm sorry, I'm really, really sorry.'

'Oh, love. You poor thing.'

In the background, she heard her mother say, 'What is it? What's wrong?' and her father reply, 'She sounds very depressed about Nick.'

'I didn't mean to cause so much trouble,' said Helen.

'It's all right, we're not angry,' her father said gently. 'As long as you're all right that's all that matters. Now, hang on there, will you, Helen? We're coming straight home.'

The prospect of her parents having to make a long drive in the dark when they were exhausted dismayed her.

'No – no, Dad, listen,' she said. 'I know – I mean, you know I'm OK now, and it's the middle of the night. We're all tired. Wouldn't it be better to wait until morning?'

'But we want to see you – '

'I want to see you too. But I'd be happier if you waited until it's light. And I'm so tired all I want to do is sleep.'

'Well, if you're sure,' her father said dubiously. 'I suppose you're right. But you make sure you lock up properly. We'll be home first thing.'

When they had said their goodbyes, Helen went into the sitting room, sat down on the sofa, and quietly began to cry her eyes out.

The mantelpiece and shelves were crowded with framed photographs; her mother dancing, her mother with ballet pupils, her father winning an angling competition, Helen at all ages from toothless baby onwards. There were photographs of the three of them together, windswept and smiling on holiday. Cadreis was slowly making his way round the room, studying each one in turn. The way he moved, the way he looked at everything with dreamy, reverent curiosity, reminded her of Rianna, drifting round the shop. He was dark and graceful and too beautiful to be human.

'What's wrong?' he said, turning to look at her.

'Nothing. Everything's all right now. My folks are coming home in the morning.'

He sat down at her side. His scent was clean and warm, as if nothing bad in the Vale of Peace had ever touched him. 'Then why are you crying?'

She shrugged. He put both arms round her and said, 'Don't weep, Helen.'

She hugged him, suddenly breathless with the need to be held. The next thing she knew they were kissing, and she could taste the salt of her own tears on his mouth.

The embrace was so sweet and natural that they might have

been lovers for ever. Cadreis warmed her, and the warmth became an ache and she arched herself against him, starving for him. He was outside everything, beyond compare.

If Martin had found in Rianna what she found in Cadreis, she could not blame him, not for an instant. It was enchantment, perfection, a dream . . .

It was only the thought of her mother and father that brought her back to her senses, and gave her the strength to pull away from him.

'I can't,' she said. 'Not in my parents' house.'

He did not try to stop her as she removed herself from the sofa and fled into the bathroom. The desire was so strong that she could hardly breathe or walk straight. She locked the door, then ran the taps and splashed cold water on her face until the heat began to fade.

She was longing to see her parents, to hug them and reassure herself that they were alive and well. But Cadreis made things so complicated.

When she went back to the sitting room he was standing by the cabinet, gazing at the doll. The room seemed to grow larger and smaller with her heartbeat.

'How on earth am I going to explain you to my parents?' she said.

He looked round at her, concerned. 'Is my presence a difficulty?'

'You could say that, yes.'

'You understood nothing in Tevera. Now I understand nothing here. But I'll be patient, Helen. I don't want to leave you.'

She walked across to the cabinet. She longed to touch him again, but instead she opened the glass door and took out the doll.

'I'm going to put this damn thing in the car. I'm not afraid of it.' She turned it to the light, sending points of purple brilliance dancing across the walls. 'I didn't notice before, but its colour is predominantly indigo. The colour of the feet, for dancing,' said Helen.

Cadreis's expression changed. He looked guarded, almost alarmed. 'Where have you heard that?'

'The Chalcenians told me. It's as if Rianna made it

specially for my mother, knowing she was a dancer.' He lowered his eyes, as if he did not wish to be reminded of the Chalcenians. She put her hand on his arm. 'Cadreis, are you sure you don't know what the doll really is?'

'No, I don't.'

'Please tell me the truth. I've got a right to know. Artienter and Sydra called it *Pelu*.'

'I had not heard the word before. I don't know what it means.'

'Considering you're their apprentice, they don't tell you much, do they?' she said, exasperated.

'I am only Sfaian.' His dark, sad eyes met hers and she had to look away, feeling the blood rising in her face. The attraction she felt for him was quite different to what she had felt for Nick. With Nick she had been slightly awed, too often on edge for fear of not pleasing him. With Cadreis there was no uneasiness, only a pure dark magnetism that would be so much easier to give in to than to resist.

Helen made herself turn away from him and walk out to the car.

Outside, the night was very still and mild; the stars were as sharp and clear as in Tevera, like drifts of white sand. An owl shrieked in a nearby wood, making her shiver.

She locked the doll in the boot, then checked three times to make sure it really was locked. She still did not know how Annie had been spirited from a display case in the shop to her house. It gave her a feeling of helplessness, as if nothing she did could keep the Pelu in one place if they wished to be in another.

A strange dream. And Cadreis was part of it. He could not be real. When she went back to the house he would be gone . . .

The thought gave her a flash of panic, and she ran back into the hall, feverishly bolting the doors behind her. She rushed into the sitting room, then felt foolish; Cadreis was sitting on the sofa with a photograph of Helen in his hand.

'This is you,' he said. 'How do they make such a likeness?'

'I'll explain later.' She sighed, partly with relief and partly with tiredness. 'I'm going to have a bath. You can have one too if you like.'

Not waiting for a reply, she went into the bathroom and turned on the taps. The water came through hot; evidently her parents had left in such a hurry that they had not bothered to turn off the heating. She was glad. She picked up a bottle from the side of the bath and poured from it a scented oil that turned the water pink and sent up clouds of fragrant steam.

After a couple of minutes, Cadreis came in through the half open door and looked over her shoulder, his hands stroking her arms. She relaxed and leaned against him, like a cat.

'What a strange bathing place,' he commented.

She looked up at him and saw that he was smiling. 'I didn't mean us both to get in at once,' she heard herself saying. 'Oh, but why not?'

She knew what was going to happen and she was beyond trying to stop it. She wanted it so much she was shaking. *I'm crazy,* she thought, and then for some reason she thought of Martin and heard him telling her that she would be even more crazy to waste the opportunity of being with the loveliest man she had ever met. Had Martin hesitated when he met Rianna?

Helen and Cadreis undressed, watching each other, hypnotised. The scented oil turned their limbs to silk, and Cadreis did not protest for long about the heat of the water.

Chapter Eleven

Helen was woken by a stripe of sunlight falling across her face through a gap in the curtains. Sleep had cleared her mind. For a few minutes she basked in the luxury of feeling relaxed and free from anxiety, but then the memories began to return. She sat up, stretching and yawning.

'Oh hell, what time is it?'

Cadreis was no longer in the bed beside her. Helen glanced quickly round the room, then saw him lying on the carpet between the bed and the window.

'I knew it was too much to hope that you were making some tea,' she said wryly, leaning over to switch on the radio. A friendly BBC voice announced that it was seven o'clock and began to read the news headlines. At that, Cadreis woke up with a start and looked from the radio to Helen, bewildered.

She turned it off. 'Sorry, I didn't mean it to wake you.'

'Where was the voice coming from?' he said.

'Well, it's a radio, it's – ' She shook her head, smiling. 'Just another thing that will take ages to explain. You'll get used to it. What are you doing on the floor?'

'The bed was too soft. I couldn't sleep.'

'I should've guessed. I think I'll ring my Mum and Dad about eight to see what time they're setting off.' Cadreis moved to sit next to her on the bed, smiling. 'You know, you never used to smile at all, when I first met you.'

He wrapped his arms round her and kissed her. 'I had no cause. But now I have.'

She returned the embrace gladly, stroking his shoulders and his silky hair. This was all she wanted, to stay with Cadreis and lose herself in him as she had the night before. The feeling was like starlight inside her, too beautiful to be expressed. She could not understand why he found her attractive, but that seemed irrelevant now; the bond between them was beyond words or analysis. A line from a song haunted her: *Drowning in the sea of love*. For the first time in her life, she knew what it meant.

I can't be in love, I hardly know him. Normally, Helen was – in her own opinion – cautious to the point of being cowardly about sex. She had never behaved with such abandon before, but this was different; she had never met anyone like Cadreis before.

'I must have gone mad,' she said softly. 'But I don't care.'

She had spoken in English. 'What did you say?' he asked.

'It doesn't matter. Look, Cadreis, my mother and father will be on their way here in a while. I can't let them see you. I don't want them to think I've run away for a week with a total stranger, or that you're some sort of maniac who's kidnapped me, and that's the sort of conclusion they might jump to. Or at least, they'd be very puzzled and worried, and even if I can think of a good excuse and they like you, what's going to happen when you go back to Tevera? It's better if they never see you in the first place.'

'Why can't you tell them the truth?'

Helen gasped. 'You must be joking. They'd never believe me.'

'Helen, do I understand you rightly? You could tell them that I am . . . a friend, or someone you know, but you are afraid to because they will think badly of you?'

Hearing it stated so baldly, she felt slightly ashamed. 'Yes. I suppose I am.'

'Why?'

'Because . . . because I just don't do things like this, or at least they think I don't. I don't want to upset them.'

'Why should it upset them?'

She shrugged helplessly. 'It just would.'

'Your world is a strange place,' he said.

'Yes, it is.' She studied his face, trying to judge whether he meant to co-operate or not. She could not tell. His eyes almost dissolved her. 'I don't know what else to say. Let's have some breakfast and try to decide what to do . . . ' As she spoke, she heard a car passing along the lane. But instead of the sound fading away it grew louder until it seemed to be almost outside the window. Then she heard the engine judder and stop. 'Oh my God,' she said, leaping across the bed to look out of the curtains. 'Oh no, they're here!'

In a panic, she struggled into her clothes, at the same time trying to smooth the bed out. Cadreis helped her, a smile hovering at the corners of his lips. Then she dashed into her parents' room, dragged a comb through her hair and took a white shirt from the wardrobe.

'Put this on!' she said, throwing it at Cadreis. 'Your trousers are all right but they'll think you're a gipsy if you wear your own shirt.'

'Are they going to see me?' He was straight-faced now, but his eyes shone as if he was about to start laughing at her.

'No!' she snapped. 'Just stay in the bedroom and don't make a sound!'

She closed the door, just as her parents opened the front door and came into the hall.

Helen ran to them and for a long time all they did was hug each other, half laughing and half crying.

Eventually Helen said, 'You're so early, I didn't think you'd even be up yet.'

'We didn't sleep too well and we were awake before six,' said her father, 'so we thought we might as well make an early start. We were going to ring you first but we didn't want to wake you up.'

'I thought you'd still be in bed, dear,' her mother added. 'You sounded exhausted on the telephone last night. How are you?'

'I'm fine, I'm perfectly all right,' Helen said, smiling. 'It's lovely to see you. I was so worried.'

'*You* were worried? Whatever for?'

'Oh – oh, you know. Because I knew you were concerned about me . . . '

'Helen, darling.' Her mother held her arms and looked at her. 'You look so pale. Whatever happened to you? We want the full story, from start to finish.'

Helen drew a deep breath and let it go. 'Wait here a minute. There's someone I want you to meet.'

In her father's shirt, which was too big for him, Cadreis looked as if he had stepped out of the eighteenth century. He sat very quietly beside Helen at the breakfast table and was no embarrassment to her; he simply imitated the way she held her cup or spread honey on her toast, and she could have sworn he was thoroughly enjoying himself. As they ate, and as Helen talked, she took frequent sips of tea as if to wash the half truths from her mouth.

'Cadreis is a friend of – well, he vaguely knows Rianna. I met him through her.'

'But surely you didn't just go off for the week with him, without telling anyone?'

'Not deliberately. Let me finish, Mum. I was so upset about Nick – I found him and went to the hospital with him, did you know?'

'Yes, the police told us that,' said her father.

'Then I had this terrible argument with Rianna. She went off and I was on my own. I wanted to ring you, but I couldn't. I just – I didn't really know what I was doing, I suppose. I went out for a walk and I didn't go home, I didn't even really know where I was.'

'Oh, Helen.' Her mother put a hand on her arm.

'Anyway, I bumped into Cadreis. I – I sort of knew him, you see . . . He was so kind to me. He just let me sleep and cry and talk until I felt better, and then – well, he persuaded me I ought to come to you. Only I didn't know you'd gone to Rothley . . . '

Mrs Locke gave her a grave look, as if she wanted to believe her but was reserving judgment. Eventually she said gently, 'Helen, it sounds as if you might have had some sort of nervous breakdown. I think you should see a doctor.'

It was easier not to argue. 'OK, I'll go as soon as I get home.'

'You're not thinking of going yet, are you?' said her father. 'We thought you'd stay here a few days, have a rest.'

Helen thought of the doll in the boot of the car, and she thought of Rianna and Cadreis. 'I'd like to, but I really must open up the shop. I've got such a lot to do, I want to get back to normal as quickly as possible.'

'Yes, I can understand that,' Mr Locke said. 'More toast, erhm – Cadreis?' He was being very attentive to the unexpected guest, as much out of curiosity as politeness. 'Does he really not speak much English? Is he Italian or something?'

'Oh, John, for heaven's sake,' Beth Locke said brusquely. 'I don't know what to make of this, Helen, really I don't. I know you've had a shock, but you've been behaving so out of character. And as for Rianna, going off and leaving you like that, just when you were going through such a difficult time – it only shows what kind of girl she is.'

'What do you mean?' Helen said indignantly.

'She was unreliable as a child, and she still is. I've spoken to the Harpers on the phone, by the way.'

'Her parents? You rang them up in New Zealand?'

'Yes, it wasn't hard to trace their number. Do you know, Mrs Harper did not have the faintest idea where Rianna was staying? Rianna had written to them, but never given them her address or more than the vaguest idea of what she was doing. You wonder why I don't trust the girl, but really, when she does things like that, can you blame me?'

Helen knew why Rianna had not wanted anyone to know her address. Mrs Locke's attitude might be justified, but the frustration Helen felt at being unable to explain was twisting itself into anger. 'Mother, you shouldn't have rung them. What right have you got to interfere in Rianna's life? She's an adult, and so am I, for that matter.'

'Then you should both behave like it.'

'What's that supposed to mean?'

'Really, Helen,' her mother said. 'She vanishes with a man she hardly knows and as for you, going off like that without telling anyone, meeting some vague acquaintance who can't even speak the language – if that's not behaving like a pair of retarded adolescents, I don't know what is.'

Helen was fuming, desperate to tell them the truth. Her father said, 'Come on now, don't argue. Helen's had a very tough time.'

'You would defend her, of course,' said Mrs Locke. 'You're both the same: secretive. I'm annoyed because I don't think she's told us everything. Helen, why can't you trust me? Do you know what you're doing? In a way you're treating me like a child, trying to defend me from something you think I shouldn't know.'

The words bled Helen's anger away, instantly. She felt

naked, transparent, as if everyone could see straight through her. She reached across and took her mother's hand. 'I'm sorry, Mum. I'm not hiding anything, honestly. I feel awful about causing you so much worry, that's all.'

Her mother relented. 'I'm sorry too,' she sighed. 'Sometimes I forget that you have your own life now, and certain things are none of my business. Help me wash up, dear. I'd like a word.'

Helen followed her mother into the kitchen, expecting a further lecture about her morals. Instead, to her surprise, Mrs Locke said, 'Rianna had a baby when she was sixteen. Did she ever tell you?'

'No,' said Helen, almost dropping a plate. 'My God, are you sure?'

'Of course. I hardly think her mother would make up a thing like that.'

'Well, what happened to it?'

'The whole thing was dreadful. It was a silly teenage affair, but Rianna refused to have an abortion. She wanted to look after it herself. Her family persuaded her to have it adopted. All the arrangements were made, and then the poor little thing was stillborn.'

'Oh, Christ,' Helen whispered. 'Poor Rianna. She never said a word to me.'

'Well, her mother said she never really seemed to grieve about it. Instead she began making those dolls. I'm no psychiatrist, dear, but you can't help jumping to conclusions . . . '

'That they were a kind of baby substitute, you mean?'

Mrs Locke shrugged. 'I feel sorry for her and all that, but it does rather lend weight to my theory that she's ever so slightly unbalanced.'

'Mum, that is my best friend you're talking about.'

'I'm not criticising her. Mental illness can happen to the nicest people.'

Helen was so taken aback that she could not even find the words to take issue with her mother's attitude. She went on washing the plates in silence, and after a few seconds her father came in waving a ten pound note at her.

'Money for petrol, love.'

'Thanks, Dad. I'll pay you back.' She dried her hands and

gave him a hug.

'I was trying to talk to Cadreis, but he doesn't seem to understand any English at all,' he said. 'How on earth do you talk to each other? Have you been going to language classes?'

'Er – well, on and off,' Helen muttered.

'What language is it, then?'

'Erhm – Finnish,' she said rashly.

He was obviously about to dispute this, but Cadreis came into the doorway and looked at Helen, grinning. 'Are they talking about me?'

'It's nothing, they just can't understand how we communicate, that's all.'

'I don't understand why you can speak to me, and they cannot.'

'Neither do I, and that's why I don't want to stay here having a discussion about it! We'll leave in a minute.'

His expression was wary. 'Must we go in the metal car again?'

'I'm afraid so. I'll try not to frighten you so much this time.' She turned to her mother. 'We really had better be on our way now.'

'Are you taking Cadreis back to Rothley?' There was a challenging edge to Mrs Locke's voice. 'Or to his home, wherever that is?'

'That rather depends on him,' said Helen, hurrying towards the guest room to fetch her car keys and tidy up. *Rianna, oh, Rianna.* Helen wondered how long it would take her parents to notice that their doll had gone. She had decided that it was simpler just to take it, and try to explain when she rang them later.

When she came back along the corridor, she overheard her father talking to her mother in the kitchen. 'I don't know what it was, it definitely wasn't Finnish, but I sort of understood it!' he said excitedly.

'I thought it sounded familiar.' Her mother sounded thoughtful. 'I could almost pick out one or two words. I don't see how you could understand it, though, John.'

'But I did. Helen said she was going to take him home, and he said something like, "Do we have to go in the car again?"!'

Helen listened, numb. Seeing her in the hall, he looked a

touch embarrassed and called, 'Isn't that what you said, Helen?'

'Yes, Dad,' she replied quietly. 'Something like that.'

It was a cool, crisp morning, summer edged with autumn. Cadreis hardly said a word as they drove back, but watched the changing scenery with a mixture of interest and alarm. Helen decided to take the country route rather than the main road, and spare him the bustle of Leicester. She sensed that Cadreis was not in a mood to talk. He had turned in upon himself again, and her own mind was so awhirl with Rianna, Martin and everything else that she did not even know where to start.

Where were Martin and Rianna? Had they really tried to find her? She had thought that once she came home, everything would go back to normal. But it was not over yet, nowhere near over.

When they reached Rothley, Helen drove past the shop on her way home. It looked quite ordinary, as if she had only just closed up. A couple of women with bags of groceries were chatting on the pavement outside. It was hard to imagine that while she had been in Tevera, life had gone on as usual.

It was only when she pulled up outside the house that she began to feel nervous about going inside. It had become a terrifying place, turned inside out and swallowed her . . . and she had no guarantee that it would not happen again.

She was trembling as she opened the car's hatchback. The violet doll still lay in the boot, its mild face turned upwards. With a mixture of relief and unease, she took it out and went to the front door.

There was a house key on the bunch with the car keys, and she let herself in cautiously, with Cadreis just behind her. Soft sunlight filtered through the windows, making it seem bright and welcoming. It had a familiar, pleasant smell that she only noticed when she had been away for several days. Home. Her spirits lifted and she walked in boldly, breathing in the clean air.

The first thing she saw was the other doll, the one Annis had possessed, lying on the carpet where it had fallen a week earlier. Helen caught her breath at the sight of it, then bent to pick it up. The jewels flickered and gleamed like stained glass.

'Look, Cadreis.' Her voice was not quite steady. 'This was the thing that took me to Tevera – or brought Tevera into my house. It came alive. It turned black and walked towards me and told me its name was Annis. Now it just lies here, looking so innocent.'

He regarded it suspiciously, but did not take it from her. 'Are you afraid of it?'

'I'm not sure. It's a bit like picking up a spider, even though you can't stand them. To prove something. Maybe I should be scared. There are some more upstairs.'

'What are they doing there?'

'Rianna made them.' She put the dolls side by side on the couch. 'I'm not going to let the damn things intimidate me. I'm going to ignore them.' Now she had got the Pelu away from her parents, she felt more angry at the dolls than afraid.

Cadreis went on staring at them, and she wished he would speak his thoughts. Did he really not know what they were? Because she had the feeling that he did know, but that it was something so awful that he could not admit it even to himself. She felt cold at the thought, and was glad when he finally turned away and went through into the dining room. Helen followed him.

'Well, this is my house,' she said. 'What do you think?'

'It's light,' said Cadreis, resting his hands on her shoulders. 'I'd forgotten . . . what it is to live in a light place.'

Helen let out a deep sigh. 'There's so much going on that I don't understand. How on earth could my father possibly understand what you were saying? Even my mother said it sounded familiar.'

'If you can speak it, why not they?'

'Yes. Well. If I think about it any more I'm going to go mad, so just until I sort myself out I'm going to put everything out of my mind.' She looked round the room, drinking in the familiar details and trying to forget the nightmare images. 'I don't know what to do first. I'm hungry again already.'

He turned her towards him. His lips were warm on her cheeks and mouth, and she reached up to bury her hands in the softness of his hair. 'So am I,' he said.

*

'So much for opening the shop,' Helen said contentedly. They sat half dressed on her bedroom floor, leaning back against the bed, with a picnic of sandwiches and wine spread out on the carpet.

'What is the "shop"?'

'The place where I work. Sell things. I'll take you there later. You must be finding all this very strange, but it's nice to get my own back.'

Cadreis stroked her arm. He seemed pensive. 'I am still a child of Artienter's teaching. This world seems nightmarish to me, so like Tevera but covered in cities full of greyness and noise . . . '

'You've only seen small towns. I should take you to London.'

He lifted her hand, absently tracing the shape of her fingers. 'But the part of me that belongs to you tells me that your world might not be as terrible as it seems. I don't know whether I can grow used to it or not. And the people . . . they are so different to the Domendrans, yet I feel that they are the same . . . '

Helen was not sure what he was trying to say, and she felt a touch uneasy. 'I think my parents liked you. Dad did, anyway. My mother's always funny with strangers. What did you think of them?'

The elusive gleam of warmth returned to his eyes, thrilling her like unexpected sunlight. His beauty made her heart ache. She could not believe she was here with him. He said, 'Your parents are . . . grey.'

'Grey?' she exclaimed.

'So are you.'

'Oh. Thank you.'

'I think I have insulted you. I did not mean to,' he said, half smiling. 'The Domendrans are dark, without colour. The Chalcenians are all colours. But the people here . . . they are also without colour, but they are grey like twilight. Or like dawn. I should have said silver. That's why I love you, Helen, because you are like light.'

'Am I?'

'In the Vale of Peace, you would not become Domendric. You could not. You rose out of the place like a bubble out of water, and you drew me with you.' Helen was startled by this, and not quite sure how to take it. He went on, 'In Tevera, you were in my hands, Helen. Now I am in yours. I trust you. I have changed because of you.'

'Changed . . . how?' She had become more and more aware that he was different, that he had lost the air of wretchedness and no longer found it impossible to smile, but she could not believe that he was happy simply because he had fallen in love. It seemed too simple a reason, and she lacked the self-esteem to make such an assumption.

'I don't know. This has never happened to me before.'

For a moment, she felt like shaking him. Everything he said seemed ambiguous. She was at ease with him as if he were part of her, yet she did not know him at all. There was an unexplored country behind his eyes, dark and strange as the city of the Domendrans.

'Can't you explain any more than that?'

'I was in a blackness from which I thought I would never escape. I was wrong, but all the things I believe in have begun to seem strange. Yet I can't believe the Aulanti's teachings were wrong . . . ' He frowned, and she touched his cheek.

'Don't,' she said quickly, 'not if it distresses you. It's none of my business.'

'It's hard to explain,' he said. 'Talk of something else, Helen.'

She said softly, 'You're only the second man I've made love to. I suppose I've led a sheltered life, but you were worth waiting for.'

'In the Vale of Death in Life, there is so little desire. A brief flame in the darkness . . . then the despair rushes back, worse than before. It is not worth it . . . '

'I take it that's why there are no children.' He nodded. 'So everyone there must have come from outside. Don't you remember anything before being in the city?'

She felt him shiver slightly. 'It's too soon. I can't think about it.'

'Sorry. I'm just trying to work out why I changed things.'

His eyes were shadowed by his long lashes, but she saw his lips soften to a smile, the kind and mischievous warmth return to his face. 'But I've told you, Helen, and I have no other answer. It was as if I was asleep, and you woke me up. You were not Domendric. You were the light of dawn.'

Later, Helen tried to ring Martin at home and at work, if only to convince herself that he and Rianna had really gone away together. All his colleagues knew was that he had taken a sudden 'holiday'.

Helen sat on the edge of the sofa, elbows on knees and chin cupped in her hands, brooding. 'I don't even know where to start looking for them. They could have gone anywhere – Wales, the Lakes . . . Maybe I shouldn't even try to find them.'

Cadreis, sitting on the floor, looked up at her. 'Might they not have tried to go to Tevera?'

'No.' She shook her head vehemently. 'Martin wouldn't risk it, I'm sure, and he'd never get Rianna near the Park anyway.'

But Helen could not stop worrying. She had to do something. She was deeply tired, so sleep came easily that night, but the next morning she was awake early, very restless.

To clear her mind, she took Cadreis for a walk round Rothley. In Tevera, he had done his best to accustom her to a frighteningly strange place and she wanted to do the same for him. More than that, she wanted him to like her part of the world . . . in the hope that he would want to stay?

In the house he had been increasingly cheerful; they had laughed together, teased each other. But as soon as they stepped outside she sensed him becoming more and more withdrawn. The outside world made him face the conflict inside himself, but he could not share it with her.

She avoided the main road and the council houses, keeping to the old part of the village. They walked along winding lanes between granite, brick and whitewashed cottages. A thin drizzle hung in the air. The slate roofs were bloomed with silver, and holly bushes leaned out over hawthorn hedges, dark and shiny. Helen breathed in the rain-scented air.

'We're in Charnwood Forest,' she told him. 'It's the only place I know that's as nice in bad weather as in good.'

'I don't see a forest,' said Cadreis.

'There isn't much forest left. It's an area of hills and woodland, with a few villages. It's only a few miles across, like a tiny highland landscape, yet there's something special about it . . . but it's no good me comparing it to anywhere else, because you won't know where I mean.'

Cadreis said, 'Except for the houses, it feels like Tevera.'

In the lane approaching the church Helen stopped to make a fuss of a tortoiseshell cat. Cadreis was as delighted as a child when the creature came to him, weaving round his legs and butting its head against his hands. 'I had forgotten about animals,' he said.

When they reached the church, however, he became quiet again. She had not told him it was a graveyard, yet as he wandered between the weathered headstones, he obviously knew. For a second she was back in the burial cave in the Vale of Peace, but she shook off the memory.

When he became withdrawn she knew he was drifting away from her, and the feeling filled her with panic. She could only guess what was on his mind: that he was ashamed of betraying Artienter and Sydra, and that he was homesick for Tevera.

The bulk of the church was dark with moisture, and trees rustled softly against the overcast sky. The grass was rich and vivid. Helen waited on the path, thinking: *If he wants to leave me I have no right to stop him*, and her heart was dancing with gladness that he was there, with terror of losing him.

When he had seen enough of the graves he came back to her, embraced her, and stood with his chin resting on her head. After a while he said, 'Sometimes I feel time rushing away from me. I am not moving. I am sitting very still yet I am dizzy, hanging on to the seat while time streams away from me on all sides. It is the same as the way I felt in the car.'

Helen turned and slipped her arm round his waist. 'I've felt like that too, sometimes. Time seems to go so fast when you get older. It always seems to be Christmas, and the whole year in between condensed into nothing.'

'I don't want to die, Helen,' he said.

'Who does?'

'But the Domendrans believe it is something we must strive towards. It's what the Aulanti have always taught us. The only use of our lives is to prepare ourselves for death, to sink so quietly into ourselves that we find peace for ever and never have to go through the pain of living again.'

'I've been through some bad times,' said Helen, 'but I've never felt so bad that I've wanted to die. I can't imagine it.'

'I have.'

'Why?' she whispered.

'I don't know.' The haunted look was in his eyes again, and she would have done anything to understand his pain and relieve it. 'I was Domendric, I never questioned the way of things. It's what I've believed all my life, but now a voice in my head is telling me that it was all lies. I don't know what to believe. I can't accept the Domendri faith any more. I want to live!'

A weird excitement went through her and she faced him, gripping his arms. 'Well, what's stopping you?'

There was hope and fear in his face. 'Nothing. But I am afraid. It is so strange to me, to feel like this, and it means I am not Domendric any more. I am not Sfaian. I have become Luthnei, transient.'

'Is that a bad thing?'

'Yes, but I – I don't know. It does not feel bad.' He suddenly hugged her, almost squeezing the breath out of her.

'We're standing here having this really depressing conversation, and yet I don't feel depressed,' she said, laughing. 'I feel as if something wonderful is beginning to happen . . . '

She broke off. There was a figure standing under a tree by the wall of the churchyard, watching them. Cadreis must have felt her freeze; he released her and looked round.

It was a stocky man in a waxed jacket, with a cap pulled down over his eyes so that his face was in shadow. But she saw the gingery hair curling over the collar, and she recognised him at once.

Cadreis said, 'Who is it, Helen?'

'Don't you recognise him?'

'No,' he said, too sharply. 'Why should I?'

He was coming towards them now. Helen's instinct was to walk away fast, but a sudden anger flamed up inside her and she held her ground, her hand tucked through Cadreis's arm. She said, 'Because he's been looking for Rianna. I think he's a Domendran. Are you sure you don't know him?'

'No, I don't, Helen, truly.'

'But I know you,' said the man, halting in front of them.

She did not think he had been close enough to hear, but their voices had carried in the still air. He used the language of Tevera. 'From the Vale of Death in Life, are you not? And your name is Cadreis, Sfaia to the Aulanti. I know you, boy, even if you do not remember me.'

'Are you Menenthonis?'

The man nodded slowly. 'And have Artienter and Sydra spoken to you of me?'

'Yes. They told me you were seeking Rianna,' said Cadreis.

Being with him gave Helen no sense of safety, only of being in the presence of two aliens. Menenthonis did not seem physically threatening, but power rolled from him like liquid ice. Under his blue gaze, all Helen's happiness fell away and the misery she had felt in the city of the Domendrans washed over her again.

'And what of you? You have won the trust of this girl, so why has she not led you to Rianna?'

'Cadreis!' Helen exclaimed. She knew that Menenthonis meant her to think she had been used, but the doubt reared up anyway.

Cadreis pressed her hand, but his eyes were on Menenthonis. He said, 'Helen, you knew I was supposed to find Rianna. And then I was to deliver her to Menenthonis to be taken home.'

'How? You didn't even recognise him.'

'He was to contact me. And he has.'

Helen was trembling. 'So was it all lies, the things you've said to me?' She turned on the ginger-haired man. 'You bastard. It was your fault I was taken to Tevera, wasn't it? You must have taken the doll out of the shop somehow and put it in my house, as a trap for Rianna. But it took me instead.'

'It was a mistake,' the man said without expression. 'We still want Rianna.'

'Well, hard luck. I haven't got the faintest idea where she is, and I wouldn't have taken Cadreis to her if I had.'

'Perhaps that is as well,' said Menenthonis. He looked hard at Cadreis. 'Do you still call yourself a Domendran, boy?'

Cadreis had turned pale. He did not seem to know how to answer. The man went on, 'I do not see one of a deep level before me; I do not see the Sfaian I was led to expect. I see one who no longer knows his own mind, who is on the verge of turning against Artienter. And for her?' He gave Helen a brief, despising glance. 'It is convenient for you that you were never faced with the decision of taking Rianna. What would you have done? You cannot answer because you are no longer Sfaian. You are Luthnei.'

Cadreis looked stricken, and Helen began to feel really afraid. Menenthonis turned to her and said, 'And you; still protecting your friend? Would you have let her go on spreading her evil creations throughout your land? Do you know what the result would have been?'

'No,' Helen stammered. 'Not really.'

'No. You cannot know. I could speak of souls being condemned to eternal torment, but I think you still would not understand. By what authority do you defy me when I say Rianna must be stopped?'

'Because she's just a vulnerable young woman and you are an arrogant bunch of – '

'Better arrogant than ignorant.' Menenthonis pulled his cap lower and thrust his hands into his pockets. He seemed at ease in the clothes as if he had been on Earth a long time. 'However, I met you this day to tell you that I shall not be troubling you again. We know where Rianna is.'

'Where?' Helen gasped.

For the first time, his lips twitched with a hint of a joyless smile. 'In Tevera, of course. Our mistake turned to our advantage, in the end. She has gone looking for you, and on our own territory she will not evade us for long.'

He turned and walked away. Helen and Cadreis stared after him as he retreated between the grey headstones. It was a long time before either of them spoke.

'How come you didn't recognise him?' said Helen.

'Because he left the Vale of Peace before I went to live there. He was sent away to hunt others like Rianna.'

'My God, you mean there are others? Who are they?'

'I don't know,' Cadreis said unhappily. 'If I had become Aulanti, I would have been told. But now I never will. What he said about me was true. I have failed Artienter and Sydra.'

'Never mind that, we have got to go to Tevera and warn

Rianna!'

Cadreis lowered his eyes. 'Helen, I have been trying to find a way to tell you: I don't belong in this limbo world. I think Anatevera must be very like this, and I cannot bear it. I need to return to Tevera.'

'I thought so,' she said quietly. 'I knew it was too much to hope that you'd want to stay here with me.'

'It's not you I want to leave! But – '

'I know, I know,' she said quickly, trying not to feel glad that Rianna's plight gave her a reason to stay with him. 'One thing: will you swear that if we find Rianna you won't betray her to the Domendrans?'

'I swear. I would not have done so anyway, whatever Menenthonis said. But Helen, listen. He will not tell us the way back. So how can we return?'

Fear was icing Helen's limbs. She had known that their idyll could not last, and now she felt guilty that they had not gone to look for Rianna immediately. They could waste no more time, but she was scared, so scared.

'Don't worry,' she said cheerfully, trying to hide the tremor in her voice. 'We can go back to Tevera the way we came.'

Chapter Twelve

The clouds were breaking up by the time they reached the Park, sunlight sifting through with a tantalising hint of warmth to come. It was mid-morning and there were already several cars dotted around the sloping, tree-lined car park. By some strange instinct, Helen had driven to the one nearest Old John hill. She pulled up at the fringe of the spinney and sat still for a moment, looking at the car next to hers.

It was Martin's MG. 'It's true, then,' she said quietly. 'Come on, Cadreis.'

They left the car and began to trudge up through the spinney towards Old John. Twigs and last year's pine cones crunched under their feet. Holly bushes massed darkly under the beeches and sycamores, and the oak leaves were edged with russet, flickering against a sky as blue and delicate as ice.

Helen was wearing jeans, sturdy boots and a waterproof jacket, and had a shoulder bag containing food and other necessities. She had lent Cadreis a grey anorak.

'I expect we're going to be too hot now, but it's better than freezing to death,' she said.

'Will we really find the gate to Tevera here?'

'I hope so. You must believe it's possible; you followed me once before.'

They went through the wooden gate at the edge of the spinney and the ancient landscape of the Park opened up before them as if they had stepped into another time. Before them, a hill swept up against the sky, rough grass scarred with rocks and crowned by the stone tower shaped like a beer tankard, Old John. On either side, acres of bracken fell away towards distant fields, separated from them by the grey line of the wall. To the right, cars flashed along the road, but everywhere else there were only the gentle uplands of Charnwood rolling towards the horizon, quilted with trees and shadows.

One or two houses nestled in the edges of the woods.

For a moment, Helen forgot why they were there. The clean, sweet air poured through her lungs, tangled her hair and stung tears to her eyes. She tugged at Cadreis's arm. 'Let's go to the top, you can see for miles.'

They gained the peak and stood by the stone tower, catching their breath. The horizon was white with mist. Slow clouds from a far-away power station stood in the air. Leicester lay glittering in a haze of greyness, but Helen only had eyes for the dew-webbed slopes of the Park below them, the trees brushed with sunlight and the yellow-green paths scored through the bracken.

Then Cadreis said, 'I believe you.'

She subdued the leap of apprehension in her stomach. She had so recently escaped Tevera, and now she was about to walk back in of her own free will. Perhaps she was mad . . . But it had been the Vale of Peace she wanted to escape, not Sheyde and Tasnian and the beautiful sea Halaranthe.

She watched a man walking his dog along the foot of the hill, and wondered why only she and Martin had so far been privileged to pass through into Tevera. *A sort of contagion I caught from Rianna, maybe* . . . She shook herself, and turned to Cadreis.

'I'm sure we'll go through soon,' she said, as if she did it every day. 'The boundary never seems to be in a specific place. If we just walk about for a while . . . '

They walked. A herd of deer watched them pass, alert but unconcerned. Helen looked at them carefully, remembering the way the weird black creature had come from their midst and chased her . . . but this time she saw only shades of brown, a couple of beauties as white as owls standing out among them.

She and Cadreis walked up and down the long slopes to the crown of trees on Tyburn, then along the top of the gorge, looking down through the trees to the river Lin and the people walking along the main path.

'It's getting quite crowded,' said Helen. 'This always happens when the sun comes out. We'll go back up the hill where it's quieter.'

The bracken had lost the freshness of early summer and was

dull green, with here and there a brown frond or a yellow one, brilliant in the sunlight. Later, as they waded through it along a deer track, she said, 'It often used to happen round about here . . . no particular landmark, anywhere on the open hill-side . . . '

But nothing happened. They wound their way almost back to Old John, and Helen knew they were still on Earth. Even without looking for the nearest sign of civilisation, she knew. She felt embarrassed, impatient, relieved. Cadreis said little, but he had a resigned look as if he had known he would never go home.

'I'm sorry,' she said unnecessarily. 'We've been trying at least two hours. I'm worn out. We might as well sit down for a while.'

'Over there,' he said, pointing across a marshy stretch of grass to a crag of rocks leaning out of the ground near a spinney.

'OK. That's the Sliding Stone Crag. All the times I've been in the Park, and I've never really looked at it close to.'

The grass was russet, hazed with purple, as soft as the sheen on a cat's fur. The ground squelched in places. Halfway across, they passed a perfectly round pond and glanced at their reflections in the green water.

There was a cluster of silver birches beside the crag, dark conifers behind. The crag towered over them, mottled with lichen and striped with bands of rust-brown rock. A couple of large boulders lay at its base and they seated themselves on the largest, arms round each other. Helen felt the chill of the rock through her jeans, but the sun was warm and she thought: *This would be so idyllic, if this was a normal day and Cadreis was just someone I'd met.* She wondered if it was worth staying any longer, or if they were wasting their time. A wire litter basket standing a couple of feet away showed her only too prosaically that they were still on Earth.

'We could try Swithland Woods,' she said half-heartedly. 'Or Beacon Hill. Martin and I went through from the Woods, you see, but when we headed towards what we thought was the Beacon, we found the sea there instead.'

'Halaranthe?'

'Yes. I told you about it, and you got upset.'

Cadreis sighed, half smiling. 'I didn't want to hear anything about the world the Chalcenians lived in, but now . . . I would like to see it.'

'Not much chance of that, at this rate.'

'Don't worry. It will be all right, I'm sure.' He put his arm round her and she snuggled against him. Their fruitless wanderings might have put someone less patient in a temper, but Cadreis was calm, if subdued. After years of coping with Nick's moods, she was more grateful than Cadreis could know. 'I'm glad you're with me, Helen.'

'So am I,' she said. 'It's nice sitting here with you.'

On their right, there was an ancient oak tree growing out of a joint in the rock. It was as lumpy and bent as a witch, thickly crowned with leaves except for one branch clawing naked at the air like a lightning whip. Its growth was forcing the crag apart. The trunk was like a torso, one leg stretched elegantly down into the fissure, the other leg severed and the stump of the hip propped awkwardly on the rock.

Helen had a sudden sense of déjà-vu, not so much that she had seen it before in real life – although she knew she had – but that she had seen it in a dream and it had looked different, with a dark cave under the roots. As she studied it, a man appeared around the end of the crag, followed by a couple of teenagers, several spaniels and a middle-aged woman. Helen sighed. Selfish it might be, but she had always liked to have the Park to herself.

The man and the youths walked on, but the woman sat down on the rock next to Helen, uttering a long, wheezing breath.

'Mind if I tek the weight off me feet?' she said in a broad Leicester accent. 'I'm that bloodeh tire-ud.'

As it happened, Helen did mind very much, but she was too well mannered to say so. 'Of course not.' She refrained from asking the woman what she expected, walking over rough ground in high heels.

Cadreis looked at the newcomer in surprise as she kicked off her shoes and flexed swollen feet.

She paused and stared back at him. 'Gorra fag, me duck?'

'No – sorry, no, we don't smoke,' Helen said hastily.

'Ooh, I'm gaspin'. Never mind.' She drew another gusty

breath, her white nylon blouse straining over her breasts. Her hair was bleached blonde. Gold jewelery dangled from her wrists, throat and ears. She wore an expensive leather skirt, at least one size too small, held round her thick waist by a studded belt which seemed to be partly responsible for her breathlessness.

Helen was wondering how they could discreetly move on without it looking too obvious, when the woman looked at her and said, 'You've bin 'ere before, ain't yuh? I seen yuh.'

'Have you?' Helen said, startled.

'Yeah. I see everybodeh 'oo guz through 'ere. Well, I should do, but sometimes I miss 'em, you know, I can't be bothered. Must be gettin' ow-uld.'

The last thing Helen felt like coping with was a mildly unbalanced stranger. She glanced frantically at Cadreis, but he obviously could not understand what the woman was saying and seemed bemused. 'Er – yes,' she muttered.

'Oh, you think I look ow-uld, do yuh?' the woman said indignantly.

'Well, no, I mean – '

'Yuh dun't know what yer on about. Yuh think yuh know everythin', but yuh dun't even remember meh.'

Helen suddenly had the unsettling feeling that this was someone she should know, but she racked her brains without success. 'I'm sorry, I really don't remember – '

'It's me own fault, I s'pose.' She tapped her head with nicotine-stained fingers and laughed as if at a private joke. 'Used to live in Leicester.' She pronounced it Lest-uh. 'Had to leave, though.'

'Why was that?'

'They built a bloodeh loada houses all over where I lived. So I come out 'ere.'

'Where – where do you live, then?'

The woman pointed around her. Her bracelets jangled. 'I told yuh! 'Ere!'

'In the Park?'

'Gorra good place to live. Scratched it out wi' me own nails, I did.' Her shoulders shook with laughter. 'Buggers yer varnish up.'

Helen was now convinced that she was deranged, but had

an equally strong feeling that if she tried to end the conversation, the woman might turn nasty.

'I don't look ow-uld, do ah?' she went on. 'Me last 'usband died.'

'Oh – I'm sorry.'

'Well, they all die, dun't they? I want anuther one, though. No chance at my age, they say. What do they know? I'm still attractive, arn' I? I dress well, keep me 'air nice. Smoke a bit, but 'oo dun't? I bin married seven times, but I got to 'ave anuther.'

'Blimey,' said Helen. 'Seven?'

'Yeah. Some seem to think that's me lot. Bugger that! Carn 'elp gettin' loneleh. I seen more life than they ever will. I seen it all. So they mek promises they can't keep, then tell me I dun't do me job properleh. But I'm tire-ud. A woman needs a man to keep 'er young, dun't sheh?'

She leaned over to Helen, who tried not to draw back. Yellow fingernails, camouflaged with chipped pink polish, closed round her arm. 'You're a pretteh girl. You 'ang on to 'im, or 'e'll be gone before you know it!'

She chuckled. Her breath had no smell, and it was cold.

'Yes – I – I'll remember that.'

'Ha! You remember bugger all else! I'd swap wi' yuh, though. Yuh dun't know 'ow luckeh you are.' Helen tried to edge away, hating the way she was leering at Cadreis. 'You dun't get called things.'

'How do you mean?'

The woman released her, and Helen rubbed at the line of bruises left on her arm. 'I get called some right things. Hag. Or black hag. I ask yuh, do I look black to yuh? This is me natural colour.' She bent her head, but Helen saw dark roots in the yellow frizz. 'Black hag, my arse.'

'Er, we really had better be going,' Helen said nervously.

'No, dun't goo, me duck. I'm enjoying our little talk.'

'So am I but, er, we really have to – '

She started to stand up, but the woman's hand snaked out and caught her. 'That's yer thanks, is it?'

Cadreis said, 'Helen, what is she saying?'

'No – please – '

'I bin good to you, girl, an' yuh dun't even know it. I

usualleh ask a price, even the little red-haired girl, *an'* she paid it. But you bin' wanderin' in an' out and I ain't said nowt. Couldn't be bothered, yuh see. Sometimes I do what they say and sometimes I couldn't give a toss.'

'Do what who say?' Helen wished Cadreis would help her instead of just staring.

'Names dun't mean nothin' to me. Men – somethin', one of 'em were called. Menenthonis.'

The word hung in the air like winter. Suddenly Helen was shivering, and all around her the bracken was turning red, shrivelling, and the leaves were streaming off the trees.

'It's up to me whether yuh goo or not, gel. Shall I let yuh goo? Yuh didn't want to last time. "Gerraway from meh!" was all you could say. Changed yer mind?'

'You – the doll,' Helen gasped. 'Annis.'

'Oh, know me now, do yuh? Did what they said, but they ain't paid meh for it.'

'You knew I wasn't Rianna.'

Annis's red lips split in a smile. 'Course I did, me duck. It were their mistake, though, an' they still ain't paid. Someone's gooin' to. You, yer cow. *You.*'

Her breath was ice; it frosted the air, blackened the branches of the ancient oak. Helen cried out and struggled, saw Cadreis through a white fog trying to pull Annis off her. The woman shrugged him off, flinging him backwards on to the frozen rocks.

'No! Let me go!'

'All right, I'll let yer goo – as long as I get to keep *'im.*'

Helen drew breath to scream, but the air was so cold it seared her lungs. Choking, she fell. The grass blades shattered like glass under her, cold stones burned her skin. The woman was gone; in her place, a dark creature reared over Helen, a creature with a sea-horse head and panther limbs. She saw the leathery udders swinging between its forelegs as it came plunging down, one clawed foot on either side of her shoulders.

She rolled on to her stomach, trying to escape. As she did so the cruel head whipped down like a cobra's and she felt the teeth meeting through the back of her jacket, sinking into the skin. Annis's breath flowed around her like liquid nitrogen.

Helen was lifted clean off the grass and flung away, but she never landed; the cold and the pain carried her away from Cadreis, from everything, out into white oblivion.

A long time later . . .

Hot light speared her eyelids. A hissing sound filled her ears, like trees moving in the wind.

A yielding surface of fronds cradled her, damp against her hands. Her back felt like one huge bruise, centred around a gash of throbbing, itching pain, but . . .

She was alive.

Helen flung up a hand to her forehead, instinctively shielding her eyes before opening them. The sun was blazing down on her. White cumuli moved across the heavens, edged with brightness. Birds flew in silhouette against them like tiny cupid's bows.

With difficulty she leaned up on one elbow and gazed through the bracken. She could see the Sliding Stone Crag and the mocking oak tree, just as they had been . . . minutes or a lifetime ago. The day was warm, the bracken green and the leaves still on the trees. Annis's winter had gone, but Cadreis had vanished with it.

She groaned. She tried to sit up, but the pain made the blood rush out of her head and she fell back, sick and faint.

'What are you doing here?' said an astonished voice.

'Mum . . . ' Helen murmured, half dreaming.

The voice spoke again, louder this time. 'You are Helen, aren't you? What has happened to you?'

She opened her eyes. There was a pale female face leaning over her, surrounded by a cloud of sunlit red hair.

'Rianna?'

A hand helped her to sit up. The burning wound in her back brought tears to her eyes, and she yelped involuntarily.

'Are you in pain? Forgive me. But what are you doing here?'

'Don't know,' Helen slurred. 'Rianna, thank God you're here. Where's Cadreis, she's taken him . . . Cadreis!' She tried to shout, but lacked the strength to raise her voice.

The peculiar silence told her that something was not quite right. She made an effort to focus, and saw that the woman kneeling by her was not Rianna. Yet she was familiar. The hair was wilder and more brilliant than Rianna's, and Helen knew that beautiful, slightly pinched and moody face.

'I thought you were . . . '

'My name is Corolea,' said the woman. 'Don't you know me?'

Corolea was one of the Chalcenians she and Martin had met by the sea, the one who had been cruelly teased by Sheyde. Even now, every moment of that strange afternoon came back clearly. 'I remember.'

'Can you stand?' said Corolea.

'I'll try. Annis bit me on my back.' Corolea's eyebrows raised slightly, as if she thought Helen was feverish. 'Christ, it hurts.' With the Chalcenian woman's help, she stood up, leaning dizzily on her.

'Annis? If you are not Gallah, I cannot understand how you came here. But we will help you, anyway.'

'Thank you. But my friends are here, I've got to find them. Where's Cadreis?' Corolea did not reply. Helen tried rephrasing the question. 'There was a young man with me, with long dark hair. He was wearing a grey jacket. He was on those rocks, he might be injured. Have you seen him?'

'No, Helen. There is only you.'

'Oh God. She really has taken him, then,' said Helen.

'Who has taken him?'

'Black Annis.'

Corolea chewed at her lower lip and took a moment to reply. 'I do not know what you mean.'

'She's – she's supposed to be the guardian of the boundary between your world and mine. That's what I was told by the – ' Helen broke off, partly with the pain of moving, partly with a feeling that she must not mention the Domendrans.

Corolea looked perturbed. 'I was riding at the back of the group when I saw you lying in the bracken. I saw nothing else. The others went on and left me behind, but we will catch them up, if you are able to ride.'

As they picked their way to the edge of the bracken, Helen's head cleared and she began to take more notice of her surroundings. If she had doubted it before, she now knew for certain that she was in Tevera. The contours of the ancient rolling hills were the same, but there was something wilder and richer about them. Bracken flowed into unbounded woodland, rocks stood proud and harsh under the sun. The sky was brushed with amethyst, and white daystars pricked the blueness.

A few yards away, a beast the size of a Shire horse stood waiting. At first sight, all she could think of was Annis in beast-shape, and her heart pounded. It had the same long head and curving neck, horse-like body and feline limbs. Its coat was almost as dark, but as it moved she saw that it had flame-coloured shading under its belly and a red and silver mane.

The first time she had been drawn into Tevera on her own, she had almost been run down by a group of such animals. She remembered their brilliance, the sparkling arrogance of their riders.

'Don't be afraid of him,' said Corolea. 'His name is Feial.'

'What are these creatures? We don't have anything like them where I come from. They're a lot different to horses.'

'They are shaliors.' The beast extended its nose towards Corolea as she approached, as friendly as the supernatural one had been vicious. 'You will have to sit in front of me.'

Helen reached out a hand to Feial and caressed his nose, just as she would have done with Destiny and Fikri. His skin was unbelievably delicate, finer than the softest deer velvet, and through it she could feel the sharp bones of his skull. The nostrils snuffled on her palm, prehensile. The eye that regarded her was unhorselike, huge and shining as a bubble of liquid black glass.

'I don't know whether I can climb up there,' Helen said. 'I'll try, but it's agony when I move.'

'It will be easy.' Corolea pulled at the delicate bitless bridle, saying, 'Come down, Feial, come down.'

And the shalior folded to the ground like a camel and sat patiently, waiting for them to mount. On his back there was a saddle with stirrups, made of some kind of stiffened material, sculpted and embellished with ornaments.

'He seems very docile,' Helen said, surprised.

'Feial is quiet today because he is tired, but he is never very difficult. Some shaliors are as mad as their riders.' Corolea said this with a straight face, and Helen did not know whether she was joking or not. She found the stirrup with her foot and, with Corolea's help, boosted herself on to the creature's back.

The effort tore at her wound and for few seconds she hung over the front of the saddle, swearing. Corolea jumped lightly on behind her.

'Are you well, Helen?' she asked.

'I'll be all right.' Helen straightened up with difficulty, then bit back a grunt of pain as Feial rose to his feet.

Corolea was wearing loose trousers of some red material like velvet or suede, and over that a shirt and a long tunic sewn with glittering red beads. Close to her, feeling the warmth of her body, enveloped by the spicy wood-scent that seemed part of the Chalcenians, Helen felt as dowdy as a tramp. A maggot next to a butterfly, she thought. The pain and the strange beauty of her situation flowed together, took her into another level of awareness that was a dream edged with nightmare.

The shalior bounded forward with breathtaking speed, swifter than any horse. He ran low to the ground like a cheetah, springing off powerful quarters in a rising and falling motion that would have been difficult to sit, had it not been so perfectly fluid. Helen's eyelids were drooping, but unless she kept them open she almost felt seasick.

When she had recovered enough breath to speak, she asked, 'Where are we going?'

'To the Heart of Life. Our city.'

'Isn't that where you were going to take us when we came through before?'

'Yes. It is not far.'

'Corolea, do you know someone called Rianna? She's a friend of mine, but she's Chalcenian. She looks a bit like you, but smaller, with darker hair. I think she's come to Tevera and I need to find her.'

'Yes, I have seen Rianna,' said Corolea. 'And your friend Martin. They are at the Heart of Life. They came there looking for you.'

The wave of relief that Helen felt at these words almost made her pass out. 'How long have they been there?'

'A few days,' Corolea said vaguely.

'Did you speak to them?'

'No. I left soon after they arrived.'

'Where have you been?'

She felt Corolea's warm breath move past her ear in a sigh. 'Fishing. Looking at the hills. Finding – ' she said something that sounded like *kir* – 'and trying to remember how pleasure felt.'

The stark desolation in Corolea's voice stunned Helen. There was a warning note in it as well: *Ask me no more.* Helen fell silent, and asked soundless questions of the landscape instead.

For a while, she was able to follow the geography of the land and relate it to that of Charnwood. She saw a dense wood like Swithland, a hill that might have led down into a nearby village, and the peak of Beacon Hill . . . But she soon lost her bearings, and it was all bracken and heath, oak and hawthorn, crags standing stark and wild against the sky. It felt like the Charnwood she knew, but it was different. It was no longer contained in a small area by roads and towns, nor sundered by the M1. It flowed out to the edges of the world. Now and again the faint, incongruous scent of the sea came to her. Perhaps, once she was beyond the area that coincided with Bradgate Park, she would no longer be able simply to 'walk' back to Earth.

She half drowsed, then came awake suddenly to find a group of Chalcenians ahead of them, mounted on shaliors.

Corolea eased Feial back to a gentle lope and caught up with the rearmost shalior, a creature bright as a kingfisher, dappled with royal blue. The rider turned to greet Corolea with a mixture of pleasure and surprise.

Helen did not recognise him. His hair was a mass of startling green curls. His face was thin and ethereal, the skin so translucent that the veins shone through.

'Corolea!' he said. 'We thought you'd deserted us. What's happened, who's this with you?'

'I found her, Nenhaliac,' said Corolea. 'She was lying in the bracken, so I stopped to help her.'

Nenhaliac looked intently at Helen. His eyes were dark blue, edged with kohl, and the whites showed slightly around the irises.

'Is she a Gallah?' he asked.

'I don't know what she is,' said Corolea. 'I have met her before, on the shores of Halaranthe. Ananthis, Tasnian and Sheyde were with me. She claimed to be from another world.'

The other riders in the group were turning to look at her now. There was no one she recognised; only a mass of painted faces and bright hair, alarming in their exuberance. Suddenly they all seemed to be talking at once, asking questions that did not seem to require any reply.

'Is such a thing possible?' said a tall woman with hair as gold as a sovereign.

'Of course not.' A crimson-haired man pulled his shalior round and rode close to Feial, reaching for Helen's hand. 'She must be a Gallah, third-born!'

Helen drew away, and Feial shied at the same moment, barging into the blue-dappled creature on the other side. For a few seconds, Corolea and Nenhaliac fought for control, while a couple of other shaliors in the group gave bugling calls and tried to bolt. Gritting her teeth against the pain, Helen felt dazzled and hemmed in.

'Give her room!' Nenhaliac shouted. The other Chalcenians laughed at him and cat-called, but did as he said. 'She seems hurt. Corolea, why didn't you call us to help you?'

Corolea shrugged. 'By the time I had dismounted, you had vanished over the horizon.'

'I shall heal her. In the Heart of Life there is no pain,' he said.

Around her the Chalcenians went on talking and laughing, but Helen was too dazed to take much notice of them. Her back felt clammy – with sweat or blood, she could not tell. She wanted the ride to be over before she fainted.

'We are nearly there,' Corolea said some time later, bringing her back to full consciousness. 'Look, Helen. The Heart of Life.'

What stood before them was not a city but the weirdest forest Helen had ever seen. They had halted on a slope sprinkled with birches and bracken. In front of them a hill rose up, dotted with clumps of granite and ancient oaks which were dwarfed by the strange trees that stood between them. If they could be called trees; their basic shape was the same, with trunk and branches, but that was the only resemblance.

Helen studied the nearest. It was leafless, and looked as if it had been created by insane wasps who had built dozens of giant nests one on another. The bole was thick and tall, the surface all irregular half-ovoids. The thick branches that splayed out from it also seemed to be constructed from huge nests or seed pods growing out of each other in clusters and rows. No two were quite the same colour; some were a sandy yellow, fresh as buds, some a ripe gold, while others had faded to beige. Like a vast organic sculpture it reared up into the sky, so strange to her eyes that it was beyond being called ugly or beautiful.

Beyond it were many others, no two the same size. Their branches were interwoven, the lines of pods forming bridges that connected each 'tree' to its neighbours. The structures were static, but between them the oak leaves flickered in the breeze, making light and shadow dance across them and turning the whole forest to a glittering, three-dimensional mosaic.

'Is this your city?' Helen said doubtfully.

'Of course,' Corolea replied. 'Welcome to the Heart of Life.'

A crowd of Chalcenians were running out to meet them. Suddenly they were all round Helen, like a sea. Their hair and garments dazzled her, a cloud of silver, red, violet and green . . . All colours were there. Her head swam with brilliance. She was sliding sideways out of the saddle, unable to stop herself, but there were hands ready to receive her, voices and smiling faces filling her head.

A familiar face, all upturned crescents. Lips and cheeks and eyes curved in a perpetual smile, a shower of bright blue hair hanging untidily over the shoulders of an embroidered tunic.

'Tasnian,' Helen gasped. His arms were round her, lowering her gently to the ground.

'Helen, is it you? What has happened to you?' he exclaimed. 'Sheyde, Sheyde, here is Helen come back to us!'

A moment later, another welcome face leaned over her. The woman's heavy brows and red lips, her exquisite pale features, had remained more strongly in Helen's memory than the others. Her irises were dark and warm as pansies.

'It is Helen!' Sheyde exclaimed.

'She is a Gallah,' said someone. 'Let us celebrate!'

'No, she is not third-born. Helen, we thought you had returned to your own world. How have you come back to us?' Helen tried to answer, but it was too much of an effort to speak. Sheyde's voice seemed to float from the far end of a long grey tunnel. 'You remember us, don't you? Hush, you are safe now.'

The physical pain was bearable, now that Helen was not alone. She felt that she was among friends. They would take her to Rianna and help her find Cadreis, she knew.

Hanging on to consciousness, she managed to croak, 'Rianna – I must see Rianna and Martin, please tell them I'm here . . . '

Then the greyness took her. The last thing she heard clearly was Tasnian saying, 'Does Ananthis know?' After that, a muddle of voices and movement was all that penetrated her swoon.

When she began to come round again she was lying face down on what seemed to be a spongy blanket. There was a fragrant smell of wood and flowers and spices all mixed up together, and a soft yellow light that seemed to filter from everywhere at once. She felt warm. Then someone touched her back and she yelped with pain.

'I am sorry, Helen, but I have to bathe and cover the wound and it will hurt until I have finished.' It was Nenhaliac's voice. 'What happened to you? The skin is all bruised and torn.'

'Something bit me,' Helen wheezed.

'I am putting a crushed root on it that will help the pain,' he said. 'Then honey to heal it. If you can raise yourself up on your elbows, I will give you a drink.'

'Oh, yes please.' She tried to smile, but it turned into a grimace. The emerald-haired man held a cup to her lips, and she recognised the taste of the drink Ananthis had given them in the boat. He had called it 'wine from the Heart of Life'. Undiluted, its fire made her gag.

'It will make you feel better,' Nenhaliac said apologetically. His face was bloodless and delicate as the victim of a vampire, and the white showing around his eyes gave him a perpetual look of surprise or alarm.

She held her breath and clenched her teeth until her eyes

watered while he tended the wound. As he worked, she felt the warmth of the drink seeping through her, distancing her from the pain.

Nenhaliac talked non-stop. 'They say Gallahs can remember nothing of what went before. Can you remember?'

'I'm not – '

'I wonder how it feels to be third-born? Some must remember Tevera, for they become part of our lives so easily, but others cannot be reached. They are only happy living wild in the forests. They say that for a very long time there were no Gallahs at all, but now they are coming back. Only a few, but they are coming back. It frightens me, but it is exciting as well. It means something, I'm not sure what, but it means something . . . '

Helen could not really follow what he was saying, but when she attempted to say anything he disregarded her comments as if he was alone and talking to himself. When the wound was dressed he eased her on to her side and asked if she were comfortable. By then she had formed the impression that he was slightly deranged.

'Yes, I'll be fine,' she said weakly. She was still not sure where she was and did not trust her perceptions. The room – if it could be called that – in which she lay was roughly egg-shaped, about fourteen feet across, with light filtering evenly through papery walls.

'I will leave you to sleep, then,' he said. As he made to stand up, Helen reached up and touched his arm. 'I need to see Rianna and Martin, please could someone send them to me?'

His smile did not change as he answered by reflex, 'There is no Rianna here.'

Helen thought she had misheard. 'Yes, there is. Corolea told me she was here.'

'Corolea must have been mistaken.'

'No,' Helen said desperately. 'She saw them. Nenhaliac, Rianna's here.'

'There is no one of that name here.'

Helen found it hard to get her breath. 'Fetch Corolea. Please. Ask Tasnian and Sheyde.'

The healer gently placed her hand back on the covers and stood up. 'Very well, I'll send them to you, Helen,' he said, moving away. 'But they will only say the same thing.'

Helen lay with her eyes closed. The room seemed to sway under her, though that might have been the effect of the liquor. She had almost drifted off to sleep when a sound made her open her eyes.

She raised her head with difficulty. The entrance at one end of the oval room was no more than a round hole, about three feet in diameter. Tasnian was crawling through it, followed by Sheyde and Corolea. She half expected to see Ananthis, the arrogant Chalcenian with white-blond hair, but there was no one else with them.

Sheyde and Tasnian knelt at her side, greeting her warmly, stroking her hands and her hair. Corolea hung back, standing with her hands clasped in front of her.

Helen tried to sit up and smile.

'Don't tire yourself,' Sheyde said kindly. 'How are you now?'

'A bit better. It's kind of you to look after me like this.'

'Joy is to be cherished,' said Sheyde. Helen did not like to ask what she meant.

Tasnian said, 'We waited such a long time for you, that day we met you by the sea. We came to look for you, but you had vanished.'

'It's a bit hard to explain,' said Helen. 'We went back into our own world. We couldn't help it, it just happened. But didn't Martin tell you?'

'Yes, he did,' said Tasnian. As he spoke, Sheyde touched his arm and he turned his head to gaze at her. Helen could not interpret the long, strange look that passed between them, but she had the feeling that Tasnian had said something he shouldn't.

'Martin is here, then!' she exclaimed, then flopped back, dizzy.

'No, Helen,' said Sheyde. Helen waited for her to go on, but she was silent.

'What's going on?' Helen said. 'First Corolea tells me they're here, then Nenhaliac denies all knowledge. Either they've been here or they haven't, so where are they?'

Her eyes still fixed on Tasnian's, Sheyde said, 'There were a Martin and a Rianna here, but now they are gone.'

'Gone? Where?'

Sheyde looked at her with a smile that was a touch too bright. 'I'm sorry that you've been injured, but you will feel well again in no time at all.'

Helen blinked, then said, 'Why are you changing the subject? I must know where they are, it's really important . . .' There was a tense undercurrent, something they did not want to talk about. 'Why did they leave?' she persisted. 'Did they go looking for me, is that it?'

Sheyde and Tasnian were like paintings or statues. Their faces were radiant and sublime, but if she entreated them for ever they would never answer her. Helen began to feel sick.

'Just a minute,' she said, 'has something happened to them? Please, you must tell me, whatever it is.'

She thought Tasnian looked slightly uncomfortable, as though she had committed some terrible breach of etiquette, and all the Chalcenians could do was to ignore it. 'Helen, there's nothing to be distressed about,' he said.

'So where are they? My God, they're not dead, are they? For Christ's sake say something! Corolea!' Helen looked pleadingly at the scarlet-haired woman. Hers was the only face that showed any appropriate emotion, a kind of grim frustration.

Corolea said, 'Tell her, Sheyde.'

Sheyde only smiled and stroked Helen's hair. 'Could you eat something, Helen?'

'No, I couldn't! Tell me what? What's happened?'

'Nothing has happened,' Tasnian replied in a voice that could have soothed her to sleep, had she not been so agitated.

Corolea took a step forward and said, 'She doesn't understand, Sheyde. How could she? If you won't tell her, I will.' Sheyde ignored her, but Helen saw anger flash into her eyes. Corolea went on, 'Rianna has gone because she was not Chalcenic.'

'But she was – she is!'

'No, she is not,' Corolea replied. 'She was allowed to stay a little while, but those who are not Chalcenic cannot stay here, can they, Sheyde?'

'Corolea – ' Sheyde said softly.

'I am only explaining our ways to Helen. Rianna was not a

Chalcenian, so she had to leave. She knew this. She went willingly, and Martin went with her.'

'But where are they?'

Tasnian said, 'They no longer exist. Don't think of them, Helen.'

Helen stared at Corolea. 'What does he mean? Please tell me what's happened to them. They're not dead, they can't be.'

They were all silent, a dreadful tableau. Then Corolea said, 'As you mean it, Helen, they are alive – as far as I know.'

Helen's heart flipped over with relief. 'Where are they, then? You must have some idea. Rianna's in danger, I've got to find her to let her know. She's being hunted by the Domendrans.'

As she pronounced the name, the atmosphere tensed as though unheard music had been switched off. The quietness rang in her ears. Corolea's lips thinned, but Sheyde and Tasnian were looking everywhere except at Helen.

'What have I said?'

'Nothing,' said Sheyde. 'It is impossible to speak of something that does not exist.'

'They do exist!' Helen cried. 'Please listen, let me explain this properly. The Domendrans captured me thinking I was Rianna. I got away, but she came looking for me. They're still chasing her. And you just threw her out to look after herself?'

Tasnian and Sheyde were still smiling, but Tasnian seemed uncomfortable and there was ice in Sheyde's eyes. They rose to their feet, and Sheyde said, 'We will leave you to rest now, Helen. Nenhaliac will come to look after you.'

'I haven't finished talking to you! Why are you pretending the Domendrans don't exist?'

'Yes, why, Sheyde?' Corolea said sharply. 'We are in private. We can say what we like. Domendri, Domendri, Domendri!'

The more venomous Corolea sounded, the more Sheyde and Tasnian distanced themselves from her, as if they could not see or even hear her. They moved to the entrance, coolly poised.

Corolea called after them, 'I'm going to tell her the truth!'

Sheyde looked round, her eyes narrow. 'The only truth is

that of Chalceny. You lost sight of it long ago, and with it your dignity and everything else. I do not see you, Corolea. I see a shadow that refuses to fade with the sun.'

'Sheyde, leave her,' Tasnian said softly. They turned away, bent to crawl through the entrance, and were gone.

Corolea knelt down stiffly at Helen's side. 'I don't care what they say,' she said fiercely. 'Sheyde has no right. When it is time I will know, but it is not time.'

Helen touched her arm cautiously. 'You were going to tell me about Rianna.'

Corolea was frowning. She did not look directly at Helen. 'Rianna became upset about something. She was weeping and she was . . . depressed. I do not think she wanted to leave, but she knew she had to. Sheyde and the others would not have let her stay.'

Helen lurched upright, ignoring the pain that tore across her back. 'Am I hearing this right? They threw Rianna out because she was *unhappy*?'

'Just so,' said Corolea, bitterly mimicking Sheyde's tone. 'Joy is to be cherished. Misery is to be rejected. It has no place here; it is the weapon of those who despise us, and those who are miserable are better to find a place elsewhere.'

Chapter Thirteen

There was nothing Helen could do.

Her only thought was to get up at once and find someone, anyone to help her find Rianna and Cadreis. But her body would not obey. Whether it was shock or whether Annis had poisoned her, she did not know, but she had begun to shiver with fever and any attempt to move made her faint with pain.

Eventually, through the haze of illness, she accepted that she had no hope of finding her friends until she was well again. Even then she could not be sure that any of the Chalcenians would help her. They had showed her nothing but kindness so far, but after their exchange about Rianna she felt she could not trust any of them. Not even Sheyde, who seemed so warm and so concerned; not even Tasnian.

After Corolea left her, Helen lay feeling wretchedly ill and wondering how long it would take her to recover. If she did not become wildly cheerful the moment she felt better, would they throw her out as they had Rianna?

The hours passed slowly, but she knew night was falling when the light shining through the translucent walls began to fade. She tried to sleep, but a growing discomfort prevented her.

'Oh God,' she murmured. 'Why on earth didn't I think to ask where the loo was before they all left? Why didn't they tell me?'

It was strange how swiftly priorities could change. Thoughts of Cadreis and Rianna now came second to physical desperation.

Shuddering, almost crying with the pain, Helen crawled from the 'bed' – which was no more than a cover on the soft, spongy floor – and made her way slowly to the entrance. Peering through it, she saw only another egg-shaped room the same as the one she was in. It had a deserted feel, and the walls were dry and papery. She had no strength to go any further. Her head spun and she slid down to the floor, utterly miserable.

A few moments later, Corolea's head appeared through the round entrance hole. She looked at Helen in surprise.

'Why are you out of bed?'

Helen was not quite beyond being embarrassed. If she had discovered that the Chalcenians were made of crystal and had no digestive systems, she would not have been surprised. But Corolea's reaction was human.

'Oh, Helen, you must forgive us. We forgot that you would not know. You may relieve yourself anywhere.'

'What?' Helen was horrified.

'But if you do not care to do so in your own kir, go into the next one.'

'On the floor, you mean?'

'Yes, anywhere. It doesn't matter in this branch; we brought you here because it is quiet and you won't be disturbed. Where there are more people, we have separate kirs for relieving ourselves, of course.' She could see that Helen still did not understand. She stroked the fibrous wall and said, 'You have never been in a kateya before, have you? It is not a dead place, like – like other cities. The kirs are alive.'

'Like a plant, you mean?' Helen was not sure whether this conversation was really taking place, or whether she would suddenly wake up.

'Yes,' said Corolea. 'Anything moist that falls on to the surface is absorbed. Indeed, without moisture the kir will shrivel into a husk and die. When we excrete, we replenish the kirs that house us.'

'Oh my God,' said Helen. 'Like watering the flowers.'

'In a way. But we live inside the seed. What we take, we give back.'

Corolea helped Helen into the next kir and left her there – with slightly more deference to her need for privacy than the Domendrans had shown – while she relieved herself, thinking that this was far worse than having to leap behind a hedge in a traffic jam. The urine vanished into the floor as if into a sponge.

When Helen was in bed again she asked, 'Why did you

come back, Corolea?'

'Someone should be with you while you are ill. Nenhaliac should have stayed. He is a good healer, but he is inconsiderate.'

'I expect he has other people to look after.'

'A few. We are not often unwell,' said Corolea. 'I came back because I wanted to look at you. To think.'

Corolea seemed different to the other Chalcenians only in that she was moodier, more introspective. Her conflict with Sheyde was something under the surface, something Helen did not yet understand.

'To think about what?' Helen asked.

Corolea's shoulders rose slightly, as if she were cold. 'Our ways must seem cruel to you. Yet they are not. I will know – I would know when to leave. Rianna knew. And your friend Cadreis would also understand that he is not ours to rescue.'

'Why? I know the Domendrans are your enemies and the others don't like mentioning them, but that isn't his fault. He's still a human being. He was sweet and kind to me and I'm so scared for him – '

She stopped before her voice broke. Corolea was frowning. 'I know what you feel, Helen. Sheyde and the others do not mean to be cruel, they truly care about you, but they know no other way. They were afraid that Rianna might be . . . Why don't I say it? Domendric. We – we do not acknowledge them, and they do not acknowledge us. I used to accept it, but it has begun to seem a ridiculous thing, because underneath we all know they are there . . . '

'Corolea, please will you help me find my friends?'

The veiled look that Helen had seen so often in Rianna's face now rolled down like mist over Corolea's. 'I cannot,' she said. 'I am a Chalcenian. I cannot.'

Helen knew that arguing was hopeless, and would have taken more energy than she possessed. She said nothing, and after a few moments Corolea went on, 'You should not be here, Helen.'

'What – what do you mean?'

'You spoke of Black Annis as if you had seen her.'

'I did see her, she almost killed me!'

'But she is a spirit, an unknown being. We know she is there but we never speak of her.'

'Why not?' Helen asked.

Corolea's voice was low, her face troubled. 'Because we only see her when we die. She guards the gate to the underworld. You claim you are not a Gallah, but how do you know? If she let you through alive, something is very wrong.'

Helen did not understand, but the fear in Corolea's tone brushed her skin like an ice feather. 'Are the Gallahs ghosts, or something? I told you, I'm from a world like Tevera. Earth.'

'I wish I had the wisdom to understand this. The higher things never mattered to me before, but now they begin to matter I find I know nothing. The Chalcenians are so stupid, they never think about anything until it's too late, and now it has been too late for thousands of years.'

'Too late for what?'

'For the Gallahs. For life. I don't know! All I know is that you and the others should not be here. Ananthis tells us we should celebrate the Gallahs, but their appearance only makes me feel desolate. There are so few. Why should I care about it? The Domendrans are right, there is no point in anything. We are going nowhere!'

She opened her eyes wide, and their wild, unfocused glitter alarmed Helen. 'What's wrong, Corolea? Please tell me . . . '

'Look at this, Helen.' Corolea held out the edge of her tunic. The last of the diffuse light, now dark as toffee, gleamed on the red beads and edged her hair with flame. 'The colour of the hands, red, red for creativity. My colour.'

'Did you – did you make the tunic?' Helen asked lamely.

'Yes – oh, yes, I made it! I make clothes and saddles and figures out of wood and clay, but what is the use of it? Why is my hair still red when my heart is dark?' Suddenly she began to tear at the edge of the tunic with her fists. Her teeth were bared.

'Corolea!' Helen exclaimed. The Chalcenian woman's frantic movements subsided. She struck weakly at her knees, then pushed back her hair and met Helen's eyes. The hem of the garment was shredded.

'It's nothing, Helen,' she said woodenly. 'I did not mean to upset you. I will know when to leave . . . but not yet. Whatever Sheyde says, it is not time yet . . . Look, I smile and I am happy!'

Helen felt out of her depth. What could she possibly say to Corolea, when she could not begin to understand what was distressing her? The darkness was almost total now. Outside, she could hear the wind blowing through the trees, and smell the clean leafy scent of the forest.

One moment Corolea was there; the next – and Helen did not know whether she had dozed off or merely blinked – she was gone, as softly as a breath.

The night was a patchwork of sleeplessness and feverish dreams. Helen was glad when dawn glimmered through the walls and Nenhaliac came to her, saying, 'Wake up, Helen. I must re-dress your wound.'

Although his presence cheered her up, she sensed in his cheerfulness a touch of mania. He said a lot, yet was hard to talk to; there was no true communication between them. When he had finished tending to her injury, he brought her some water and a bowl containing a sour, creamy drink like yogurt. Its taste was pleasant, but she had very little appetite. To stall for time, she asked what it was.

'It is the milk of the kir,' said the healer. She looked questioningly at him, and he went on, 'Our excretions feed the kir. In return, they give back this juice. This kir is old and dry, but even the sweat of your body has created a little moisture . . . ' He ran a hand down the wall that curved up beside the bed, and a few droplets of white liquid oozed over his fingers.

Helen stumbled out of her bed, through the entrance into the next chamber, and was sick, narrowly missing Tasnian's feet.

The blue-haired Chalcenian man looked at her in surprise, verging on laughter. 'This is no way to greet a friend,' he said.

'I'm sorry,' said Helen, gulping air to subdue her stomach. The vomit had disappeared into the floor of the kir, leaving only a slight stain. 'Nenhaliac just told me what – what I was eating.'

Tasnian took her arm and helped her back into her kir. 'Why has that upset you?'

Nenhaliac, looking displeased, was pouring out a drop of

the 'wine' which they apparently used to cure everything. Tasnian took the cup from him and said, 'Leave me with her, Nen. I will look after her.'

'As you wish, as you wish,' said the healer. He swiftly gathered his herbal ointments and ducked through the entrance.

When Helen had swallowed the spirit, she was able to explain what had made her ill. Tasnian listened gravely, then said, 'Do you think we are unclean, Helen?'

'Er – er, I don't know, I mean, no, of course not – '

'The kirs are living things. They feed us, but they have to be fed in turn. Do you not eat fruit and plants that have been nourished with animal droppings? Don't you eat honey?'

'Well yes, but – '

'It is no different,' said Tasnian. 'Whatever moisture the kir receives is distilled and changed within its own cells before it is given back as milk. We make everything from it, curds and cheese and wine.'

'You mean it's the only thing you eat?'

'No, we have other foods – fruit, seeds and fish – but almost everything is mixed with it. I don't want you to starve, Helen. The kir-milk is good.'

'I believe you,' she said. 'I'll eat anything you say when I'm better, only please stop talking about food . . . '

Tasnian smiled at her, stroking her hair. His presence was soothing. He radiated serenity and she felt she could say anything to him. Yet the previous night he had disregarded her questions about Rianna as cold-bloodedly as Sheyde had, if less pointedly. 'I am sorry. We'll talk of something else. You will soon be well again. Nenhaliac is a good healer, a bringer of grace.'

'Yes, I noticed the hair,' she said. 'Green, for grace. Do you remember, in the boat, you told me about the colours?'

'Yes, I remember. We will go out to sea again when you are well. Would you like to see the Oa again?'

A pleasant memory, blue sunlight and green scales flashing through the water. 'Oh, yes,' she sighed. 'I would love that.'

'We want you to be happy in the Heart of Life, Helen.'

'Why? I'm not even from Tevera.'

'That doesn't matter. Either you can enter Chalceny or you

cannot, and I think you can.'

She paused, then asked, 'Did you say that to Rianna, too?'

'You will love the Heart of Life. There is so much to show you. I will teach you to ride the shaliors . . . '

He had passed over the mention of Rianna as if he had not heard it. 'Tasnian, listen. I don't want to upset anyone here, but I don't know your ways yet . . . '

'There is not much to know. We are what you see.'

'Yes, well, everyone interprets what they see differently, don't they? I don't want to jump to any wrong conclusions.'

Tasnian laughed. 'I think your colour will be gold.'

I must have made some progress, Helen thought. He meant it as a joke, and she understood it; gold was the colour of the head, of thought. 'Oh no, not gold,' she said. 'Thinking isn't my strong point. Just the opposite.'

'If the opposite of the head is the feet, you must be a dancer.'

She grimaced. 'I ought to be. My mother did everything she could to teach me, but I was a lost cause.'

'Your mother?' His smile faded momentarily. She remembered how Cadreis had claimed not to know his own family.

'Yes, on Earth children usually live with their mother and father until they are old enough to look after themselves. Don't the Chalcenians do that?'

'No. We do not know our parents. When a woman has a baby she gives it up, and all the children are brought up together by any childless Chalcenian who wish to look after them.'

'It sounds chaotic. I don't believe mothers would just give up their babies like that.'

'But they do. It is the way things are. It is not good to form strong bonds. Imagine, if a child had only its parents to love it, and then they went away, how hurt it would be. But living in the group they are always loved and protected.'

'But don't they even know who their brothers and sisters are?'

'No. Why should it matter, Helen? We are all one. We all love each other.'

'You mentioned people leaving,' Helen said cautiously. 'Why would they leave?'

'Oh, to travel, to visit other Chalcenians. For the sheer joy of life.' Tasnian's lips were still curved, but he was not meeting her eyes.

'Not for any other reason? Would someone have to leave because they weren't happy, like Rianna?'

There was a pause, brief but sharp as ice. 'Tevera must seem very strange to you. Would you prefer to go back to your own world?'

'I don't know. Feeling like this, I wish I was tucked up in bed at home. But the time Martin and I met you on the beach, I didn't want to go home at all. And now I can't, not until I know what's happened to Cadreis and Rianna.'

Again the feeling of walking on to a step that was not there.

'There is so much for you to discover in Tevera, such beauty – '

'Tasnian, please don't change the subject!' Helen was almost at the point of screaming with frustration and the misery of feeling ill. 'Look, I admit I don't know what your conflict with the Domendrans is about, but why do you pretend they don't exist? Cadreis wasn't like the others. You've helped me, why can't you help him?'

He did not reply for several seconds. The Chalcenians' dismissal of the Domendrans seemed an automatic reaction, something they did without thinking. Then he said, 'We care about you, Helen. We would like everyone to be happy in the Heart of Life, but it cannot always be.'

'And if I can't be mindlessly happy, will you turn me out to fend for myself?'

'Mindless?' He shook his head as if in wonder. 'Is that how we seem to you?'

'No, of course not,' she said impatiently, wishing he would not pounce on the most irrelevant part of her questions. 'But would you?'

She had pushed him too far, but he did not fight back as Nick would have done. He only became more vague, like a boat drifting away from her. 'If someone must leave, they understand when it is time. But it is different for you, because you are from this other world . . . '

'Yes. Earth.'

'Earth . . . ' he echoed thoughtfully. He rose to his feet, and she knew if she tried to ask him anything else she would soon be talking to thin air. 'All my life I believed there was only Tevera and Anatevera. Now there is Earth. I don't know what to make of that, or of you.'

His face was sublime, the da Vinci saint again. What was going on in his mind, Helen could not begin to guess.

For two days, Helen lay on her sickbed, hardly able to move. Sweat fell from her and vanished into the floor below; drops of white dew formed on the curved roof above her. Nenhaliac was with her the most, but she was rarely left alone for long. Sheyde and Tasnian were endlessly kind to her, and other Chalcenians also came to see how she was.

Corolea, however, did not come back.

On the third morning Helen woke to find that the sting of her wound had faded to a dull ache. Her temperature had fallen. She felt limp but refreshed, and the air seemed to have the clarity of spring. She could not wait to go outside.

When Sheyde came to see how she was, Helen was already out of bed and putting her clothes on. The Chalcenian woman did not ask if she was sure she felt well enough to get up; she only lifted Helen's hand to her forehead, then hugged her.

'You are feeling better,' said Sheyde. 'This is wonderful!'

'Well, yes, a bit,' Helen said, taken aback. Apparently the Chalcenians would tolerate illness – if not unhappiness – but the sooner they could brush it aside, the better.

Sheyde picked up Helen's jacket. 'But there's no need for you to put these old garments on again. I will bring you some Chalcenian clothes, you will be more comfortable in them.'

She left, and returned a few minutes later with an armful of shining material. There was a pair of trousers, a shirt and a long tunic, made of a woven stuff like a mixture of wool and silk. The colours were predominantly red, blue and gold, sewn with swirls of beads.

As Helen changed, she asked, 'Have Rianna and Martin come back?'

A frown momentarily touched Sheyde's dark brows. 'No.'

Helen had not expected good news, but her heart still sank. She was a little in awe of Sheyde; her dark-and-light beauty, her sheer physical *presence*. She did not know how far she could risk pushing the Chalcenian woman. 'Corolea is still at the Heart of Life, isn't she?'

'Yes,' Sheyde said stiffly, helping her to arrange the folds of the tunic. 'Why do you ask?'

'It's just that I haven't seen her for two days and I was a bit worried. She seemed rather upset.'

'Helen, stop.' Sheyde spoke hardly above a whisper. 'I know this is hard for you, but it is ill-wishing to mention those who have left – or who should leave.'

'You don't think it's wrong to care about people, do you?'

Sheyde looked angry, then her face softened. She teased Helen's hair, making it stand up from her head. 'No, but some are not ours to care for. Don't question our ways; they are as they must be. You know, you would be pretty if your hair was not so dull.'

Again Helen wondered why it was so hard for them to mention certain things, and how she could make Sheyde explain. She was sure their reticence was not malicious, but that made it no less frustrating.

When she was dressed, Sheyde said, 'I suppose Nenhaliac was right to leave you in a quiet place, but I never want solitude even if I am unwell. Now you are well again you can leave this branch and stay with me in the main trunk.'

Sheyde led her from the kir and through one egg-shaped chamber after another, angling downwards. The structure seemed to sway under them, and Helen had the feeling there was only thin air beneath. Seeing a window, or rather a hole hacked in the spongy fibre of the wall, she looked out and saw where she was.

She found herself looking at one of the great 'trees', which the Chalcenians called kateya. The main body of the trunk was in front of her, and she and Sheyde were in one of the branches, a string of the seed-pod shapes sticking out of the trunk like beads threaded on a wire. Helen had been in the very tip of the branch, and the ground looked a long way below.

'Oh, God,' she said, swallowing. 'The branches don't ever break off, do they?'

'Sometimes,' Sheyde said off-handedly. 'When they are very old and dry. This is a dry one, that is why there is no one here. Nenhaliac could have put you nearer the centre, but if he had put you too near, you would have been disturbed by people coming and going through your kir.'

That would have been preferable to plummeting to the ground in the middle of the night, Helen thought, but her mouth was too dry to say so.

In the main body of the trunk, the circular entrances between kirs had been enlarged, so they could walk upright, rather than squeezing through. There were openings in floor and roof as well as in the walls, and fibrous ropes hanging down so that it was possible to climb vertically as well as horizontally from one kir to the next. Warm grainy light shone through the walls. Here and there, a window let through a shaft of clear daylight, blue against the gold. Further into the trunk, the light deepened to honey.

Sheyde led Helen downwards. Other Chalcenians passed them, more overpowering in this confined space than they had been outdoors; all shining hair and energy and laughter. When they paused to exchange words with Sheyde, Helen felt an indefinable excitement in the pit of her stomach, a sense that all things were possible.

It took only a few minutes to reach the base of the trunk, then they came out through a wide, ragged hole in one of the kirs and into the forest. The sun was high, the air clear as glass. Through the oaks and birches Helen could see the otherworld landscape, alien yet heart-rendingly familiar, rolling to a distant horizon. All at once she felt like running and dancing, yet at the same time she was too choked to speak.

Sheyde took her hand and led her through the forest of trees and kateyas. Leaf shadows danced on the sandy-gold structures. The Heart of Life extended beyond the peak of the hill and over the other side, much larger than Helen had realised. At the base of the far slope, there was a freshwater spring where several Chalcenians were bathing and gathering water. They were like tropical birds, Helen thought, bright and hauntingly different.

'I never imagined the Heart of Life was like this,' she said.

'No doubt your world would seem as strange to me,' said Sheyde. 'We think it is beautiful.'

'Oh, yes, it is.' As they talked, Helen's eyes were

everywhere in the vain hope of spotting Rianna. She did not want to alienate Sheyde by persisting with questions she could not or would not answer. In her own clothes, Helen might have felt more belligerent, but dressed in the Chalcenian garments she felt inexplicably vulnerable. 'Where do the kateyas come from? If – if it's all right for me to ask.'

'Of course it is.' Sheyde sounded surprised.

'It's just that usually when I ask a question I feel I've said something wrong.'

Sheyde did not seem offended by the remark. Her lips were curved, her eyes warm. 'Surely there are unspoken things in your world, things you take for granted, that you would find it hard to explain to a stranger?'

Helen thought of Cadreis. Warm memories, then the coldness of Annis's breath. 'Yes,' she said faintly. 'I suppose my world is worse, if anything.'

'Well then, I shall explain as best I can. The kir are the pods of a great plant that grows by the sea. The plant is called the Flower of Cahantias. We bring the kir back and build the kateyas from them, and as long as they are fed they live and sustain us. Look – ' She pointed through the trees, and Helen saw a group of Chalcenians tearing a small kateya to pieces. The pods split like dry, rotten wood, scattering dust and fibres. 'They dry out and die eventually, but then we dismantle them and build another. The Flowers of Cahantias also give us the fibre we spin and weave for our clothing. They give us almost everything.'

'Have you always lived here, Sheyde?'

'Oh, yes. For as long as I can remember, I have lived here. I remember nothing else.'

'How long has the Heart of Life been here?' As Helen asked the question she sensed a restlessness about Sheyde, as if her attention were drifting.

'I don't know. We take little notice of time. It passes in the same way whether we count it or not. Some may count the seasons, but even they could not tell you exactly, because the Heart of Life itself is not always here.' Sheyde moved away a couple of paces, staring out through the trees. In the distance Helen caught sight of a group of riders, but they were a long way off, and she wanted to continue the conversation.

'Not always here?' Helen said. 'How do you mean?'

'The Heart of Life is not a place. It is the Heart of Chalceny. It is wherever we are. As it decays and is rebuilt, it shifts its position. Parts of it split away and become separate cities with other names, but they are still part of the whole. If we wished, we might take the whole city to pieces and rebuild it somewhere else, and it would still be the Heart of Life.'

As she spoke, Tasnian came running towards them, followed by Nenhaliac and two women whom Helen knew by sight, if not by name. One was silver-pale, the other golden skinned with bright eyes and hair dark as holly.

Tasnian kissed Sheyde on the lips, then said, 'He is coming back.'

'I know, I can see them!' Sheyde rose on tiptoe, gazing at the distant party of shaliors.

'Who – ' Helen began, but Sheyde was no longer paying her any attention. Suddenly the Chalcenian woman flung off her outer tunic and sprinted away down the hill, leaving Helen standing. The discarded garment lay on the grass, a heap of glittering indigo. Helen was about to start after her when Nenhaliac caught her arm.

'No running,' he said. 'You will make yourself ill again.'

He was right; Helen already felt shaky and tired just from walking. Nenhaliac and his two companions, however, did not stay with her but hurried after Sheyde. She watched them ruefully, then realised Tasnian was still beside her.

'I will walk with you, Helen,' he said cheerfully. 'It is always a cause for joy when someone comes back to the Heart of Life.'

A couple of hundred yards down the hill, Sheyde halted in a clearing that was flooded with sunlight. There she began to dance.

The dance was balletic, exaggerated and almost cartoon-like in its fluidity. Helen had never seen a human body bend into such curves or leap so high. Pure joy in living blazed from Sheyde's body. Helen was spellbound, but another image formed in her mind; her mother, in a dusty ballet studio, forcing herself stiffly through the extreme stretches that her limbs were no longer supple enough to accomplish. Unexpected tears pricked her eyes.

Word of the riders had spread quickly, and Chalcenian men and women were running down the hill, shouting and laughing. Some began to dance with Sheyde, others went on towards the riders. A few yards away Helen heard high-pitched voices and she turned to see a crowd of children, as colourful as the adults, trooping between the trees.

'This is the first time I've seen the children!' she said.

Tasnian put a hand on her shoulder, and the touch sent an involuntary thrill through her. Despite his kingfisher hair, he was as beautiful as Cadreis. 'You look different in those clothes; almost a true Chalcenian.'

Helen was watching the children. Except for their outlandish clothing, they could have been a crowd of schoolchildren let loose on an outing. They were of all ages, and some had babies or toddlers in their arms. She could see only one or two adults with them. 'Where are their parents?'

'Whose parents?' said Tasnian.

'The children's.'

'Their parents are all around you,' he said.

'I can't understand it, not wanting to look after your own children. Don't you love them?'

'Of course we love them, Helen. They are the first-born, blessed by Cahantias. But we do not possess them.'

'Who are the adults with them, then?'

'They are the Shefri, the Chalcenians who care for them. I am a Shefri myself, sometimes.'

She did not often have to consciously think about the language she was using, but she could not find the Chalcenic words for 'wife' or 'husband'. She could hardly ask Tasnian if he was married, and from what she had seen, none of the Chalcenians went about in couples. Instead, she asked, 'Do you have any children, Tasnian?'

He seemed taken aback by the question, then he laughed. 'I don't know, Helen. Quite possibly.'

There was so much she wanted to ask him, but she sensed the same wandering of attention that she had noticed with Sheyde. 'I haven't seen any old people at all,' she said. 'Where are they?'

'We do not live to be old, Helen,' he said.

Then he was hurrying away from her, lost in the crowd that

was surging forward to greet the riders. Helen could just see Sheyde, at the very front, dancing wildly. The group of seven shaliors came to a prancing halt, and the Chalcenians on their backs cheered her.

Helen instantly recognised the lead rider as Ananthis. His copious white-blond hair caught the sun like a mirror. He rode an ice-white shalior, with the other six forming what could only be described as an entourage. The Chalcenians seemed too anarchic to have leaders, but there were inevitably some who attracted others to them. That was human nature, Helen thought, and the Teverans were human.

Behind the riders two huge sandy-coloured ovoids rested on the grass, tied to the shaliors' saddles. Helen recognised them as kirs. Every small thing that began to make sense raised her spirits.

Ananthis took his time dismounting, evidently enjoying being the centre of attention while at the same time pretending to be irritated by it. Eventually he jumped down from his shalior and warmly embraced Sheyde, Tasnian and all those nearest to him. Pushing her way towards them, Helen was surprised and relieved to see Corolea, all smiles again, with the others.

She drew closer. Ananthis was leaning against his shalior with affected elegance, lazily slapping its head away when it tried to bite him. He was deep in conversation with Sheyde, and took no notice of Helen. She went to stand unobtrusively at Tasnian's side, and realised she was listening to an argument.

'I was told she had come back,' said Ananthis. 'So where is she?'

There was a silence, just like the one that had greeted Helen's questions. Then Sheyde said, 'I trust you had a delightful journey?'

'That goes without saying.' Ananthis's eyes narrowed languidly. 'Don't play games with me, Sheyde. I must know where she is.'

Sheyde had her back to Helen, so she could not see her face, but her shoulders lifted with tension or indignation. 'Ananthis, you cannot be asking me – '

'Sheyde, don't be ridiculous. It's me you're talking to. Is

she here or not?'

The Chalcenian woman seemed to find it almost impossible to answer. Eventually she said stiffly, 'She does not exist.'

Ananthis closed his eyes and uttered a heavy sigh. 'I see. Was it you who let her leave? Or you, Tasnian? You all look equally guilty to me.'

'It was as it should be,' said Tasnian. 'She knew – '

'Oh, you fools.' His lids swept up, and Helen saw that his irises were gold. His expression was one of utter exasperation. 'I really thought you would have had more sense. Didn't you realise who she was?'

'What do you mean?' Sheyde said faintly.

'She is the Pelumayis! The last one we have!' He stared haughtily around the crowd. 'Half of you do not even know what I mean, do you?'

'Ananthis, we did not know, we did not think – '

'Just so. You did not think, beloved dancer. Spare me the excuses, I really can't be bothered to listen to them. I suppose I must sort this disaster out for myself. And then – then I shall make sure you all understand who the Pelumayis is!' He began to stride away, then saw Helen and stopped. 'Well, if it is not the girl out of the Earth again. Wherever do you keep springing from?'

He said this in a tone of such boredom that Helen did not know how to react. Before she could say anything he was sweeping past her, whispering something into the ear of a purple-haired woman that made her roar with laughter.

The Chalcenians were on their way back to the Heart of Life again, singing and dancing to welcome the travellers home. Helen, giving up hope of pinning someone down to tell her anything, followed.

The shaliors were led up the hill, with the two kirs bouncing along the ground behind them. Ananthis stood for a while with his hands on his hips, looking around at the kateyas, then he appeared to make a decision and pointed up at the sunny side of one of the trunks.

At once, the Chalcenians began to haul the kirs towards its base. As workers, they were totally disorganised; they were all trying to help at once, but somehow, through sheer enthusiasm, they manoeuvred the kirs to where they were wanted.

They climbed on each other's shoulders, on the shaliors' backs, even up the outside of the kateya itself. The huge pods were then manhandled up the trunk until they were about twelve feet above the ground, then attached in some way that Helen could not make out. She had the impression that they clung to each other naturally. Now she could see that the entire kateya had been constructed in this way, one pod on another, like cells in a honeycomb.

It took only a few minutes to place the kirs where Ananthis wanted them. Helen held her breath as some of the Chalcenians hung precariously from the trunk. They seemed to have no regard for their own safety, and some of them looked certain to fall. But they climbed down easily, and then a head appeared through a hole in a kir next to the ones the Chalcenians had just attached.

It was a woman with a heart-shaped face and yellow hair. She looked annoyed. 'Who has done this?'

Ananthis looked up at her, laughing.

'Oh, it's you,' she said, apparently not impressed. 'Why did you have to put these kirs here? You've blocked out all my light!'

'So move to another one, dear Sukeyle,' Ananthis called. 'Move to mine.'

'You snake,' she said defiantly. 'I shall do exactly that.' The blonde head withdrew. A few moments later, Sukeyle came out of the base of the kateya and threw herself on Ananthis, who received her with an embrace so passionate that Helen had to look away.

She could hear Martin saying, *They're all bloody mad.* Perhaps they were, but still she felt she would have done anything to be one of them, to share their sublime joy in life.

Each of the Chalcenians had a kir that they considered their own, if only as a place where they could leave their clothes and few personal possessions. That evening, Sheyde insisted on Helen staying with her, and Helen did not argue; she had no wish to go back to the isolated tip of a branch that might have broken off at any moment. They built parts of the kateyas in fantastic and dangerous shapes apparently just for the sake of it.

Sheyde's home was in the trunk of a large structure, about eight feet above the ground, with a window cut in the wall. It was larger than the one Helen had been in before, some twenty feet in diameter. The walls were a fresh sandy colour, the air warm and slightly moist, fragrant with the spicy scent that Helen now realised came from the kirs themselves. There was very little in it; only a few bedcovers woven from spongy kir-fibre, a pile of garments, a few flasks and bowls.

Sheyde called it her own kir, yet as the evening went on Helen was amazed to find other Chalcenians going back and forth through it almost non-stop. Some stayed, sitting cross-legged on the floor, making Helen feel very welcome among them. They had brought food and wine with them and shared a huge meal. Helen had overcome her initial revulsion for the kir-milk, and was so hungry that everything tasted delicious. From time to time, others simply went straight through the kir as if it were a public corridor.

When Helen asked Sheyde if she minded, she laughed. 'We are all one, Helen. We move about the Heart of Life just as we please.'

What Helen was learning about the Chalcenians was more by observation than by being told. They seemed to have no organisation and no discipline. Some worked hard, even obsessively, at the various tasks needed to support the community: weaving, gathering food and so on. Others appeared to do nothing at all. Yet it worked. They painted and danced and sang; they rode their shaliors or sailed on the ocean for the sheer pleasure of it, and they were happy.

One thing she still did not understand. When travellers returned, they were greeted with overwhelming joy. But when they left, no one took any notice, no one spoke their names, and the question 'Where is – ?' was never answered.

Eventually the crowd of Chalcenians left Sheyde's kir, and Sheyde disappeared with them. Helen was on her own. Sighing, she found a cover to wrap herself in and curled up on a comfortable part of the floor to sleep.

There was a figure standing over her. She sat up, wide awake with alarm.

'Well. Helen.' She recognised Ananthis's lazy voice. 'Your

name is Helen, isn't it?'

'Er – yes,' she said, edging back so that she was leaning against the wall. She was not exactly afraid of him, but his sudden appearance disconcerted her.

'What an excellent memory I must have,' he said. 'And how are you, Gallah-who-is-not-Gallah? I heard you were injured.'

'Er – I'm getting better. Did they – did they tell you how I came to be here?'

In the blue-black gloom, she thought she saw him smile. Starlight from the window feathered his hair with frost. 'Corolea told me some garbled tale about Black Annis.'

There was a pause. Nervously, she said, 'What do you want?'

'I would like to know what you are, Helen. You came through from Anatevera, did you not? So by rights you should be a Gallah.'

'I'm not, I mean, I didn't. Anatevera is what you call the afterlife, isn't it?'

'A place where our spirits go. Where we are born for the second time,' he said softly. She sensed that he was trying to discover things without telling her anything in return.

'Well, how could I possibly have come from there? I thought I told you, Martin and I come from a place called Earth.'

'A place called Earth, of course. But the Gallahs do exist, Helen. Some are wild and savage, but others are civilised enough to live among us.'

'I don't know what you're getting at.' The warm haze of wine had left her, and all the misery of losing Cadreis, Rianna and Martin returned.

'I am trying to establish that you and Martin are not Gallahs. If you have been allowed through the barrier alive, without making a bargain with Black Annis, it means that she is behaving very strangely.'

'How do you mean?'

His shoulders lifted minimally. 'I do not know. Perhaps she is going mad.'

Desperate, without much hope, Helen decided to throw herself on his mercy. 'Look, the reason I'm here now is to find Rianna. I can't get anyone to talk to me properly, I don't suppose it's their fault but I can't make anyone understand that three of my friends are in danger and I've got to find them. Why is that so difficult to understand?'

'It's quite simple, Helen. Anyone who is not Chalcenic does not exist.'

'But this is different, surely they can see that?'

'You and I can see it,' he said conspiratorially. She felt he was mocking her. 'Sheyde, Tasnian and the others were too concerned with being correct Chalcenians to stop Rianna leaving. Rianna should not have come back to Tevera in the first place. It was foolish of her to have done so, but I don't blame her. It is the fault of the others.'

'You mean the Domendrans?'

'Yes, Helen. You will forgive me if I do not speak the word.' For the first time she sensed a seriousness under his flippant exterior, and there was something sinister in it. 'I blame Menenthonis. That cursed Menenthonis, chasing her back here. Those damned – others.'

'Ananthis, who is Rianna?'

'She is the Pelumayis. If you do not understand, I shall not explain until I find her. I presume you have not seen her since you came to Tevera?'

'No,' she said, 'and I'm worried sick about her. The Domendrans want her.'

'I know. But I want her as well. It is essential that I find her and talk to her . . . '

Warnings flared in Helen's mind. She did not trust Ananthis. Whatever he wanted with Rianna, she was sure it would not be in Rianna's interests. 'I'll help you find her – ' she began, but he cut across her.

'I don't need your help,' he said dismissively. 'They will have gone towards the Vale of – of the others. I only hope they have not reached it. A word of advice: do not keep asking questions about her or about others for whom you feel concerned. Forget them. However you feel, appear to be happy. That way you will survive here.'

With that he withdrew into the darkness.

'Just a minute – ' Helen cried, but he left without a backward glance, and she knew – as always – that the more she demanded of him, the less he would tell her.

*

'I'm going to find Rianna,' Helen said to herself.

It was dawn. Yellow light filtered softly through the walls, outlining two sleeping forms; Sheyde, curled up with a ruby-haired man whose name Helen did not know. She had not heard them return. She had slept soundly, but now she was wide awake.

In the centre of the trunk were the uninhabited kirs in which the Chalcenians relieved themselves. All excreta and any kind of liquid that fell on to the surface was absorbed, leaving no smell and no trace. What had seemed horribly primitive at first to Helen she now accepted as a perfect and hygienic system.

Back in the main kir, Helen washed in a bowl of spring water and tipped the water on to the floor to feed the kir. Sheyde and her companion did not stir as she dressed quickly and left. Outside, there were already several Chalcenians going about their business in the dawn light, but Helen could not find the one man she wanted.

She wandered about for an hour, growing more and more restless, before she saw a familiar form with long, untidy hair that shone peacock blue. 'Tasnian,' she called, running to meet him. She was still unfit and the effort made her short of breath. 'Tasnian, you said you would teach me to ride a shalior.'

He looked pleased. 'Yes, and I meant it.'

'Good, because I want you to teach me now.'

He stared at her, then laughed. She was behaving like a true Chalcenian. 'Why not? Come, then. We have to catch them first.'

Riding the shalior felt very different from riding a horse, but the principle was the same and Helen swiftly grew used to it. Tasnian rode a creature dappled in rich shades of blue. The mount he had chosen for Helen was a female the newly minted sovereign colour of a palomino, with a cobweb pattern of amber all over its coat. Helen's heart was in her throat, more with excitement than fear. The neck that arched up in front of her was so high that she had to look round the side of it rather than between the ears. The long loping gait was like nothing she had experienced before. All the time she was aware that she was in another world, on a creature more fabulous than a unicorn; the awareness was like crystal air in her lungs, so sweet that it verged on pain. Riding the shalior brought the alienness and the beauty of Tevera home to her as nothing else had done.

Tasnian was pleased with her progress. 'I forgot that you were riding when we first met you,' he said. 'What were those animals called?'

'Horses,' said Helen.

'Yes. So you have the skill already; I don't think there's much I can teach you.'

'I wouldn't say that. I was never a very brilliant rider at the best of times.'

'But you are happy on Hlah? She goes quietly for you.'

'Yes, quite happy. She's an angel,' Helen replied. She had the feel of the shalior now, and felt reasonably confident of controlling her. All the time they had been riding over the hills round the Heart of Life, Helen had been noting landmarks and trying to orientate herself. Now she pulled Hlah to a halt. 'I've got a confession to make, Tasnian.'

'Oh? What is that?'

'I wanted the shalior for a reason.' She spoke firmly, and she gathered the reins to gallop if Tasnian tried to stop her. 'I'm going to try to find my friends. I'd like you to help me.'

Tasnian looked at her with his head slightly on one side. For once he was not smiling. 'You might get lost, Helen.'

She tried not to sound angry, but bitterness crept into her voice. 'You wanted Rianna to get lost, didn't you? Of course, I realise you can't come with me. If my friends don't exist there's no one to look for, is there? So don't worry about me. I'll be quite all right on my own.'

She neck-reined Hlah and trotted away, trying to bite back her anger at Tasnian, to put him from her mind. A few moments later, she heard the pad of hooves on grass, the rattle of saddle ornaments behind her.

'Helen, I'm coming with you,' said Tasnian.

Instinct took her towards the hills that corresponded with Bradgate Park. The Vale of Peace lay not far from there, she knew, though she was not sure exactly where it was. The thought of going anywhere near it frightened her, but Ananthis had sounded so certain that they would have gone that way.

It was further than she had thought. By noon she was exhausted and dispirited, although the shaliors were as fresh as ever and seemed capable of going on all day.

She recognised the familiar lines of Bradgate, and at once she wanted to turn back. What if she was drawn back to Earth, Tasnian and the shaliors with her? That would be no use to anyone.

'This is hopeless. A needle in a bloody haystack,' she said in English.

'What was that?' said Tasnian.

'Nothing. Look, are you sure you can't think of a specific place they might be?'

Tasnian looked away, not answering, and she knew. He also thought they had gone towards the Vale of Death in Life, but he could not bring himself to name the place. The idea that Martin and Rianna were actually inside the city by now turned her cold. She could not face going inside it again. 'Oh, God,' she said.

'Come back to the Heart of Life,' Tasnian said gently. 'You can achieve nothing by distressing yourself. People leave. It is better to let go, to forget.'

'I can't.' But she followed him anyway. He found a shorter way back, through the sunlight and deep shadows of a wood that was just like Swithland. She would rest, she decided, and then she would try again . . .

It was Martin's glasses that caught her eye. She would never have seen him in the shadow of foliage under a rocky overhang; she would have passed them by and gone wretchedly back, still tormenting herself about them. But just for a second, the sun caught his glasses and two white circles of light flashed out like twin beacons.

Helen almost fell out of the saddle in shock. She was too breathless to say anything to Tasnian. She gesticulated dumbly, then sent Hlah cantering towards the rocks.

She was on her feet before she had brought the shalior to a proper halt, stumbling through the grass and brambles.

Martin saw her coming. He was on his feet, waving, his mouth open with delighted astonishment.

'Helen! Helen!'

Behind her, Tasnian hung back as if he did not want to acknowledge Martin or Rianna. Helen took no notice. She was almost at the overhang, and it was Rianna who ran out to meet her; Rianna, her hair blowing back like an autumn tree shedding its leaves, her face streaked with tears.

'Helen,' she cried. She was in Helen's arms, warm and slender as a bird, and she was shaking and sobbing uncontrollably. 'Oh, help me. I have done something terrible.'

Chapter Fourteen

Rianna's hands were very tight on Helen's and her eyes were red and shiny with grief. 'I've done something so terrible, Helen. All these years I'd forgotten about it. But the moment Martin and I came through to Tevera, I remembered . . . I remembered everything.'

'What is it?' Helen said gently.

'I had a baby, a long time ago, when I was sixteen.'

'I know. Your mum told mine.'

'I gave it to Black Annis, Helen.'

The quietness was filled with the voices of birds, a soft breeze stirring the grass. The gentle sounds rang in Helen's ears. 'You did what?'

'Black Annis took my child. She devoured it.'

'No – Rianna, hang on – the baby died at birth. That's what your mother said. I know it was a dreadful thing to happen but you mustn't blame yourself . . . '

Rianna stared at her. Tears were running down her cheeks, but her eyes were sane. 'Listen to me, Helen. I haven't gone mad. I wish it weren't true, but it is. It was the bargain I made with Black Annis when I first came to Earth. She would let me through the barrier, if I promised to give her my first-born child.'

'Oh, God,' Helen breathed.

'I was only a tiny child, I didn't know what I was promising, but I promised her anyway. Then I got pregnant, some stupid boy at school. It didn't have to happen. I did it for Annis. Then they told me the baby had died, but I knew, I knew Annis had got her part of the bargain . . . ' She was weeping soundlessly, in such terrible pain that she could not articulate it.

'It wasn't your fault, Rianna,' Helen said. 'You were just a child, you didn't know what you were promising.'

'It doesn't matter now, does it? The baby died. I murdered it. I sold it and I murdered it.' Helen and Martin held her as she cried, helpless to console her. In all her images of reunion, Helen had not expected this.

'She's been like this since we left the Heart of Life,' said Martin. He looked haggard. His face was blotchy, and behind his glasses there were dark hollows under his eyes. 'I can hardly get any sense out of her.'

'Thank God I've found you,' Helen said. Martin looked at her. His mind had obviously been on Rianna, but now the surprise and relief of seeing Helen came home to him. 'Thank God *you* found *us*?' he exclaimed. 'Oh, Lord. We didn't know what had happened to you. You just vanished, we didn't know what to think.' He reached for her and the three of them formed a circle, hugging each other. 'You're all right, aren't you?'

'Just about,' said Helen. The semi-healed bite was stinging, making her catch her breath.

'But what are you doing here?'

'It's a long story.'

'Ditto,' said Martin.

'I see you haven't managed to lose the glasses yet.'

'No, thank goodness.' He gave a shaky smile and pushed his brown curls off his forehead. He and Rianna were both wearing jeans, jumpers and coats which looked slightly the worse for wear.

'Have you been sleeping outside?' Helen asked.

'Not as such. We found an abandoned kir – you know, those pod things – so we weren't cold.'

'It must still have been awful.'

'It wasn't so bad, was it, Rianna?' Martin said cheerfully. 'You're looking at a fully qualified boy scout. Shame I forgot my Swiss Army penknife. But we've survived.'

'Well, you look like a down and out.'

'Thank you very much. And you look like something that's fallen off a Christmas tree.'

Helen laughed, but there was not much humour in it. Rianna was still crying softly, leaning against Martin. Insects winged around them; huge butterflies, velvet black and violet, scarlet-striped bees and wasps as bright as flame. Everything seemed edged with light and with danger.

'I see Tasnian still isn't speaking to us,' Martin said resentfully. The Chalcenian man was standing a few yards away with his back to them.

'It was all I could do to get him to come with me. At least he hasn't deserted us,' said Helen. 'But I'm still confused about why you left the Heart of Life. Aren't you going to tell me what's been going on?'

'Yes, but I want to hear what happened to you,' said Martin.

'I know what happened to me! I can't face going over it again just yet. Come on, tell me your story first.'

'OK,' he sighed. They sat down on a rock, and Helen was glad to rest.

'By the way, I saw Jo. She told me . . . er, that you and Rianna had gone off together. And I found your car in Bradgate car park.'

'Ah,' said Martin. He sounded very slightly sheepish. 'That night you vanished, Rianna came knocking on my door and said she was really terrified of this guy called Menenthonis finding her. Then we discovered you were missing and we panicked a bit. To start with, we thought of going to Scotland, somewhere he wouldn't think to look. But Rianna thought that if Menenthonis could trace her from New Zealand, he could find her anywhere. Then she started saying she was sure you were in Tevera, that Black Annis had possessed the doll and taken you in mistake for her.'

'She was right.'

'So the only thing to do was go to Tevera and try to find you.'

'Whose idea was that? If ever I tried to mention it, Rianna denied that Tevera existed and said she'd forgotten how we used to come through when we were kids.'

'It was my idea,' said Martin. Rianna, sitting beside him with her arms round him, appeared to be lost in her own thoughts.

'How on earth did you get her to go in the Park?'

'She just came with me, no argument. I think she was afraid to be left on her own. So would I have been. So we went into the Park and it turned into Tevera, just as it did before.'

'Did you see . . . anything strange as you went through, like a woman with dyed blonde hair, or a black shalior?'

Martin looked puzzled. 'No, nothing like that.'

'Never mind. Go on.'

'Well, until we went through the boundary – wherever that was – Rianna was fine. A bit nervous, you know, but all right otherwise. Then, when we were in Tevera, she went really quiet. Almost as if she was in a trance or something. She took me straight to the Heart of Life as if she knew where it was.'

'And you met Tasnian and Sheyde again?'

'Yes, and Corolea. We got to know a few others as well. Of course, we asked about you, but they hadn't seen you, had no idea where you might be, and so on. I really didn't know where to start looking. I thought Rianna was OK, just a bit tired. All the time, something must have been building up inside her. She suddenly had a kind of breakdown, wouldn't stop crying, kept telling me – well, what she just told you.' He pushed his hair back. He looked, Helen thought, five years older. 'The next thing I know, she announces that she has got to leave the Heart of Life. It was ridiculous, she wasn't rational, she was really quite ill, but she insists on leaving and the sodding Chalcenians – well, Sheyde and Tasnian gave me no help at all. They just kept saying that if she wished to leave, she must.'

'They didn't actually kick you out, though?'

'Not as such, but I had the distinct impression that Rianna wasn't welcome there any more. I couldn't for the life of me work out why. For being upset, for Christ's sake?' Helen put her hand on his arm. He went on, 'That was about three or four days ago.'

'You must have left only just before I arrived.'

'Maybe,' he said. 'Anyway, Rianna had this idea that there was a special place she must go to. She was so vague about it that I wasn't sure that it really existed. Eventually I persuaded her not to go any further, but she wouldn't go back either.'

'Were you going to the Vale of Peace, Rianna?' Helen asked.

'The Vale of Peace,' Rianna whispered. 'Death in Life. They were the names I couldn't remember!'

Helen reached across Martin's knees to hold her friend's hand. 'Did you think I was there? I was, but I got out.'

'I – I don't know what I thought. I just felt I had to go there . . . '

'Well, you definitely mustn't. That's where Menenthonis comes from, and the Domendrans are trying to catch you. It will be safest if we go back to the Heart of Life.'

'I agree,' said Martin. 'I've been at my wits' end. I don't know what to do for her. I love her.' There was a short silence, then he added, 'By the way, what did Jo say?'

'She wasn't exactly thrilled.'

'Oh dear. You know, I never meant to hurt her. It just happened. You understand, Helen, don't you?'

Suddenly, Helen felt very strange. She was only too aware of the closeness between Martin and Rianna. She wanted to say: *Martin, I always thought that if ever you left Jo, it would be . . . well, not for Rianna.* She missed Cadreis so much that it was like a bereavement, iron bands squeezing her chest.

'Yes, I understand,' she said. Speaking quickly to obliterate the feelings, she told them what had happened to her. As she finished, they heard voices and looked up to see Ananthis, mounted on his white shalior, talking to Tasnian. With him were Corolea and Nenhaliac.

'Good grief, isn't that Ananthis?' said Martin.

'Yes. He told me Sheyde and Tasnian should not have let you leave. He wants to see Rianna, but I don't know why.' Helen felt an odd mixture of annoyance and relief. Ananthis would have found Martin and Rianna if she had not, so they would have been all right; but her mistrust of him would not be subdued.

'So, you got here before us,' Ananthis was saying. 'Why are you wasting time standing about here?'

'I'm waiting for Helen,' said Tasnian.

'Had it not occurred to you to take them straight back to the Heart of Life? Surely you are not still shunning Rianna?'

'She is not Chalcenic,' Tasnian said mildly.

'Give me strength.' Ananthis rolled his eyes. 'Did I not explain that it does not matter? Go and fetch them, and don't be an idiot.'

Tasnian turned and approached them, leading Hlah and

the blue shalior. Martin gave him a less than friendly look, and Helen was glad it was not in either of their natures to start a fight.

Martin said, 'Hello, Tasnian. You remember Rianna, don't you? Or maybe you don't.'

'I am sorry,' Tasnian said quietly. 'We should not have let her leave. An exception should have been made, but we did not realise.'

He sounded so contrite that it was impossible for Martin to argue with him. Ananthis, following him, said sarcastically, 'Dear Tasnian, it was a mistake anyone would have made. I blame myself for being absent. It was too bad of me to expect Chalcenians with heads full of air and sunshine to be capable of making a sensible decision.'

Tasnian appeared to take no offence at all at this, and Helen found herself envying his equanimity. She knew he was not a fool.

'So you are Rianna,' said Ananthis. 'Do you remember me?'

Rianna straightened up, wiping her eyes and pushing her hair back. 'I'm not sure,' she said. 'Some things I remember . . . others are hazy.'

With an unreadable smile, Ananthis drew a flask from his white and gold robes and handed it to her. 'Take one sip. It will make you feel better.'

'What is it?'

'Wine from the Heart of Life.'

'Oh, yes,' said Martin. 'It cures everything by giving you such a shock that you forget what was wrong in the first place.'

'Exactly,' said Ananthis.

Rianna swallowed a mouthful of the liquor and shuddered. Then she murmured, 'I've tasted it before. A drop on his finger, to quiet us if we wouldn't sleep . . . '

Ananthis took back the flask and stoppered it. 'Many things entertain me, but standing about in a damp wood all day is not one of them. It's time we left. Rianna had better ride with Tasnian, and Martin with Helen.'

'I'll take Rianna. I can ride,' Martin said firmly, then turned and whispered to Helen, 'They *are* just like horses, aren't they?'

'More like a cross between a panther and a Ferrari,' she said. 'Good luck.'

Martin and Rianna on Hlah, Helen sitting behind Tasnian on the blue, they followed Ananthis, Nenhaliac and Corolea through the trees. Presently Corolea held her shalior back until she was alongside Helen.

'Hello,' said Helen. 'I've been quite worried about you. Are you all right?'

'Oh yes, I am very well,' Corolea replied with a smile as bright and brittle as glass. 'I was – not myself when I saw you, but now I am whole again.' Once more Helen sensed a hidden tension which she did not yet understand. Corolea's face was a mask of happiness, but her eyes were screaming.

Tasnian glanced sideways at her and said, 'Rianna knew when it was time to leave. How long can you go on lying to yourself?'

'What do you know about me?' Corolea said angrily. 'Don't you dare condemn me, when you have been in the darkness yourself!'

'I do not condemn you,' Tasnian said gently. 'But if you would only admit it – '

As he spoke there was a commotion in front. There were figures running through the trees ahead of them. Ananthis, in the lead, spurred his white shalior forwards and the others bounded after him.

'Gallahs!' he and Nenhaliac shouted in unison.

'What's happening?' Helen said, then gasped as Tasnian's mount leapt into a gallop and almost caught her off balance. She saved herself by catching hold of his tunic.

'We are following the Gallahs!' he cried.

Shouting with excitement, the Chalcenians pursued the human shapes.

Leaves scattered light through the deep brown shadows of the wood. Helen could not make the figures out clearly, but she counted six. They were naked, their skin glistening and streaked with dirt. Their hair was wild and tangled. They looked round at the Chalcenians, bared savage teeth at them and ran on through the undergrowth. Whooping, Ananthis raced in pursuit.

'What's Ananthis trying to do?' Helen said breathlessly.

'He's scaring them!'

'No,' said Tasnian. 'The Gallahs are third-born, sacred to us. We take as many as we can to live among us. They are not afraid, only empty-minded.'

The Gallahs were all adults, and quite young, from the smoothness of their lithe bodies. They leapt in the air like deer as they ran; they climbed trees and flung themselves off the branches to land unhurt; they laughed like children, and the Chalcenians were laughing with them, delighting in their exuberance.

'They are not beautiful, they are more than beautiful,' Tasnian said. 'Some call them savages, but they are wrong. They are the jewels of the earth, they are proof that there is no death. Helen, have you ever seen such joy?'

His emotion was infectious; she shared their excitement, but with it she felt fear. If there was joy in the Gallahs' wildness it was a raw, savage thing. A sense of something unspeakably weird, like an irrational but very real feeling in a dream, shivered through her. They were like newborn creatures, torn shining not out of a womb but out of the earth. Their minds were cleansed of knowledge. All they knew was that they *were*, and from that knowledge poured their wild pleasure in being.

'Where are they from?' she said, knowing the answer, not believing it.

'From Anatevera.'

No, she told herself. *He's telling me they're from limbo, that they've been reborn. But it can't be, the Chalcenians are mistaken, it's some sort of primitive tribe that they've attached this belief to . . .*

'Now I know why you couldn't have mistaken Martin and me for Gallahs,' she said.

Nenhaliac's shalior overtook Ananthis. His excitement seemed to be going beyond euphoria into madness, and he would have crashed through the middle of the Gallahs, had Ananthis not yelled at him to stop.

'Don't be a fool, Nenhaliac! The idea is to bring them back alive!'

Now it seemed a game was developing between Chalcenians and Gallahs. Ananthis could have overtaken them at any time; instead he held back, and the chase became gentle, almost teasing. He let the Gallahs remain a few paces ahead, and in return they turned to laugh and cavort mockingly. Their faces shocked Helen. They were so ordinary. They were grimy with mud, but under the dirt they were faces that could have belonged to people she knew; a young man, three women, and – despite the lithe body and wild hair – a man who looked seventy at least. His age still shone like a skull through the skin, but the lines had been smoothed out. Old, but young again . . .

I'm dreaming. A nightmare.

Suddenly Corolea shouted, 'Ananthis, stop!' Helen had been taking no notice of the red-haired woman, assuming that she shared the others' enthusiasm. But now Helen saw that her face was white, her mouth distorted with revulsion. 'Stop!'

'What, Corolea?' His shalior plunged round in a circle and he rode alongside her.

'They are disgusting. Come away from them.'

Ananthis gave her an unpleasant look. 'You have seen Gallahs before. You used to rejoice in them.'

'Not now.' There was a hysterical note in her voice. Something about the Gallahs had broken her mask, brought her despair rushing to the surface. 'They are vile. They mock us. They are not living things, they are a mockery of life. Why can't you see it?'

'Be silent!' said Nenhaliac.

'No, I won't! They are an abomination, and I can't bear it!'

'Enough,' Ananthis said quietly. Corolea stared wildly at him, like someone who had involuntarily admitted to an appalling crime. 'Corolea, as dear as you are to me, I think you must know now that it is time.'

Ananthis, Tasnian and Nenhaliac looked steadily at Corolea. A rush of fear went through Helen; for a moment she thought they were about to turn on her physically. But they did not move, and after a few seconds Corolea simply turned her shalior and began to ride away. She caught Helen's eye as she passed, and the desolation in her face almost made Helen weep.

'Tasnian, where's she going?'

He did not reply. Helen struck his shoulder. 'Talk to me, damn it! How can you just let her go when she's so upset? She needs to be helped, not rejected.'

'Please, Helen.' Tasnian spoke softly, and he sounded as if he was suppressing tears. 'It is not easy for us, but it has to be borne. She may come back, but for now she has ceased to exist.'

'Let us go on,' Ananthis said brusquely. The Gallahs were drifting away through the trees. Helen suddenly wanted the ride to be over. All she could think about was Corolea, and every movement of the shalior dragged at the wound in her back. She felt tired, confused, uncomfortable.

What happened next was a bad dream, creeping up with understated slowness. The Gallahs were still running through the sunlit wood. The Chalcenians began to catch up with them, but too late they saw dark figures appearing through the trees from the other direction. They were on foot. There were more than twenty of them and they carried ropes and clubs.

Helen knew the drab, hooded cloaks, the grim expressions. They were Domendrans. Before anyone could react or anticipate what was going to happen, they had cut off the Gallahs' line of flight and were spreading out to surround them.

Shocked, the Chalcenians pulled up sharply, Ananthis and Nenhaliac shouting in protest. They had unintentionally driven the Gallahs straight into the arms of the Domendrans.

It was over in moments. The Gallahs tried to scatter, but not realising the danger, they had left it too late. The Domendrans moved in swiftly, binding them tightly and hitting those who tried to struggle. The Gallahs stood huddled in a group between their captors, not understanding what had happened to them.

Nenhaliac, yelling in fury, sent his shalior galloping at the Domendrans. His green hair flew out, wild as seaweed.

'Wait!' shouted Ananthis. His own shalior was prancing and trying to rear, but he restrained it. Turning to Martin, he said fiercely, 'Take Rianna away from here and take her *now*.'

'But what – ' Martin began, staring at him.

'Don't argue, *go!*' He flicked the sleeve of his robe on Hlah's rump and she spun round and sped away, almost unseating Martin and Rianna. Helen turned to watch them as they dwindled between the trees.

'Oh my God, is there going to be a fight?' she said.

Tasnian answered, 'We cannot fight those who do not exist.'

'Come on, they're standing in front of us, clear as day! You know who they are, don't you?'

Tasnian did not reply, but as Ananthis rode after Nenhaliac, he went with them. The air was filled with shouts. Nenhaliac was harrying the Domendrans, but he was unarmed and they were swinging ropes and clubs at him. His shalior was in danger of being brought down. Ananthis forced his own beast alongside the healer's and seized its bridle.

'Cease!' he said. 'We cannot fight them physically. Just block their path.'

Nenhaliac's eyes were wild, but he obeyed and pulled back. The Domendrans were doing their best to ignore the Chalcenians. Ananthis and the others wheeled round in front of them, forcing them to stop.

'Attend to me!' Ananthis cried. 'How dare you capture the Gallahs? What are you doing?'

With their heads down, the Domendrans simply changed course and took their captives another way. The Chalcenians followed and blocked them again.

'I am not invisible!' Ananthis roared. 'Answer me!'

One of the Domendrans stepped forward and looked up at him. With a dreadful shock, Helen saw that it was Artienter. That grave, lined face, with its black beard and mournful eyes, was the one that had brooded over her in the darkness of the Vale of Peace. She hid behind Tasnian's back, desperately hoping that he would not see her.

Nenhaliac was silently seething with anger, but Ananthis was suddenly very still and calm. Everything about him – his colouring, his bearing, his voice – seemed as dazzlingly sharp as the flash of sunlight on ice.

'Remove yourselves from our path,' Artienter said gruffly.

'You have not answered my question.'

'We are taking these Gallahs away.'

'I can see that,' Ananthis retorted. 'I wish to know why.'

'If you thought for one moment, you would know why. Their existence is an abomination.'

'But you cannot slay them! They have been through death,

they cannot be killed again.'

Artienter's lips thinned. 'Perhaps not, but we can keep them in darkness. We can keep them from the Sea.'

'You have no right,' said Ananthis. 'There are so few Gallahs. Is it too much to ask that you leave them be? For thousands of years the Domendrans have had their way in everything. Is it not enough? What right have you to break the natural cycle of life, to go on and on breaking it?'

'Who says it is natural?' Artienter said grimly. 'You have even less right to inflict rebirth on poor creatures who should be at rest.'

'Rebirth is life, and life is everything!' Ananthis exclaimed. 'The natural way of things must be reasserted. You and I are at the beginning of the cycle. How can we know the Gallahs' feelings, when they are so far beyond us? How dare you presume that they hate life as you do? You and your kind are no less than murderers. Murderers!'

'No!' Artienter took a step forward. 'It is out of love we do this, love for poor human souls. The Chalcenians are the destroyers of peace. You are the ones who would rend eternal rest for the sake of the brief and pathetic pleasures of living!'

'Only pathetic to you, Artienter, who never knew how to live.' Ananthis leaned forward in the saddle and spoke softly. 'If death is so sweet to you, may you find it swiftly. Leave the rest of us to our pleasure. Let the Gallahs be.'

'It is you I pity,' Artienter replied. Helen's stomach turned cold, because she could feel the words crawling inside her. 'How can you claim to possess such wisdom, when you have never tasted the darkness? And when you come at last to taste it, how you will mourn that you did not listen to me. I wish you no harm. I wish only that you could understand.'

Ananthis gathered up his reins, and the shalior tucked in its delicate head and pranced on the spot, like a cat. 'I understand. I have every sympathy for the Domendrans. But that cannot excuse the infinity of deaths for which you and your kind have been responsible. Begin to make amends; let these Gallahs go.'

Artienter gave him a sneering, dismissive look and beckoned to the other Domendrans. They moved off again, evading the shaliors. There was nothing the Chalcenians could do to stop them; they were only three against twenty. But Nenhaliac and Ananthis tried. They circled round and round the group, dodging ropes and clubs. The Domendrans began to run, dragging the Gallahs with them.

Tasnian held back for Helen's sake, but his shalior was leaping about, trying to join the others. For a few seconds of chaos, it was all she could do to keep her seat. Then she noticed another human flitting between the trees.

Tasnian saw it too. 'Ananthis!' he called. 'Come away, you cannot stop them!'

Ananthis spun his shalior round and made it rear. It seemed a creature of crystal, shedding icy light, while Ananthis was a white and golden fire. 'Destroyers!' he yelled. 'You have not defeated us yet!' The Domendrans fled before him, flightless birds whose cloaks flapped like wings.

'Ananthis!' Tasnian shouted again. 'Come here, quickly! It's important.' Ananthis and Nenhaliac wheeled round and cantered back to him, while Artienter and his people vanished into the wood.

'What is it?' Ananthis said impatiently.

'We have just seen another Gallah. There may be more. We must go after them before the – the others find them.'

'Which way?'

Tasnian pointed, and Ananthis pushed past, causing the blue shalior to shy and race after the white one. Only a few yards further on they saw four Gallahs. Ananthis pulled up sharply.

Tasnian's shalior, thoroughly overexcited by now, plunged to one side and reared, flinging both him and Helen from its back. She landed on grass and lay winded, too shocked to move. There was a blur of movement above her. The blue shalior and the white one circled round her; she heard Ananthis cursing. Tasnian was bending over her, asking if she was all right, but she could not reply. Something in the grass hypnotised her. A heap of rainbow jewels . . . one of Rianna's dolls, lying limp and flat like a discarded skin. No, it was just a costume. The doll's body was no longer within it. *The colours to guide us home and then . . .*

'Helen, answer me, please!' said Tasnian.

Her head cleared. She was aware that the Gallahs were

slowly edging in, staring at her with bright, curious eyes.

'Yes, I'm all right,' she said.

She sat up and found herself looking straight into Nick's eyes.

He was one of the Gallahs, a man of less than thirty, with blond hair and clear green eyes. There was dirt smeared on his face, as with all the others, but she saw through that to the arrogant, angelic features that were so familiar to her, so loved and so hated. She could not have mistaken him in a million years.

It *was* Nick.

Helen tried to scream. Her stomach twisted up inside her. She peeled herself off the ground, staggered against the nearest tree, and hung on to it with her ears ringing and lights exploding across her eyes.

Tasnian's hands were on her shoulders. She could not explain what was wrong. She clung to him, and all she could say was, 'Christ. Oh dear Christ. Help me, please help me.'

It was Ananthis's voice that brought her back to her senses, like ice water. 'It is one of those days, Tasnian, when it seems everyone in the entire world except myself has flown out of their minds. What is wrong with her?'

She turned round, shuddering and pushing her hair off her face. The bite-wound had opened up like a starfish radiating acidic arms across her back.

Nick was still there, naked, crouching in the grass and staring at her. The expression in his face was slightly different now. Wonder was being replaced by bewilderment.

'Nick?' said Helen. Then, 'No. I'll wake up in a minute.'

Nick frowned, blinked, and rubbed at his forehead. He stood up straight, looking around him, his fingers still pressed to his eyebrows. Then he said, 'Helen? What the fuck am I doing here?'

Chapter Fifteen

Helen's head was spinning, her hands and feet numb with pins and needles. Nick stood staring at her, looking so shocked and confused that her heart went out to him. It was impossible, but it was happening.

'Do you know this Gallah?' Tasnian asked incredulously.

Helen nodded.

'How can this be so?' said Ananthis.

'What the hell's going on?' Nick sounded frightened now. Helen remembered the phone call, which had been the first time she had ever heard that terror in his voice.

She wiped her mouth, and took a deep breath. 'I – I knew him on Earth, Ananthis. I thought he was dead.'

'He seems to remember you, yet I have never known a Gallah able to recall his or her previous life,' the blond Chalcenian said off-handedly. 'I should be interested to talk to him. He shall come back to the Heart of Life with us.'

The presumptive way he spoke infuriated Helen. She ignored him. What she and Nick had to say to each other – if anything – was private.

She went cautiously up to Nick and took his hand. It felt cold. 'Are you – are you all right?' she asked.

'I don't know.' He peered at her. 'It is you, Helen, isn't it?'

'Yes.'

'Thank God for that. Who the hell are these characters?'

'Erhm – just a couple of people I know. Nick, what happened to you? Can't you remember?'

He scratched his head. Then he suddenly glanced down at himself. 'Shit, where the bloody hell are my clothes?' He began to sound angry. 'What is this, Helen? Your idea of a joke, or what?'

'It's not a joke, Nick, and it's not my fault.' The defensive reaction was automatic. 'We just came along and found you.'

'Found me?' He blinked. 'Wait a minute. There must be something I should remember. A party. God, I must have been pissed. I suppose some joker thought it would be funny to bring me out and dump me in Swithland Woods.'

'What?' said Helen.

'I can't think of any other explanation. That's scary, I don't drink that much, never enough to black out. Someone must've spiked my drink. I'm just trying to work out who'd do that, I'll murder the bastard.'

'Nick, please. We're not in Swithland Woods. There wasn't a party, you weren't drunk, and I . . . '

'You what?' he said accusingly.

'I've got a hell of a lot to tell you. I don't even know whether I should.'

'You'd better tell me. God, I feel strange.'

He looked suspiciously at Ananthis and Tasnian. Then his gaze moved to the shaliors. His mouth opened and closed, but he made no comment.

Ananthis said, 'Tasnian, you had better lend him something to wear, as he seems unduly modest. We'll take him to the Heart of Life.'

Tasnian handed Nick his shimmering blue tunic. Nick put it on slowly, his eyes flickering nervously in every direction.

'The Heart of Life?' he said. 'Helen, that guy spoke another language and I understood it. Somebody's drugged me, they must have done. I was having this stupid dream that I was racing through the wood with a load of weirdos and I was incredibly, ridiculously happy. And before that . . . ' He suddenly clutched Helen's hand. 'Oh God. I was on the phone to you . . . oh, God.'

He wrapped his arms round her like a frightened child. His cheek pressed against her hair, and he was almost crying. She tried to soothe him. 'It's all right, it's all right,'

'Tell me it didn't happen,' he said. 'Oh, Helen, tell me it didn't happen.'

Most of the way back to the Heart of Life, Nick was quiet. He refused to mount the shaliors, but walked along between them, barefoot. Helen walked with him. He was not visibly distressed now, only deep in thought, and after a time he began to talk.

'You'll have to help me, Helen.'

'I'll do my best.'

'It's no good, I still don't understand what happened. The last thing I remember was being in the flat. I'd come home from work early, I wasn't feeling too good that day. I had a blinding headache. I thought I'd have a lie-down then cook myself some tea. I didn't get that far . . . I couldn't seem to see properly. I put all the lights on and it was still dark. I lay down for a few hours, I think, I don't really know. All I can remember is thinking that I was going to die and I didn't really mind, I just felt sleepy and calm.

'Rianna's doll was on the chest of drawers opposite the end of the bed. I opened my eyes . . . ' He frowned with the effort of remembering. 'The doll was the only thing I could see properly. Everything else was sort of black and glaring at the same time, but the doll shone. You know how the sun shines through a glass or something and makes a rainbow on the wall? It was like that, like someone had trained a rainbow spotlight on it. Then it moved. This must really sound like a load of crap. I'm not saying it's what happened, it's just what I thought I saw.'

'It's OK. Go on.'

'Right.' He breathed in, sighed. 'So, I saw the doll stand up. It started dancing on the chest of drawers, like a little ballerina on a stage. I was confused, I thought I was watching the telly and it was one of those amazing puppets where you can't see the strings. I remember thinking: *How do they do that?* and then I suddenly felt this cold sweat streaming all over me, like my body had realised a split-second before my brain that I wasn't watching telly. It was really happening, or at least I thought it was.

'I was terrified. I've never felt so scared in my life. One minute I thought I didn't mind dying, the next it was the last thing I wanted to do and I knew, I just *knew* the doll was waiting for me to die.

'Then it spoke. Shit, the bloody thing spoke.'

'What did it say?' Helen prompted.

'It kept saying my name. "Nicholas". Only my mother calls me that, for God's sake. "Nicholas". I thought I'd gone mad. I panicked, I had to call someone for help. I don't remember picking the phone up, I must have dialled automatically. The next thing I knew, I could hear your voice, but I couldn't explain what was wrong. My mouth wouldn't work. That happened to my grandfather when he had a stroke. Did I really ring you up, or did I imagine it?'

'No, you rang me. You said it was dark, and something about Rianna's doll.'

'Somehow I'd got off the bed and I was standing up. Then I saw the thing make a flying leap from the chest on to the floor and start walking towards me. It climbed on my foot. I tried to shake it off, but I was so dizzy I fell back on the bed again. It was climbing up towards my chest. I couldn't fight it any more, I was passing out, but it seemed to be telling me that I shouldn't be afraid . . . I don't know how to describe it. It was like being given an anaesthetic, that last moment when you fight to stay awake, you're scared to let go, but as soon as you do you're awake again and everything's all right, the operation's over?'

'Yes,' said Helen. 'I've only ever had teeth out, but I suppose it's the same.'

'I've had appendicitis and a broken arm,' said Nick. 'It's stupid, I can remember that from when I was a kid, but I can't remember exactly what happened that night . . . The doll was round my neck, sort of hugging me. I could feel its little hands. They felt kind of soothing, in a way. Then I thought I *was* the doll, and I was looking down at myself lying flat out on a bed . . . I don't recall what happened after that. The next thing I was aware of was running about in the woods. I felt as if I'd always been there and everything was fine. I was cold but it didn't matter, I couldn't really feel it. I didn't have a thought in my head. I was happy. Then suddenly I saw you and it was like someone had shaken me awake. I started to remember things. It was the bit where you sit up and go, "Oh, it was all a dream!" only it wasn't a bloody dream, was it?'

'No.'

'Well, how the hell do you explain it? Did someone put LSD in my coffee, or what? Where the hell are we?'

'I've got some difficult things to tell you,' said Helen.

'You'll probably find them hard to believe.'

'Try me,' said Nick. 'I mean, what are these animals? I've watched all the wildlife programmes and I have never, *never*, seen anything that looks like that before.'

'We're on another world. It's called Tevera.'

'David Attenborough should be here.'

'Look, I don't really know where to start, because I don't understand most of it myself,' Helen said. 'But that night you phoned me, I came straight round to your flat. I found you unconscious and I called an ambulance and went to hospital with you. The doctors pronounced you dead.'

'Yes, and then what?'

'Then, nothing. You were dead. They said it was probably a brain haemorrhage.'

'How do you mean, dead?'

'Dead! You know, dead! How many meanings does the word have?' she cried. 'Oh, I'm sorry. I didn't know how to tell you. But it's true. I had to tell Gina. Your funeral was last week, but I missed it.'

'Funeral?'

'Yes.'

'But I'm still alive.'

'Not on Earth, you aren't,' she said.

It was a long time before he spoke again. He reached out and squeezed her hand so hard that she gasped. Then she knew that he believed her; perhaps he even remembered something that told him it was true. 'And you came round and found me?' he said.

'Yes.'

'I wanted you with me. It was you I rang, not Gina. I thought if you came and sat with me, I'd be all right.'

'I did,' Helen whispered. 'I sat on the bed and held your hand, but you didn't know I was there.'

'And you got an ambulance for me.'

'Yes.'

'Poor Helen,' Nick said quietly. 'Poor Helen.'

They put their arms round each other, and went on towards the Heart of Life in silence.

When they reached the city of the Chalcenians, men and

women came running out to meet them, as they always did. It was a tide of friendship and welcome which, for the first time, gave Helen a feeling of returning home. There was still so much she had to tell Nick . . . she looked round for him, but suddenly he was no longer at her side. They were surrounded by colour and life and noise, separated by it, and he had vanished into the midst of a knot of Chalcenians.

She tried to push through them, but a hand restrained her.

'Leave him,' said Tasnian. 'Let them clean him and feed him. Ananthis wishes to talk to him.'

'But – '

'You will see him again later,' he said, walking away.

'Helen?' Martin was beside her. 'Thank God you're back.'

'Mm,' she said, rubbing her arms. 'Where's Rianna?'

'Talking to Ananthis. I think he's trying to calm her down.' He sounded anxious. 'Oh, it's a elief to see you. We didn't know what had happened to you.'

'Something weird,' she said. She pointed to the group of Chalcenians who were taking Nick up the hill towards a kateya at the summit. 'That's Nick. We just found him.'

'Who's Nick?'

'My ex, how many Nicks do you think I know?'

'But he . . . '

'Don't say it, please.'

Helen tried to explain. The words came with difficulty and seemed jumbled, but Martin listened patiently. She was infinitely glad that he was there. By the time she had finished, most of the other Chalcenians had wandered away, but Tasnian and Sheyde were approaching them with bowls of food.

'Are you well, Helen?' Sheyde asked, her eyes warm and concerned.

'Sort of,' she said. Tasnian stroked her arm. He never seemed to change; he was always quiet and smiling and patient. She felt she could forgive him anything, even the way he had behaved to Corolea.

'You must both be tired and hungry,' he said. 'Come and eat with us.'

Helen and Martin went with them and sat against the trunk of an oak tree, looking out over the rugged hills, all gold, green and silver-blue in the afternoon light. Sheyde and Tasnian gave them bowls of a thick, creamy kir-milk, mixed with seeds and nuts. After, they drank water and wine and ate small, sweet apples. Helen was famished, but she could not relax. She felt she was burning with nervous energy, and if she did not move she would go mad.

Eventually Martin said, 'What's up? Is it Nick?'

'No. It's partly that, but I can't stop thinking about Cadreis. I've got to go and look for him.'

'You cannot leave now, Helen,' said Sheyde. 'You're tired.'

'I'm fine,' she said fiercely.

'Sheyde's right, though,' said Martin. 'What could you do?'

'Just – just look for him, that's all!' She tried to sound reasonable. 'I can't sit here and do nothing. I think I know where to look.'

'Where?' Martin said, surprised.

'The rock where Cadreis and I met Annis. It exists in our world and in Tevera. I think she lives under it. I've got to go and look and I really need your help, Martin. No one else will help me.'

She tried not to direct this remark too pointedly at Sheyde, but Martin glanced at the Chalcenians. The strength of Helen's feeling must have come through in her voice, because he stopped arguing with her.

'I suppose if I don't come, you'll go on your own?' he said.

'I'm not being awkward. I've got to. If it was Rianna – '

'It's OK. I'm coming with you.'

To Helen's astonishment, Sheyde said, 'Tasnian and I will come too.'

The light was deepening towards evening as their four shaliors moved across the hillside, but the colours grew richer, not paler. Now they were doing something positive, Helen felt less agitated. The anxiety was still there but she was floating above it, detached. She rode Hlah, flame-golden in the dusk. Sheyde's mount was a dark brown with red and violet lights moving on its coat; Martin's the mixed hues of a peacock's tail. Tasnian rode the dappled blue. Shaliors and Chalcenians glowed like jewels, enamel figures set in the landscape and edged with gold.

It was a long ride back to the place where Corolea had found her. She knew they would not return to the Heart of Life before dark. She tried to blank out the nagging thought that she had made a terrible mistake.

After a time she recognised the contours of Bradgate Park . . . the Park as it was in Tevera. Riding at her side, Martin said, 'You know we could be drawn back to Earth, don't you?'

'I know,' she said. 'But riding the shaliors, I feel there's less chance of it, don't you?'

'Maybe,' he said. She knew he dreaded leaving Rianna behind; so did she, but Martin was sensitive enough not to make Helen feel worse by talking about it. 'What made them change their minds about helping you?'

'Who, Sheyde and Tasnian?' said Helen. 'I think they must feel responsible for me.'

'I didn't think a sense of responsibility was the Chalcenians' strong point,' he replied dubiously.

From a distance the landscape seemed easy to recognise. Closer at hand, the difference in the size and spread of the copses was confusing. But Helen saw the hill which in her world was called Old John, and from there she easily located the Sliding Stone Crag.

She was sweating and shivering as they approached it. Hlah picked up her nervousness and began to prance and leap.

'Is this the place, Helen?' said Sheyde. Her voice seemed to ring through the quietness; if Annis was there, she must have heard it.

The rocks were a solid stack against the trees and sky. The solitary oak leaned out of the split. Under its roots, as in her vision, Helen saw the thin black mouth of a cave.

'Yes. This is it,' she said.

There was no sign of life within, no sound. They sat and looked, and Helen was thinking: *I can't go in. I can't ask the others to go in, either.*

'Do you want me to go in and look?' said Martin.

Helen jumped. 'No,' she said quickly. 'No, please don't, it's dangerous.'

'Well, it doesn't look like anyone's there. Are we just going to stand here?'

She hesitated. Sheyde and Tasnian waited patiently, saying

nothing. Then, desperate, she shouted, 'Cadreis!'

The silence prickled like static. The shaliors flattened their ears and bunched their muscles. Helen should have known better than to shout again, but she could not help it.

'Cadreis!'

Hlah snorted and sat back on her haunches. A voice came out of the black slit: 'Who's mekkin' that row?'

'Bloody hell,' said Martin, startled. Something moved in the cave mouth, but what came out of it was not a woman.

It was a storm.

A wild, bitter wind tore into them like an explosion. Trees creaked, thrusting black branches at them like witches' fingers. Leaves and twigs battered them, and the shaliors screamed and went wild, spinning in a whirlwind.

Helen never knew how she kept her seat. She simply hung on to the pommel with all her might, gagging and gasping against the bitter ice of the hurricane. The sky turned lurid yellow, and against it a shape rose up, a shape like a tree cut from flapping black paper, but which shook and undulated its branches like human arms.

Above the roar of the wind, a voice shrieked, ''E 'as ter come willin', dun't 'e? Gerrout of it, yer bitches! Nobodeh crosses my border, nobodeh, unless I says so. Dun't you ever come near 'em again, I wun't let yer through!'

Martin's shalior was the first to break loose. It tore past Hlah, bumping into her, and she spun and bolted with it. Sheyde and Tasnian were only a couple of feet behind, and there was nothing any of them could do to stop and face Annis. The wind pressed viciously at their backs, then it condensed itself into a jet-black shalior with malevolent eyes, leapt over their heads and was gone.

The sudden silence and the inrush of warm air was almost as much a shock as the sudden storm had been. They brought the shaliors back to a walk, staring around them and at each other, speechless. Tears were streaming down Helen's face, partly from the cold and partly from shock. Coughing, finding her breath again, she wiped them away.

'She's gone,' said Tasnian. He rode the blue in a circle, looking at the hills behind them. He spoke more in wonder than fear. 'We faced her, Black Annis of the Boundary, and we are unhurt!'

'Speak for yourself,' Martin muttered. He reached out for Helen's hand. 'It's no good. Even if she's got Cadreis, I don't see how we can get him back.'

She nodded. Martin was right. If they wanted proof that it was impossible to challenge Annis, they had received it. 'I wonder what put her in such a vile mood?' she said shakily.

'God knows. You must have woken her up.'

'Did you hear what she said, that she won't let us through the borders again?'

'Don't worry about it, Helen,' Martin replied gently. 'She probably didn't mean it. When Rianna and I came through, I don't think she even noticed. Let's go home and have a rest.'

'You said home,' she murmured.

'Slip of the tongue.'

Fear and cold had burned the nervous energy out of Helen, and she felt exhausted now. She was relieved that Hlah had calmed down, because she did not have the strength to stay on if she played up. Sheyde and Tasnian rode side by side, talking about what they had seen, but so quietly that Helen could hardly hear them.

Presently Martin said, 'We have to talk, Helen.'

'Yes,' she said, but he did not go on. Eventually she asked, 'Are you religious, Martin?'

'Not in the slightest,' he said. 'My family are Roman Catholics. All that religion at an early age put me off it for life. I was a wonderful altar boy, though.'

She smiled in spite of herself. 'I can't picture that. So you don't believe in God?'

'Not now. I must have done once, I suppose, until science and cynicism took over.'

'I don't either. At least, I didn't. Now I'm not so sure. What's a woman who can call up storms and turn herself into anything she likes, if not a goddess? Then there's Nick. He died, but now he's walking around alive again. How do you explain that?'

'Oh, Helen, I wish I had an answer. Are you glad?'

'Of course I'm glad. I never wanted him to die! I'm just so confused. I was convinced that Rianna's doll had somehow killed him. Did the doll also bring him back to life here, or what? I don't know what to think now. There were two other people who died, and maybe others I don't know about. Are they alive in Tevera as well?'

'I don't know,' Martin said helplessly.

'Hasn't Rianna told you anything?'

'Not much. It's not her fault, I don't think she can. She says her memory's come back, but all she could talk about was the baby. Her mind must have blocked it out somehow. It must've been a hell of a shock for her, suddenly remembering that.'

'Don't you mind?' Helen asked.

'Mind what?'

'That she'd had a baby.'

'Why should I mind?' said Martin. 'This isn't *Tess of the d'Urbervilles.* I only mind that it upsets her so much.' He paused. An animal the size of a badger wandered across their path. Its fur was russet with white tips that gave it the look of being covered in a web of stars. 'Look at that.'

They watched the creature until it was lost in the undergrowth. Then Martin went on, 'You were saying about what happened to Nick with the doll. But when you were brought to Tevera, we didn't find you dead, and the doll itself was still there . . . '

'That's because it wasn't the same. I think when Menenthonis found out where we lived, he brought the doll back to the house – unless it spirited itself there, because I don't see how he could have broken into the shop and the house. Black Annis must have needed something to use as a sort of channel to get at me. She took possession of the doll and mimicked what they do. That's the only explanation I can think of, anyway. You know, I still feel so terrible about that argument I had with Rianna, but then I think, what the hell was she doing, making those dreadful things? If only she'd say something to explain it!'

'Well, she's told me nothing yet,' said Martin. 'Helen, you don't mind about Rianna and me, do you? I never thought it might upset you.'

'It hasn't,' she said, rather too sharply.

'I couldn't help it,' he said. 'I never knew it was possible to fall in love with someone overnight, but that's what happened.

I can't explain it. Rianna is – '

'You don't have to explain,' Helen said quickly. 'I felt the same about Cadreis. There's something about Teverans.'

'Must be magic,' Martin said with a half smile. 'I don't know whether she feels the same about me, or whether it was just because she was scared and I was there. I don't think about it.'

Helen nodded. 'I've got to find Cadreis,' she said. 'I suppose the Chalcenians didn't want to help me find him because he's a Domendran. The enemy. But I don't know what side he's really on; I don't think he knows himself. If he's still alive.'

'Come on, Helen,' Martin said gently. 'We'll think of something. At least we've discovered that we can't fight Annis directly; she'd eat us for breakfast.'

A sob escaped Helen. 'Literally,' she said, without humour. 'Isn't that what Rianna said happened to the baby? I mean, I wouldn't have believed her, I couldn't, but I've *seen* Annis. That bitch is capable of anything. Where Cadreis is now, I can't bear to think. I wish I was stronger, Martin. Nick always said I was spoilt, and I suppose my parents did give me too easy a life. I'm hopeless at keeping a stiff upper lip. I just feel like falling apart.'

'You haven't, though, have you? You're stronger than you think, Helen, really.'

'But what am I going to do? What the hell is Annis, anyway?'

'I don't know, but I've heard the name before. It's Leicestershire folklore. She was a wind-hag who lived on the edge of Leicester. That's all I can remember.'

'Good grief. I remember her saying they'd built houses over where she used to live, so she moved to the Park and dug a cave with her own nails. She said it ruined her nail varnish.'

Martin burst out laughing at this, and Helen did too, a release of tension that verged on sobs. She went on, 'Annis was playing a character. She can take any shape she wants. She lives on the boundary between Tevera and Earth; or it exists wherever she is. But the Domendrans told me that she also guards the gates of Anatevera.'

'Anatevera . . . I've heard that before, what is it?'

'What they call limbo. The underworld, I suppose. Even after everything I've seen, that's one place I really can't believe in.'

'So they believe in an afterlife, but not in a God?' said Martin.

Helen sighed. 'I don't know what they believe in. It's so hard to get them to talk. I don't know anything about them, really.'

'You probably know more than you realise,' he said thoughtfully. 'You think there are secret things going on under the surface, but maybe there aren't.'

Helen looked up at the sky. It was almost dark now, but the stars and a half moon washed the landscape with silver. And the constellations seemed the same as those of Earth, only more brilliant. She said, 'That afternoon we came to Tevera and they took us on the sea . . . I could have stayed here for ever.'

'Yes.' Martin scratched his head, as if he was trying to remember something.

'But should people be able to walk from one world to another? Cadreis said it meant something was wrong, and so did Corolea.'

'I don't know, Helen,' he said. 'I was trying to imagine how I'd feel if we really couldn't go home.'

'And?'

'I think I could bear it. I feel . . . I feel as if I belong here. Look, this sounds incredible, I know, but I've got to say it. I'm sure I've lived in Tevera before. I can't remember anything clearly, but it all feels so familiar. Whenever someone tells me something, I think, "Yes, I knew that." Do you believe me?'

'Well – if you say it's so, then – '

'But don't you remember living here before?' Martin said impatiently.

'No. Not a thing,' she said. And for no reason, a terrible feeling of being outcast, of belonging nowhere, swept over her, and it seemed to be the same feeling that she had seen in Corolea's eyes.

When they arrived at the Heart of Life, there was still no sign of Rianna or Nick. Sheyde took them to her kir, saying they were welcome to rest if they needed to. Helen was only too glad to crawl under a cover and fall asleep, but she slept fitfully, and some time later she found herself wide awake, staring at the deep blue gloom.

She knew by the soft snoring on the far side of the chamber that Martin was asleep. But in the centre, two figures in silhouette sat talking in low voices.

'I cannot stop thinking about what happened today!' said Tasnian.

'Weren't you afraid?' Sheyde sounded cool, affectionately mocking.

'It is not Chalcenic to be afraid. What we saw today was something that only the highest of the Chalcenians may see.' He sounded excited.

'Any Chalcenian may see her when the time comes,' Sheyde said drily.

He caught her arms. 'Sheyde, did it not affect you at all? Don't you understand? Annis guards the gate of Anatevera. Today we have confronted and defeated death!'

'She let us go.'

'No! She could not destroy us, because we are Chalcenic! I understand Ananthis now, I could even aspire to his level.'

'Tas, beloved, don't you realise we are not supposed to know he is any higher than us?' Sheyde said. Helen could hear the smile in her voice. 'He pretends to be nothing out of the ordinary, but how he loves us to notice that he is.'

'He's higher only because of knowledge!' Tasnian exclaimed. 'And I want that knowledge. I want to paint it. I want to fly!'

'Hush. You'll wake the others.'

'How can they sleep? I can't!'

'Then don't,' Sheyde said softly. She leaned forward and kissed him, and the two of them sank down into the shadows and began to make love without self-consciousness, without inhibition.

Chapter Sixteen

Helen slept late the next morning, but even as she surfaced through a comfortable doze she sensed that something was happening. There was a bustle of activity round her, excitement sparking in the air. By the time she woke fully the kir was deserted. Why hadn't Martin woken her? She sat up, listening to the murmur of Chalcenian voices outside in the forest with the distinct feeling that she was missing something.

A few moments later Tasnian came into the kir, dressed in a garment of shimmering peacock blues. He seized her hands and pulled her to her feet. 'Helen, you're awake at last. Dress quickly, and come with us!'

'Where? What's happening?'

'We are going on to the ocean Halaranthe.'

'This minute?' she said. 'I'm still half asleep. Where's Martin?'

'You must come. It is in Rianna's honour.' His face was as serene as ever, but she could sense a wild excitement under the surface. It was infectious.

'I'd love to, but I can't go without Martin, and I want to see Nick again.'

'They will come with us. Hurry, Helen. The others won't wait!'

She dressed quickly, uneasy at Martin's absence. But as she followed Tasnian out of the kateya, he appeared at the entrance.

'Where have you been?' Helen exclaimed.

'Looking for Rianna,' Martin said unhappily. 'They won't let me see her. They keep on about some ceremony in her honour. It's ridiculous.'

'It is not ridiculous,' said Tasnian. 'Come with us and you will see her!'

All around them the Chalcenians were flocking from the

Heart of Life to the open hillside, like multi-coloured flamingos on the wing. 'Where are they going?' Martin asked.

'To the ocean, to call the Oa,' said Tasnian. 'As we did the first time you came to Tevera, do you remember?'

Martin looked at Helen. The magic of the first trip could never be forgotten. In their hearts they both longed to see the Oa again. 'I can't go unless I know Rianna's all right.'

'Of course she is! Martin, you cannot miss this. We may see the Transfiguration, the Cahantias. Ananthis says that has not happened in thousands of years.'

'I don't know what you're talking about,' Martin said tersely.

'I can't describe what I've never seen,' said Tasnian. 'If it happens, you will know. It is what we have always hoped for. Rianna might make it happen. Come on, hurry!'

The Chalcenians were crowding around a shalior on the hillside. Tasnian quickened his pace towards them, but Martin hung back and pulled at Helen's arm.

'What's got into him?' he said.

'How should I know?'

'Well, it's making me nervous. One minute they don't want to know Rianna, the next they're treating her like the Queen. Are they mad or is it just me?'

'I'm as much in the dark as you are,' she said. 'Don't worry, I'm sure they don't mean any harm.'

Martin glanced at the Chalcenian men and women running past him. 'This doesn't make you think of one of those films where they're about to burn the witch or make a human sacrifice?' He made it sound like a joke, but his face was full of anxiety.

'Don't be daft.'

'If I could just see her . . . '

They reached the crowd and pushed their way through to the middle. A pure white shalior stood there, with Tasnian, Sheyde, Nenhaliac and Ananthis grouped around it. In the saddle was a slender figure, decked from head to foot with flowers.

'Rianna!' Martin cried, starting towards her. Sheyde blocked his path.

'You cannot speak to her now. Be patient.'

Martin protested, then reluctantly went back to Helen's side. Rianna's appearance awed them slightly. Her body was covered in blue-petalled flowers, blending through purple to indigo on her legs. Those twined round her arms were green, and even her hands were covered with crimson blossoms. A yellow-gold wreath sat on her coppery hair. No longer upset, her face had no expression beyond a vacant tranquillity, and when she turned her wide eyes on Helen and Martin, the look did not change. She was as distant and unreachable as a rainbow above them.

'What have they done to her?' Martin whispered.

The Chalcenians were cheering her with more than their usual enthusiasm. Ananthis raised his hands to quiet them, then leaned towards Nenhaliac. Helen heard him say, 'Make the speech, Nen. However sincere I feel, I never seem to sound it. You will be better than me.'

The healer nodded and stepped forward. His hair was a wild mass of emerald, his eyes ringed with black and white. Helen shuddered to think that she had had to trust her life to him.

'This, our honoured guest, is the Pelumayis, Rianna,' he began. 'She is the last one, the only one we have. She has been in the Otherworld and she will go there again for us, to create the pathway to the third life. For this we honour her and name her Lifegiver!'

Helen had to cover her ears against the roar of adulation. The Chalcenians' sudden passion for Rianna was almost frightening. Rianna did not react, but her silvery-pale eyes slid from side to side as if she felt trapped.

'Now let us bring her to the ocean Halaranthe,' said Nenhaliac. 'Although she was born here, this will be the first time she has seen the Oa, and her time in Tevera will be short. Let us make it a time she will never forget. For if we bring the Pelumayis to the Oa, who knows if we will not see at last the transfiguration and the Cahantias?'

As the Chalcenians began to make their way towards the sea, everyone went on foot except Rianna. With startling humility which seemed quite out of character, Ananthis himself led the white shalior to ensure that it went quietly for her. She shone in the centre of the crowd. The mood of euphoria was impossible to resist and Helen found herself caught up in it.

'There's nothing to be afraid of,' she said, squeezing Martin's shoulder. 'They love her, they won't hurt her.'

'This is like being at the bloody dentist,' said Martin, 'when they keep smiling at you and saying "This won't hurt". Translation: "This is going to be unspeakably nasty, but please don't inconvenience us by making a fuss."'

Helen saw no sign of Nick until they reached the beach, when she caught sight of him with a group of women. His appearance startled her. Dressed in Chalcenian robes, his beauty blending with theirs, he could have been taken for a Chalcenian himself. The women hung on his arms, making a fuss of him, while he laughed and joked with them as if he had known them all his life.

Helen did not go to him. He was a long way from her, and definitely not in need of her company. She kept her concern for Rianna.

The beach was washed with gold under a bluebell sky. On the sea the butterfly-wing sails of the boats bobbed and glittered. Gentle waves smoothed the sand.

The crowd halted at the water's edge, cheering again as Tasnian and Sheyde reached up to help Rianna down from the shalior. As she moved to dismount, all the flowers suddenly unfurled wings and lifted into the air. Helen gasped. They were not flowers but bright-winged insects. Like a flock of birds they peeled away from Rianna, revealing the pastel shimmer of the robe she wore underneath. A few still clung, here and there, like jewels.

Ananthis beckoned to Helen and Martin. 'There are not enough boats for everyone,' he said with a condescending smile. 'You may come in ours, with Rianna. I hope you realise how privileged you are.'

The moment Rianna's feet touched the sand, she ran into Martin's arms. The Chalcenians did not try to stop her. They only smiled as he hugged her, exclaiming with relief. Seeing them embrace, Helen felt a pang of jealousy and longing. She knew the feeling was childish, reprehensible, but she could not suppress it. She had thought of Rianna and Martin only in relation to herself, as *her* friends, but now there was something between them that excluded her. She wanted Cadreis desperately, but he was gone and she was alone.

She shook the feeling off. Tasnian's and Sheyde's arms were round her; how could she feel sorry for herself when she was surrounded by love and standing on the shore of Halaranthe?

Martin looked at her over Rianna's shoulder, as if to say, 'Sorry I doubted you. Everything is all right after all.'

Their second voyage had all the glamour of the first, and more. The very air seemed effervescent. The little boat was crowded, with Ananthis, Tasnian and Sheyde taking up the rest of the room, but Helen did not care. Rianna was safe between her and Martin, and their fears had been unfounded.

Twenty boats set sail across a sea as green and smooth as glass. The laughter of the Chalcenians rose above the gentle lapping of water. Helen looked around for Nick, but she had a feeling he was with the many who had had to stay on shore.

For a while she felt that everything was perfect and there was nothing to say. But presently Rianna said, 'Helen, can you forgive me?'

'Whatever for?'

'For running off and leaving you alone that night. It was a dreadful thing to do. I'm so sorry.' Her hand slid into Helen's.

'Oh, Rianna, it doesn't matter. Can you forgive me for letting you go off on your own? I was upset and I said things I didn't mean . . . '

'I know.' They looked at each other. Rianna smiled. They both knew the argument was over, forgotten and forgiven; it no longer mattered. Helen felt an unspeakable relief and calmness simply at being with her again.

'Do you feel better now?' Helen asked.

'Yes. I've been talking to Ananthis. It helped.'

Helen found it hard to imagine that talking to Ananthis could help anyone, but she did not say so. 'Rianna, would you tell me something? When you claimed you'd lost your memory, that you really couldn't remember how we used to go into the Park, was it true?'

'Yes,' Rianna said, slightly ashamed. 'I – I really couldn't, Helen. But I think I forgot because I wanted to. When I came back to England, I was scared to go in the Park, because I knew that if I did, I'd remember things I didn't want to. And I was right. As soon as Martin and I came through, I started to remember. When you and I used to play in the Park, for me it wasn't playing. I was standing on the boundary, wishing I could go home.'

'Can you tell us what you remember now?' Martin said gently.

'I'll try. It seems such a long time ago.' Although Rianna was calm, she was very pale. 'I was born in the Heart of Life. When Martin brought me back, I knew where to find it, and I recognised it as if I'd never been away.'

'And did you know any of the people?'

'Not – not really. I was only a little child when I left. Some I recognise, but they might as well be strangers . . . We have no families, you see. The children are all brought up together by guardians they call Shefris.'

'Yes, Tasnian told me,' said Helen.

'It's not that the Chalcenians don't love each other, you mustn't think that. But they can't tolerate possessiveness, even that of a parent for a child. But some people form special bonds all the same . . . '

'Was there someone you loved?' Martin asked.

'Yes. My Shefri. I can't say I thought of him as a parent, because I did not know what a parent was . . . but that's what we were like, father and daughter. And I didn't even know his name. He was simply Shefri to me. I can see him so clearly, even now.'

Helen glanced at Ananthis and the others, but they were too busy talking among themselves to listen. She put a hand over the side of the boat and trailed it in the water as Rianna went on, 'I was happy as a child. I knew I was loved, I never doubted it. There were friends all around me, and my Shefri. I thought he would always be with me, until I got up one morning and he was not there any more.'

'What had happened to him?' Helen asked quietly.

'I had no idea. He had simply vanished. I thought it was my fault, because we had been too close and the other Chalcenians did not like that. I thought he had had to go away because I loved him too much. When I asked about him, they ignored my questions. I learned very painfully that when someone goes away you must never ask about them, but I didn't understand why.'

'You mean he had died,' said Martin.

Rianna frowned. 'I – that's what I thought. I didn't know what death was, but an older boy took me aside and told me that my Shefri was dead. At the time I thought he was being cruel; now I think perhaps he meant to be kind, to make me forget. He told me that my Shefri had passed on to Anatevera, the afterlife.

'I understood so little. The Chalcenians don't think of death as being final, and I got the impression that Anatevera was a real place I could go to. So I decided to find my Shefri and bring him back, and I ran away from the Heart of Life.'

'You poor thing,' said Martin. 'You must have been terrified.'

'Yes, I was. I got completely lost, then I saw this old woman sitting on a rock. I had never seen anyone really old before. She was so ancient that she was like a papery old tree . . . except for her face. Her face was like granite. She seized hold of me with long spiky fingers and demanded to know what I was doing.

'I said, "I'm looking for a man." She gave a really nasty laugh and said, "So am I."'

'That couldn't be anyone but Black Annis,' Helen said grimly.

'I tried to explain, but she said I could only go to Anatevera if I died. I was frightened. I remember I kept saying, "I don't want to die, I just want my Shefri back," and in the end she said, "I like you, girl. I don't want to kill you. But if I let you through alive, you've got to give me something in return."

'I said I'd give her anything.' Rianna's voice was as quiet and dry as the wind rustling the leaves. 'She thought, then she laughed and said, "Give us your first baby." Well, I didn't know what I was promising, I didn't understand . . . '

'It's all right,' said Martin, stroking her head.

'So I agreed, and she said, "All right, you can go through, but old Annis will always be watching you." Then she vanished. I didn't see anything change, I just went on walking until it grew light, but suddenly there were strange people around me, iron gates and machines made of metal. I didn't know where I was or who I was. This couldn't be the afterlife; Annis had tricked me, sent me to a horrible world instead.'

'Where you couldn't even speak the language,' said Martin.

'No. I was put in a children's home, while they tried to find out who I was. I hated it. The cold white walls, the cruelty of the other children . . . I was only there a few months, then a man and woman came and adopted me. My Mum and Dad.' She pressed her fingers to her forehead. 'It all seems so weird . . . having lived in one world, then forgotten it and grown used to another.

'Annis stole something else from me. My memory. Or at least, she blurred it. I knew I was trying to find someone, but I couldn't remember who. I didn't know where to start. The more English I learned, the more Tevera seemed like a dream. Helen, do you remember those times in the Park?'

'Of course I do. They were beautiful, Rianna.'

'I could go into Bradgate Park and just walk about on the boundary between our worlds. I don't know why Annis allowed it; perhaps she didn't notice or care. We never saw her, did we?'

'No, thank God,' Helen murmured.

'While I was there, I would begin to remember things, very vaguely. A beautiful people called the Chalcenians, the names of the animals of Tevera. But I couldn't go back. Perhaps I was afraid to, afraid of Annis. I still knew there was something I had to do first, if only I could recall what it was.'

Rianna was silent for a time. The boats were circuiting a small island. Weird plants grew along the shore, with long silver-green leaves and huge flowers that looked like bells made of crumpled yellow tissue paper. The fruiting heads trailed along the ground, sprouting vast seed pods.

'Look, they're kir-plants,' said Martin.

From the other end of the boat, Sheyde said, 'They are the Flowers of Cahantias.'

'Tasnian said something about seeing Cahantias. Is this what he meant?'

'No,' Sheyde laughed, leaving them utterly confused. 'He meant we might see the Cahantias itself!'

The island slid past and was left behind. The swell of the waves increased, and the sails swayed against a jewel-bright sky. Martin said, 'Go on, Rianna. Keep talking, then I won't think about feeling seasick.'

'Where was I? Well, my parents – and I really did think of them as parents now – decided to emigrate. I was never really happy in New Zealand. But I became very good at pretending I was, because I had this dreadful feeling that if I did not, I would be sent away. Where did I get that idea? Not from my Mum and Dad, although I knew they worried about me if I seemed unhappy. It was something I'd retained from Tevera. I could never forget completely. Annis would not let me, not when I was still in debt to her and old enough to do something about it.' Rianna closed her eyes. 'So I had a baby. Not for me, not for its own sake. For her.'

'But if Annis lives in England, how could she take the baby from New Zealand?' said Helen.

'Annis lives wherever death is,' Rianna whispered. She opened her eyes very wide, staring at the sky. 'However she did it, she took the child and even then I knew she wasn't finished with me. I could just hear her saying, "I like you. Old Annis will be watching you."

'I was in a mental ward for a few weeks after the birth, did my mother tell you that? So my fears came true in a way; I was depressed, so I was exiled. But my poor mum and dad, how on earth could I explain what had happened? Everyone thought I was crazy as it was.

'While I was recovering, I made the first doll. Don't ask me where the idea came from; somewhere very deep inside me, or maybe from outside. My family and the doctors were delighted that I was taking an interest in something, a sort of occupational therapy. By the time I'd finished the doll, I'd forgotten about the baby. I'd forgotten Tevera. My mind had blocked it all out. But the doll . . . I always had this feeling Annis was angry that I'd made it, and she was using it to watch me. Annis had taken over the doll, so it was spoiled and I daren't part with it. But I made more dolls to be given to other people. I felt there must be thousands, millions of dolls, everyone in the world must have one, and I was the only person who could do it.'

Rianna breathed in, held the breath, let it out softly. 'That kind of thing is regarded as a delusion, isn't it? A symptom of schizophrenia, or something similar. I knew that, because whatever anyone thought, I was not mad. So I was very sane about it. When I left school I got a nice, sensible job in an office and I made and sold the dolls as a hobby. And everyone was so pleased that I'd made such a good recovery.'

Helen said, 'What were the dolls for?'

'I didn't know. Nothing happened to most people who had them. There were just a few who – who died unexpectedly.'

'Just a few?' Helen choked.

'I know how it sounds. A voice always seemed to be telling me that it was all right, but I was scared sometimes. No, I was scared all the time, but every time I tried to stop the voice would tell me: *It's all right. You must make the Pelu . . .* ' She hesitated. 'That is their true name. Ananthis told me.'

'Yes. Go on.'

'How can I explain? I hated making the dolls. Yet I only felt right while I was working on them. As long as no one tried to stop me, I was almost happy. But then, last year, the man began to follow me.'

'Did you know his name was Menenthonis?'

'Not at the time, no. I didn't know anything about him, but *part* of me knew him . . . the dark part of me that seems to know things without ever telling my conscious mind. Does that make sense? Anyway, I had to escape or he would stop me making the dolls, and worse than that, he would take me away to a dreadful, dark place. I couldn't have explained any of this to anyone, I just *knew*. So I left my job and made up some story to my parents about going off to work in Europe. They were shocked at first, but it was the sort of thing a lot of my schoolfriends had done, so they didn't really think there was anything odd about it. After that, it was automatic to come back to Leicestershire and to find you, Helen. I was working my way back to where I belonged.'

Rianna closed her eyes, seeming exhausted by the effort of telling the story. As gently as she could, Helen asked, 'But don't you know what the dolls are now?'

'Not dolls. Pelu.'

'But what are they?'

'Helen, no more, please!' She squeezed Helen's hand. 'I'm sorry. Ananthis will tell you later; he promised he would. I can't talk any more, I'm so tired.'

'Don't worry,' said Martin. 'Just put your head on my knees and go to sleep.'

As he spoke, the boat began to rock violently, and they all sat up in alarm. Tasnian was climbing up one of the masts, his bright blue hair swinging like a pennant and his garments flapping. The mast could not bear his weight. It was bending like a sapling, making the sail crumple and the rigging sag like a cobweb under the weight of dew. Tasnian seemed unconcerned.

'He'll capsize us!' said Martin.

Ananthis and Sheyde did nothing to restrain him. Despite the pitching of the boat, they were cheering him on. Martin was the only one who shouted at him to stop.

Tasnian took no notice. 'The Oa!' he cried. 'The Oa!'

The mast held. He slid down it and threw himself over the side of the boat, fully clothed. The little boat kicked through a wave, scattering foam, then righted itself. Helen hung on to the side, breathless. None of the others followed Tasnian, but she saw distant figures in the other boats disrobing and diving in.

'Sheyde!' Martin called. 'What's wrong with him?'

She stared at him, laughing with astonishment. 'Nothing!'

'Nothing?' he exclaimed, but only Helen was listening. 'He was so quiet before. What's got into him?'

'I've no idea,' Helen said, straining her eyes to keep sight of him. 'Oh, God, he'll drown himself. Can you see him?'

'Don't worry, Helen,' said Rianna. She suddenly seemed happier. Her eyes were shining, and there was healthy colour in her cheeks. The wind whipped strands of hair around her face. 'He is in Elation. No harm will come to him. I remember this . . . '

She tried to stand up, but Martin quickly held her down. She seemed transfixed. Then Helen saw the emerald shapes sliding under the surface of the water, the quicksilver flash of scales, and she forgot Tasnian.

'They are called the Oa,' said Rianna excitedly. 'I *have* seen them before, my Shefri brought me. They are the givers of grace and joy . . . '

The sea creatures circled playfully round the boat then

dived again, trailing foam along the waves. A powerful feeling came over Helen that everything was exactly as it should be. The sky was a sphere of blown glass, blue and silver, delicate but infinitely enduring. Everything beneath it was cherished and safe . . .

The next thing she knew, Ananthis was hurling himself across the boat at Rianna.

'They are leaving!' he cried. 'Help me call them back!' He seized Rianna and began kissing her. Martin stared at them for a moment in total astonishment, then pulled Rianna away. The boat plunged alarmingly. The Chalcenians in the nearby vessels whooped and cheered. Rianna hung stretched between Ananthis and Martin for a moment, then she cried, 'I'm not a doll! Let go of me!'

'Then call the Oa!' Ananthis exclaimed as he let her go. 'Call them, Rianna!'

Rianna slumped over the side of the boat, stretching her hands out above the water. She was breathing fast. Almost at once, seven shining creatures broke through the surface, scattering spray over everyone. Helen's heart somersaulted. The Oa seemed different now, frantic. They thrashed the waves stiff as egg-white, sliding over and round each other until they were tangled into a knot. Then they rose up, dancing on their tails like dolphins, faster and faster until their soft golden eyes turned dull with exhaustion.

'Cahantias!' shouted Ananthis. *'Cahantias!'*

Others took up the cry. Helen leaned out beside Rianna, the edge of the boat pressing across her ribs until she could hardly breathe. The Oa were yearning wildly towards something, but they could not attain it and the effort was tormenting them.

'Let them stop!'

'No, call them, Rianna!' said Ananthis. 'The Transfiguration must take place!'

'I can't! I don't know what you want of me!'

'Try!'

Rianna was gasping for breath, straining towards the Oa. For one dreadful second Helen though she would go over the side. Then she flopped back into the bottom of the boat, her chest heaving. At once the Oa crashed back into the water, disentangled themselves and dived out of sight.

The mood had changed. From the other boats there were light-hearted cries of disappointment, but Helen had the feeling the other Chalcenians had no more idea of what should have happened than she had.

'What the hell were you trying to do?' said Martin, gathering Rianna in his arms.

Ananthis sat back in his place, as cool as if nothing had happened. 'Obviously the time is not yet. Never mind, Rianna. It will be soon.' Giving Martin a scathing look, he added, 'It is sexual energy that is needed.'

The vessel lurched again. Tasnian was climbing in over the side, his clothes streaming with water and so heavy that it took Sheyde and Ananthis a good deal of effort to help him in again. He was the only one who did not seem at all subdued by what had happened. His eyes were shining and he did not stop talking all the time it took them to sail back to the shore.

'This can't be happening, can it?' Martin said as they walked slowly along the beach towards the cliff paths. Rianna walked arm in arm between him and Helen. Whether the Chalcenians felt Rianna had let them down in some way, or whether they were simply being their fickle selves, they had transferred their attention to Tasnian. 'But it's so real. I never experienced anything so real. I feel as if I've always been part of it. Don't you, Helen?'

'I don't know,' Helen said. 'I just – I don't know what to think.' For once, she did not feel like talking. She felt wildly excited, happy, confused, disturbed, all at the same time, and she could not put any of it into words. Tasnian might have calmed her, but he was behaving so strangely that he seemed like a different person. Many of the Chalcenians were running and dancing with him like children, inspired by his wild mood.

Martin said, 'I wonder why he's like that. He's not just in high spirits, he's manic.'

'You think he's ill?' said Helen.

'Well, he's definitely irrational. It's impossible to talk to him.'

'I know, I've tried.'

Rianna said, 'He's not ill. Elation is a higher state. The

Chalcenians revere it.'

Her words brought back a less pleasant memory to Helen: dark shapes standing or sitting motionless in a barely lit cave. Domendrans in the level they called Nohm, unspeaking, unable to move or communicate. She imagined Tasnian like that, then shook the image off quickly.

'Why?' Martin asked.

Rianna shrugged, closed and opened her lips. 'It is a higher state. It is closer to the Oa. Euphoria.'

'That's all very well, but his antics nearly tipped us all in the water. Elation is bloody dangerous, if you ask me. Ananthis wasn't much better. What was he trying to make you do?'

Rianna shrugged vaguely. Helen thought she genuinely did not know. 'Did you hear Tasnian and Sheyde last night?' Helen asked, then added hurriedly, 'Talking, I mean.'

'No, I was fast asleep,' said Martin.

'Well, whatever's got him in this state was something to do with Annis. He was on about how he'd confronted and defeated death.' As she spoke, they saw Tasnian, in the distance, beginning to climb up a steep, rocky part of the cliff. 'Look at him now.'

Tasnian climbed with the poise of a dancer and the agility of a squirrel. It was all Helen could do to watch. The near-vertical face would have daunted an experienced climber, yet he never put a foot wrong. He shone like a kingfisher against the rocks.

When he reached the top safely, she breathed again. He waved both arms wildly above his head, and the Chalcenians, watching from below, cheered in response.

Tasnian was shouting to them. He was obviously breathless, and the wind carried his words away. Helen could only just make out part of what he was saying.

'Annis cannot bind us. Anatevera cannot hold us. Death cuts us down and we spring up again, flying like birds. We are in Chalceny . . . we shall fly!'

And he flung himself off the top of the cliff.

The air currents rippled fiercely through his garments. Two never-ending seconds, then the beach received his body with a dull thump.

The Chalcenians' voices were cut off in mid-cry. Silence fell, thick as sand, pierced here and there by a gasp, a smothered cry. For a moment they froze, and then, as one, they flowed forward to form a half circle around Tasnian. Helen did not want to look, did not want to push through them, but she and Martin went forward with them as if hypnotised.

The first ones to reach him had turned him on to his back. Tasnian lay utterly still, his eyes wide open, blue as the sky. He was still smiling, but the expression was a carving in wax. Sheyde and one or two others knelt beside him, while Nenhaliac the healer bent to listen to his heart.

Helen glanced at her companions. Martin had gone white, but there was no emotion at all expressed on the faces of the Chalcenians, and Rianna reflected their detachment. The only sign they gave that they cared was their sudden, total silence.

Nenhaliac rose. He said, 'The portal has received him. May he live again in Anatevera.'

'May he live again,' echoed the other Chalcenians.

Then they turned and began to move slowly and quietly away.

'No,' Helen whispered. She felt Martin's arm around her, supporting her. 'Is that it?'

'Helen – '

'They can't – they can't just leave him there. What are they doing?'

'Helen,' he repeated, quite sharply. 'Don't say anything. If it's their way, we have to respect it.'

'But – ' She was straining towards Tasnian's body. 'He might not be dead – '

Martin's arm restrained her. 'Come away,' he said firmly. 'Come on, Helen.'

She felt Rianna's hand on the small of her back, warm and light as a bird. 'It's all right, Helen. They will come for his body and take it to – '

'Where?'

'Take it away. But Martin is right.'

Rianna's voice was calm, her face tranquil, but tears were flowing down her cheeks.

They walked back to the Heart of Life without speaking.

Helen could not cry. She felt she had done all the crying she was capable of, over losing people and finding them again. Now there was only a heavy sense of disbelief and confusion, like a boulder lodged in her stomach.

She could not look at Sheyde's serene face and ask, 'Don't you care?' The way the Chalcenians chose to express or contain their grief was not hers to question or judge. Rianna understood; so, with startling instinct, did Martin. Helen felt like the only alien among them.

Back at the Heart of Life everyone dispersed quietly and went about their usual business as if everything was normal. Helen was desperate to speak to someone, but Sheyde and the others slipped away from her like the Oa through the waves. No one would ever ask, 'Where's Tasnian?' She could not bear the finality of it, the coldness.

'Didn't anyone guess what he was going to do?' she said to Martin. 'Why didn't someone try to stop him?'

'Don't ask me.' He put a comforting arm round her, but she was not comforted. 'Come on, Helen, there's nothing you can do.'

'I hardly knew him,' she said. 'I always felt there was so much to find out, and now I never will. Have you ever had that feeling that you really love someone – I mean, not as a lover necessarily, as a friend – or that you were just growing to love them, only suddenly it's too late?'

'It's no good upsetting yourself about it,' Martin said helplessly. She knew his mind was more on Rianna than anything else. Misery flew up into her throat like strangling rage.

'Someone's got to be upset for him!' she cried, turning and marching away. 'I'm going to make some bastard in this place talk to me!'

She found Ananthis inside one of the kateyas, by sheer determination rather than luck. He was alone, to her relief, but she had forgotten how intimidating he could seem. He was taller than Nick, his chiselled features accentuated with paint, his hair white-gold like the sun.

'I'm sick of being treated like an idiot,' she said. 'Why is it so hard for anyone to answer my questions?'

'It grieves me to see you in such a state,' he said. 'How can I help you, Helen?' His cool superciliousness made her even more angry. She felt powerless.

'Just talk to me! Or if that's too much trouble, at least have the decency to admit you cared about Tasnian.'

His face softened slightly. 'Of course I cared. But these things happen.'

'Is that all you can say?'

'What do you wish me to say?' He crossed the kir towards the entrance, and she followed him.

'Just tell me why! What was wrong with him?'

'Nothing was wrong. He was in a state we call Elation.'

'Well, where I come from we call it mania. It's an illness,' Helen said grimly. 'Either that or he had taken some kind of drug. Don't walk off while I'm talking to you!'

'I am not. There's something I wish to show you,' he said mildly. 'Tasnian was not ill or drugged. It is something inside us. Elation may happen to anyone; it is euphoria. We welcome it.'

'But it results in death?'

Ananthis gave her an ironic look. 'Only if the Elated one throws himself from a cliff, or something similar. It is not inevitable.' He led her through a long series of kirs where Chalcenian men and women sat weaving the silky kir-fibre into cloth. Hanks of fibre made a small forest on the ceiling. Two children, who were painting tiny clay beads, grinned at Ananthis as he passed.

Further on they came to a large, light kir. The walls were covered in paintings. There were tranquil scenes of the sea and the Heart of Life; a serene portrait of Sheyde and another of Ananthis, studies of flowers. Ananthis led her into the next kir. There the paintings became progressively more strange and disturbed. Skies became ragged, seas wild. Elongated birds swooped over breathtaking drops. Vague rainbow figures haunted weird landscapes. The last ones were such a chaotic blur that she could not even interpret them, yet they filled her with a sense of the painter's excitement, the scent of the sea.

'Did Tasnian paint them?' she asked.

'Yes,' said Ananthis. 'What do you see in them?'

'I think . . . I think he saw something beyond . . . '

'Beyond what?'

She lifted her shoulders helplessly. 'Beyond this life.'

'So, why feel sorrow for him? Perhaps he found it. Death is not the end. One day he will come back to us, Helen, though you and I may never see him again.'

Helen could not take her eyes from the paintings, which so clearly mapped the change in Tasnian's state of mind. 'How . . . how can he come back?'

'Did Rianna not tell you?'

'No,' said Helen. 'She said that you had promised to tell me about the Pelu.'

Ananthis gave a lazy smile. 'But my favourite pastime is breaking promises.'

'What? Look, all I ask is that you be straight with me, and instead I get – '

'You should know by now that I am never straight.' He placed a hand on her shoulder. 'Helen, don't look at me like that. It frightens me and takes away all my pleasure in tormenting you. Come with me.'

Ananthis took her to his own kir. Rows of shining garments hung from the walls and the air was sweet with aromatic oils. On one wall there was a painting which made her stop and stare. It showed a yellow, burning desert with a few trees straggling along the horizon. In the foreground stood three African tribesmen, all but naked, their skin shining black under a relentless sun.

'Where did this come from?' she exclaimed. 'It's a painting of Earth.'

'No, Helen, it is Tevera,' said Ananthis, the merest touch of surprise in his voice.

'But where? Tasnian didn't paint it, it's not his style.'

'No. It is very old and I don't know where it is from. I have never travelled that widely. Perhaps I should. No doubt some Chalcenian brought it back from his travels . . . '

Helen looked more closely, and now she could see the Chalcenian traits in the figures: the subtle differences in bearing, the beauty that was not quite earthly. A creature like a scarlet feathered lion was crossing the landscape behind the figures.

This part of Tevera is so like Charnwood . . . another, like Africa.

Maybe every part of Earth has its equivalent in Tevera.

Ananthis showed her a comfortable place to sit, and poured her a cup of watered wine. She found herself watching his every graceful movement, fascinated by him. Handing her the cup, he sat beside her. 'Poor Helen. Brave Helen,' he said.

'Why do you call me that?' she said, uncertain of whether he was mocking her or not.

'It seems to me you have suffered a great deal over your friends, yet you are still Chalcenic.'

'I would love to think I'm one of you, but I don't see how I can be.'

Ananthis laughed, shaking his head. 'Have you misunderstood all this time? Chalceny is not our race. It is a state of mind.'

'Happiness?' she said.

'If you want to be simplistic, yes.'

'But I'm not happy at the minute. I'm bloody angry.'

'But anger is a sign that the spirit is alive. You are full of passion and hope. Rianna means much to you, doesn't she?'

'Yes . . . but I don't know what to make of her. I don't want to believe anything bad about her, but on Earth she was making dolls that seemed to be causing people's deaths. Nick died, then I find him alive again. Please tell me what it means, because if you don't I think I'll go mad.'

'That would never do,' Ananthis said with a half smile. 'The dolls' true name is Pelu. To explain what they are, I must tell you of the cycle of life. We are born for the first time in Tevera, and when we die we pass to the Otherworld, Anatevera. That is our second life.' He suddenly reached out and touched Helen's forehead and for a second she thought she had gone blind. She started in panic, but Ananthis held her still and she realised that she was seeing a vision. It was all shadows, a clearing in a forest with a fine rain hanging in the air, turning everything silver-grey. Human figures crouched in a circle, their naked skin painted with strange patterns. Helen had the feeling of a lost time, a chasm of years yawning away into a past so ancient that her mind spun. A woman moved round the circle, giving to each a doll made of twigs and leaves. In some hands, the dolls began to twitch.

'God, what is it?' she gasped. She felt Ananthis's hands on

her, cool and firm.

'Nothing to be afraid of. In Anatevera, every person is given a Pelu. When they have lived out their life there, the Pelu will bring them back to Tevera where they become the third-born, whom we call Gallah.'

Now Helen was seeing a man dying, while the doll in his hands came to life and danced on his chest before vanishing. The scene changed subtly. She was looking at a forest floor. Leaves and soil erupted and the Pelu wriggled out, shedding its leafy costume until it was a gleaming figure of white, stripped wood. It began to grow, to take on human shape and flesh. The man who had died stood before her eyes again, recognisable but wholly renewed, shining and perfect.

'Stop,' said Helen. The image faded and her eyesight cleared. 'How can this happen? What are the Pelu?'

'They are a focus for the elemental form of the soul. They catch the soul and bring it back through the barrier of death, which otherwise it could not cross again.'

What Helen was hearing sounded like purest peasant superstition, yet she had seen too much proof to disbelieve him. She was still confused. Was there a limbo shared by Earth and Tevera? 'Where do the Pelu come from?' she asked.

'They are made by one with an instinctive skill: the Pelumayis, who is always a Chalcenian who has crossed to the underworld alive . . . ' For the first time she saw a touch of sadness on his face. 'I speak as if it were still so. But it has not been so for thousands of years. In all that time there have been no Gallahs, because there have been no Pelu to bring them home.'

There was a silence, which to Helen seemed full of desolation. 'But if they didn't come back to Tevera – what happened to them?'

'What else is there for them, except oblivion – true death? Without the Pelu, the cycle of life is ended.'

'What went wrong?'

'The others – of course, I can name them to you – the Domendrans stopped the cycle. They had their reasons, which no doubt they truly believe are right, but I care nothing for that. They have committed a great evil for which they can never be forgiven, an evil which must be put right. They have had their way for thousands of years, but it is not too late.'

'The Domendrans deliberately prevented people being reborn? But how could they do that?'

'By bribing Black Annis,' said Ananthis. 'She guards the gate of death. What she is, I do not know, but her appetites seem human enough. They supplied her with lovers, and in return she let them through the barrier alive to pursue and destroy all the Pelumayis until there were none left.'

'Wasn't there anything the Chalcenians could do to prevent it?'

'Very little.'

'Why not?'

He pursed his lips, and leaned over to refill her cup. 'I hoped you would not ask. The reasons are complex. Annis should be neutral, but she is not; she co-operated with the Domendrans for her own reasons. She would be bought by them, she would not be bought by us. But the fault lies also in the nature of the Chalcenians themselves. We are not perfect. Ignorance, apathy and disorganisation are not least among our numerous vices, and we never made a proper resistance. Too busy living for the moment, no thought for eternity. Besides, we do not fight the Domendrans openly. The truth is, we fear them . . . '

'I don't blame you,' said Helen. 'They scared the hell out of me. But how did Rianna – '

'I am coming to that. I have lived . . . about thirty years, I believe. I have perhaps another twenty, if I do not follow Tasnian. I have taken the trouble to learn and understand far more than most Chalcenians here, but how can my wisdom be complete after so few years? Black Annis, now, is as ancient as time. Would you expect her always to be the same, or to change as the world changes?'

'I don't see why she shouldn't change, if she's human in other ways,' said Helen.

'Good. Because she has changed. Perhaps even she can become old and forgetful. The Domendrans failed to keep a bargain with her and that displeased her. For the first time in aeons, she let Chalcenians through her gate alive, and we were able to send several Pelu-makers to the other side.'

'When was this?'

'Around the time I was born, I think. Those who sent the Pelumayis were my teachers; they are gone now. But after the Pelu-makers were sent through, the Gallahs began to return. Only a few, but it was a start. Unfortunately, the moment our grim friends found out, they pursued and captured every Pelumayis we sent, until there were none left.'

'Except Rianna,' said Helen.

Ananthis stroked his cheek with a long finger. 'Mmm. Now, little Rianna. She was strange, you see, because we did not know about her. She was a small girl when she vanished. Talking to her, I discover that she was making the Pelu purely by instinct and did not even know what she was doing. Now she is the only Pelumayis we have at present. The Domendrans must not have her, under any circumstances. All our hopes rest on her, and she must go back to Earth.'

The suspicion Helen had felt of Ananthis returned. She remembered how he had shouted at her in the boat, and her stomach turned cold.

'I see,' she said coldly. 'The Domendrans want to destroy her, and you want to use her. Have you asked Rianna how she feels about this?'

'How she feels is irrelevant. She must be our Pelumayis.'

'But what if she doesn't want to go back to Earth?'

'She will go!' Ananthis said irritably. 'She knows her duty. I can't understand why you're arguing about it.'

'It just seems a hell of a responsibility to put on her, that's all! She's had a dreadful time and she's vulnerable.'

His eyes glittered, and she saw no empathy in them at all. In his way, Ananthis was as single-minded as Artienter. Helen suddenly felt desperately afraid for Rianna, seeing her dragged this way and that like a rag doll.

'I understand your concern for her,' he said. 'Particularly as it is my fault that she ran away from the Heart of Life in the first place.'

'Yours? You mean you were the child who told her that her Shefri was dead?'

'I am afraid so.'

'Why tell her something so cruel?'

'Unpleasant though I must have been as a child, I did not mean to be cruel. I hoped it would help her forget him.'

'But was he dead?'

'It was a long time ago. It is of no relevance now. The important thing is that Rianna must make the Pelu. If she does not, there will be no return from Anatevera for anyone.' Helen climbed to her feet. 'Where are you going?'

'I've heard enough. It's too much for Rianna. There must be someone who can help her!'

'I hope there will be, but for now she is on her own. You can change nothing by running away, Helen!' His voice followed her as she left the kir. 'Without her, Tasnian will not live again. Neither will you! So which is the greater sacrifice? Rianna's happiness or life itself?'

The following day and night were wretched for Helen. After she left Ananthis she could not face being with anyone. She had to be alone to gather her thoughts, but at the same time she had never felt more isolated. She spent the night in a deserted kir, but could not sleep. The images whirled through her mind like a film loop; the wild joy of the Gallahs, the Domendrans conspiring with Annis to end the cycle of life, Rianna crying out as she was pulled and pushed between opposing sides, '*I am not a doll! Let go of me!*'

Helen rose before dawn and rode Hlah into the hills. Shafts of sunlight fell in glory between soft, bright clouds, and unearthly animals scampered in the light. She thought: *I'm doing what Corolea did. I'm running away. Is this how she felt? I wonder what made her so miserable. The Chalcenians welcome you when you return, but they never try to stop you leaving.*

She turned and went back eventually, knowing Martin would be worried and not wanting to cause any more distress. Tevera's beauty had calmed her, as Bradgate Park had always calmed her when she had been upset.

When she arrived back at the Heart of Life a group of Chalcenians ran out to greet her. Nick was with them.

'Helen, I wanted to see you,' he said with a broad smile. 'Can we go somewhere and talk?'

'We can go anywhere you like and talk. We can go riding, if you want,' she said.

He looked disgusted. 'What, on those animals, shaliors? You must be joking. You know I can't stand horses.'

'They're not horses.'

'Don't split hairs. They bite, they throw you off; that's close enough for me. Come on.'

She dismounted and walked between the trees with him, leaving Hlah with the others. His appearance was very different from when she had found him in the woods. His hair – which he had always kept fashionably short – was tousled but freshly washed. He wore the loose trousers and tunic of the Chalcenians, sewn with glittering beads in a design that spiralled from red to violet through the colours of the rainbow.

'What do you think?' he said, pirouetting for her, self-mocking.

'Very nice,' Helen replied. 'I always said you should be a male model. You certainly seem happy here.'

'I'm the happiest I've ever been. I could never have imagined anywhere like this. It must be heaven!'

They found a place at the crest of the hill, a rock warmed by the sun and clasped in the embrace of tree roots. It always seemed to be summer in Tevera. Helen wondered if the breath of Annis's winter ever touched it.

'I feel so weird,' said Nick as he sat beside her. 'I can remember everything before I died – doesn't that sound stupid? – "before I died". You know, I'm still *me*, but the strangest thing is that I'm sure I've lived in Tevera before. A previous life. I lived in a place very like this before I lived on Earth, and now I've come home. Does that make sense? I belong here. I am Chalcenic!'

Again the sense of alienation tugged at her. 'When did you work that out?'

'It just sort of came back to me, like recalling bits of a dream. Ananthis talked to me for quite a while. That helped, even though he is an arrogant bastard.'

'Yes, I know,' said Helen. 'I've been talking to him as well.'

'Oh, what about?'

She began to explain about Tasnian and Rianna, but she soon sensed that he was not really interested. His mind was on his own experiences. She lost her impetus, and trailed off feebly.

'Ananthis was on to me about this life cycle,' said Nick. 'He said I was a Gallah, which meant I'd died and been down to limbo and been brought back to life. Normally, you'd think someone who told you that was a crackpot, but when you *know* it's happened . . . Can you believe it?'

'Don't have much choice, after the things I've seen.'

'One thing I wasn't sure of was whether the doll had actually killed me,' he went on. 'But I don't think so. I think I would have died anyway. I was lucky that the Pelu was there to catch me as I fell, if you see what I mean. Either that . . . or it called me, and I was ready to go.'

'Rianna's off the hook then,' Helen said ironically.

He laughed. 'Even if it had been murder, she would have done me a favour.'

'I'm glad you're so pleased about it.'

'Makes a change from being a bad-tempered bastard, doesn't it?'

'You said it.'

He took her hand. 'Look, Helen, that's one of the things I wanted to talk about. Us. The things that have happened . . . it's made me realise what you must have gone through when we got divorced. I was so selfish. I'd say anything to get my own way, I never thought how much it was hurting you, and I tried to make out it was all your fault. But it wasn't. You know that, don't you? It was all me.'

'I managed to work it out,' she said faintly.

'I'm really sorry. I don't know how to make you believe it, or make it up to you. I had no right to put you through that.'

She hardly knew what to say. 'I – I thought it was because you didn't love me.'

'I thought I did. I suppose I loved myself more. I shouldn't have married you, Helen.'

'Why did you?'

'You were there, I liked you, you'd do absolutely anything for me, it just seemed a good idea . . . '

'A whim.'

'No, of course not. I thought I loved you, then I thought I loved Gina, but . . . the way you came to me when I phoned, the way you tried to save my life. You sat with me while I was dying . . . Helen, what I'm trying to say is that I was wrong. I do love you. Only I hadn't realised it until now. I wasted all that time, thinking Gina was "the real thing", throwing you away . . . and all the time it was you who really cared for me. It's you I love, Helen, not her.'

Helen could not speak. All the years she had longed for him to say this, dreamed of it . . . and now, after she had spent so many painful months getting over him, he finally said it. Now it was too late.

'I can't expect you to believe me,' he said. 'But I mean it. It's funny, I actually had to die to realise what a fool I've been . . . '

'You told me a lie,' she choked out.

'I expect I told you lots of lies. Which one do you mean?'

'You said Gina had left you, when she hadn't. She was away looking after her mum. I actually felt sorry for you!'

He looked ashamed. 'I was feeling sorry for myself. She'd been away weeks, she thought more of her mother than she did of me. And I still like your company, Helen. I always did.'

'You had a bloody funny way of showing it.'

'I know. But it's true. You made me feel safe.'

Safe . . . like a mother? Resented by a man who thinks he'd prefer to live dangerously . . . 'You're just a little boy, really, aren't you?' she exclaimed.

'Yeah,' Nick said sheepishly. 'I'm trying to grow up though, Helen, and nothing does it quicker than dying. I need you.'

'How do you mean?' She was suspicious. She was over the relationship, and yet she was not. She did not want it to start all over again, but Nick did seem different. It was impossible to reject him, a cruelty of which she was not capable. 'Do you want to start again?'

'I don't know. How can I know? If you could just . . . be with me.' He leaned back against the tree. 'I love the people here, the way they love without being possessive. The air feels full of possibilities . . . '

She said quietly, 'Nick, you're part of this world now. I'm still part of Earth, and I've got so many things to worry about . . . '

He was not listening. He was sitting forward, looking down the hill. 'Someone's arriving,' he said. 'Who is it?'

Helen saw a figure walking up the hill, and a group of young Chalcenians running to meet him. 'I don't know,' she sighed.

'Let's go and see!' He seized her hand and pulled her with him. They ran down the hill and mingled with the others, but all Helen wanted to do was to get away from the shouting, laughing Chalcenians. She shook herself free of Nick and began to fight her way out of the crowd.

As she did so, someone grabbed her. It was so unexpected that there was nothing she could do to resist. Breathless, she found herself turned round by strong arms, embraced, her chin lifted and another mouth pressed to hers. The kiss went on and on, and she could not break away even to draw breath.

At last the stranger's lips left hers and he hugged her tight to him. 'Helen, Helen,' he whispered in her ear. Over his shoulder she saw Nick staring at her with a mixture of astonishment and annoyance.

'Let me go,' she said. 'For heaven's sake let me go, I can't breathe.'

The stranger's arms loosened their hold, but his hands held on to hers as she stepped back to look at him. He was a young man with hair brushed wildly back from a fair face, with dark eyes and heavy brows. His hair was dark, with a sheen of red and purple on it. He seemed vaguely familiar, but she could not put a name to him.

His face fell. 'Helen, don't you know me?'

She knew the voice, and shock shivered through her from head to foot. She had only seen him looking dark and haunted, his hair brushed forward as if he wanted to hide behind it. It was the happiness of his expression that was strange to her, but now she recognised him without doubt.

It was Cadreis.

Chapter Seventeen

'Cadreis, it is you, isn't it?'

In reply he lifted her and whirled her round and round in the air. When he set her back on her feet, the landscape went on spinning. 'Yes, Helen! Oh, I'm so glad I've found you!'

She was half laughing and half crying, almost in shock with relief. 'I thought Annis had – I don't know what I thought. We came to look for you. I've been so worried!' She hung on his neck, returning his kisses gladly.

At her side, a dry voice said, 'I take it you two know each other?' Nick was looking at her with the cynical smile that she knew – and hated – of old. It had always appeared when she had displeased him, a look that said: *Once again you've proved yourself a complete prat, which is exactly what I expected of you.*

'Nick, this is Cadreis, he's – a friend of mine,' she said.

'So I see. Hello, Cadreis,' he said pleasantly, then returned his gaze to Helen. 'Well, you didn't waste much time, did you?'

'What do you mean?'

He raised one eyebrow. His attitude was teasing, but under it there was real resentment. 'Obviously you've already forgotten what we were talking about just now – unless it didn't mean a damn thing in the first place. You know, for a few minutes there I really thought we could be friends again.'

'Of course we can! What was that you said about not being possessive? Look, Nick, you don't understand, I thought Cadreis might be dead!' *Why am I making excuses?*

'Oh, I think I understand all right,' said Nick. 'Have fun, Helen. I'll see you around.' He began to walk away. Her first instinct was to go after him. She had spent most of her married life trying to justify herself to him, make him admit that she had actually done nothing wrong. She had always failed, but the anger, the instinct to try, was as strong as ever.

Several of the Chalcenians ran to catch up with Nick. She watched him greeting them, laughing with them, and she was infuriated. It was still one law for him, another for her. Why shouldn't she have found another lover? He had no right to be jealous, even less to pretend to be, just to hurt her.

'Helen, why are you arguing with your friend?' Cadreis said innocently. She looked at him, and her heart melted. Nick was playing games, giving her a choice of following him or staying with Cadreis. There was no contest at all.

'It doesn't matter.' Her anger vanished, and she wrapped her arms round his slim body. 'He's just being an idiot. People don't change, do they?'

'But they can.' There were still other Chalcenians around them, but Cadreis smilingly evaded them and led Helen away on her own.

'You certainly look different,' she said. 'I didn't know you, you look so cheerful. What happened to you? I was so sure Annis had caught you.'

'Did you think she had killed me?'

'Either that, or she was holding you prisoner.'

'You thought that all this time? Helen, I'm sorry. She did not catch me.'

'What did happen then? The last I saw of you was when you tried to pull her off me, and she flung you on to the rocks. Were you knocked out?'

'Only for a moment. Then I saw her coming at me in the shape of a shalior and I jumped up and ran until I thought my heart would burst. I daren't look round. I thought that if I did, she would claim me. All the time I could hear her saying, "You're mine, you're mine."'

A tremor of disgust went through Helen. 'How did you escape?'

'I'm not sure. I fell and a shadow leapt over me. I thought it was the end, but when I looked up, she had vanished.'

Helen thought of their confrontation with Annis, and her words, '*'E 'as ter come willin', dun't 'e?*' Hesitantly, she said, 'You know, I don't think Annis could have captured you unless you'd agreed to it.'

'Agreed?'

'Yes. She wanted you but she could only have you if you

went with her willingly.'

Cadreis looked horrified. 'Who would go willingly with such a creature?'

'Exactly. That would explain why she was in such a foul mood, that time we tried to find you . . . ' She looked up into his large, dark eyes. 'But Cadreis, where have you been since? Annis nearly killed us! Now you turn up as if nothing's happened.'

'Don't be angry with me, Helen. I was not ready to come here any sooner. I was going to go back to the place where I first met you.'

'The Vale of Peace, you mean?'

He nodded uneasily. 'But I realised I no longer belonged there. Menenthonis was right, I had become Luthnei. I had not realised it could cause such great pain.'

Helen was disconcerted. 'How do you mean? Mentally or physically?'

'In my mind.'

'And you were on your own? Oh, I wish I'd been with you.'

'No one could have helped; the change has to be faced alone. But when I awoke this morning, I felt different. The pain had gone and everything filled me with joy, and I knew that if I came here I'd find you.'

This startled her so much that she could not think what to say. 'Oh, dear. I'm just so glad you're here, and you haven't forgotten me.'

'I could never forget you, Helen. You have brought this happiness to me. Without you, I might never have changed.'

He pressed his mouth to hers, cutting off any reply. Warmth spread though her, filling her with fierce joy. Cadreis was back. She was no longer alone. Nothing Nick, or Ananthis, or anyone did could hurt her.

This was Tevera: joy, and threaded through it, fear.

The next few days were the happiest Helen had ever known. Cadreis hardly left her side. They rode in the woods and walked on the beach; by night they shared a kir of their own. She was astonished at how like the Chalcenians he had become, his joy in life so strong that it was a radiance, hypnotising her.

Yet the longer she was with him, the less she seemed to know about him. He was more complex than she had realised. There was a mischievous quality in him, though none of Nick's guile. They could tease each other happily for hours. Yet in some indefinable way she felt that he was on a different level to her, a shade beyond human, like all the Chalcenians.

She tried to tell him how she felt, but she had the impression he did not fully understand; not because he was unintelligent, but because he genuinely thought there was no reason for her to be worried. 'You know, it's strange,' she said. 'On Earth, there was only Rianna who was an alien. Now it seems everyone around me is part of Tevera, even Nick and Martin. I am the alien now.'

'Not to me, Helen,' he assured her. 'You belong here as much as I do.'

And he did belong now, and she drowned herself in his love to forget that she did not.

Helen saw very little of Nick, but she had seen enough to know that he was taking full advantage of Chalcenian society. Although they formed strong friendships, they had no kind of marriage, and made love to whomever they fancied as the whim took them. She was still unable to come to terms with it, but it suited Nick perfectly. Sometimes she feared that once the novelty of being with her had worn off, Cadreis too would seek other company. If she had said as much, he would have denied it, but even with Cadreis words and actions might be two different things. There was no point in risking their idyll by voicing her insecurity. She simply treasured every hour with him as if it was her last.

When they were not on their own, they spent much of their time with Martin and Rianna. The four of them would often walk round the Heart of Life together, or sit watching light and shadow chase each other across the landscape.

'If only you could have explained about the dolls, Rianna,' said Helen. She had repeated everything Ananthis had told her, if only to establish that it was the same explanation as he had given Rianna. 'I can't tell you how awful it was, thinking you might actually have been trying to kill people.'

'I wish I'd known,' said Rianna. 'It was even more of a relief to me when Ananthis said the Pelu do not kill directly.

They call . . . but only when the person is ready to go with them.'

They were sitting in their favourite spot, on the bank of a stream sheltered by a rise in the ground. Sunlight streamed through the trees and flashed on the ever-moving water. A pair of Halats, ferret-like creatures with sapphire fur, were snuffing at Cadreis's hands. Animals were drawn to him, and his childlike love of them always delighted Helen.

Cautiously, Helen asked, "How do you feel about going back to Earth to go on making the Pelu?'

Rianna gazed down at a grass stem she was twisting between her fingers. Her hair was a curtain of brilliant, coppery silk: Helen could not see her face. 'How I feel about it doesn't matter.'

'Of course it does! Tell me.'

'All right,' said Rianna. 'I don't want to go. I'm scared. If I could stay here, the Domendrans would probably leave me alone. But if I'm really the only one with the power to make the Pelu, I can't refuse to go back. It wouldn't be fair. On the other hand I can't do it all alone, there have to be millions of Pelu and I can only make a few hundred at best.'

'Maybe it's something you can teach to others,' said Helen.

'Maybe,' she said, unconvinced. 'I must try. But I don't think Black Annis will let me through the barrier again. I will never offer her another payment like the last. Never.'

Martin said, 'I'm not convinced it's Earth they mean to send you back to. This other place, Anatevera . . . Is it a limbo shared by both our worlds, or what? It doesn't make sense. Cadreis, don't you know the answer?'

Cadreis was reluctant to speak of his life in the Vale of Peace, but at least he did not try to pretend it had never happened. 'I did not reach a deep enough level to learn such things.'

'But if I've lived in Tevera before, I ought to remember.' Martin sat up, excited by the train of thought. 'What if Anatevera *is* Earth?'

Helen stared at him. 'Well, why shouldn't it be?' he said defensively. 'Because it doesn't fit our image of what limbo should be like? But if I did live in Tevera before, Nick too, what if being born on Earth was our second life? And now

Nick's in his third. Earth's the place we wait to come back to somewhere better . . . '

The images Ananthis had put in Helen's mind returned, like a fuzzy television picture ghosting up out of the ancient past. Earth . . . a grey limbo, a place of drabness and suffering. Children playing with dolls, priests speaking of heaven; all that was left of a fragmented race memory? It was a long time before she could speak. 'I know,' she said. 'I don't know when I realised. It's too much to take in. There have been no Pelu for thousands of years! It's us, *us*, who haven't been able to come back to Tevera.'

'Without the Pelu, we just – die,' said Martin. 'Is that it, Rianna?' She nodded. 'Bloody hell. All this time, paradise was here, only we weren't allowed in. I can't cope with this.' He stood up and went to the stream, looking down into the silver-white water.

'I think that makes the Domendrans worse than murderers,' Helen murmured. 'Sorry, Cadreis, I didn't mean – '

Cadreis stroked her arm, half smiling. 'I am Chalcenic now, Helen. I don't know how I could ever have thought Artienter and Sydra were right.'

Martin turned round, then Helen saw him glance up the slope and freeze. 'Oh my God,' he said. 'Hide! Hell, they've seen us.'

Coming over the rise were the hooded figures of six Domendrans. They walked in two rows like pall-bearers, carrying a body between them. A seventh Domendran walked behind. Helen and the others jumped to their feet, but they were too late to get out of sight or run away.

The Domendrans, however, did not even look at them. They slow-marched down the slope towards the stream, eyes fixed ahead. The corpse they carried was concealed from head to foot in a black robe, but a stray lock of bright blue hair betrayed its identity.

'Oh, Martin, it's Tasnian!' Helen whispered. 'What are they doing? They've no right to take him!'

Cadreis's hand was on her arm, restraining her. 'No, Helen, they've every right. The Domendrans bury the Chalcenian dead, they always have done so.'

Helen leaned against his shoulder as the procession went

by, biting her lip to stop herself crying. As the Domendrans reached the edge of the bank and began to wade the stream, the one bringing up the rear glanced up and looked straight into Helen's face.

It was yet another shock. As with Cadreis, it was someone she knew but changed almost beyond recognition. She started forward, then hesitated.

'Corolea?' she said uncertainly.

'Yes, Helen, it is me. I thought you would not know me,' said the woman. The other Domendrans went on their way without her, not looking back.

'Only just. You – you look as if you've been ill,' Helen said lamely. She was horrified by the deterioration in Corolea's appearance. She had changed so much that she looked as grim as a true Domendran. Her face was like parchment stretched over bones, her eyes lifeless in pools of grey shadow. Her hair, escaping from the edge of her hood, had lost all its brilliance and was as dull as earth. 'Corolea, what are you doing with these people? Please come back to the Heart of Life, you look so ill.'

'I cannot.'

'Are they forcing you to stay?'

'You don't understand,' said Corolea spiritlessly. 'It is by my own choice that I am with them. Have you never been in darkness, Helen? There is no point to anything. Do you know what it is like to look at the sun through the trees, hear birds singing and to feel nothing but blackness inside? Beauty mocks me, because all it does is emphasise the darkness in my mind, and love mocks me because it can give no comfort.'

'What happened to make you feel like this?'

Corolea frowned. 'Nothing happened, Helen. The sadness found me out of nowhere.'

Martin said over Helen's shoulder, 'It sounds like clinical depression.'

Corolea did not hear him. 'I went to the Domendrans because I needed darkness and absolute peace. It is all I can bear.'

'And have you found peace there?' said Helen.

'I am beginning to. I am accepted there.' She began to turn away, then looked back at them. 'I should not tell you this.

Chalcenic beliefs are no longer mine, but you tried to help me, Helen, when no one else would. So I will warn you. Menenthonis has come back to the Vale of Peace. The Aulanti know that Rianna is here, and they will come for her.'

'How do they know?' said Martin.

'I told them,' Corolea replied. With that she pulled her cloak tight around her and waded after her companions.

'There is no reason to panic,' Ananthis said placidly.

'How can you be so sure?' Martin demanded. His usual kind expression had been replaced by one of intent concern, the only sign that he was furious. Helen stood beside him, facing the blond Chalcenian man, with Rianna, Cadreis and Sheyde around them. 'Corolea changes sides, for some reason of her own that I can only guess at, and now everyone knows where Rianna is! You must know what the Domendrans are like, you seem to know everything else!'

Ananthis leaned against a kateya, a bored king lolling in a throne. 'What do you suggest?'

'That we take Rianna away from here, now!' said Martin 'There must be somewhere safe we can go.'

'Why do you think I had her brought back here before, and was so annoyed that she'd been allowed to leave? There is nowhere safer for her than the Heart of Life.'

'Safe?' Martin exclaimed. He reached for the kateya and tore out a handful of plant fibre. 'How safe is a place that's more or less made of paper?'

'The others cannot take Rianna without attacking us, and that they will not do.'

'How do you know?'

Ananthis' golden eyes became cold and dangerous. 'We do not fight. We have never fought physically, and we never shall.'

'What about when the Domendrans attacked the Gallahs? They weren't worried about using violence then. There's always a first time.'

'Listen to what I am saying,' Ananthis said in a thin, sarcastic tone. 'They will not attack the Heart of Life.'

'Ananthis is right,' Sheyde said. 'There is nowhere safer for Rianna than here.'

'And if you attempt to take her away, you will have to bear the consequences,' the blond Chalcenian added. 'Let us keep her here – until a way can be found to persuade Annis to let us send her back to Anatevera.'

There was no arguing with him. Rianna said nothing, but her face was white.

After Ananthis had left them, they walked through the forest in silence for a while. Then Martin said, 'Sod Ananthis.'

'But he's probably right,' said Helen.

'Why? Why must Ananthis always be right? I don't give a damn what he says. I'm taking Rianna away from here.'

'Martin, that's stupid!'

'No it isn't,' he replied calmly. Martin was only stubborn when something really mattered to him; stubborn, or determined.

'I think you might consult Rianna about this,' Helen said acidly. Rianna glanced up, but remained silent. 'Cadreis, what do you think?'

'I think the Domendrans will find her wherever she goes.' Cadreis spoke with a slight smile, as if his happy frame of mind could not be eclipsed even by Rianna's predicament. Helen felt like hitting him. 'But if you decide to leave, I will come with you.'

'I've decided,' said Martin.

'For heaven's sake, think about it,' Helen said desperately.

'All right, I won't go against Rianna's wishes. If we can't all agree on it, then we'll do what she thinks best. Agreed?' Martin turned to her. 'What would you prefer to do, love?'

To Helen's surprise, Rianna said shakily, 'I want to leave. I am not Chalcenic. I'm scared.'

Ananthis had been overconfident, expecting them to obey him and failing to keep an eye on them. It was not hard to slip away from the Heart of Life unnoticed; other Chalcenians came and went all the time. Before leaving, they had changed into their own clothes, jeans and jackets. Helen's heart was in her mouth as she and Martin caught two shaliors, trying to convince herself that it was not stealing because the Chalcenians did not own anything.

Shaliors would make them more noticeable, but at least they would have the speed to escape if necessary. Martin wanted to take two dark ones, but in the end the only ones they could catch were Tasnian's dappled mount, which Helen called Blue, and the golden Hlah.

Helen riding with Cadreis, and Rianna with Martin, they left the Heart of Life behind and struck out into the wildness of the hills, where the wind breathed through the trees and the light edged the bracken with gold. By an unvoiced, mutual instinct they made for the area they knew best; the part of Tevera that blended with Charnwood Forest. There was always a chance that they might evade the Domendrans by returning to Earth. But the boundary was closed, Black Annis silently keeping her word that no one would pass through.

'We're too close to the Vale of Peace,' Helen said uneasily. She pointed to a forest a couple of miles distant. 'I'm sure it lies under those trees.'

'Yes, you are right,' Cadreis said.

'Then we'll turn around and ride directly away from it,' said Martin. 'I don't fancy going into unknown territory, but we'll have to.'

When it grew dark they made camp in a dense wood of oak and holly, tethering the shaliors where they could graze on the tussocks of grass. Rianna was morose, and Helen did not feel much better; she had a sense of futility, and longed to sleep in a proper bed. Martin's attempt to be cheerful was becoming strained, and only Cadreis had any natural animation about him. He was like a dark, cool fire, not human enough to be truly concerned with what was happening . . . and Rianna was like a white crystal leaf, trembling, so fragile that the slightest thing might shatter her.

The four of them sat close together, wrapped in the warm Chalcenian blankets they had brought. Sleep seemed impossible.

Eventually Martin said, 'Where the hell do we go? There must be another city like the Heart of Life that we can make for.'

'There are many, but they are quite far apart and I don't know the way to any of them,' said Cadreis. 'But we may meet other Chalcenians on our way.'

'Or we could get completely lost and starve,' Helen muttered. Martin frowned at her. 'Sorry, but it's true. How long is our food going to last? What if one of us gets ill?'

'What's the alternative: to go back and give ourselves up? Look, it will be all right, Helen. Let's try to get some rest. We'll have a think in the morning.'

They lay down to sleep, and something strange began to happen.

If it was a dream, they all shared it. Helen was sure she was not asleep. Every sight, every sensation was too vivid to have been imagined, yet if it was real she could find no logic and no meaning in it.

Rianna lies on her back, naked. Her arms and legs are stretched out and she gleams owl-white against the grass. Her eyes are closed, her chin tilted up to the stars.

Out of the shadows the wild animals come. First is Talui, the Giver of Grace: a lizard with one huge, grass-green eye, who wraps himself round her left arm, like a bracelet. His eye is a cabochon glowing with the grace and affection that the embrace of the arms bestows. Then comes the badger, his red coat webbed with stars, to lay his head gently on her right palm. The badger is called Aeni, the Maker. Rianna's hand closes like a flower to caress his nose.

Halat is next: Halat the Bestower of Love, long as a weasel, soft-eyed and sharp-toothed. His fur is as bright as Tasnian's hair, blue for love and hate and all other emotions. He curls up over Rianna's heart.

For the legs comes an indigo creature, a Blesser of the Dance. His name is Suis and he is a glittering fish, hauling himself along on his fins like a mudskipper. Resting on her feet, he opens and closes his mouth and has no grace; but in his own element he would be a true dancer.

Now there is a crashing noise in the undergrowth and Rhoam, the wild boar, shoulders his way into the clearing. His head and chest are massive, his eyes fierce, and he is coloured the electric purple of lust. As he lays his snout along Rianna's groin she twitches and sighs, arching her back.

Now the circle is almost complete. Golden for the colour of thoughts and dreams, Hlah pads soft as a lion through the trees and drops her head to rest in a velvet kiss on Rianna's forehead.

With one voice that has no sound, the beasts begin to sing of Tevera.

They sing of a bright people who sprang from the ocean and built a civilisation surpassing any of Earth. Their society was created then torn apart by the irreconcilable difference between them . . . The Chalcenians, bright as butterflies, loving life and burning themselves out through love of it . . .

And the Domendrans, a dark race, loathing their existence, burdened with the desolation of spirit that descends from nowhere, for no reason, but which cannot be reasoned away. The Chalcenians were too carefree, too fragile to fight; the Domendrans too soul-weary. Thus their civilisation, over countless turns of the sun, disintegrated into isolated settlements. And they found peace and a way to co-exist.

It was a Chalcenian, his name long forgotten, who first defined the rhythm and pattern of Life. Humans were born in Tevera; they died and were reborn in Anatevera, a place of sadness and trial; then they died again and the Pelu brought them back to Tevera to live once more as the third-born, the Gallah. But at the heart of the Domendrans there were always a few who retained the energy and conviction to pursue their beliefs. They fought for an end to the cycle of life. And they sought it not out of malice but as a merciful thing, a euthanasia that would bring peaceful oblivion. And the Chalcenians did not have the strength to defeat them . . .

Who knows where it begins and where it ends? sing the animals. We are part of Tevera and Anatevera; we are in your bodies and your souls for ever. How many animal souls blend to make one human, how many humans to make one Cahantias, how many turns of the sun before we are all one . . .

There is one more colour, the hidden one that is all colours mixed. Brown, if it is of the earth; white if it is of light. The hue of the soul.

The animals dissolve into pure pigment. Rianna is a crystal figure, her head golden glass, her emerald arms blending into ruby hands. The brilliant blue of her chest melts into the violet flame of her loins and the indigo of her legs. Her feet gleam almost black, starred with amethyst. White wings beat across her, and the swan named Fi rises up out of her, created from the core of her soul. Even the swan's feet and eyes are white, and its beak shines like diamond.

The animals have turned into light. An aura shines from Rianna's body, and its heat envelops all of them. Bathed in the radiance, she sits up and reaches for Martin.

He falls on her. Helen and Cadreis are in each other's arms, famished, melting into each other in the heat and sweat. Time ceases within the rainbow. None of them knows when or how it happens, but for a while, Cadreis is with Rianna and Helen with Martin, then all four of them are knotted together . . . and the light grows paler with every heartbeat until it explodes into whiteness, and the rays of the sun fall through it in needles of golden fire.

Helen woke up with the battered feeling of having drunk too much and slept too little. It was all she could do to open her eyes. Cadreis lay across her, warm and heavy; she woke him as she stirred, and sat up to see Martin already awake, staring ahead of him with an expression of bemusement and worry.

Their eyes met. Helen tried to smile, but it turned into a grimace. Martin simply looked embarrassed.

'Did it really happen?' he asked.

She pulled the blanket around herself, aware that she was all but unclothed beneath it. A few yards away, Blue and Hlah grazed as if nothing had happened. But Helen's back ached, and between her legs she felt sore and wet. 'I'm afraid so,' she said.

'This must be what they mean by the cold light of day,' said Martin. She was not sure how to take the remark. As he turned away to wake Rianna, she struggled to dress herself, while Cadreis watched her with a tenderness that actually partly relieved her embarrassment.

The memory of the dream – or whatever it had been – flowed back in full, and she shut her eyes. *Oh God* . . . Feeling Cadreis move to stand up, she caught his arm and said, 'What the hell happened to us last night?'

He turned his dark eyes upon her; so beautiful. 'Helen, I wish I knew. I feel like a newborn child. I've lived almost all my life in darkness. I've only just come out into the light and I want to forget everything that went before. It's the same for you, isn't it, Rianna?'

Rianna was sitting up now, her bare shoulders thin and pale above the blanket, her hair an untidy cascade of russet. 'Yes,' she said, 'in a way.'

A sudden recollection of the night's bright images made Helen catch her breath. Suddenly she understood, and the changes she had seen in Cadreis and Corolea were no longer quite so strange. 'The Chalcenians and the Domendrans,' she said. The others looked at her. 'They're not two separate peoples, they're the same people. You knew, didn't you,

Cadreis? Why didn't you tell me?'

He looked perturbed. 'The knowledge is part of us. We never speak of it, because there is no need.'

'And because we would like to pretend it isn't so,' Rianna said quietly.

'Martin, did you realise?'

'Only last night. I didn't know before, honestly.' He addressed a point in space rather than look directly at Helen. 'It brought more of my memory back. I started to work things out, then I found I could actually sort of remember it.'

'I've got things right, though, haven't I? Chalceny and Domendri are both states of mind. The Teverans change from one to the other. But how? Please explain it to me, Cadreis. These things you take for granted, I wish you'd realise I need them spelled out!'

'I will try,' said Cadreis. 'I was born in the Heart of Life, among the Chalcenians, as we all are. I became Domendric when I was very young, I don't even remember anything about it. They must have seen that I was a very sad child and taken me to the Vale of Death in Life, and I never became Chalcenic again until I met you.'

'But why did it happen?'

'I don't know. The Chalcenians are a joyful people, but sometimes a misery comes over them out of nowhere. It cannot be controlled. All they can do is take themselves away to the Vale, where the other Domendrans can help them.'

'It's what I said before,' Martin put in. 'It's like clinical depression. If you're susceptible to it, it doesn't matter how wonderful your life is, it hits you and that's it. It's an illness.'

'We are not ill,' said Cadreis. 'It's the way we are. We change physically as well as mentally. Some Chalcenians never suffer the darkness at all. Artienter and Sydra have been Domendric almost from birth, and may never come out into the light.'

'But they've found a way of living with it,' said Martin.

'Yes. But many Chalcenians change from one state to another at least once in their lives, some many times. While they are Chalcenic, they belong in the Heart of Life, but while they are Domendric they can only bear to live in darkness.'

'What about the Luthnei?'

'They are called transients because they hover between one state and another. The Domendrans do not trust them because they might become Chalcenic again at any moment.'

'And the other Domendran levels . . . I think I understand them now.'

'Sfaia are those who are still able to work, and who are trusted not to change; not for a time, at least. Aulanti is the deepest level to which they may be initiated.'

'And the Nohmics . . . ' Helen could never forget those motionless figures, so deep in misery that they could do nothing at all.

'Sometimes they recover,' said Cadreis. 'Sometimes they die.'

'But why does there have to be such absolute segregation between the Vale and the Heart of Life?' Helen asked. 'You never even mention each other if you can help it.'

'It's the way things have always been.'

'It's because the Chalcenians are terrified of becoming Domendric, isn't it? They think they can prevent it by ignoring it, and when it happens to someone like poor Corolea, they don't want to know. They just needled her until she left.'

'Because she would not accept what was happening. She is best cared for in the Vale of Peace. I can understand how it seems to you, but we do care. Where do you think the Domendrans obtain their food? The Chalcenians bring it for them.'

Helen stared at him, opened her mouth, said nothing. He went on, 'But you are right, the Chalcenians are afraid, and so are the Domendrans. I have often seen newcomers arrive in the Vale. When they become Domendric, they think they have found the truth, that life is pointless agony. Then they despise the Chalcenians for what they see as foolishness and ignorance. The two sides have to live apart. They cannot tolerate each other.'

Martin turned to Rianna, perhaps speaking before he thought. 'Rianna, your Shefri. He wasn't dead, was he? He'd become Domendric and gone to the Vale of Peace, but no one would tell you. The best they could do was pretend he was dead!'

She shivered slightly. 'I expect so. Perhaps he is still there. I shall never know.'

'Was that why you wanted to go to the Vale when you were upset?'

'No. I didn't consciously know I wanted to go there. It was instinct . . . because I was depressed.' She pushed her hair back. A slight smile lit her pale features. 'But I am better now. I think I know what happened last night. It was a ritual, a kind of blessing. We became part of the Circle of Cahantias. It's something all the Chalcenians long for; but it cannot be made to happen. Ananthis would be mad with jealousy . . . '

'But why did it happen?' said Helen.

'Because I am the Pelumayis. The animals came to confirm it. I am the only one who can make the Pelu.'

As Rianna finished speaking, Cadreis went across to her, lifted her up and kissed her. Helen had never known Martin to lose his temper openly, but from the expression on his face he came close to hitting Cadreis. Helen was unsure of her own feelings; the kiss was an affirmation of what had passed between the four of them, and the feeling of closeness still lingered. But she had not yet managed to accept the Chalcenians' utter lack of jealousy or possessiveness.

'What are you doing?' Martin sounded incredulous.

'Kissing Rianna,' Cadreis replied, smiling openly at him. He was the only one of them who seemed overjoyed rather than stunned by what had happened.

'I can see that,' Martin said, scratching his head. 'Look, whatever went on last night – well, it's over now. Finished. Rianna!'

'What's wrong?' Her eyes had a misted look, cobweb silver.

'That was then and this is now! The more time we waste the more danger we're in,' he said grimly. 'How do you know that the – ritual, whatever it was, wasn't some trick by the Domendrans? Or even Ananthis? Not that I can see how they did it. I don't believe in magic, I'm a bloody scientist.'

'Not magic. The Circle of Cahantias,' said Rianna, reaching out to take his hand. Cadreis went back to Helen's side and put an arm round her, at which Martin visibly relaxed.

'Whatever it was, I don't pretend to understand it, but we can't stand around talking about it all morning.' He removed his glasses and polished them on the sleeve of his shirt. 'We'd better have a quick breakfast, then be on our way.'

'Have you decided where we're going?' Helen asked.

'Any bright ideas?' he said. She shook her head. 'Let's just ride. Fast, and in a straight line.'

It was the strangest time Helen had ever known. The enchantment of the previous night permeated all they said and did, edging everything with a flaring aura of warmth. But through the aura, persistent flashes of reality kept intruding. Martin studiedly avoided speaking to Helen, and his obvious guilt and shame upset her more than anything. Her mind locked on to it, unconsciously trying to block out the fear of what lay ahead.

Autumn was coming to Tevera, stealthily, almost overnight it seemed. Only now did Helen notice that the bracken and the trees were turning to fiery copper, while the hillsides were sheeted with dew and fallen leaves. There was a sharp chill in the air. *We're back on Earth!* she thought with a pang, but then she looked at the crisp, star-flecked sky and knew they were not. There was no sign of any other Chalcenian settlements, or any kind of human life at all; only the wooded hills and ancient granite crags, like Charnwood Forest with all softness and civilisation torn away.

Later, as they walked to rest the shaliors, Helen left Cadreis to lead Hlah and edged up to Martin's side.

'Aren't you speaking to me?' she said uneasily, trying to be light-hearted.

'Yes, of course.'

'Don't you think it's a bit pointless?'

'What?'

'This – this journey. It's OK now, while we've got a fair amount to eat and we're not tired, but what's going to happen when our food runs out? We'll have no choice but to turn round and go back. We're wasting our time. I'm not getting at you, Martin, I'm just being realistic.'

He sighed, but he did not sound angry. 'I know. I'm not Conan the Barbarian, Helen. I wasn't even a very good boy scout, if you must know. But I don't know what else to do.'

'Why wouldn't you listen to Ananthis?'

'Because I don't trust him. The Heart of Life wasn't safe.'

'Maybe not, but this is worse. Rianna and Cadreis have no more idea of where we are than we have. No one's going to pop up and rescue us.'

'I know. But I'm not going back. Those bastards are not getting their hands on Rianna.'

'Martin, about last night – '

'Try to forget about it. I have.'

'Forget?' she began, but he was striding ahead of her, leaving her alone and fuming. She did not want things to have changed between them, but they had. They had made love, involuntarily, as if in a dream, and it was something Martin could not face up to.

A moment later, she felt a slender hand slide through her arm.

'Are you all right, Helen?' said Rianna.

'I would be if Martin would talk to me.'

'You were talking to him a minute ago.'

'He was answering my questions. That's not the same thing as talking. He's avoiding me, because of last night.'

'I think men find it more difficult than women to accept things like that.' Rianna seemed so tranquil that Helen was concerned for her.

'Cadreis isn't like that with you. Just the opposite.'

Rianna lifted her shoulders. 'Cadreis isn't Martin.'

'Bloody men,' said Helen.

'But it was beautiful, wasn't it? It's so hard to feel scared now. I ought to, but everything looks golden. I don't feel like running and fighting any more . . . I think it gave me the courage to turn and face what I have to. You're not still frightened, are you?'

Helen scraped her teeth over her lip, and took a breath. 'I'm frightened of you, Rianna. Those animals came to you. You didn't even look human any more. I don't know you.'

Rianna looked puzzled, then rested her head on Helen's shoulder. 'It's just me, Helen,' she said.

Sunset came rimmed with orange flame. The light died but the orange brightened, and there were flakes of burning ash skimming overhead.

'Fire,' Cadreis said, alarmed. It was the first time Helen

had seen him look serious since she had met him in the Heart of Life. 'The Chalcenians do not use fire.'

'What is it, then?' said Martin. 'Are there any people apart from Chalcenians and Domendrans around here?'

Cadreis shook his head. In the time it took them to reach the peak of the nearest hill, the flames, swift as burning paper, had subsided. In the distance, singed oaks stood with sparks slithering round their limbs like red-gold snakes. Between them, the interlocking web of kateyas was ruined. A few dry limbs still hung in lines of black powder that would be blown away by a breath, and the shrivelled stumps of the trunks were still smouldering. Every now and then a kir would crack, sending up a firework shower into the twilight.

'It's another Chalcenian city, isn't it?' said Martin.

When neither Rianna nor Cadreis replied, Helen said, 'Looks like it.'

'We'd better go down, and see if anyone's hurt . . . '

Hlah and Blue jibbed and sprang about like skittish cats, nostrils wide at the stench of burning. *Bonfire night, that's what it smells like*, thought Helen, her heart pounding. Her eyes began to stream with the smoke. When they could calm the shaliors down for a moment, they dismounted and continued on foot.

'It looks – it looks – ' Helen gasped, but her throat stung and she could not control a spasm of coughing. 'Martin – *Cadreis* – '

She reached out for someone's arm, but they slipped out of her grasp and ran on. She followed through a fog of smoke into the heart of the kateyas. Ash plastered itself like tissue to her face. Black stumps loomed at her out of the haze, smouldering red at their hearts and radiating intense heat.

No – it can't be –

The city of the Chalcenians was deserted. There were no signs of life, no bodies. The fire must have swept through the kateyas as if they were made of cardboard. Nothing looked the same in the half light, smoke and ruin distorted even the most familiar place, but the dreadful feeling inside Helen kept swelling and growing until she knew, she *knew* –

God, am I the only one who realises? I can't be. No, they know!

'Rianna!' she choked, seizing her friend's thin arm. 'You

recognise this place, don't you?'

Rianna's eyes were streaming and the tears were washing white streaks through the soot on her face. She could not speak. She raised a hand, and Helen spun round to see Martin and Cadreis in front of her, and coming towards them – rising out of nowhere, like ash-streaked ghosts – Ananthis and Sheyde.

Ananthis's hair was half the length it had been, shrivelled by fire. Sheyde's face was blistered. They were waving at the four, waving and crying out, 'Why did you come back? *Why did you come back?*'

Martin turned to face Rianna, his hand to his head. 'Did you know we were going round in a circle?'

'Yes,' she replied.

'But we can't have been! It's impossible, this can't be the Heart of Life!'

'But it is,' said Rianna.

Ananthis flung himself at Martin, his robes flying. 'Get out. Don't stand there like a roasted tree, go, *go!*'

Martin stood his ground and fought him off. 'Ananthis, calm down, tell us what happened here.'

'Run, you fools!' he screamed, then subsided abruptly. He composed himself, folding his arms as if nothing had happened, while smoke and sparks swirled all round him. 'Too late. Never mind.'

Cadreis was with Helen, sombre and protective again, as he had been in the Vale of Death in Life. 'Is anyone hurt?' he asked.

'No,' Sheyde replied, though she did not sound sure. 'Most – most escaped.'

'For heaven's sake, Ananthis, will you tell us what happened?' said Martin.

'I would have thought it obvious, but if you insist. The Domendrans came to find Rianna. Yes, I know I said they would not dare; I was wrong,' Ananthis said in bitter self-mockery. 'We told them she was not here but they did not believe us. They told us all to leave, or they would burn us out. And then they set the city afire, just to prove to themselves that Chalcenians are not liars. A savage experiment, which I trust gave them joy.'

'But no one got caught in the fire?'

'No. They gave us the chance to leave, as I said, though they insisted on taking any Gallahs prisoner.'

'So why are you and Sheyde still here?'

'You shouldn't have come back!' Sheyde cried, but Ananthis placed a hand on her arm to quiet her.

'They made us stay,' Ananthis said quietly. 'To bait their trap. Now, if you had fled when I told you, you might have had a chance of escape. Alas, you elected to hold a conversation instead . . . '

Then Helen saw the movement all around them, piles of black ash rising from the ground and resolving themselves into cloaked forms. They were surrounded by Domendrans. She saw Sydra's hard, heart-shaped face, framed by dark hair. Beside her was Artienter. His expression was the nearest it could come to joy; a grim, cold gloating. And Rianna was walking slowly towards them, her head bowed, like a doe towards a hunter.

Martin started forward and seized her by the arm.

'Run!' he shouted, and for a chaotic moment they tried to make a break for it, thrusting through the ranks of Domendrans. Then the dark figures closed in, hands snatched them out of mid-flight, and a wooden stave came thumping down on Helen's skull.

Chapter Eighteen

The Vale of Death in Life; a veil of rock and earth, sundering them from light and freedom. Helen remembered nothing of how they had been carried there. Her head felt huge, like a cave filled with whispering shapes, shadows moving against a dull glow, conspiring against her . . . She was trapped inside her own head, and her skull was made of solid rock that ached, ached right through to the world's core.

Somewhere to her right, a voice kept saying, 'Where the bloody hell are we?'

She tried to move, became aware of a hand clasping hers. Through the pain she felt deadly calm, and she knew exactly where they were.

'In the Vale of Peace,' she said, but her voice was slurred.

'Helen? Oh, she's come round, thank God.' It was hard to focus but she recognised Martin's voice, knew it was him at her side. 'What did you say?'

'This is the Vale of Peace, the city of the Domendrans.'

'I know,' said Martin.

She struggled to sit up. The effort sent a dizzy wave of sickness through her. 'Shit,' she gasped. 'I thought I heard you asking where we were.'

'That was about half an hour ago,' Martin said, startled. 'Cadreis told me. Don't worry, Helen, just try to rest.'

Feeling came back to her body, and her head resumed its normal proportions. A bowl of fresh water was held to her lips. Rianna was at her side, next to Martin, her face horribly white in the gloom. Cadreis was sitting on Helen's left. She was too dazed to make out much beyond their small circle, but it seemed they were alone in the cave.

'They hit Martin as well,' said Rianna.

'Did they?' Helen looked at him anxiously. 'Are you all right?'

'Yeah, I think so. I was only out for a few seconds.'

'What about you, Rianna?' said Helen.

'I'm not hurt,' she replied, but her voice was shaky. Helen reached across Martin to take her hand and Rianna hung on to her as if she were a lifebelt in a wild sea.

Cadreis said softly, 'You remember this place, don't you, Helen?'

She looked around and realised that the cave was actually a pillared chamber, like an ancient crypt gouged out of the earth itself. She recognised it at once. 'We're in Bayn.'

'What's Bayn?' said Martin.

'A sort of church or temple,' Helen answered. 'You tell them, Cadreis.'

Cadreis's eyes glimmered in the darkness, light brimming in them like tears that could not escape. 'It is a place where the Domendrans meet to find peace. When I brought Helen here before, she could not bear the darkness. I could not understand how she felt, but now I do. I want to go out in the light again.'

'Well, what's to stop us?' said Martin. 'Do you know the way out?'

'Yes. But . . . ' Cadreis pointed to the lightless arch of the entrance, and they saw the shadowy forms of Sfaians standing there.

'You must know them,' Helen said urgently. 'Couldn't you speak to them or something?'

'It would be of no use. They know I am no longer Sfaian, that I became a transient and left. They cannot acknowledge my existence, let alone think of me as a friend.'

'Jesus, I don't believe this,' Martin murmured. 'Friendly lot, aren't they?'

'You don't understand them,' Cadreis said sharply.

'I also don't understand how we could have travelled round in a circle and gone back to the Heart of Life. I was watching the position of the sun, we were definitely going in a straight line – unless I was under some sort of delusion. I don't believe in that sort of thing, but I can't find any other answer. Someone fooled me, and led us round in a circle.'

He looked straight at Cadreis, who said, 'Are you accusing me of leading us to the Domendrans?'

'I'm just trying to eliminate possibilities. You were originally working for what's his name – Artienter – and you were trying to find Rianna for him!'

'But not now,' Cadreis said fiercely. 'I am no longer Domendric. For Helen's sake I would never have betrayed Rianna. I did not – '

'It was me,' said Rianna. Martin turned to her, protesting, but she put her finger to his lips. 'You were dazed from the previous night; we all were. You did not really know where we were, and it was easy to lead you back.'

'Rianna, why?'

'There was nowhere for us to go, Martin. Only wilderness. The Domendrans would have caught us eventually; them or Annis herself. Whatever they want of me, Martin, I have to face them. That is all.'

There was a long, static pause, as if Martin did not know whether to shout at her or console her. Eventually, very quietly, he said, 'Yes, but it's not just you and me, is it? It's the others as well.'

'I'm sorry.'

Another silence. Then Helen said, 'None of us would have let you face this alone, Rianna. I'd rather be with you than anywhere else.'

'I know. Thank you,' Rianna whispered.

'But why have they brought us to Bayn?' Helen added. 'It's a strange place to put prisoners . . . '

Cadreis looked over to the Domendrans guarding the entrance. 'Someone is coming,' he said.

There was movement in the tunnel. The guards parted and two black figures came gliding between them as if they had solidified from the darkness itself. Artienter and Sydra. Following them came Sheyde and Ananthis, their clothes shimmering in pale contrast, their heads held high in defiance. Ushering them in came a third Domendran, and as he put his hood back, Rianna uttered a faint cry as if fear had wrung all the breath out of her. It was Menenthonis. He fixed his eyes on Rianna and said not a single word.

Ananthis and Sheyde came to sit with Helen and the others. Their faces were serious and they did not speak. As Martin began to whisper questions at them, Sydra shouted, 'Silence!'

The walls snapped out a dull echo which hung in the air, sinister. Standing between Artienter and Menenthonis, Sydra raised her arms and said in a sing-song drone, 'You have been brought into Bayn to be brought into darkness. You must be brought into peace. You must find understanding . . . '

The very greyness of her voice triggered Helen's memory of her last visit here; the monotone chanting that dragged her down and down into a desolation where nothing mattered and nothing hurt. She was spiralling down into it already, and she seized Cadreis's hand so hard that he jumped.

'Understand that we do this not out of malice,' Sydra went on. 'We act for your good as well as our own; we act for mankind.' To Helen there was an underlying note in her voice that could have been sarcasm or bitterness. 'But we cannot expect you to believe us, who have always been Domendric, invisible to you. Listen instead to one of your own, who was with you but now has found her way into darkness.'

A slender woman entered, cloaked, her delicate features pulled into a lined mask by misery. The hair that had once been so much brighter than Rianna's was now dull as tarnished brass, as if the colour had leeched out with her joy in life. Again Helen was shocked at Corolea's appearance.

Sheyde said nothing, but Helen heard her breath hiss softly between her teeth.

'Corolea, my beloved friend,' Ananthis said loudly. His world-weary tone, as always, did not betray what he really felt. 'Did we not make you welcome while you wished to live in the Heart of Life? Did we try to prevent you from leaving when you tired of your life with us? I must be mistaken, for we obviously did something very terrible to you to make you betray us. Perhaps we should ask to be forgiven.'

'You did nothing, Ananthis,' Corolea said dully. 'I changed. I was only remembering happiness, not feeling it. The Chalcenians seemed such fools, like glittering insects, mindless and pointless. What is the point of life? We are going nowhere.' Her voice rose with anguish. 'Nowhere! We live such a short time, and then there is only Anatevera waiting to receive us. Another life, a living nightmare far worse than this. And while we wait, there is only pain. How could I ever have been Chalcenic? I see this so clearly now. Life is nothing but meaningless torment, and there is only one way out of it for all of us. To end the cycle of life in a way that will bring peace. That is why I had to tell them where Rianna was.'

'Oh well, that excuses everything,' Ananthis said caustically.

'They would have found her anyway. Listen to me. I am finding quietness in the Vale of Peace. There is healing in the darkness; the soul can find silence here, and let go of all that causes pain. It's all we can hope for, because we have nothing else.'

A voice rang out, 'No!' Cadreis had leapt to his feet. 'I once felt as you do, Corolea,' he said. 'I'd felt like that all my life. I thought I would live in darkness for ever, that there was nothing else, but I was wrong. It is the other way round! You've gone into the darkness and you think it will be for ever, but it is not so, you will come out into the light again. It has happened to many others. I did not even know until I left this place. *They* will never tell you' – He pointed to Artienter and Sydra – 'but it is true. If it can happen to me, it can happen to anyone. You'll change and be happy again.'

'He is right,' said Ananthis. 'Have you ever lived in the light, Artienter?'

Artienter and Sydra shook their heads. 'No,' said Artienter, 'but those who never change are needed at the heart of things. If we were all Luthnei, there would be chaos.'

'Perhaps,' said Ananthis, 'but all it proves is that you have never experienced what it is to be Chalcenic. So what entitles you to judge us by your own unfortunate feelings? How dare you assume the right to take life from us, who love it?'

'And you, Ananthis,' Sydra said furiously, 'you have never known what it is to be Domendric.'

'True, but – '

'Then how can you presume to tell us we are wrong? You understand nothing at all.'

'None of you understand!' Cadreis exclaimed. 'You talk of dark and light, but there are only Corolea and I here who can speak for all the others who know what it is to feel both. Joy is nothing without sorrow.'

'And how dare you treat the Luthnei as outcasts,' Corolea said with sudden passion, 'when they cannot find their true place through no fault of their own? We seal our mouths, and walk away, and are forgotten.'

'But you would be welcomed if you come back,' Sheyde said gently. 'Only the Domendrans speak of "transients", not the Chalcenians.'

Sydra looked angrily from Sheyde to Corolea. 'That is enough,' she said. 'The purpose of Bayn is not only to bring peace, but to teach understanding. This is why you are here; so that before you die, you will at least comprehend the truth of what we believe.'

Die? Helen thought, glancing at Martin. But he did not look at her; he was hugging Rianna to him, as if trying to protect her from the cold unwavering gaze of Menenthonis.

Ananthis stood up suddenly, all the faint light in the place seeming to gather in his hair. 'No, *you* understand,' he said. 'Imagine human souls wandering lost in the underworld. They know they have lost the beauty of Tevera; their only hope is contained in the Pelu, which when they die may carry their spirits into a new life . . . '

Artienter's voice rose over Ananthis's like the low thunder of the sea. Sydra recommenced her hypnotic chant. They were angry, but they turned anger into a mental weapon that even Ananthis could not resist. Over thousands of years, the Domendrans had made a state of mind, depression, into a religion. Nihilism. The Aulanti were priests of nothingness, controlling the other Domendrans' beliefs. Perhaps they controlled those of the Chalcenians, to some extent; why else did they have charge of burying the Chalcenians' dead?

Ananthis fell silent, slid back to the floor. In the grey trance, Artienter's words shaped themselves into visions. Briefly they saw a glittering sea, a sweep of blue sky and a group of Chalcenians dancing on the sand, and a voice said, 'The purpose of joy is only to make you mourn the loss of it.'

Then they saw bent figures wandering through the unlit caverns of the Vale of Peace. Their eyes were lifeless; they could barely move themselves to carry out the most basic tasks of survival. Some had ceased to function altogether and were in catatonia, the state of Nohm.

'This is the reality of life,' said Artienter. 'Sorrow. And when we die, can we expect relief?'

A brief glimpse of corpses half buried in sand, and then there was a sense of falling, dislocation from one world to another.

'*Anatevera*,' he whispered. 'Rebirth into a limbo more appalling than Tevera.'

And Helen found herself staring at a fuzzy, black and white nightmare of a scene: buildings towering into a grey fog, rain hissing down on to roaring machines, smoke drifting thickly along desolate pavements. She saw children as thin as sticks wailing in a desert, and a slow, dark river where dead fish floated among the rubbish.

It is terrible, yes, she thought, and she was laughing inwardly with a hysteria that was one step beyond grief.

'And at the end of this, we die again. Then, at last, we find a way back to the oblivion from which we came. But not if the Pelu are allowed to carry our souls back to Tevera and begin the process again!'

A voice, rough as tobacco, rustled in Helen's ear. 'Dun't 'e go on?'

Helen was no longer in Artienter's vision. She was physically in another place, as if she had been flicked there without warning, without any kind of awareness of the process.

She was walking on the bare rocks at the summit of Beacon Hill. At her side, a middle-aged woman in a short fur coat and shorter skirt struggled along in high heels, her bare thighs whipped red by the wind. Leicestershire rolled out below them in every direction, the hedgerows stark black against fields that were hard and white with frost. The hill seemed mountainous, the earth very far away. Clouds of mist and smoke billowed from Annis's mouth as she spoke.

'Whassup, me duck? Cat Annis got yer tongue?' she said, laughing chestily. 'I said, that Art-whatsisname goos on a bit.'

'Yes. Yes he does,' said Helen.

'Yer recognise me this time, dun't yer?'

Helen nodded. 'You're Black Annis.'

'Not so much of the "Black". I wanted to talk to yuh. Gorra message I want passin' on.' She flicked a long finger of ash from her cigarette.

Helen did not know what to say. She knew she must be dreaming, but there was no way she could escape from the dream. It was happening, it was *real*, so real that she could barely speak for the cold.

Annis said, 'Yer not scared of meh? Yer've gorra kind face. Thought I could talk to yuh, you know, woman to woman, like. I can, can't ah?'

'Y-yes,' said Helen, her eyes widening.

Annis scratched at the hairs on her upper lip. 'It's downhill, like a one-way valve,' she announced.

'What is?'

'From Tevera to Anatevera. I can't catch 'old of the souls comin' through that way. Like soap, goo straight through me 'ands, they do. Tek their memories, though. One thing ah can do is tek the bastards' memories. Then they dun't remember nowt about Tevera, y'see, so they dun't know they want ter goo back. 'Cos they can't get back, unless they got summat to carry 'em.'

'You mean the dolls – the Pelu?' Helen said through chattering teeth.

'Yeah. Yer caught on, gel? Bleedin' Pelu. Bloodeh nuisance, ah'm not 'avin' it.'

'Why not? Why are they a nuisance?'

Annis's eyes narrowed. She blew a stream of smoke from her wrinkled red lips. 'What d'yer think I am, gel?'

'I don't know. Er – a goddess?'

'Hah! Goddess? Bleedin' gatekeeper, that's me. Like on a turnstile at a football match, letting the sods in, lettin' 'em out again. Bet yer can't guess how long I've bin doin' it, either.'

'No . . . '

'Neither can I. That's the joke, ennit? Centurehs. Thousands and thousands of years. Can't imagine it, can yuh? But I don't know where ah come from. I've always bin there, on the boundary, always alone and bloodeh loneleh. But the world won't last for ever, will it?'

'No, I suppose not.'

Annis chuckled unpleasantly. 'Do yer 'ave ter agree with everything I say? No, world's gettin' older and so am I. Hard job for an ow-uld woman. No one realises. Hard and loneleh, an' ah'm gettin' bleedin' sick of it.'

The bleakness in Annis's voice was genuine. Helen began to feel sorry for her. 'You said you had husbands . . . '

'Oh, them. That were part of the bargain.'

'What bargain?'

'With them lot – the Domendrans. I were dead angreh, the first time they come, intrudin' on me privaceh. Said they wanted to come through the boundary *alive* so they could destroy them Pelu, stop the third-born comin' back. Well, I were all fer that, but I wasn't goin' ter let on. So ah said there's a price, an' they said what? An' I said I want an 'usband but 'e's got ter be willin'.' Confidentially she added, 'Can't keep 'old of 'em unless they're willin' . . . ter start with, anyhow.'

'So the Domendrans bribed you – with a husband?' said Helen.

'Bribe's a dirteh word, me duck. Paid. So ah got two things I wanted. A man, and no more Pelu botherin' meh.'

'When was this?'

Annis shrugged. ''Bout eight thousand year ago. I dunno.'

'Eight thousand?' Helen gasped.

'Means a lot to yer, that much time? Don't mean so much ter me, only a lot of standin' about, gettin' colder an' older, watchin' them souls slide through, smug bastards. Good ter know they can't get back now. It were all right when I 'ad a man, but they onleh live about five minutes, dun't they? In all that time, I've onleh 'ad seven. Seven 'oo come willin' – ones I fancied, I mean. 'Ad a load of others ah couldn't gi' a damn about. Men are shits, aren't they, duck?'

'Some are. Some are OK.'

'Yeah, you know what it's like ter be loneleh, ah can tell.'

'Yes,' said Helen. She was nervous now, wondering how long Annis would keep her here in the bitter wind, if she would ever let her go.

'Anyhow, where was ah? Long time since I 'ad a man. Domendrans say they can't find me a willin' one. But I got ter get one. I'm desperate.' Annis took out another cigarette and lit it with difficulty. Her hands were shaking, and there was a terrible sly bitterness in her eyes that chilled Helen more than the cold. 'Didn't realise I were gettin' ow-uld 'til them others, the Chalcenians, started sneaking through me gateway without 'avin' the decency to die first. Sneaked through alive, and the next I know is, the Pelu start reappearin'.'

'When?'

'When, when,' Annis said impatiently. 'About thirty year ago, I s'pose. Only a few, mind, not like before. So I lets a few Domendrans through to stamp it out, but this time the bastards ain't paid.'

'They promised you another husband?'

'Look, what's the basics of life? Sex and food. Ah may not be human but I still need 'em. They gev me a few kids to eat an' said the man'd come later, but they let me down. Then there was the little girl. Shouldn't 'ave let her through, that was a mistake. Should 'ave just eaten her there an' then, but I were soft-hearted, she 'ad such pretteh red 'air. An' she offered me such a good price. 'Ad to wait a bit, but I got it.'

'What was it?' Helen whispered.

Annis grinned, showing nicotine-stained teeth. 'Oh, the best thing of all. A new-born babeh. I squeezed it 'til its soul shot out. Shot out like a blackhead, it did! An' no Pelu ter tek it 'ome.'

Helen's stomach turned over, and she hugged herself. Her face felt solid with ice.

'Please can I – please can I go now? I'm freezing.'

Rage flashed into Annis's face and she seized Helen's shoulder. 'Thought you understood. Too much trouble to keep an ow-uld woman companeh, is it? Listen, you cow, I ain't finished the message yet, I'm workin' up to it. About the girl, Rianna – I didn't know she could make the Pelu. I'd never 'ave let 'er through if I 'ad. You can tell 'em all from me – I ain't lettin' 'er through again, no way. Dun't care if the Chalcenians offer me six men.'

'I thought you were desperate.'

'Cheekeh cow! I got me principles. Tell 'em! Anyone tries it, they've 'ad it.'

'I'll tell them,' Helen said, shuddering.

Annis reached up to squeeze Helen's cheek, her nails piercing the numb flesh. 'I ain't finished,' she hissed. 'I've 'ad enough of all this. Bloodeh humans, like fleas, always pesterin'. I don't want 'em comin' through me gate night an' day, I've 'ad enough. I'm goin' ter do somethin' about it.'

'What – what are you going to do?'

'Think about this, gel. When the Pelu got stopped, it meant

they couldn't goo back ter Tevera. But they still get two goes at life, an' that's two too many. So, first I kill everybodeh on Tevera. Then I kill everybodeh on Earth. An' then I can retire. 'Cos when the folk on Earth die, they ain't goin' nowhere!' She swung her fist and landed it hard against the palm of her other hand, making Helen jump. 'Nowhere! Into blackness they go, into my cave, for ever! Yer've helped me make me mind up, duck. That's where they're goin'! Tell 'em that!'

Helen felt the sick sensation of faintness creeping over her, saw the grey landscape break up into dancing black and white dots. The rocks came rearing up to meet her, but she never felt the impact; instead she was falling into the blackness of a cave, Annis's cave, which she had so dreaded. And now she knew what the cave was. Death. And it was what she had always feared it was: nothingness, oblivion. The full despair of that knowledge flooded through her and she fell into a whirlpool of blind, glazed terror.

And only the terror told her she was still alive.

The vision ended. Helen tried to scream, could not, then opened her eyes with a sense of shock, as if someone had slapped her to wake her up. She was back in the darkness of Bayn.

Wherever she had been, the others had not shared it. Artienter's voice droned on, while his captive audience blinked and looked about them as if they had just been released from his terrible images of Anatevera.

'It *is* Earth,' Martin said faintly.

Artienter did not hear him. 'Isn't this enough?' he cried. 'Must we go through this life cycle over and over again? If I could prevent souls going to Anatevera I would. The least we can achieve is to ensure that the Pelu never take hold again. It is an obscenity that we cannot find rest when we die. The dignity of a peaceful end is what the Aulanti have always fought for, and we will not cease our struggle until it is achieved.'

Helen saw Ananthis, in profile, look at Sheyde. For once he seemed too shocked to form a caustic reply. 'You are biased, Artienter. How do we know Anatevera is really as dreadful as you make out?'

'It isn't!' Martin exclaimed, louder this time. 'Anatevera is

Earth, where Helen and I come from. It's not just a grim shadow of Tevera, it's a whole world in its own right.'

Artienter and Sydra looked angry, as if they had not expected this interruption. Artienter said, 'If you are so wise, please tell the Chalcenians whether the images I showed you are true or false.'

'True,' Martin said reluctantly, 'but – '

'Then there is nothing more they need to know.'

'But there is! Earth isn't all ugliness, there are good things there as well. It's not so different to Tevera, in some ways.'

Sydra said, 'From your own lips – Anatevera is the opposite of Tevera; similar enough to be a mockery, but full of pain and ugliness.'

'She's twisting what I say. Oh, this is hopeless. Helen, tell him he's wrong – ' Martin turned to her, and trailed off. 'You look awful. Are you all right?'

They were all looking at her now. Very shakily she rose to her feet. She was still rigid with cold, but the marks of Annis's nails in her cheek felt like fire.

'I have a message from Black Annis,' she said. 'The Domendrans haven't kept the bargain they made with her. She's furious about it and she's threatening to destroy us all.'

The words sounded ridiculous, banal. They all stared at her as if she had gone mad, and she could see that Artienter and Sydra did not believe her; they probably did not want to. She felt too weak to argue.

'You still refuse to accept the truth,' Sydra said gravely. 'We have done all we can; there is no place for you in Bayn, if you will not listen.' She turned to Artienter. 'Shall they be taken away now?'

'Yes,' said Artienter. 'Let them meditate on what I have shown them. Then they may find peace as they draw closer to death.'

The darkness was not quite total. Just enough light spilled down from the fungal lamps to reveal the ragged outlines of corpses, the faces stretched in eternal screams and the sand crusting their half-decayed forms.

Twelve Domendrans had brought them to the cave that Cadreis had called the Centre of the Vale; the place where they laid their dead. They forced the prisoners on to the edge of the rock shelf that ran round the cave, and ordered them to jump.

They looked apprehensively over the edge. It was ten feet down to the skeleton-littered floor, but it was clear that if they did not jump voluntarily, they would be pushed. 'I'll go first,' said Martin. 'I'm used to falling off horses, I know how to fall without breaking anything.'

He jumped. Cadreis followed him, and between them they caught the others as the Sfaian guards all but shoved them over the edge.

They landed without injury on sand that was full of bones. The dead lay centuries deep below them.

Ananthis immediately began to talk of escape.

'There is no way out,' said Cadreis. 'We could only escape if we could climb back up to the shelf.' They looked up at the rim of rock where the twelve Domendrans patrolled listlessly, watching them with dead eyes.

'I intend to see for myself,' Ananthis replied.

'If you need proof, I'll come with you,' said Cadreis. He and Ananthis walked away into the shadows and began to make a slow circuit of the cave. Helen watched them, wishing they would come back, wishing she was anywhere but here. Tasnian's body must lie here somewhere; she did not want to see it.

In the dimmest recesses of the cave, pale shadows moved and whispered. 'There's someone else in here as well,' she said nervously.

'Helen, they are Gallahs,' said Sheyde.

'The ones the Domendrans caught in the woods? Why are they here?'

'They are third-born, they cannot be slain.' Sheyde's dark brows fell into a frown and her eyes were pensive, shadowed. She scratched absently at her left forearm. 'All the others can do is to imprison them.'

Helen kept a nervous eye on the Gallahs, not knowing what to expect of them. It was hard to see clearly, but one of the figures detached itself from its companions and went towards Cadreis and Ananthis.

'We ought to find somewhere to sit,' Martin suggested.

'I couldn't sit down on – on this,' said Helen.

'It's only calcium,' he said, attempting to be practical. But none of them moved. Ananthis and Cadreis came out of the darkness, and with them was Nick.

'What are you doing here?' said Helen, startled.

Nick was still dressed in Chalcenian garments, though their grimy condition betrayed that he had narrowly escaped the fire. Apart from that, he seemed his usual self, incongruously unconcerned by his situation. 'The Domendrans caught me and stuck me down here with those bloody Gallahs. Hopeless lot. None of them remember a damn thing about Earth; half of them can't even talk. It was a relief when I saw Ananthis, I can tell you!'

'You have nothing to be relieved about,' said Ananthis. 'Cadreis is right, there is no way out. They have left us here to die.'

'There is no need to be so brutal!' Sheyde said coldly.

'But it is the truth, my dear. We have no food and no water. Now they have stopped Rianna from returning to Anatevera, we are of no further use to them. Doubtless they think it's for our spiritual benefit to die slowly, reflecting on our folly as we do so.'

'Stop it,' said Martin, sounding too calm.

'Or what? What will you do to silence me? Kill me?'

'I just can't see the point of making things worse.'

Helen almost yelled at both of them to shut up, but Ananthis subsided. Rianna was turning round slowly, hugging herself and staring into the musty darkness. 'Is this all?' she said.

'Is what all?' Martin asked.

'I thought they were going to do something terrible to me.'

'Isn't this terrible enough for you?' He was so astonished that he almost laughed.

'I mean – I thought they would single me out, take me away and – I don't know.' She leaned her head against Martin's shoulder and he stroked her hair. 'But they did not even speak to me.'

'Did you want them to?' said Helen.

Rianna sighed softly. 'I didn't want all of you to be punished for what I have done.'

Ananthis raised his head sharply. 'For what you have done? For trying to bring back the life that the Domendrans stole from us? Oh, a most punishable sin, I'm sure.'

'Ananthis, be quiet,' said Sheyde. She looked as pale as Rianna, her tranquillity eroded to a bare self-control.

'How long have we been here now?' asked Rianna.

'Er – I don't know,' said Martin. 'Seems ages already.'

'I wonder how long it will take? What will it be like to die and be born again in Anatevera?'

'Don't think about it,' said Martin, but Helen's head was spinning with the thought. The Chalcenians were bound to fear death, the unknown, but at the same time they knew they would be reborn; the one-way valve to the Otherworld. But for her and Martin it was the end; there were no Pelu to carry their souls to a third life. And she had seen oblivion . . .

'What was it you tried to tell us about Annis?' Cadreis asked suddenly, shaking her out of her reverie.

Helen related the experience. Discussing it achieved nothing, except to take their minds from their situation for a while. Nick did not bother to listen. He wandered to and fro in the background, giving an impression of intense boredom rather than fear.

'Could Annis do what she threatened?' said Martin.

'I suppose so, if she has the power to kill.' Helen was feeling the wintry cold again, shaking even though Cadreis was holding her.

'Well, it hardly matters, does it?' said Ananthis. 'There is nothing we can do, and if we are to die anyway, why should we care?'

Quietly, Sheyde said, 'You do not mean that.'

'Whether I mean it or not is of even less importance. Annis has gone mad, and from what Helen has told us of her wretched life, I can hardly blame her.'

'Annis should not have the power to kill,' Rianna said suddenly. 'She should only be a gatekeeper. In time gone by, the Cahantias bound her to her proper duties.'

Ananthis stepped forward and gripped her shoulder. 'How do you know this?'

'I learned it in the Circle of Cahantias,' she said, flinching slightly.

'You have undergone that?' He released her with a bitter smile. 'Well. You are fortunate indeed. But there is no Cahantias now. We tried, didn't we, Rianna? But there are not enough Oa. That, too, is the Domendrans' fault. If Annis will run wild, no one has the power to bind her.'

There seemed to be nothing more to say. Tired from standing, they sought the cleanest patch of sand they could find and sat down in a close circle, seeking warmth from each other. The Gallahs stayed apart on the far side of the cave.

For a time, Helen thought she could stay calm. But as another hour went by she realised that nothing was going to happen, no one was going to help them. The darkness pressed fiercely on her. Sheyde was in obvious discomfort, alternately rubbing at the blisters on her forehead and scratching at her forearms as if they itched unbearably. Helen could hardly stand to watch her.

'What are we supposed to do in a situation like this?' Helen said. 'Pray? You ought to know some prayers, Martin.' Almost in tears, she jumped up and walked away from the group.

Martin followed her to the cave wall. 'Hey, we're all in the same boat, you know.'

'It's at times like this I really regret being an atheist, but I've never felt less like believing in God.'

'Yes, I get the feeling He's slipped out for a very long lunch hour,' Martin sighed.

'I think cold's quicker than starvation, isn't it?' she said, rubbing her hands together. 'I've heard it's just like falling asleep.'

'Don't,' he said, but so patiently that she felt ashamed.

'I'm sorry, Martin. I'm not coping with this very well, I'm afraid.'

'None of us are. I think we're doing as well as can be expected.'

'The stupid thing is, I don't feel scared so much as angry. Helpless. We should be digging a tunnel or knocking the guards flying, like *Escape from Colditz* or something, but things aren't really like that, are they?'

'No,' Martin said. 'One thing I ask of you, Helen: don't start saying, "All this is my fault." That really drives me mad.'

'I wasn't going to!' she said indignantly. 'It's not my sodding fault, is it? I don't know whose it is.'

'Nobody's,' he said, giving her a brief hug. 'That's better.'

'And if there's one thing that makes me mad, it's people trying to make me smile or get angry and then saying, "That's better"!'

'Sorry.'

'Martin, what are we going to do?'

'I don't know. Think. Talk. Make our peace with God.'

'I suppose that's what Artienter and Sydra want, isn't it? They're like the Spanish Inquisition. The worst kind of religious fanatic.'

'All this hasn't convinced you that there's *something* out there?'

'Martin, a few hours ago I was walking about on Beacon Hill with a woman out of folklore who's hundreds of thousands of years old! Now I'm here in another world again! There must be something . . . After that night with us and Rianna, I don't know what to make of anything.'

Martin cleared his throat. 'I meant to talk to you about that.'

'Oh?'

'I didn't mean to avoid you the next day. I was just so embarrassed. I mean, just to leap on someone like that, I've never done anything like that in my life. I always thought, if you and I did ever make love, it would be . . . well, more romantic.'

'Oh, you *did* think about it then?' she exclaimed, then stopped before she said anything even more stupid.

'Well, sometimes, but – oh God. I'm just trying to say I'm sorry.'

'Why be sorry? I wasn't in control any more than you were. Anyway, it was nice.'

He caught her eye, managed to smile. 'Yes. To be honest, I was bloody annoyed about Cadreis and Rianna, as well.'

'Jealous?'

'I suppose so. Stupid, really. Perhaps I'd get used to the Chalcenians' ways if I lived with them for about twenty years . . . Oh well.'

'I was jealous, too,' said Helen. 'I couldn't help it, but in another way I understand the Chalcenians. I love all three of you so much . . . '

There were tears in her throat. Martin shook her arm and said teasingly, 'Was I as good as Cadreis?'

'I'm not saying,' she replied. 'It wasn't a competition.'

For a few minutes they had managed to shut out the darkness and encircle themselves in memories, but a voice breached the fragile walls.

'Hi, Helen.'

She almost leapt out of her skin. Nick was leaning against the rock wall next to them. She had not heard him approach. His stance was confident, and his face and blond hair were radiant in the darkness. But there was something in his eyes she did not like, the look he had when he was about to be particularly unreasonable.

'Hello,' she said. 'You made me jump. Are you OK?'

'Fine. Fascinating conversation you were just having,' Nick said sweetly. 'I would never have thought it of you, Helen.'

'You were standing there listening?' she gasped, what little heat there was in her body rising to her face.

'I couldn't help it. I'm really amazed at you. First Cadreis, now Martin; is anyone safe? Funny, Helen, while we were married I could have sworn you were frigid.'

'You what?'

'Come on, admit it; sometimes you were about as exciting as reheated porridge, and you wonder why I left you?'

Helen was all but speechless. The attack on her was nothing new; what floored her were the circumstances in which he had chosen to do it, as if they were at home and nothing had changed at all.

'As you seemed to think the best time to go to bed was just after a blazing argument – '

'Come off it, arguing and sex have got nothing to do with each other.'

'Oh yes they have – ' She mastered herself. Martin, unsure whether to defend Helen or leave them to it, was uneasily quiet beside her. 'Look, I can't believe we're standing here having this conversation. What does it matter? We could all be dead soon.'

Nick smiled. 'So? You're much more fun when you're angry.'

'I know what's wrong with you. You want everybody in the world to love you. So even when you don't want me, I have to go on loving you, and I'm not allowed to love anyone else because you can't bear that.'

'Got all the answers, haven't you?' He had a slightly hurt, disdainful look which meant she was right, but he would never admit it.

'Nick, for heaven's sake. I thought you'd changed, that time we found you and took you to the Heart of Life. I really thought you'd learned something and grown up. Didn't it mean anything to you, the fact that you'd actually died and been given another chance at life?'

'Oh, I see. I'm supposed to have sprung out of the grave as a fully matured saint, am I? But I'm still the same Nick. I might not have remembered who I was if you hadn't reminded me, and I'd have been the same as that brainless lot over there.' He pointed at the other Gallahs. 'You don't get it, Helen, do you? Of course I've changed. I've had time to think about things. I died and I'm still alive. I have defeated death. Look at you two, white as sheets and sweating ice because you have a fair chance of dying down here. But I'm not scared, because I know I can't die again and I know I am going to get out!'

'So you don't give a damn about us,' Martin stated.

'Not really,' said Nick, and walked away towards Sheyde. Over his shoulder, he added, 'I hope Rianna's better in bed than Helen is.'

'I'm going to kill him,' Helen said quietly. 'No, I'm not. He only says it for effect.'

'Bloody funny effect,' said Martin. 'Why not kill him anyway, just to prove him wrong?'

Sleep seemed impossible, but Helen dozed off eventually, with her head on Cadreis's knees. It seemed only a few minutes later that she woke up. Her mouth was sticky, and she was so desperate for a drink that she felt ill.

Now it begins. She remembered how she had felt the first time Artienter and Sydra had imprisoned her, and a stab of fear went through her. *I don't want to die, please God, don't let us die . . .*

Something had woken her; Cadreis stirring, the sound of voices. 'What is it?' she said, sitting up blearily.

Rianna was on her feet, her gaze fastened on the rim of rock above them. Her face was ash-white with terror.

'What's wrong?' said Helen, standing up. She could see no sign of the guards. There was only one silhouette moving on the ledge.

'He's coming for me after all,' whispered Rianna.

A rope snaked over the edge of the shelf, and down it climbed the cloaked shape of a Domendran. He reached the ground, turned and approached them, and Helen also felt the rising of the involuntary fear that he had always inspired in her. His eyes cold and piercing, Menenthonis came towards Rianna.

Martin was at Rianna's side, hugging her to him. The closer Menenthonis came the more she shrank back into herself, and Helen had a sudden, horrible intuition that the second he touched Rianna, she would die of terror. She knew it could happen, that people who had been cursed would die simply because they believed they would.

She wanted to throw herself in Menenthonis's path, but she could not move. It was as if she, Martin and Cadreis offered no more protection to Rianna than sheets of paper. If they tried to interfere, they would be torn away. They did not even exist. There was only Rianna and Menenthonis, staring at each other through a veil of icy white fire.

Menenthonis stopped, a couple of yards in front of her, and said, 'Rianna, come to me.' He held out his hand and she moved towards him, pulling herself out of Martin's arms and ignoring his protests. The Domendran's fingers hovered a few inches from hers, and she froze. 'Are you so afraid of me?'

'Don't touch me,' she whispered.

'Why? Don't you know who I am?'

'You are Menenthonis.'

'You know my name, but you don't know me?'

'I know enough. You are the life destroyer.'

He blinked, as if Rianna had said something that disturbed him. Then he said in a low voice, 'I have been searching for you for such a long time, Rianna.'

'Now you've found me. So leave me alone.'

Ananthis strode up to Menenthonis, and Helen silently blessed him for going to Rianna's defence. His Chalcenic radiance seemed very bright and very fragile before the Domendran's cold aura. 'Black Annis is on the rampage,' said Ananthis. 'Do the Aulanti know? They should, it being their fault. She knows how the Domendrans have used her. If she decides to take revenge, who shall stop her? Surely not you, so smug in your suffering.'

With that, Ananthis turned and strutted away, as if he knew exactly what Menenthonis would say in reply, and did not want to listen. Helen's hopes sank leadenly in her stomach.

Menenthonis, however, only glared after Ananthis for a moment before returning his gaze to Rianna. 'I had no wish to frighten you,' he said, 'but it was my task to stop you making the Pelu.'

'I didn't even know what I was doing.' Her voice was unsteady but defiant. 'I kept thinking the Pelu were something bad, but in my heart I knew, I *knew* they were good. You had no right to stop me.'

He shook his head. 'I did not even know who you were until the first time I saw you. Do you still not know me?'

'I don't know what you mean.'

'The first time you saw me, you did not recognise me? You still don't realise who I am?'

'No.' Her shoulders rose and fell, faster and faster. 'I don't understand.'

'I knew you when you were a child,' he said. 'I used to look after you.'

'No,' she whispered. 'That's impossible.' She tried to back away, but he caught her hand. She did not faint, but she visibly wilted at the touch, a fading white flower.

'It is true. I lived in the Heart of Life. I was Chalcenic then. We were close, you and I; you cannot have forgotten. I was your Shefri.'

'But – but I – I remember what my Shefri looked like. You are not like him.'

'Are you sure?' He leaned towards her. For the first time,

Helen sensed something different about him. His voice was less harsh, his eyes almost imploring. 'Look at me carefully, Rianna. I am older. But the main change is that I was Chalcenic, and I have become Domendric. That changes the face, the colour of the hair; everything.'

It was a long time before Rianna was able to speak. Then she said, 'Your hair was redder. Your eyes were warm and you used to smile . . . '

'Most of all, it changes the soul.'

'But I came looking for you!' she cried. 'You left me. I thought they'd sent you away because I loved you. They told me you'd died, so I went to the underworld looking for you . . . ' She broke off, pressing one shaking hand to her face.

'No, Rianna. I left because of myself. I was happy once, I never wanted to leave you. But a terrible gloom came over me. I can only describe it as a tearing away of illusion, a knowledge that the reality of life is suffering. You understand now that I could not stay among the Chalcenians. I had become a Domendran, I had to go to them. But you were too young to understand. I could not explain where I was going; I never thought you would try to follow.'

'So you came to the Vale of Death in Life . . . '

'Yes. I had fallen so deep that I knew I would never become Chalcenic again. Artienter and Sydra knew it too, so they apprenticed me to them and after a time they trusted me enough to send me to Anatevera to hunt the Pelu-makers. Ten years I have been on Earth, Rianna. I never knew you were there before me.'

'My Shefri,' she said faintly. 'And didn't you know it was me you were chasing?'

'Not until the first time I found you. I had never forgotten you.'

'But you – you went on hunting me. You sent Annis after me and Helen, you – '

'Yes, Rianna. Because stopping the Pelu was more important than my love for you. Knowing who you were did not change right and wrong.'

'You are not my Shefri,' she breathed. 'He was warm-hearted. You are so cold. That's why I'm frightened of you. You are cold and I don't know you any more. I gave a baby's life to find you again! I dreamed – I dreamed of our meeting, I imagined what we'd say to each other. If I'd known it would be this, I would have died. I shall die.'

Menenthonis's gaze did not waver. 'It is sad. But life is sad, child.'

'Why did you have to tell me? I wish I'd never known, then I could have remembered you as you were. My real Shefri. Why did you come here?'

His voice became quieter, losing strength. 'I came to help you let go and find oblivion, where there is an end to this pain. I wished to show you that the Domendrans were right – '

'Artienter has already shown us,' she said.

'So now you believe?'

'How can I? I am not Domendric.'

'But you will enter Domendri in this cave, as death creeps in to take you. All of you will. That was why I came to you, to help you and guide you along the journey . . . '

Oh God, Helen thought, *like a priest come to give us the last rites.*

Rianna tilted her chin up and her eyes glittered. 'That's the reason you came? Not to see me?'

Menenthonis took several moments to answer. In that time, Helen saw an intangible reversal of their relationship. Rianna grew in strength, while Menenthonis diminished and his convictions dripped away like water into the sand. He said, 'Those reasons were the ones I gave myself for seeing you again. But since I saw you in Bayn, they became a lie. You are so young, so full of life. I cannot let it be extinguished in this place.'

He looked vaguely round at the others. His eyes had lost their staring look, the ice melting to simple misery. His voice was throaty. 'The Luthnei say that the first stage in changing from Domendri to Chalceny is like walking on thorns. Every movement and every thought burns like fire. Light shines in your eyes after years of darkness, but all you feel is pain. I have to say that they are right.'

'That's how it was with me!' said Cadreis.

For a long moment no one else reacted. Ananthis and Nick were like stately blond twins on either side of Sheyde, who still scratched absently at her arms until Helen's skin crawled in sympathy. Rianna, no longer pulling away from

Menenthonis, hugged him briefly and awkwardly. He stroked her hair. 'Little Rianna. My light.'

'Am I understanding this correctly?' said Ananthis in a dry, matter-of-fact tone. 'You are no longer Domendric?'

'I do not know what I am!' he flared. His anger was born of shame at betraying his beliefs; Helen had seen Cadreis go through the same conflict. 'I only know that it is wrong for you to die. There is a purpose to life after all.' He pointed up at the ledge and said evenly, 'I have sent the guards away. I am taking Rianna out of this place and I shall leave the rope, for any who wish to come with us.'

In the rat-black tunnels beyond the cave, Helen's pulse hammered in her throat and fear seemed to sweat from the very walls. But there was excitement in the fear, the irresistible drug of hope. Weak from lack of food and sleep, she ran with the others in a haze of adrenaline.

'I know a way to the upper levels, but we must make haste,' said Menenthonis.

'No, we are certain to be intercepted if we go upwards,' said Cadreis. 'We must take the river tunnel to the sea.'

'It is the longest route.'

'But the best. It's the last place they will search for us. Believe me; I was Sfaian once, I know every inch of the Vale.'

'Very well. Take us, quickly.'

Cadreis led them through a series of narrow, twisting side passages until they heard the dull thunder of the river Shabdaranth. They paused to drink from a spring; Helen had rarely been so desperate for water. Meanwhile Cadreis ensured that the main tunnel was clear, and called them to follow him.

'We are well below the bathing areas,' he said. 'There is no cause for anyone to come this far downriver, so there should be no one to see us.'

'Famous last words,' Martin said into Helen's ear.

Cadreis had collected a couple of fungal lamps on their way, so they were not travelling in absolute darkness. The light splashed dimly on the rugged stone bank. At first the roof arched high above them, echoing the rush of water, but soon it swooped so low that they had to bend double, sometimes walking in the water itself. The rocks were treacherous, the current ice cold and powerful. Their progress became slower and slower. Nick went on ahead and was lost to sight; none of the others would leave the group, so their pace was measured by the slowest of them. No one complained of tiredness. No one mentioned the cold. But it was a long journey, and Helen began to fear she would collapse before they ever gained the sea.

It was Rianna who sensed the pursuit, long before the others could hear it. She kept glancing back, saying, 'Someone's following.'

'I can hear nothing,' said Cadreis. 'There's no one there.'

'Yes, there is.' Her eyes were wide with alarm. 'Hurry. She will catch us . . . '

They drove themselves hard for a while, then slowed again, partly from exhaustion and partly from certainty that Rianna was wrong. That was when the first faint sound slid after them, so subtle that at first it was hard to separate the dull rumble from the noise of the river. But then it began a slow crescendo, like a roll of thunder rising from the world's roots and swelling horribly up the register into a scream; a screeching, deafening scream on a hundred different notes.

Helen pressed her hands over her ears. Something that sounded like a low-flying jet was hurtling along the tunnel behind them. The rock shook; a wind roared past them, a wind full of stones and scratching twigs and the smell of winter.

Menenthonis was shouting, but he could not be heard. They tried to run, skidding on the rock as the force of the storm hit them and skimmed them into the savage current of the river.

In the split second it took her to fall, before the water received her with a vicious slap, Helen saw their pursuer. It was a wild, twisted shape, ancient as rock and black as nothingness . . . And screaming along behind the storm, like a cloak torn from the night sky, came Black Annis.

Chapter Nineteen

The world became a roaring grey chaos, bone-cold and choking. Helen fought to reach the surface, could not find it. Her head felt full of water. Annis's scream howled away down the tunnel, a solid sheet of sound that churned the river white in its wake.

Panicking and floundering, Helen felt air on her face and tried to breathe. Water caught in her throat. She struggled weakly to keep her head above the torrent, the breath bursting from her lungs in explosive coughs.

A side current caught her and flung her into a rock. The water was shallower there, and somehow she found a hand-hold and hung on like a grounded boat. She spluttered, heaving for breath. A white hand drifted past her, a dark ripple of hair, bubbles of material where air was trapped in the clothing . . .

Helen flung herself back into the river and seized the floating form. It was Rianna. The current took them both, dragging them under, but this time she was ready to swim against it. She pulled backwards, lifted Rianna's head clear of the water and struck hard towards the left bank.

Her feet hit rock. She lost her balance, found it again, and with desperate strength hauled Rianna into the shallows. The rocks were sharp and unforgiving, but she was so numb that she hardly felt the pain. All that mattered was getting Rianna on to the bank.

It was years since she had learned lifesaving at school, and having no cause to put it into practice she had scarcely thought about it since. Now she acted by instinct, turning her friend on her stomach and bearing down rhythmically on her back. Water trickled from Rianna's mouth. Then her body convulsed into a long, wrenching spasm of coughing, and she began to breathe again.

Helen sat and held her as she gulped wheezing lungfuls of air. Rianna's eyes bulged, and she shook from head to foot. It was a long time before she was able to speak. 'Helen – '

'It's all right.' Helen hugged her, almost crying with relief. 'I'm with you.'

'Where are the others?'

Helen looked back and forth along the tunnel, her teeth chattering with cold and anxiety. A dim light broke like rough diamonds on the surface of the water, but she could see no sign of anyone else. No bodies. 'I don't know.' She felt terror and grief rising inside her.

Rianna climbed to her feet and stood shivering on the rocks. Her skin was pearled with water, her hair dark and dripping. 'We must find them.'

'Rianna, you need to rest.'

'I can't. Not until we know what's happened to the others.' They looked at each other. 'Be strong, Helen.'

'Yes,' said Helen, taking her pale, icy hand. The knowledge that she *had* to cope helped her subdue the fear. 'We'll be strong for each other. Come on. Oh God, please let them be all right!'

The rock bank was narrow and slippery. The river had carried them a long way, and from the faint illumination Helen realised that the end of the tunnel was not too far ahead. The river grew wider and slower as it neared the sea.

Exhausted and aching, they rounded a last curve and saw the grey glimmer of the sky, a half circle framed by the tunnel mouth. It was dawn or dusk, Helen could not tell which. The sudden daylight disorientated her. There was a strange dark shape moving against the grey light . . .

Rianna's hand tightened on hers. 'What's that?'

The shape was that of a black shalior. Helen recognised the creature that had terrorised her in the Park . . . 'Black Annis,' she whispered. Then she frowned, confused, because the shalior was not at the end of the passage but prancing in the sky itself.

Helen broke into a half run, pulling Rianna with her. Water splashed under their feet. As they reached the end of the tunnel they halted and pressed themselves back against the stone.

The ice-silver light of dawn lit the shore. The tumbled rocks edging the river gave way to shining sand which swept down towards the waterline. The sea Halaranthe filled the horizon, the colour of granite, roughened by a cold wind that carried the scent of Annis's winter. Huge waves rose and fell with deceptive sluggishness, loosing streamers of foam from their crests.

'Look!' Rianna stretched out a trembling hand. 'They're on the beach, they're alive!'

On the shingle beyond the end of the river-tunnel stood a large group of people, some bedraggled, some in dark cloaks. Helen strained her eyes to identify them. Menenthonis, Ananthis, Sheyde, Martin, Cadreis . . . and Nick. They were all there, but mingled with them were ten or eleven Domendrans. Helen and Rianna looked at each other with a mixture of relief and dismay.

'They made it. Thank God,' said Helen. 'But the bloody Domendrans . . . How the hell did they manage to catch them?'

'Perhaps they were already guarding the tunnel.' The wind took Rianna's words away. It was hard to hear anything above the rushing of the river and the roar of the sea. The group were motionless, staring at the sky where the monstrous shalior cavorted against the clouds.

It was a vast silhouette, rearing up from the horizon and increasing in size by the second. The cold wind issued from its mouth. Its neck undulated like a snake, the claws on its cat-like feet were iron twigs, raking the sky. Every movement radiated a fury and madness that were more dreadful than the wind itself.

'Rianna,' Helen said hoarsely. 'Annis meant what she said. She must have lost her mind . . . '

They clung to each other, staring at the apparition. It covered a quarter of the vast sky now, and the dawn light darkened to steel grey. Suddenly Rianna gave a yelp of fear that went through Helen like an electric shock.

Helen jerked round. Artienter stood behind them with his hand on Rianna's arm, his eyes as unforgiving as the sea. There were three Sfaians with him; young men with dead-fish eyes.

'You unleashed Black Annis,' said Artienter, pointing a bony hand at the sky.

'What?' Helen exclaimed. 'How can you possibly blame Rianna for this?'

'I do not blame her alone. All of you are responsible. Rianna, the Chalcenians, and you, Helen Locke. By breaching the gate that should only be crossed by the dead, you have caused this.'

'Now hold on – '

'Have you understood nothing of what we tried to teach you?'

Helen was too furious to be frightened. 'I tried to warn you about Black Annis, but you just wouldn't listen. You are the ones who've been making suspect bargains with her. Sending victims to her in payment – that makes you murderers, doesn't it? Obviously the Domendrans don't think murder is wrong, but where I come from it's the greatest crime – '

'None have gone to Annis who were not willing, whether to feed her or to serve her.' His gaze was unwavering, his tone severe. He believed totally in what he was saying.

She said, 'Annis told me that the reason she is angry is that you promised her a husband, but you haven't kept the bargain.'

'She cannot keep one who does not go to her of his own free will. Few are willing, but if she had been patient, the promise would have been kept.'

'But she's not patient, is she? She's not human!' said Helen.

'The reason is deeper than that,' said Rianna. 'She needs an equal force to keep her in her place. But the last Cahantias left long ago and there have been no more to take its place.'

Artienter turned his lightless gaze on her. 'You are a clever child; I thought only the Aulanti still had this knowledge. But it no longer matters. If we do not have the power to bind Annis, we have brought our fate on ourselves, and above all we are fatalists. If she makes good her threat to destroy us all, then the cycle of life will be ended and we will all find peace. Thus Annis will serve us.'

Then Helen realised that Artienter was not accusing them, but obliquely thanking them. She stared at him. 'You're as mad as Annis is! I don't care what you say, you can't really want to die that badly. Maybe you do, but what about the rest of us?'

'The infliction of life is the infliction of suffering. It was stupidity that made you rouse Annis to this rage, yet all creation will have cause to thank you for it.'

'I can't believe what you're saying!'

He gave them a despising look, as if he had dismissed them as being unable to match his intellect or comprehend even the simplest elements of his philosophy. 'Foolish children,' he said gravely. 'Come with me.' He looked up at the dark shalior, and his expression changed horribly. It was as if his soul had poured into his eyes for the first time, revealing all his sorrow and twisted self-hatred, which he had only mastered by the power of his will; and his face became a grim parody of a saint seeing a vision of God.

Artienter and his three Sfaians took Helen and Rianna on to the shore to join the others. Sydra, already there, turned to greet her fellow Aulanti, while the other Domendrans bowed to him.

Martin and Cadreis were the first to see Helen and Rianna. They rushed towards the two women, their faces transformed with astonishment and delight.

'Oh God, we thought you'd drowned,' Martin said hoarsely.

'I almost did,' said Rianna. 'Helen saved me.'

Martin took them both in his arms. He was soaked through and shaking from head to foot. Cadreis, his hair dripping, hugged and kissed Helen first, then Rianna. Ananthis and Sheyde came running up to encircle them with welcoming arms. Then Helen felt Nick's hand on her shoulder, heard him say faintly, 'Thank God you're all right. If I'd stayed with you . . . '

The rest of what he said was lost amid other voices. Menenthonis stood slightly apart, his expression sombre, unmoved. But he was gripping Rianna's elbow with one hand, and the tendons shone white through the skin. Silently, their cloaks flapping in the cruel wind, the Domendrans shifted their position to keep them surrounded.

'How did this lot catch you?' Helen asked. She could hardly

speak for the cold. Only Nick seemed to have escaped a soaking. The rest of her companions were wet through and shivering.

Martin took off his glasses and wiped his eyes. 'They were waiting for us at the end of the tunnel. They fished us out of the water. I don't know if they were here by coincidence or if they knew.'

'We knew,' said Sydra, turning her tight, hard little face towards them. 'We never thought you would betray us, Menenthonis. Not you, who seemed so steadfast. But you could not keep the change within your soul a secret; it was so strong that we felt the shockwave of it.'

Overhead, Annis's twistings grew more frantic. Her shape thrashed into other forms, mockeries of earthly animals. The wind wailed forlornly across the waves.

'Can't we take shelter?' said Martin, but no one answered him.

'Do not condemn me, Sydra,' said Menenthonis. 'Neither side is wrong, but there is more to life than misery.'

'And if even the deepest of us change on a whim, who will be left to care for the true Domendrans, who cannot help their fate?' said Sydra. 'Who will feed and clothe the Nohmics?'

Ananthis interrupted sardonically, 'What do you care? By your own philosophy, you should leave them to die, and then they will be happy!'

Sydra stared at him angrily. What Helen had taken for meanness in her eyes suddenly appeared as heartfelt passion. 'How easy the Chalcenians find it to condemn us as life haters, the Vale of Peace as a self-inflicted hell,' she said. 'You are so wrong! We revere life in our own way. How would those who become Domendrans survive without us? They would wander in despair and kill themselves. But the Vale is a place they know they can come to, where they will be understood and looked after . . . until they become Chalcenic again.'

Silence followed her words. *Have I misunderstood everything?* Helen thought. After a moment, with a strangely icy politeness, Martin said, 'If you care so much, you'd let us take shelter before Helen and Rianna freeze to death.'

'Do not move!' Artienter said sharply. 'Coldness is nothing! Our duty is to watch Annis. And if she offers us danger, we shall welcome a swift end. If not, what have you to fear?'

As he spoke, Black Annis swooped.

She was a black sheet flapping across the sky. They all flung themselves to the ground. But as she descended on them she was all claws and fur; claws rattling like winter twigs, raking down through the air and into flesh. Bitter screams shrilled out, and Annis spiralled away into the sky, an inky shape borne on vast, crackling wings.

'That were just the start. Yer want it quick, yer'll get it slow!'

They broke and ran for the tunnel mouth. Annis dwindled with preternatural speed until she was no more than a speck in the sky.

'Wait!' shouted Ananthis. Most of the others stopped and turned back, but some of the Domendrans went on running. Artienter and his Sfaian guards were still standing on the beach, untouched, but two bodies lay where Annis had struck them down.

Sydra was dead. Her scalp had been all but torn away. Next to her lay Sheyde. Her face was gouged by four long claw-marks which continued down her chest. Blood was seeping orange-red through the slits in her wet clothing, but she was still alive and struggling to sit up.

Ananthis went to Sheyde, knelt down beside her and touched her hair. Swallowing her distress, Helen went to help.

'Stay with her,' said Ananthis. He straightened up, marched over to Artienter and seized him by the shoulders of his robe. 'Sydra's dead! Is that what you wanted for her? Is it what you want for all of us? We must bind Annis. Help me, before she kills us all!'

'She cannot be bound,' said Artienter. He seemed unmoved, but his eyes were full of ghastly, manic pain. With a shock, Helen saw something in him that reminded her of Tasnian. Was it possible that the changeless Artienter *had* changed, switching from deepest Domendri to suicidal Elation as swiftly as lightning? Perhaps it was only one step. Perhaps the whole sequence was a circle.

'Help me, damn you!' Ananthis cried, shaking him.

'There is nothing to be done.'

'There must be!'

'No!' Artienter shouted. 'Let her have her way! Let it end!'

Menenthonis pulled Ananthis away. 'There's no time to argue. She's coming back.'

Above the ocean, Black Annis was increasing in size, diving and looping in hellish glee. She clawed at the clouds and four long slits appeared, as if the fabric of the sky was no more than tissue. The ground trembled. The air turned grainy, and everything began to swirl as if beginning to break up.

Between them, Ananthis and Menenthonis lifted Sheyde. She was groaning and writhing, raising her hands to tear at the claw wounds as if they gave her unbearable agony. Her face was a mask of blood.

Helen and Cadreis tried to help, but it was all they could do to keep Sheyde's hands from her face. They began to hurry towards the mouth of the river to take shelter, leaving Artienter on the shore. Except for the three loyal Domendrans who remained with him, the others had vanished into the tunnel.

'No!' cried Sheyde. 'No, don't take me there.' She pulled her hand from Helen's grasp and pointed along the beach, to the right of the tunnel mouth as they faced it. 'Further – '

'Hush, there's no time to find a better place,' said Ananthis.

Sheyde's eyes were wild in her ruined face. 'No, you must listen to me. Take me along the beach. There is a cave. You must take me there, please.'

'But you're in pain – '

'No, not pain. It itches. The cave – Ananthis, you know where it is. I must go there.'

'Do as she says,' said Menenthonis. Going as swiftly as they could without making Sheyde any more uncomfortable, he and Ananthis made their way along the base of the cliff. Helen fell back to follow with Cadreis, Martin, Rianna and Nick. The hole Annis had torn in the sky seemed to have no specific location; it was in front of them whichever way they ran. It was growing larger, the edges tearing and blowing away like ash. Through the hole, Helen saw the landscape of Anatevera. Earth. Red bracken massed around the roots of ancient rocks. Beyond, the wintry landscape stretched down to a sea of mist in which the grey towers of a city glittered dully.

The wind storm was raging on Earth, as well. Both worlds were trembling, breaking up like raindrops. And Black Annis had seen them, toiling desperately towards their refuge.

'There's the cave,' said Ananthis. 'Hurry.'

Just as they scrambled over the scattered boulders towards the hollow in the cliff, Annis swooped again. They felt the arctic draught of her wings; something hard caught Helen's ankle, scratching painfully but not quite breaking the skin. In a paroxysm of terror, she flung herself into the cave mouth alongside the others.

They were all shocked, but safe. When they looked out at the beach, Annis seemed to have vanished. 'Where is she?' said Cadreis.

'Oh God, look,' said Helen. 'She's there . . . '

There was a doll dancing on the sand. It was a mockery of a Pelu, all brown and grey and black, with a tiny version of the ravaged face that Helen knew so well.

Annis's whisper cut through the gale. '*It wun't be that easeh to hide from meh, when the 'ole world turns into dust and blows away. The one ah want is in there. If he comes to meh willin' . . . I might think again.*' She took a few mincing steps towards the cave. They flinched and she looked gratified at that. She curtseyed and smiled. Then she speared away into the sky, and the gale came howling into their refuge.

'She means me,' said Cadreis. His face was set, his eyes wide. 'If I go to her, perhaps she will stop.'

'Over my dead body!' Helen cried. 'Don't be so bloody stupid!' She grabbed his arm and he hugged her, stroking her hair.

'No, don't even think about it,' said Martin. 'We won't let you go. There's no guarantee it will help.'

'There's no guarantee she means Cadreis, either,' Nick said drily.

Ananthis sighed, pushing his wet golden hair from his face. 'She is wild, it will take more than that to calm her,' he said wearily. 'Look after Sheyde. I am going on to the beach.'

'Why?' said Martin.

Ananthis shook sand off his garments and gave him a haughty look. 'Someone must stop Annis. There is only me, as usual.' He ran out of their shelter and sprinted towards the sea, tearing off his clothes as he went. In half a minute he reached the waterline and kept going, a pale figure dwarfed by the waves. The sea swallowed him.

'I don't believe it,' said Helen. 'What on earth is he doing?'

'Calling the Oa,' said Cadreis. He stared out at the sea as if hypnotised. 'I must help him . . . '

Menenthonis gripped his arm. 'He means to summon the Cahantias. He will fail. You must not go.'

'Shefri!' cried Rianna. She looked so frail that Helen could hardly believe she was still standing. 'You told me you believed in life. It's the only hope we have. Don't accept defeat before we have even tried.'

Menenthonis went to her, placed his hands on her shoulder and stared into her eyes. Helen sensed tortuous pain between them, warmth laced with years of loss and misunderstanding. Then he said, 'If you believe it is possible, Rianna, then I will try.'

He and Cadreis ran out after Ananthis before the others could do anything to stop them.

Annis was not in sight. The hole she had torn between the worlds hung above the sea like a picture pasted on the sky, shimmering and swirling with dots of colour.

In the cave Nick was pacing about with his arms folded, terrified but trying not to look it. 'All this self-sacrifice is making me feel sick,' he commented.

'Just shut up!' Helen flared. 'What have you done that's any use? Either help us with Sheyde or sod off!'

'Charming,' said Nick. 'Look, I'm sorry. I'm scared and I don't know what's happening.'

'Welcome to the world,' said Martin. He and Rianna were kneeling on either side of Sheyde, trying to make her comfortable. Helen could hardly bear to look at her face. Blood dripped down her neck and pooled on the sand. She seemed rational, but all the time she was restlessly clawing at her own flesh as if driven mad by the pain.

'Sheyde, don't, you'll make it worse,' said Rianna.

'I can't – I can't help it. It itches,' she sighed. 'I will be all right if I lie down . . . '

'You are lying down,' said Martin. 'Try to rest . . . '

Outside, patches of the landscape were breaking up into mosaic pieces, then re-forming, only for another area to dissolve. The whole world seemed insubstantial. At the edge of the sea three small figures emerged from the waves and stood looking out at the horizon. Helen sensed – rather than heard – a psychic wave flowing from them, a desire so strong that it became a call.

'Will the Oa come?' said Helen. 'I don't see what they can do against Annis.'

Sheyde raised her head with difficulty. 'The Transfiguration. But Ananthis is not strong enough, there are too few Oa . . . '

On the tideline the waves began to foam wildly. Helen thought she saw flashes of green, slender heads rising through the wave crests. Wishful thinking. But then Nick said, 'Am I seeing things? I don't think I want to know about these Oa. They look like snakes.'

'They're nothing like snakes,' Helen said quietly.

Cadreis was running up the beach towards them. Panting, dripping with seawater, he came into the cave mouth and said, 'We need one of you to help us.'

His eyes were on Rianna. Helen tried not to mind, tried to tell herself that it must be Rianna because she was the Pelumayis, but she knew she would never forget the image; Cadreis holding out his hand to Rianna.

'I will go,' Rianna said. She started towards Cadreis, but Martin seized her arm and held her back.

'No, you won't! You've already nearly drowned once.'

'It will have to be Helen, then,' Cadreis said. 'Take off your clothes, they will only weigh you down in the water. Quickly!'

Helen could not refuse him. Beyond modesty, she peeled off her shirt and jeans. She took his outstretched hand and ran with him on to the storm-torn beach.

When they reached the tideline he did not stop, but pulled her into the waves with him. She was already so cold that the water felt lukewarm, and so far beyond fear that all she felt was a strange excitement.

She lost her footing and was swallowed by a wave. When she surfaced the Oa were all around her.

They were as green as leaves, their eyes as golden as the sun. They radiated an innocence and gentleness which filled Helen like physical warmth, and for the first time she understood the overwhelming joy that the Chalcenians found in swimming with them. Their scales brushed her limbs like silk. They were a mystery to her but she embraced the mystery gladly, knowing that the truth within it was something perfect . . .

Water hit her face, bringing her out of the trance. Something was wrong. The Oa were beginning to twist wildly, thrusting their long bodies out of the foam and falling back, over and over again. The movement became a weird writhing dance. They seemed intent on weaving themselves together, as they had the last time Helen had seen them. There was a desperate urgency in the ritual. The closer they interwove the less easily they could swim, and their fluidity of movement deteriorated into a frantic thrashing. For the second time that day, Helen was close to drowning.

'Helen!' Cadreis was pulling her back to the shallows. She leaned on him, coughing. Ananthis and Menenthonis stood in the edge of the waves, heads back and eyes closed. She could feel the power of their silent song to the Oa.

'What do you want me to do?' she asked.

'Only this.' Cadreis's mouth closed on hers. She was taken so much by surprise that she could not ask why. They overbalanced. The tide gushed around them and he was outside her and inside her, like a flood of sunlight.

Ananthis had said, *Sexual energy is needed.* Without it, the Transfiguration would fail . . .

Helen was in Cadreis's mind and he in hers; and their pleasure was so intense that they seemed to be at the centre of everything, floating on a spire of light. It was more than sex. It was the celebration of life, it was life itself; and as their pleasure blazed to its peak, the knotted Oa made one last desperate surge out of the waves.

This time they did not fall back. They hung half in air and half in water, and they began to change.

Terrified, euphoric, Helen and Cadreis scrambled out of the tide and ran to Ananthis. As they reached him he caught them by the arms, spinning them round to face the Oa.

'Watch!' he said.

The knot of shimmering creatures was resolving itself into a distinct shape. The central mass elongated into a trunk from which several Oa writhed outwards, closely twisted, to create an impression of a head and arms. The torso split halfway up to form two legs. The shape they created with their serpentine bodies was human, more than twice the height of a man, rising to float impossibly just above the surface of the water.

Helen watched with incredulous awe, wondering why they had taken that shape and how long they could hold it. Then her stomach tightened in shock. The Oa were beginning to fuse. Their scales melted like wax and lost their colour. Their long bodies flowed together, becoming muscle-ropes, the contours of a single, perfect human form.

'What is it?' Helen whispered.

'The Transfiguration,' Ananthis said raptly. 'The Oa become the Cahantias.'

At first the figure was translucent, pale as quartz. Then the colours came, swelling up through the depths of its body like slow fire. Indigo flowed up from the feet, melting to luminescent purple at the groin and brilliant blue over the chest. The green of the Oa reappeared along the arms, changing suddenly at the wrists to red. The hands were like ruby flowers. Finally the head blazed golden, and the figure stood placidly on the surface of the sea, its tranquil face bent towards them and its hands spread wide.

If the Cahantias was a living creature in human shape, it was more god-like than human. It breathed warmth into the frigid wind and stilled the waves.

'Black Annis!' Ananthis yelled suddenly. 'Behold the Cahantias!' His hair blew back from his face. His strong features were bone-white, but he was laughing savagely. He caught Helen up and kissed her, and she tasted salt on his tongue. 'Helen, as long as I live I shall bless you and thank you for this. You made it possible . . . '

Artienter was running across the beach towards them, his face distorted with fear and rage. 'Fool, Ananthis!' he cried. 'What have you done? You fool!'

'On what grounds do you call me that? You and I have never seen the like of this creature. We witness a legend. Do you feel no awe, no privilege? And it is only one Cahantias, where once there were thousands.'

'It will be the last,' Artienter said bitterly. 'Do you imagine you can set it against Annis? You idiot. It cannot slay Annis.

Nothing can!'

Ananthis thrust his face close to the Aulanti's. 'Can't it? Shall we find out?'

There was a crack of thunder like the earth tearing apart, a heart-stopping shriek. Annis rose up out of nowhere, a cloaked figure with a face like stone, covering the sky. Her hands were like winter trees, blackened, bitter spikes. She saw the Cahantias and she swooped.

On the ocean, the figure began to spin. It shone like glass lit by rainbow fire as it pirouetted faster and faster towards Annis.

At the last second Annis swerved away from it and dropped like a stone on the group at the water's edge. Artienter and Menenthonis went down under her claws. The others scattered. Helen looked back over her shoulder to see Annis whirling away into the sky and flitting round and round the Cahantias like a huge, taunting crow.

Menenthonis was climbing to his feet, but Artienter remained where he had been struck down. Wrapping his cloak tightly round himself, Menenthonis staggered to the body of his former friend and stood staring down at it until Ananthis pulled him away.

'Don't weep for him, Menenthonis,' said the Chalcenian. 'He has what he wanted.'

Cadreis was tugging at Helen's arm. 'There's nothing we can do,' he said. 'We must take cover!'

'Yes, save yourselves!' shouted Ananthis.

As he spoke, Black Annis dived again. This time she plunged on to the Cahantias like a vampire bat. The shining figure looked very small beneath her. There was a noise like the snap of leather wings as the two met, but the Cahantias took the impact without wavering. It went on spinning, carrying Annis with it. She hung on, locked her hands round its waist, and began to squeeze.

The Cahantias made no sound, or none they could hear above Annis's shrieking. Harder and harder she squeezed, and suddenly both figures were tumbling, tangled together, into the sea.

Their fall flung up a vast wave which came tearing up the beach like an iron-grey wall edged with red and blue fire.

Helen and Cadreis ran before it. They gained the cave mouth just as the wave exploded into froth on the boulders behind them.

When it had gone, a thick and eerie silence came down. Water left the sand as bright as a mirror. Ananthis and Menenthonis had withstood the wave and remained on the shore, sole-to-sole with their reflections, dwarfed by the sweep of the beach and sky. The ocean Halaranthe boiled ponderously, spitting flashes of colour as if a giant kaleidoscope were turning in its depths.

'Helen, are you all right?' Martin said.

She jumped, suddenly becoming aware of the others in the cave. 'I think so,' she said, quickly groping for the clothes she had shed before the calling of the Cahantias. Her shirt was still unpleasantly damp, the jeans stiff with salt and sand.

'We couldn't make out what was happening out there. Where did that incredible rainbow-creature come from?'

'From the Oa,' said Cadreis. He gave Helen a very private smile. 'Ananthis believes it can defeat Annis.'

'Is there anything we can do?'

'No. Only wait. How is Sheyde?'

'Worse,' said Rianna, looking at Helen with wide, haunted eyes.

Helen and Cadreis knelt by Sheyde. The Chalcenian woman's eyes were very bright, and her whole body was rigid with suppressed pain.

'We ought to clean some of this blood from your face,' Helen said gently.

'It's better not to, the wounds might start bleeding again.' Martin's voice sounded shaky.

Helen put her hand to Sheyde's forehead, where the skin seemed undamaged. It was only a gentle touch, but she felt an unpleasant slippage under her fingers and a lump of Sheyde's skin came away. Underneath there was a patch of glistening pearl-green.

'Oh God,' said Helen. She jerked away, but Sheyde caught her wrist.

'She's – she's like that all over her arms and chest,' Martin said. Helen noticed how white he was, as if he was only managing to control his stomach out of compassion for

Sheyde.

Cadreis gently pulled down the shoulders of Sheyde's robe and looked at the wounds. Her skin was in shreds, and scales gleamed palely underneath. He put the material back in place. 'I did not know,' he said.

'Know what?' said Helen. She felt that she had taken all she could stand.

'It is all right, Helen,' said Sheyde, still holding her wrist. 'I have something to tell you all. Only Ananthis knows. I am not Chalcenian. I am third-born, a Gallah.'

There was a long silence, then Nick stepped forward, looking ill. 'A Gallah – like me?'

'Yes. Like you, I lived in Tevera once. I remember so little of it; only the depths of sorrow and the flights of joy. And like you I must have been reborn in Anatevera, though I remember nothing of it. All I know is that I was very lucky.' She smiled through her discomfort. Her radiance was still there, masked only by pain – or made sharper and more vivid by it. 'A Pelu brought me back and the Chalcenians found me, as they found you, Nick. I loved them so much that I wanted to live among them and make myself a true Chalcenian again.'

'But what's happening to you?'

'Take me further back in the cave. I must lie down . . . '

Martin and Cadreis lifted her between them, and did as she said. The cave meandered back into the rock, banded with red and white. Along a narrow passage, it opened out into a second cavern, dimly lit by reflected light.

All around the edge were shelves of rock. On almost every one lay a creature like a carved statue. Some were recognisably human, despite the pale leaf-shimmer of scales all over their bodies. Others were more serpentine and of a richer green. All slept under a crust of salt, chrysalises undergoing a slow transformation.

'Find a space,' said Sheyde. 'Lie me there.'

They found a rock dais that was unoccupied, but Martin began to protest. 'This is ridiculous, we can't just leave you here. You need proper treatment. We should find the healer, what's his name, Nenhaliac – '

'I am not ill,' said Sheyde. 'The wounds don't matter. I am so tired.' She yawned, and the skin around her mouth tore and sloughed away. She scratched at it absently. 'Just let me sleep here . . . '

They laid her on the rock and she looked up at them with her dark-lashed eyes. Helen found herself trying not to cry.

'Is this going to happen to me?' said Nick.

'In time,' Sheyde replied.

'How long?' He put his hands to his face, anxiously feeling the skin.

'I cannot say. It may be tomorrow or it may not be for many turns of the sun. I have been back in Tevera . . . oh, I don't remember. A long time.' She smiled. 'I think Annis attacking me made the change begin . . . but no, it had started before that. It must have been the fire. It doesn't matter. It will happen anyway, Nick.'

There was a movement behind them. Menenthonis came into the cave, drenched with sea-spray and holding his wet cloak around himself. Helen could sense the profound change he was undergoing from Domendran to Chalcenian. The ice in his eyes had become blue fire, but he looked disturbed and weary.

Seeing Sheyde, Menenthonis went to her and sank into a sitting position beside the dais. Rianna was immediately at his side.

'What's happening out there?' said Martin.

'The struggle goes on. I fear Ananthis has misjudged the Cahantias's strength. It does not know how to fight,' he replied. His voice cracked with exhaustion. 'Sheyde – I did not know. Ah, but look round this cave. They say that once there were thousands of Gallahs sleeping along every beach round every coast. Now there are only a handful.'

'What's happening to Sheyde?' Nick demanded.

'Do you not know? She is becoming an Oa. This is what happens to all Gallahs; it is the next stage of life.'

'That's what I thought,' Nick said quietly.

Menenthonis was looking at Rianna, holding her hand. 'Once I thought this an obscenity. Only yesterday, was it? Now it seems the most precious and desirable thing . . . '

'You must be joking,' said Nick. 'I don't want to turn into a fish!'

'Nick, for heaven's sake,' said Helen. 'It's not like that.'

'How the hell would you know?'

'I've been out there with the Oa, they are full of joy in being alive. I can't describe it. You're a Gallah, you must feel it!'

Nick looked uncomfortable. 'I'm not sure. It doesn't mean I want to turn into one! No, no way is that happening to me.'

Menenthonis looked up. Some of Sheyde's blood had run down the dais and pooled round the hem of his cloak, but he took no notice of it. 'This would not trouble you if you could not remember Earth,' he told Nick. 'And you should not be able to remember it. Who brought your memory back?'

'I did,' said Helen.

'You know, he's right? I was perfectly happy with the other Gallahs until you reappeared,' Nick said venomously. 'I might have known I'd have you to thank. But I don't care what anyone says, I am not going through that.' He pointed at Sheyde. 'I'm going back to Earth.'

'You cannot!' said Menenthonis. His voice sounded strained, and he closed his eyes briefly. 'You are third-born, you cannot go back.'

Nick sighed and fell silent. Helen knew there was no use in trying to talk to him; she would only receive another mouthful of abuse.

Rianna said, 'Shefri, you know I have to go back to Anatevera and make the Pelu, don't you? You do understand?'

Menenthonis took her hand and held it to his cheek. 'Yes. When you are gone, I may become Domendric again, and perhaps then I shall cease to understand. But I will never again try to stop you, I promise.'

Rianna bowed her head against his shoulder. 'Come with me.'

'I can't, my beloved child.' She started to ask why; he put a finger to her lips. 'Hush. You will have your friends with you.'

As they went on talking quietly, Sheyde beckoned Nick to her. He went a few steps closer and stood looking at her apprehensively, as if her condition might be infectious. 'Listen, Nick,' she said. 'You should welcome the change, not fear it. It is the gateway to immortality. In time, each group of Oa combine to become a Cahantias; that is what we know from legend, though Ananthis only proved it today. No one knows what the Cahantias is or where it goes, but it is right that some knowledge should be beyond us. We called the Oa, we brought them to the Transfiguration, but in time it would have happened without us.'

Menenthonis glanced up. 'The tragedy . . . ' He winced, closing his eyes briefly. 'The tragedy is that since the Domendrans began making their bargains with Annis, there have been so few Oa. And it is my fault there are not more . . . '

'Somehow I am going to find a way to teach others to make Pelu,' said Rianna. 'No one has the right to break the life cycle, not the Domendrans, not Annis. No one.'

Sheyde raised one limp, ragged hand to stroke Rianna's head. 'Forgive me,' she said through stiffening lips.

'Why?'

'For being such a fool, making you leave the Heart of Life. I was too busy with being a correct Chalcenian to see beyond. Tell Ananthis . . . '

'What?' said Rianna.

'Just tell him.' After that, Sheyde said no more. She lay stiff and motionless on the rock; not dead, but metamorphosing.

A second later, Ananthis came into the cave. He looked down at Sheyde without reacting; he glanced round the others, then sat down on a boulder, pushing his white-gold hair back from his face.

'Well?' said Martin.

'You had better hurry,' he said calmly.

'Where to? Has the – the Cahantias won?'

Ananthis tapped the boulder with long fingernails. 'I can see no end to the fight. However, as we are still here, Annis obviously hasn't won yet. I think we had better send Rianna through the tear in the boundary while Annis's attention is elsewhere.'

'Are you sure about this?' said Martin.

'No, I am not sure! Would you prefer to sit gawping at me like idiots while we lose the only chance we have? Come on!'

Helen looked anxiously at Cadreis. 'Will you come with us?'

'To the boundary, Helen. Not back to Earth. I do not belong there.'

'But we – but after – ' She waved helplessly in the direction of the sea. Had it meant anything to him? The Pelumayis was not essential to the Transfiguration after all, yet Rianna had been Cadreis's first choice . . . She could not bring herself to ask why. He was a Chalcenian now; he could love everyone without sentiment or favour.

'Please,' she said pathetically.

And Cadreis said, 'All right, Helen, I'll come.'

Tears of relief burned her eyes. She hugged him, but Martin's hand was on her shoulder. 'If what Ananthis says is right, we really had better hurry.'

'I'm bloody well coming too,' said Nick. No one argued with him.

They all began to leave the cave, except Menenthonis, who remained slumped by the rock dais. 'Shefri,' Rianna said anxiously. 'Come with me, at least to the boundary.'

'I can't. Go on, quickly.'

But Rianna hesitated. 'Why?' She knelt by him, pulled the cloak away, and revealed the terrible marks of Annis's nails. His flesh had been rent from shoulder to hip. They had thought the blood soaking into the sand below him was Sheyde's, but they had been wrong.

Rianna's mouth opened and closed with shock, but no sound emerged. Menenthonis caught her arm, pulled her down to him, and kissed her cheek.

'Shed no tears for me, beloved child,' he said. 'I shall be born again in Anatevera. With all my strength I shall hang on to my memory so that I can look for you again and remember the Pelu. Now go – go!'

And Rianna fled, the others with her.

As they ran on to the beach the battle erupted from the sea like a volcano. They had no time to take cover. They could only fling themselves down as the sky filled with multi-coloured lightning and a storm of sound. Through showers of seawater, glittering like millions of tiny prisms, they saw the Cahantias and Annis soaring overhead.

Annis had diminished in size, as if to concentrate her strength. She was a ragged wing, so intensely black that she reflected no light at all. She was pure oblivion. Her long fingers were still locked around the waist of her opponent, squeezing so powerfully that the Cahantias had taken on an hour-glass shape.

Yet it did nothing to defend itself. It was utterly passive, its emerald arms held by its sides.

'I did not help it into being just for it to be destroyed,' Ananthis said under his breath. 'Why does it not fight?'

'It can't!' said Rianna. 'You must have known it can't!'

Like liquid glass, the Cahantias was being forced out of shape. Helen had a horrible vision of Annis breaking it in two and throwing the halves on to the rocks, where they would be smashed to pieces, like a glazed figurine. Her nerves stretched and stretched like wire as she waited for it to happen . . .

The end came suddenly, explosively. Terror burst from Helen's throat in a short scream, which was lost in the wind. The Cahantias did not break; it shattered. From head to foot it crazed into fragments as tiny as jewels, and those fragments burst outwards into a cloud of blue, red and green raindrops. They hung in the air for a few seconds, glittering. Then, like rain, they began to fall.

Annis gave voice to a deafening wail of triumph. She had seen Ananthis and the others cowering on the beach; she began to swirl slowly down towards them, curtseying in mid-air, turning lazy somersaults, mocking them.

As she drifted down, the jewel fragments attached themselves to her. She tried to brush them away, irritably at first, then frantically as they clung and thickened. She became encased in a skin of coloured glass, and within it she was shrinking.

The glass thickened, took on a familiar shape. The Cahantias re-formed around Annis, absorbing her. By the time it touched the sand it was complete again, perfect, and Black Annis had gone.

Ananthis was the first to move, urging his companions to their feet. The rainbow being stood before them, in a human shape as faultless as a Michelangelo statue. It was formed of something that was not glass, nor even diamond, but an infinitely subtler, richer substance. Its aura was of both tranquillity and the fire of life; and when it opened its eyes they were white as stars.

Helen remembered the words of the Teveran animals: *How*

many animal souls blend to make one human, how many humans to make one Cahantias, how many turns of the sun before we are all one? . . . We are in your bodies and your souls for ever . . .

The cycle of life had no end. The Cahantias was only the next stage after the Oa, the last one about which anything was known.

Speechless, they bowed to it. There seemed nothing else to do.

Then the Cahantias closed its eyes and rose on one pointed toe. With its arms held at its sides it soared up into the air and arrowed out over the sea until it was lost to sight.

As it went, a crumpled dark heap fell on to the sand. Helen did not even realise what it was. She was thinking: *Where did that old sack come from?* when the 'sack' began to move.

It was Annis, not in supernatural form nor even as the bleached blonde whom Helen knew too well. She was an old, old woman, tiny and frail with age. She stared up at them with colourless eyes and Helen felt an overwhelming pang of pity. Then Annis bared her teeth and spat, 'You gits'd like ter do for meh, wun't yer? But I ain't dead yet. Catch me if yer can!'

With that she was up and running away, like a kite blown on the wind. They stared after her for a second, then Ananthis shouted, 'Follow her! She'll close the boundary!'

Black Annis could no longer fly, but she could still outpace them. While they were struggling to find a path up the cliffs, she was already gaining the top and vanishing from sight.

'I thought the Cahantias had killed her,' said Cadreis as they toiled up the rocks.

'Only weakened her,' said Ananthis. 'The Cahantias is pure life, but she is not pure death. She has too much life in her ever to be destroyed.'

The window on to Earth was still visible, now hanging above the cliffs. It was smaller, but its edges were so frayed that it was hard to tell where Tevera ended and Anatevera began. Even as they climbed towards it, it was dwindling. Annis was fleeing back to her lair, dragging the torn boundary behind her. By the time they were almost at the top, Helen knew she would not have the strength to pursue Annis all the way to her hiding place. It was too far . . .

But at the top of the cliffs waited a huge crowd of

Chalcenians, all those who had been driven from the Heart of Life by the fire. The next thing she knew, she and Cadreis were being hoisted on to the back of a shalior, and Martin and Rianna were riding alongside them.

The wind still blew, but the storm had contracted in on itself, a small whirlwind that darted along just below the ragged window. It took Helen a few minutes to realise that the whirlwind *was* Annis. Diminished, but still angry. Still alive.

The landscape flew by. It was Charnwood and it was Tevera; she knew the air, frosty and poignant with the scent of bracken, the hills rolling wild to the horizon and the ancient, ancient rocks . . .

I don't want to go back, she thought. *Close the boundary, Annis! But I have to go back. I have to stay with Rianna, and there's Mum and Dad . . .*

They could hardly see the window now; it was a fuzzy patch of greyness, drawing them along behind it. Helen saw the Sliding Stone Crag with a dreadful sinking sensation in her stomach. There was the tree, with its bent trunk and one twig-finger pointing at the sky, and the dark slit in the rock underneath. Black Annis's bower.

They were still a hundred yards away as they saw the whirlwind vanish into the blackness, and the fuzzy greyness sucked in after it.

'We're too late,' said Helen.

'No!' Ananthis cried. She looked at him and that last impression stayed in her mind for ever; the pale hair flying back from his face, the beautiful face and golden eyes that were the essence of Chalceny; fierce joy. 'Follow her, you fools, *follow her!*'

Helen had no choice. Cadreis was off the shalior and pulling her down with him, then Nick was suddenly seizing her arm on the other side. She could not face going into that darkness, could not bear it, but she went because Rianna's hair was like a red beacon in front of her and because Cadreis was with her.

They climbed down into the thin cave. There was not even time for a last glimpse of Tevera before the blackness swallowed them like a throat.

A door slammed.

Helen and Martin stood alone in a small, dingy front room. A pair of grubby orange curtains were drawn across the window, letting through a single, dust-festooned shaft of daylight. The room was overcrowded with mismatched furniture, and in the corner an old portable television stood forlornly on a table with spindly teak legs. Three ducks flew up the wall above a tiled fireplace, lost in the green and brown excesses of the wallpaper. The carpet had been liberally used as an ashtray.

Martin looked at Helen. 'This is a dream, isn't it?' he said without any trace of amusement.

'I don't think so.'

'Where the hell are we?'

'Where are Rianna and Cadreis?'

Martin went to the window and jerked the curtain open. 'There's just an ordinary street outside. Council houses.'

At the same time, Helen dived towards the door, terrified she would find it locked. It opened on to a hall. 'Jesus,' she whispered.

Sitting on the stairs, with his head in his hands, was Nick. 'Sorry to disappoint you, but it's only me,' he said, trying to grin. He jumped to his feet and came towards her. 'Truce; I promise I'll be nice to you, only for God's sake tell me what's happened. This house looks so familiar.'

Helen did not respond. She ran to the kitchen door and threw it open, calling, 'Cadreis!'

A large middle-aged woman stood in the kitchen, her arms folded. A low-cut leopardskin top revealed the reddened, wrinkled flesh of her chest. Her bleached hair stood up from her head as if she had slept on it, and her eyes were smudged with mascara and tiredness.

'Lookin' fer yer toy?' she said. She barged past Helen into the hall. Helen shrank away, then tried to open the door into the dining room. It was locked. 'Do yer normalleh gi' yerself a guided tour of other people's houses wi'out bein' asked?'

'What the hell have you done with Cadreis and Rianna?' she shouted.

'Dun't raise yer voice ter me, gel,' Annis said flatly. She marched into the front room, sneering at Martin as she passed. 'I'll show yer. I'm nothin' if not fair.'

'I thought she lived in a cave,' Martin said faintly.

'You would think that, wouldn't yer?' said Annis, moving to the back wall of the room. 'Dun't see why I should live in an 'ole wi' nowt in it. Times change. Gorr'ave a few mod cons, ain' I?'

In the wall was a glass connecting door. Helen had not noticed it before; in fact, she was certain that it had not been there. Annis ran her hand over the frosted panes and the frosting vanished like mist.

On the other side was a room with flocked red wallpaper, a blue and brown carpet and a teak dining table. Rianna and Cadreis stood staring through the glass.

'Let them through,' Martin said furiously. 'Let them through!' He began to shake the handle, but Annis knocked him aside with a casual flick of her hand that sent him flying over the back of a sofa.

On the other side, Cadreis picked up a chair and flung it at the door. The glass rattled; the chair bounced off. Annis laughed unpleasantly.

Then Rianna came to the door and began tugging at the handle and clawing the glass. 'Helen,' she cried faintly. 'It's no good, she won't let us – '

'Shut it!' Annis barked. 'Listen. This is how things are gonna be. Them what belongs in Tevera – that means you an' you ' – she stabbed a finger at Cadreis and Rianna – 'are goin' back there, out me back door. Them what belongs on Earth are goin' out me front door. I'm mekkin' a fresh start, a spring clean, like. Nobodeh wanderin' in an' out of me borders what shouldn't be. An' no more o' them bastard Pelu! I dun't want ter see none o' yer again until yer die.'

Martin said, 'What happened to destroying both worlds and killing everybody?'

Annis pursed her lips and shrugged. 'We all 'ave our off days, dun't we, me duck? Say yer goodbyes.'

Helen felt as if the floor had been torn away from under her. Already the panes of glass were misting over. She would never see Cadreis again. Never see Rianna. There was no time to say anything at all. Martin called out, 'Cadreis! Look after her, won't you?'

Cadreis nodded. He and Rianna had their arms round each

other like frightened children, and for ever afterwards Helen remembered that frozen scene and their bewildered, angry, beautiful eyes.

The glass frosted over. Helen rubbed her eyes, wanting to cry but unable to.

'Ooh, fer God's sake!' Annis exclaimed, 'no harm'll come to 'em. Nor to you, neither, if yer sensible. Ah could do wi' puttin' me feet up, after all that excitement. Fanceh a cuppa tea?'

'No,' said Helen, almost retching.

'Yer may as well goo off 'ome then.' Annis propelled them into the hall. They heard the back door slam. She opened the front door and held it open for Helen, Martin and Nick, for all the world like a maternal aunt seeing them off after a visit.

Outside, as Martin had said, was an ordinary street that could have been anywhere in Leicester; anywhere in the country. But the daylight looked oddly pale, and mist blew about in the unkept front garden.

They hesitated on the doorstep.

'Where's this Black Annis, then?' said Nick.

'What?' Martin gasped. 'We've just been talking to her!'

'Really? I didn't see anyone. I've had about enough of this. I'll be glad to get back to normal.'

'Didn't you see – ' Helen began, but another voice drowned hers.

'Nick,' it said.

Nick turned round. Standing in the doorway where Annis had been was a dark, very pretty girl in a tailored suit. He stared at her in disbelief.

'Gina?'

'Yes, who were you expecting to see in my mum's house?'

'Oh God, of course,' Nick said dazedly. 'I thought it looked familiar. Your parents . . . Sorry, I'm not with it at all. Can I come in?'

'Yes, please come in, Nick,' said Gina. 'Something funny's happened and I feel a bit scared.'

'Nick, don't!' Helen exclaimed. She caught his arm but he shook her off.

'What's the matter with you, Helen?'

'It's not Gina.'

He looked at her as if she had gone mad. 'Don't be stupid, do you think I don't know Gina when I see her?'

'Nick, please – ' He ignored her. He went up to the dark-haired girl, hugged and kissed her.

'You'll stay with me for a while, won't you?' Gina said softly.

'As long as you like.' Nick put his arm round her and they went into the house together. 'Now, what's been going on?'

The door banged shut, cutting off their voices.

Helen dived after them, but she suddenly seemed to be moving through glue. Her limbs felt like sponge; her fists made no sound as she pounded feebly on the door.

'No!' she cried. 'Nick!'

Everything began to shimmer. Martin was pulling at her arm, mouthing her name in slow-motion panic. He dragged her away from the door and along the concrete path until they could see into the front window of the house.

Nick's face was pressed against the pane, white with a look of absolute horror; and looming up behind him was the grinning, painted face of Annis, radiant with triumph.

The garden and the house blew away into the mist, leaving Helen and Martin on a cold, bracken-covered slope.

Chapter Twenty

The storm that had shaken Tevera still buffeted Earth, wailing thinly as it played out the last of its strength. Night was falling. Rain drove down from a smoky-black sky, and before them loomed the dark mass of the Sliding Stone Crag.

Terrified, furious, Helen threw herself at the rocks, struck at the trunk of the crooked tree. 'Annis!' she yelled. 'Rianna! Nick!'

There was no response. The crag stood silent against the sky, as it had for millions of years, as if nothing supernatural had ever touched it.

Martin shouted too, but gave up before Helen and pulled her away. 'It's no use,' he said. 'It's over.'

'How can you give up so easily?' she said, pushing her wet hair off her forehead.

'We can't make Annis do anything she doesn't want to. She's sealed the boundary. Now come on, we're going home.'

She knew he was right, but she could not bear the knowledge that they had failed, that there was nothing they could do to release Nick or to bring Rianna and Cadreis back. The grief pushed up into her chest and stayed there, like a boulder. Martin's face was wet with rain and tears.

The darkness disorientated them, and it seemed an age before they reached the tall wooden gate and the path leading through the copse to the car park. The oaks and birches had been stripped of the last of their leaves. A few trees had fallen. It looked as if a hurricane had torn across Charnwood.

The car park was deserted, except for the red MG and the blue Renault, which stood where they had been left.

'My car will never start after all this time,' said Helen.

'Never mind, we'll go in mine.' Martin started towards the MG, then halted, patting the pockets of his jeans. 'It's a miracle,' he said. 'I've still got my keys.'

'And thank God you haven't lost your glasses, either,' said Helen.

As they drove back to Rothley the news on the car radio was of the freak wind that had swept across the Midlands, bringing down power lines and causing general havoc.

There was very little traffic on the roads, other than police vehicles and tractors moving a couple of fallen trees. Fifteen minutes later they drew up outside Helen's house. Rothley was in darkness, and as she entered the front door she tried the light switch without much hope of it working.

'Power's off,' she said. She went to light the gas fire in the dining room and they both huddled in front of it. The touch of heat made them shiver violently.

Helen was almost too tired to move, but forced herself through the essential tasks of finding towels and dry clothes, while Martin made soup and toast. Eventually they sat wrapped in dressing gowns and blankets in front of the fire, sipping hot drinks in a slightly uneasy silence.

Martin said, 'We have to talk about it, Helen.'

'What's the point?' she snapped bitterly. 'There's nothing we can do, is there? Annis trapped Nick, and he's probably stuck with her for ever! Sorry, Martin, it's not you I'm angry with.'

'I shouldn't worry about Nick too much. Annis can turn herself into anything she wants, can't she? If she pretends to be Gina all the time, he'll be perfectly happy – much happier than he deserves to be.'

She smiled shakily. 'Maybe. But if Annis is content now she's found herself a man, she'll be happy to go on doing what the Domendrans want.'

'No, she does what *she* wants.'

'Same thing, isn't it?' said Helen. 'She won't let Rianna, or anyone who can make the Pelu, through to Earth.'

Martin nodded. His face was flushed in the firelight, his eyes red-rimmed. 'It's one of those things that makes your brain hurt to think about. The Domendrans stopped the Pelu *before written history began.* Children play with dolls, witches stick pins in them, and no one ever thought it might have some other significance.'

'Like a race memory?' said Helen.

'Could be. But think of all those thousands of years in between, when no one has been able to return to Tevera, and mankind didn't even know. We didn't know. We got religion instead.'

'False promises.'

'That's the way it's always seemed to me, but I'm biased. To be an atheist then find out there *was* an afterlife after all, only we've had it taken away from us . . . ' He shook his head helplessly. 'I think it's a tragedy. A bloody great silent tragedy.'

Helen started to cry. He edged closer to her and put a blanketed arm round her. 'I'm sorry. I shouldn't be so maudlin.'

'Why not? We've got enough to be miserable about. I feel like crawling back to the Vale of Death in Life and signing myself in.'

'Never. A world that has gas fires and instant hot chocolate can't be all bad, can it?'

'I suppose not,' she said, wiping her nose on a tissue.

'I'm sure Rianna and Cadreis are all right. And . . . ' Martin did not speak the thought, but it had been there between them all the time; that, even if they had not been separated, Cadreis and Rianna would slowly have drifted together. It had already begun.

Helen reached for the telephone, found the line dead, and replaced the receiver.

'Who were you going to phone?' Martin asked.

'My Mum and Dad. I left a really pathetic excuse for disappearing again. It would have kept them calm for a few days, but they must be going frantic by now. As soon as the line's back on, I'll call them.'

'What are you going to tell them?'

'The truth,' said Helen.

Martin looked taken aback. 'Helen, they will never believe you! How could they?'

'I can't help it. I'm absolutely hopeless at lying, and I can't bear them to think I would be callous enough just to drift off and not bother getting in touch. That was one of Nick's favourites in an argument, saying I was still tied to Mother's apron strings, but I don't care; they're my family and they're all I've got. I owe them the truth.'

'Perhaps you're right, but they'll think you've cracked.'

'They might not,' Helen said with a ghost of a smile. 'When they met Cadreis, even though he was speaking a language they'd never heard before, my Dad understood him and my Mum said she could pick out a few words. And we could speak the language fluently, couldn't we?'

'Yes, but – '

'Because we've all lived in Tevera before.'

'Yes, but can you remember being there in a past life?'

'No,' Helen said, bowing her head.

'They won't remember either. That's the point, no one remembers, because Annis wipes everyone's memory clean.'

'But it's all the proof I've got!' Helen said stubbornly. 'How can they possibly argue with it? I don't care what they think, I have got to tell them.'

'OK,' Martin sighed. 'And I'll back you up. But there's something worse we have to think about, and that is what we are going to tell Rianna's family.'

'Oh God.' Helen was quiet for a few moments, then she said, 'The same.'

'Helen, it's not that simple. Look at it from their point of view; their daughter vanishes, then they get some wild nonsense over the phone from England. How can we possibly prove that she's not dead, or even that we didn't kill her?'

'Any story we try to invent would be even more disastrous if it went wrong. We have got to tell them what really happened.'

Martin looked up at the ceiling. 'Helen, I don't fancy our chances of repeating the story in court. Besides, it would be even worse if anyone did believe us.'

'How?'

'Because we'd be like those nutters who reckon they've been in an alien spaceship, and use it to start a religious cult.'

Helen laughed. 'If we expect people to swallow what's happened to us, we've got a cheek assuming that those "nutters'" experiences weren't real.'

'That's not the point. People wouldn't believe it because it was true, they'd believe it because they need some way-out thing to believe in. I couldn't bear Tevera to be trivialised like that.'

The feeling in his voice seemed to go right through to the root of her soul. She gripped his hand. 'But it won't come to that. I'm sure Rianna's folks will believe us.'

'Why?'

'Because they know her better than anyone. They know how she was found as a child. They probably know things about her that we don't. Trust me, Martin.'

'I do,' he said gently. 'I couldn't have got through any of this without you. Oh God, I'm going to miss her.'

Helen drew a breath. 'I shall miss all of them,' she said softly. 'Even Ananthis. Even Menenthonis. Did you hear him before he died, saying he would try to hang on to his memory? I wonder if he will. I shall be looking at every baby I see, wondering if it's Menenthonis reborn. Or Tasnian.'

'Don't do that. You'll drive yourself mad,' said Martin.

'If I'm not mad by now I never will be,' she sighed. 'It's late, and we're both exhausted. You'd better stay here tonight.'

'Thanks. I'll be fine on the sofa.'

'Don't be silly, I've got a spare bed.'

'Rianna's room?'

'Ah. Er . . . yes.'

Martin made a non-committal, gulping sound.

In the end, Helen did not even look in Rianna's room. She could not bear to. She and Martin cuddled up for warmth in Helen's single bed and fell asleep immediately, so bone-weary that they slept until twelve the next day. By then the electricity was restored, the telephone in working order.

Helen called her parents. She weathered their tears and their anger, but she only found herself able to say, 'I can't explain things over the phone. Can you come and see me tomorrow? I'll tell you everything then.'

When her mother had calmed down, she said, 'By the way, Helen, something odd has happened. You know the doll Rianna gave us? It's disappeared, but we're sure we haven't had a burglary.'

'I know,' said Helen. 'I took it. I'm sorry; it's part of all the other things I've got to explain.'

When she had put down the receiver, Martin looked at her and said, 'We'd better go and fetch your car. Then I'll call work and see if I've got the sack yet.'

'It's Saturday,' said Helen.

'Is it?'

'Yes, honestly. At least no one can sack me, but I'll probably have no customers left by now.' She felt dead inside, yet there was comfort in having Martin with her. She was at ease with him, as she had never felt with Nick; and she could talk to him, as she had never been able to talk to Cadreis. But in one sentence Martin destroyed the mood and virtually ended everything between them.

'I've got to go and see Jo,' he said. 'You do understand, don't you?'

He did not try to discourage Helen from going to the farm with him, so she went, not out of bloody-mindedness but because she wanted to see Jo herself. Unless the Pelu had taken her as it had taken Nick . . .

They found Jo in the stable yard. She was mucking out one of the loose boxes; Destiny, Fikri and the yearling were grazing peacefully in the field. They looked small and colourless after shaliors, yet Helen's heart ached at the sight of them.

'Hello, Jo,' said Martin.

Jo was startled, then her expression became hostile. Her breath clouded on the air and her nose was red with the cold. She leaned on her fork and said flatly, 'If you'd come earlier you might have been some use. I had a sodding barn blow down yesterday!'

'I'm sorry,' said Martin, 'but – '

'Where's Rianna?'

'I wanted to talk to you about that.'

'Well, I'm damn sure I don't want to hear it, any more than you want to hear about me and the vet.'

'You and the vet?' said Martin, thrown off balance.

'Never mind. Where is she, then?'

'She – she's, er, gone home. She won't be coming back,' Martin said quietly.

'That didn't last long.' Jo went into the loose box and began shovelling manure into a wheelbarrow with unnecessary vigour.

'Listen, Jo, I want to explain.'

'No, you listen,' she said flatly. 'I don't care what you've got to say, however interesting it is. I don't want to hear it. No one uses me, Martin. You think I've fought for everything I've got, just so some bugger can come here when it suits him, ride my horses, go off with the first girl who takes his fancy, then come back when it doesn't work out? You have got another think coming.'

'Jo, you know it wasn't like that!'

She put her head on one side, almost smiling. 'Maybe it wasn't. Maybe I was using you as well. But I've had time to do a lot of thinking while you were away and I've made a decision. I don't need you. I don't need anyone. Animals are reliable; people mess you about, and I've had enough. So get off my land, Martin. I don't ever want to see you again.'

Jo was obviously saying it because she meant it, not because she wanted him to argue with her. Martin knew.

'Well, er, if you feel like that, I'd better go,' he said.

'That's right,' Jo said triumphantly. 'Goodbye.'

'Can I say goodbye to the horses as well?' he asked, calmly meeting her eyes.

Jo threw her fork down on the straw. 'Yeah. Take as long as you like. Helen, can I have a word with you?' She marched away towards the house.

Helen glanced at Martin, who was leaning over the gate to call the mare and gelding, then ran to catch up with her. 'Jo – '

'Don't say a word about Rianna, don't make excuses for Martin, just leave it, OK?' Jo said as they entered the kitchen.

'Right,' said Helen. 'So why did you want to see me?'

'It's a bit embarrassing,' Jo said, rubbing the side of her nose. 'There's nobody I can tell except you. It's about that doll.'

Helen felt a trickle of cold electricity go through her. 'What about it?'

'Well, you tried to warn me about it killing people.'

'Yes, but I'd got things wrong, I – '

'So I did what you said, I made a bonfire, and I took the doll out to burn. Took it out on a pitchfork as well, felt a right idiot. I was about to shove it on the fire and the damn thing spoke to me.'

'What did it say?'

'"What did it say?"' Jo mimicked. 'Oh, you kill me, Helen. Anyone else would have asked me how much I'd had to drink. Only about half a bottle of brandy, actually, which had been in the pantry since 1968. But I wasn't drunk. It said my name. I was so shocked I dropped it, and it picked itself up and walked back up the pitchfork like a little tightrope walker. It almost stood on my hands. I was paralysed. And it told me . . . I don't know, I can't remember what it said exactly, but it was something like, "The time is not yet. But when it comes, everything will be well." Oh, I don't know.' Jo looked away, embarrassed.

'It's OK,' said Helen. 'I'm not laughing at you. Go on.'

'It said a lot more. Some of it I can't remember and some of it was between me and the doll. It just left me with this overwhelming feeling that things were going to be all right. I would get over Martin, I didn't even want him any more, I would be fine on my own. I just felt really happy. I haven't felt like that since I was a kid. When the doll had said its piece it went lifeless again, so I dusted it off and brought it back inside the house. I couldn't burn it after that, could I?'

'Where is it now?'

'That's the odd thing,' said Jo. 'Yesterday I couldn't find it. It was on the mantelpiece in the morning, gone in the afternoon. Maybe some kid crept in and nicked it, but I don't think so.'

'Did you want me to help you find it?' said Helen.

'Good grief, no. It doesn't matter. In fact it almost seems right that the doll's vanished. It's gone, but the feeling's still here. And that's why I don't want you to tell me anything about the dolls or Rianna. I don't want anything to spoil the good feeling I've got.'

'Well, it – well,' Helen floundered. Jo was right, what was the point in explaining? 'All right.'

'Thanks for listening. For believing me.'

'It's nothing.'

'By the way, that mouthful I gave Martin; take no notice. Not that he didn't deserve it, but underneath he's all right.'

Helen nodded, managing a smile. 'Now, go and drag him away from those horses, will you? I've got work to get on with.'

By the time they had fetched Helen's car and returned to her house she was trembling with an irrational anxiety. It was not fear; or at least, only the fear of discovering one more mystery.

She had prematurely broken up Martin's farewell to the horses, and now she felt guilty. He had not complained, but his very quietness betrayed how much the Arabians had meant to him, how much it hurt – on top of everything else – to know that he would not see them again. As for herself, Helen felt that she was going to miss them as much as she missed Cadreis and Rianna. Everything hurt, no emotion was qualified.

She parked the Renault and dashed into the house. The previous night she had hardly thought about the two dolls that she had left on the sofa, nor the half-finished ones in Rianna's room. She checked the sofa, then ran upstairs. A few seconds later, Martin came through the door and stood looking at the chest of drawers. 'What's wrong?' he asked.

'The dolls have vanished,' she said. 'There was a pile of them on there. And the violety-coloured one I brought from Mum's has gone too.'

She felt his hands on her shoulders. 'Must be something to do with Annis. Never mind.'

'But there's one left,' said Helen. 'The one Rianna brought with her when she first came. It's still in the front room. Why would Annis leave just one Pelu?'

'I don't know,' he said thoughtfully. 'Perhaps Annis has a soft spot for you. She left the Pelu so you can go back to Tevera after all.'

'No. She wouldn't do that,' Helen whispered.

They went downstairs to the sitting room and Martin picked up the doll. Helen had almost forgotten how beautiful it was, glittering with the rainbow fire of the Cahantias. But she could not bring herself to touch it. Martin said, 'Whatever the reason for it being here, you ought to be glad. Treasure it.'

'I can't. I'm still scared of it. Too many bad memories. I

feel as if Annis has contaminated it.'

'Of course she hasn't,' said Martin. 'She only borrowed it to scare you. You know the true reason for the Pelu now, doesn't that make a difference?'

'I know it should,' said Helen, 'but it doesn't. Maybe Artienter had a point about finding peace instead of trying to live for ever. I don't want to go back to Tevera without you.'

'Without me?' Martin said, surprised.

'Without you, without my Mum and Dad! I don't want to go back on my own. It's not fair. Why should I have the chance, when no one else has?'

'Don't get upset about it – '

'Why not? Look, I don't want the thing. Do you want it?'

Martin hesitated. 'No. It wouldn't feel right. Rianna left it for you.'

'Then I'm going to get rid of it.'

'How? Don't be silly, Helen.'

'I'm not being silly,' she said in a low voice. Suddenly she did not want Martin there, trying to rationalise with her, did not want to go on wondering whether he had gone to see Jo in order to patch things up between them. 'Do you mind leaving?'

'Well I do, really. I'm worried about you.'

'I don't want you staying here because you're worried about me! Please, I'll be OK. I just want to be on my own.'

After Martin had gone, Helen felt worse. There was no reason for her to have all but thrown him out. He had not suffered any less than she had; he was just better at hiding it. Feeling wretched, she went to bed early and tried to sleep off her profound exhaustion.

The next morning, her parents came. They had already played out their rage over the telephone, and something in Helen's manner made them realise that what she had to tell them was deadly serious. They listened in silence as she told them everything. They did not interrupt or argue, and for that she was eternally grateful. When she had finished, her mother covered her own face with her hands. Helen thought she was weeping.

Her father said weakly, 'Er – well, the way you tell it sounds very convincing, but . . . '

'I can't prove it, I know. But just explain how you could understand what Cadreis was saying.'

Her mother lowered her hands. Her face was dry, but she looked stunned. 'I remember Tevera,' she said.

'You what?' said Mr Locke.

'I was a dancer there, as well. That's all I can recall; dancing on the sand, the amazing colours of the sky . . . but I was there, John. And I died very young.'

Much later, after her parents had gone, Helen sat looking at the last Pelu. It looked back serenely, saying nothing.

'It's you or me, kid,' she said softly. 'If you don't take me now, you won't be around to do it tomorrow.'

She had tried to give the Pelu to her parents; they had refused, as Martin had, saying it was hers. She wanted to give her mother the chance to go back to Tevera again . . . but her mother, even if she believed in the doll, did not want to go back alone. 'The doll is not yours to give away,' she had said.

Perhaps she was right.

Helen studied the doll, marvelling at the rainbow lights pooling on its satin garments. The Pelu of old had been clay or wooden figures. It was not the form that mattered, but the power breathed into them by the maker. Every time Rianna had made a Pelu, she had shed a little bit of her soul. The making of them would have destroyed her in the end.

'She'll be happier in Tevera,' said Helen through her tears. 'It's best for her.'

First thing the next morning, she took the doll to Bradgate Park. The russet hills were deserted, ragged and desolate. She walked to the Sliding Stone Crag and wedged the doll in the branches of the crooked oak tree.

'Annis can have you back,' said Helen. 'If she doesn't want you, maybe someone else will find you.' She turned away. Her breath clouded on the air; it was autumn now, but already it felt like winter. The frosted red beauty of the Park touched her more deeply than the lushness of summer ever could. *This endures*, she thought. *This landscape has been here for thousands of years, and when I am gone it will still be here . . .*

The thought gave her immeasurable comfort.

She walked back to the gate, let herself through, and began

to cross the spinney towards the car park. Halfway along the path she found her way blocked by a dapple-grey Arabian. The mare raised her head at Helen's approach and pricked her delicately curved ears. Her eyes were large and kind, almost flirtatious under a long, silky forelock.

'Destiny?' Helen called. She would recognise the mare anywhere. It was not impossible that she could have jumped out of her field and wandered into the Park; unlikely, yes, but not impossible. Helen had a responsibility to catch her and take her back to Jo.

The Arabian waited placidly as Helen went up to her and began scratching the dappled neck. She was fumbling to remove the belt from her jeans for a makeshift halter, when the mare spoke.

'It's no good, me duck, you can't 'ave 'im back.'

Helen leapt away as if she had been burned. 'Annis! You bastard!'

The mare bared yellow teeth, and laughed. 'Eh up, I'm not as black as I'm painted. Went through a bad patch, I did, but our Nick's made me feel young again.'

'Young?' Helen gasped. 'You can't keep him prisoner, you *can't!* I saw his face in the window, he looked terrified. You've got to let him go, please – '

'Oh, shurrup yer moanin'! What's the matter wi' yuh? 'E come wi' meh of 'is own accord, din' 'e?'

'You tricked him.'

'So what? 'E's a mardeh git. Says ah wear 'im out.' Annis curled her lip lewdly. 'If 'e's good, I gi' 'im a treat; I pretend to be Gina. Sometimes I pretend ter be you. But what I like best is ter be me own beeyootiful self, an' see the 'orrible face 'e pulls!'

'Oh, God,' Helen said faintly.

'I'll tell yer one thing; as long as 'e stays wi' me, 'e can't turn into an Oa. I think I've finalleh got one what'll live for ever.' Annis chuckled, and winked one large black eye. 'Dun't worreh, me duck. I'll be as decent to 'im as 'e was ter you.'

Helen swallowed. The more she showed her distress, the more Annis would laugh at her. She forced herself to sound calm. 'Now – now you've got Nick, couldn't you let Rianna and Cadreis through to Earth?'

'Why should ah do that, me duck?'

'Because of the Pelu. Surely it can't matter to you that much. And because I miss them.'

'Selfish,' Annis said mockingly. 'I like that. It's honest. But it's too late, y'see. Rianna's happeh in Tevera wi' Cadreis, where she belongs. An' I blurred her memory a bit, ter mek things easier for 'er. She dun't remember owt about the Pelu now, an' ah think I ought ter do the same fer you.'

'No, don't,' said Helen, backing away. 'Somebody's going to remember. One day someone else will come who has the power to make them!'

'Not while I 'ave owt ter do wi' it,' Annis said smugly. 'Look, this is the last time yer'll see meh – in the Park, at any rate. Me onleh real 'ome, see, is the border where life meets death. So until then, this is me partin' message. Before this little outbreak, there weren't no Pelu fer thousands o' years. Nothin's changed. Let it be, me duck. Let it be.'

With that the mare galloped away from Helen, soared over the high gate, and vanished into the Park. She left a swirl of mist behind her, a mist that was more in Helen's mind than outside her.

But her memory was not taken away. Instead, she remembered. The memories were a swelling gold and silver fire in her head, and she cried out and ran back into the Park. She went on running all the way back to Annis's crag, with her heart hammering and her lungs sore to bursting.

But the doll, the last Pelu, had gone.

Later, Helen drove to Loughborough and went to Martin's house. There was plenty of parking space in the tree-lined street, and then it struck her that he was probably at work. But his car was there . . .

He opened the door, looking delighted to see her.

'Hello,' she said. 'Have you got the sack?'

'No. I managed to sort it out with my Head of Department. He's too soft for his own good. But I've come down with the flu or something, so now I'm on sick leave.' He showed her into the small, book-strewn lounge. 'How are you?'

'OK, I think,' said Helen. 'I've come to apologise.'

'What on earth for?'

'For being such a sod to you, kicking you out. I was being selfish.'

'Hey, it's all right. We were both a bit fraught.'

'Just a bit,' said Helen, half smiling. She perched on the edge of a couch, with Martin sitting in an armchair opposite. 'Something happened to me today. I went in the Park . . . ' She told him about Annis and the Pelu. 'And now my memory's come back.'

'I wasn't aware that you'd lost it,' Martin said seriously.

'My memory of living in Tevera! My first life! I didn't live in the Heart of Life, but it was a place very similar, further along the coast. It was called "Trees in Light", I think . . . and my name was Siloca, or Clioci, something like that. It feels like a dream I had a hundred years ago, but I know it was real. I was always in boats or swimming in the sea, I think I must have been a fisherwoman. One thing I'm sure of is that I became Domendric twice, but both times I became Chalcenic again.'

'I don't know whether I did or not. I wish I could remember my own life in that much detail,' said Martin.

'I've sometimes been depressed in this life, but it was always for a reason. But in Tevera it was an uncontrollable thing that completely overwhelmed me. It didn't matter how brightly the sun shone, how beautiful everything was. It didn't make any difference. All you could do when you felt like that was go to the Vale of Peace, where people understood and tried to help you. Now I remember how it felt, I know why Artienter and Sydra were like they were. I don't even think their beliefs were wrong. But I can remember what it felt like to become a Chalcenian again as well.' Helen smiled. 'It hurt, yes, but it was also the most beautiful feeling in the world. To feel like living again, to come out of the Vale of Peace and find that nature is about ten times more beautiful than you remembered it. I wish I could recapture that feeling.'

'What makes you think you can't?' said Martin.

Helen sighed. 'We can't go back to Tevera. Not much point in dwelling on what's past.'

'Helen, we're privileged to remember living there,' said Martin, leaning forward. 'And we've had incredible, beautiful experiences that most people could never have dreamed of. I feel privileged to have known the Chalcenians, don't you? Especially Rianna.'

'Yes, I do,' she said.

'You were glowing while you were talking about Tevera. Now you've gone back to looking as rotten as I feel.'

'Thanks a bunch.'

'Come on, you know what I mean. Yes, we've got things to be unhappy about, but think of the good things that happened.'

Helen looked down at her hands. They were still red with cold; red for creativity, she thought, but she no longer felt like smiling. 'We had some fun,' she said acidly, 'but was it worth it? We've discovered that there is a kind of paradise, but we're not allowed to go there. Great. I wish I didn't know. I wish I'd never met Rianna.'

'No,' said Martin, 'you don't wish that.

Helen shook her head. 'Of course not. Everything I am is because of her, one way or another. No, I'd hate never to have known her. You really loved her, didn't you?'

'I couldn't help it. And you loved Cadreis.'

'I think so,' Helen said quietly. 'I mean, I loved him but I didn't really know him. Can you truly love someone you don't know? I miss him like mad but it's like missing a dream. As if he was never really there in the first place.' She hugged herself against the chill of loss.

'That's exactly how I feel about Rianna. It's the truth, isn't it? We could never have held on to them. It was too perfect to last.'

Their eyes met. Helen felt she was going to break down, and she could not face making a fool of herself. 'I think I'd better go now.'

Martin left his chair and sat beside her. 'Please don't go.'

'I can't think of much more to say.'

'Something's bugging you, and you're not saying what it is,' he observed.

Before she could stop herself, Helen interrupted harshly. 'When you went to see Jo, was it because you wanted to start again with her?'

'So that's it,' Martin said softly. 'Helen. Oh, Helen.' He

took both her hands in his own, and the warmth that flowed into her from him was so comforting that she could not break away from it. 'No. Even if I'd wanted to, I wouldn't have had the cheek. All I wanted to do was to explain, sort of set things straight between us. She wouldn't listen; fair enough, that was up to her. But I didn't want to go back to her. My relationship with Jo – it was a sort of partnership. We were together because we both loved horses. Not that I didn't like her, of course I did, but it meant I had access to Destiny and Fikri. God, this makes me sound like a complete bastard.'

'You're not that,' said Helen.

'You see, I didn't know what real love felt like until I met Rianna. But it made me realise I love you as well. I don't want to make you sound like second best – it's not like that – oh, God, I'm hopeless at this.'

'No, it's OK. Carry on.'

'I'm just trying to say that you and I have always got on well, and I'd like us to stay together.'

The warm shock of his words hit Helen in the stomach, mixing with the coldness and the tears, making it hard for her to reply. Eventually, trying to sound calm, she said, 'One thing I learned from the Chalcenians is that it is possible to care about more than one person at the same time. You know you mean a lot to me, you always have.'

'That sounds like a gentle let-down. I don't blame you. I was never sure whether you saw me just as a friend or – '

'Martin, you're as bad as me! Listen. I was jealous of Jo and I was jealous of Rianna – even when I was with Cadreis. I know that's selfish but I couldn't help it. I love you too.'

'So let's get married.'

Helen stared at him, startled. 'I don't know about that. I've hardly got over the last one.'

'I know, I'm not rushing you. But something you said to me in Tevera has always stuck in my mind.'

'What was that?'

'It was about Tasnian. You asked me if I'd ever realised that I loved someone, only to find out it was too late. Well, it's happened to me now. I think I've always felt like this about you, only I didn't realise. Let's do something about it before it's too late.'

'I'd like to. I want to. But . . . '

'But what?'

'It's just that everything seems so pointless now. Maybe Artienter was right, living for ever isn't such a good thing. But at least the Pelu gave us a choice. Now there's no choice. You die and there's Annis waiting on the boundary to slam the door in your face. So why bother to go on living?'

Martin sat back in exasperation. 'Are you always this optimistic? There's everything to live for. Nothing's changed. All that's different is that we know.'

Helen stood up and went to the window. The sky was silver-blue, leaves were lying like bronze coins on the pavement and birds were singing on the bare, shining branches. She could smell the sweetness of distant spring in the air. When Martin came to wrap his arms round her, she leaned gladly into the embrace. 'But do we know?' she said. 'We only know what people have told us. What if they were lying, or wrong? If we can't go to Tevera when we die, where might we go instead?'

Martin lifted her chin and kissed her. 'With any luck, we've got years and years and years before we find out.'

FREDA WARRINGTON

A BLACKBIRD IN AMBER

The great serpent M'gulfn was dead, its power dispersed and all save one of its demon-servants destroyed.

Now was the time when the power of sorcery might be harnessed for good or for evil.

Journeying disguised to Gorethria came Mellorn, daughter of Silvren and Ashurek, by training and by will eager to use that latent power for good.

But to Gorethria, summoned by the usurper Duke Xaedrek, there came also the demon Ahag-Ga in the guise of an old woman. Together they plan to use the power: he to rebuild the terrible authority of the old empire; she, silently vengeful, determined to unleash the dark forces of Chaos on a world that, saved, is yet in peril.

A Blackbird in Amber, sequel to *A Blackbird in Darkness*, is the third in the series begun with *A Blackbird in Silver*.